LAWLESS LANDS

TALES FROM THE WEIRD FRONTIER

LAWLESS LANDS

TALES FROM THE WEIRD FRONTIER

Edited By
Emily Lavin Leverett
Misty Massey
Margaret S. McGraw

Falstaff Books
Charlotte, North Carolina

Copyright Notice

Cover Image - "West Side" by Mateusz Ozminski
Ebook & Cover Design - John G. Hartness
Print Book Design - Susan H. Roddey www.shroddey.com

ISBN-10: 1-946926-06-X
ISBN-13: 978-1-946926-06-7

Published by Falstaff Books
Charlotte, North Carolina

Acknowledgments

Special Thanks to Melissa Gilbert at Clicking Keys for her assistance with this project. www.clickingkeys.com.

We couldn't have brought you these wonderful stories without the support of our fantastic Kickstarter backers. The following people had faith in our project, and we're very grateful!

Alea Henle, Alex Bacon, Alexander Bennett, Ali Tink, Alice Bentley, Alice Ma, Alisha Henri, Amy Bauer, Amy Lea Mills, Anders M Yterdahl, Andrew Hatchell, Ann Robards, Anna Wick, Anne M Rindfliesch, Antoon Telgenhof, April Steenburgh, Ariel Jaffee, Axisor and Mike, Barbara Hasebe, Ben & Cynthia, Betty Law Morgan, Bill Collins, Bill Sykes, Brian Webber, Brit Colgan, Bryce O'Connor, Camilla Cracchiolo, Carla Holler, Carol J Guess, Carol McKenzie, Caroline Gaudy, Cat Rambo, Catherine M, Catherine Sharp, Chad Bowden, Charlotte Henley Babb, Cheryl Preyer, Chris Callicoat, Chris Classen, Chris Mitsinikos, Christina Stiles, Christine Swendseid, Christopher Francisco, Christopher Sanders, Chrys VanDerKamp, CL McCollum, Crazy Lady Used Books & Emporium, Cullen Gilchrist, Cynthia Gobert, Cynthia M, D Wes Rist, Dan Shaurette, Darin Kennedy, Darrell Grizzle, Darren G Miller, Dave Hermann, David Arthur, David C Ridout, David J Baer, Deirdre T, Dejsha K, Denise Murray, Dino Hicks, Don Kinney, Don, Beth & Meghan Ferris, Douglas Molineu, Dru Pagliassotti, EC, Edward Ellis, Elaine Tindill-Rohr, Elena Beghetto, Eliza Wilcox, Elizabeth Bennefeld, Elizabeth Hyatt, Eric Rose, Erin Penn, Evan Nitz, Franny Jay, Fred Dingledy, G Nakayama, Gail de Vos, Garret Myhan, Gary W Shelton, Grace Spengler, Hendel Thistletop, Holly Daugherty, indianajewel, Isaac Alexander, Isabel, James Harding, Jamie Michels Smith, Janine K Spendlove & Ronald T Garner, Jason and Melissa Gilbert, Jay Barnson, Jay Zastrow, J E Donovan, Jen1701D, Jen B, Jen Woods, Jenn Whitworth, jennielf, Jenny Langley, Jeremy Seeley, Jess Beaushene, Jessica Fisher (Minikitty), Jim "The Destroyer" Bellmore, Jim Ryan, Jo Good, Joe Rixman, Joel, Jonathan Castro, Jonathan Turner, Joseph Hoopman, Joshua Palmatier, Joylyn Davis, Joysann, Judy Bienvenu, Julian Murdoch, Julio Capa, K Nelson, Kaijutron, Kalayna Price, Karen, Karen Dubois, Karen Flanigan, Katerina Reisdorf, Katherine Malloy, Katherine S,

Kathleen Condo, Kathy Jolly, Katy Holder, Keith Setzer, Kelley, Kenesha Williams, Kenn Gentile, Kerra L Bolton, Kerry aka Trouble, Kevin Menard, KixieKat, Kristi, Kristy K, Krystal Windsor, Larisa LaBrant, Lauren Harris, Lee Dalzell, Lesen, Lily Connors, Lisa, Luc Ricciardi, Lynn Kramer, Lynn Rushlau, M Kent Anderson, M Phelps, M Rian, Madison Metricula Roberts, maileguy, Margaret Coin, Mark Newman, Marta Kowalska, Matthew & Amy Nesbitt, Matthew W Quinn, Max Kaehn, Megan E Daggett, Megan Linton, Melissa Tabon, Merry Barton, Michael Cieslak, Michael Hockey, Micheal "The Axeman" Axe, Michael Zenke, Michelle Carlson, Michelle Iannantuono, Michelle S, Mike Miller, Missy Katano, Missy Pratt, Molly Findley, Moo moo, Morgan S Brilliant, Nathan French, neal bravin, Netha Kane, Nick Williams, Nicole Nickerson, Nile Etland, Nova B, Pat Hayes, Pat Reitz, Patrick Russell, Paul Derda, Poppa Connelly, Rachel Gollub, Rachel McNulty, Rachel Shell Vance, R E Stearns, Rebecca Poole, Regenia Liles Alcock, Renee Grimmett, Rhel ná DecVandé, RJ Beem, Rick Smathers, Rob Gaddi, Robert Moulton, R Olson, Rose Zukley, Roy McEvoy, Russell Ventimeglia, Sally Schoonover, Samuel Aronoff, Samuel Montgomery-Blinn, Sandra Seaman, Sarah Hale, Scott Drummond, SFC Marti Wulfow Garner, Retired, Sharon Wood, Sheryl R Hayes, Simo Muinonen, Skullgarden, SL Puma, SL Ryan, Smashingsuns, Stephen Graham, Steven Mentzel, Sue Anne Merrill, Susan Carlson, Susan Simko, Susan Feldman, Susanne Driessen, S Williams, T Eric Bakutis, Taryn Faust, Tasha Turner, Tera Fulbright, Textivore, The Mysterious G, The Pevners, Theresa Glover, Thomas Reed, Tina Bowerman, Tina Connell, Tom Berrisford, Tom P Powers, Tomas Burgos-Caez, Tommy Acuff, Tracy Kaplan, V Hartman DiSanto, Valentine Wolfe, Veronica Kavanagh, Victoria Pepe and Brianna Nickerson, Wakey, Yvonne Kuhn

TABLE OF CONTENTS

Introduction..1

Desert Gods - *Aubrey Campbell*....................................3

Railroad - *Matthew J. Hockey*......................................19

Pixie Season - *Seanan McGuire*....................................35

The Men with No Faces - *Alexandra Christian*..............51

Lost Words - *David B. Coe*..69

Boots of Clay - *Laura Anne Gilman*..............................85

Trickster's Choice - *Jo Gerrard*.....................................97

Wolves Howling in the Night - *Faith Hunter*................105

To Hear a Howling Herd - *Gunnar De Winter*..............127

Calliope Stark: Bone Tree Bounty Hunter - *Edmund R. Schubert*...141

Cards and Steel Hearts - *Pamela Jeffs*..........................163

Bloodsilver - *A.E. Decker*...171

Volunteered - *B.S. Donovan*...189

The Stranger in the Glass - *Dave Beynon*......................203

Belly Speaker - *Nicole Givens Kurtz*............................223

Walk the Dinosaur - *John G. Hartness*.........................241

The Time Traveling Schoolmarms of
      Marlborough County - *Barb Hendee*....................259

Rainmaker - *Margaret S. McGraw*................................279

Out of Luck - *Jeffrey Hall*..293

Rollin' Death - *Jake Bible*...305

About the Authors & Editors..327

INTRODUCTION

Everyone imagines something a little different when they hear "the wild west." For Emily, it's childhood memories of Clint Eastwood in *The Outlaw Josey Wales, the Good, the Bad, and the Ugly,* and *High Plains Drifter*--hard men and women searching for a bit of peace in an unjust and lonely world.

For Misty, "the wild west" invokes hot sunlight in a painfully blue sky, the soft creak of leather, and the occasional whiff from the horse as she rides toward a horizon that never gets any closer. She thinks of black iron locomotives pulling wooden cars painted red and gold and herds of buffalo thundering over seas of golden grass.

To Margaret, "the wild west" is freedom, mystery, opportunity, and danger. It's natural magic, or old spirits and gods that were out there long before white men ever set foot across the Mississippi. It's Coyote the Trickster sitting just on the edge of the campfire's light. It's dying of thirst or cold or heat and stumbling into the mouth of the dark cave, or down the sandy ridge to find the hidden spring...and whatever else may be there.

The wild west is a frontier, a land of possibilities: fresh starts and new beginnings made in dangerous and distant country. In *Lawless Lands* the frontier extends into the fantastic, a world of magic, faith, and futuristic science. The worlds are weird, not only strange and unfamiliar, but touched by the fates and filled with the impossible and supernatural.

Creating an anthology means facing our own kind of frontier. As editors, we start with a vague map of expectations, but the travel from the call for submissions to the final print always takes us to unexpected places. We received around three-hundred submissions for the open call, from which we selected ten stories--an incredibly difficult task given the high quality of the submissions.

We give you this book as your ticket to the Lawless Lands--twenty different weird frontiers to explore.

Misty Massey
Margaret McGraw
Emily Leverett

Desert Gods

Aubrey Campbell

THE DESERT BREATHES. TINY GRAINS OF SAND DANCE IN THE WIND, hissing and rattling along like miniscule tumbleweeds. Knocking against windowpanes, asking to be let in. When entrance is denied, the grains slip through the cracks anyway. A constant reminder that the desert gods no longer demand sacrifices. They simply take and take again.

Jackson had more than her fair share of run-ins with these desert gods. And she spent more than her fair share of time in saloons because of it, just as she did now.

Seeker's Pass wasn't much of a town. It sat too close to the edge of destruction—about to be swallowed down the gullet of the hungry desert at any second—to be considered a proper town. The inhabitants were too thin, too few and far between, and too haunted to even enjoy a proper drink, let alone stand in defiance against the gods looming on the horizon, waiting to strike and wipe this smudge of a town from the map. But there was nowhere else to go. The sands were everywhere, the gods not far behind. And when the gods were done, there was nothing left to build on, let alone any survivors. Nothing but sand. Endless sand.

Then again, Seeker's Pass had a saloon and what Jackson supposed could pass for a stable, though it looked about ready to pitch over and fold in on itself at any moment. In her opinion, a town didn't require much else.

Jackson sat at the bar of The Wraith's Kiss saloon and threw back another shot of White Fire whisky, gritty with sand as usual. A soft whisper started somewhere at the back of the saloon, a question posed low and quickly chastised into the suffocating silence again.

The city saloons still held a little friendly buzz of chatter, warm with life and the possibility of survival. But the cities…eventually, they came to be just like Seeker's Pass. Broken down and scrubbed away with the abrasive assault of the sands and the promise of death, waiting. Always waiting. The Wraith's Kiss was silent, save for that one brave whisper and the clink of glass.

Jackson didn't like silence. It never lasted long. And when it broke, generally all hell broke loose with it.

Out of habit, Jackson rested one hand on the butt of her six-shooter at her left hip. With her free hand, she pulled a cigar and a match from her vest pocket. Slowly, each movement measured and unhurried, she put the thick, earthy cigar between her teeth and dragged the match across the counter with a rasping scratch and a flare of light.

Touched the match to the tip of the cigar.

Inhaled.

Let out a cloud of smoke on a tired sigh.

A reek of desperation tainted the bittersweet flavor of her cigar, a stench Jackson had smelled so many times in her life, she had long since lost count. The reek of desperation had started with that faint whisper. All too soon, the desperation would grow into a plea for help, just like the last town, and the town before that. Endless, like the sands.

Footsteps, heavy and thunderous on the floorboards, entered the saloon. That would be O'Reilly then, after finally intimidating the stableman into a dirt cheap price, just for the fun of it, only to tip him generously to annoy him. She settled onto a stool on Jackson's left with a creak of her leather holsters, a hiss of metal as her blades shifted against her back.

Jackson poured another shot for herself, then slid the bottle of whisky down the bar. O'Reilly gave a wild smile, green eyes still bright with excitement over the smallest taste of an argument from the stableman, weak though it must have been in a place like this. It didn't feel like the folks of Seeker's Pass had much fight left in them to give. But for the moment, O'Reilly got the fight she craved—no matter how easily won it might have been—and she tossed her head back as she took a long swig from the bottle.

"Where's Imala?" Jackson asked.

O'Reilly set the bottle on the bar and wiped her hand across her mouth. "Takin' a tour 'round the place," she replied, the words rough and heavy with her Irish accent. "Said there'll be two storms in the next day."

Jackson nodded, calculations flying through her mind at this piece of information. Three gods to a storm meant six gods were looking to take Seeker's Pass and every measly, ghost-like soul who still lingered in this hellhole.

O'Reilly leaned back against the bar, bottle draped from her fingertips. Her short, curly hair caught a few slivers of light from the lamps of the saloon and gleamed wicked red, like fire in the dim, smoky atmosphere, matching the all-too-eager glint in her eye.

"Two-to-one odds," Jackson pointed out.

"We've fought worse and come through fine," O'Reilly said.

"The last time we faced four. I was laid up for a month from one of those things rammin' a poisoned barb in my leg."

O'Reilly's smile turned into a smirk, a knife's slash of confidence and teasing and a challenge on her lips, all at once. A dangerous, dangerous mixture if ever there was one.

"Losin' your touch, old girl," O'Reilly replied.

Jackson stiffened, though not at O'Reilly's teasing. The whispers had started up again at her back, this time insistent and determined despite the chastising. The impending plea for help was coming, no stopping or escaping it now. She went rigid as she sensed a hand reaching out toward her shoulder, a faint presence hovering just out of her line of sight.

"If you don't want your fingers blown off, boy," Jackson said, "best keep 'em to yourself."

The boy snatched his hand back. He was a thin, grubby little creature, well acquainted with hunger and the hard, unforgiving life of the desert like most folks these days. His shock of blond hair held a thin coating of dusty golden sand, and his clothes hung on his slight frame, three sizes too big for him.

"Are you...I was wondering..." he stammered.

Jackson raised an eyebrow and turned toward him. She propped one elbow on the bar while her other hand pushed her black duster aside to reveal the massive six-shooter on her hip. The boy's eyes bulged, and his mouth dropped open, words forgotten. O'Reilly chuckled and took another long draw from the bottle, watching the interchange play out.

"That's what you want, isn't it?" Jackson asked the boy.

His gaze flicked up to meet hers. Solid. Unwavering. She had to give him credit for that. Most people were too scared to look her in the eye.

"Is it true?" he croaked. "Can you really kill a god?"

Jackson let her coat drift back into place, and she waved her cigar at him. "What do you think? You wouldn't be here if you didn't believe it was possible."

He shifted, uncertain. "The last bartender here, Mr. Stockman, he tried to kill a god with his sawed-off shotgun."

Jackson stifled a groan and slid her glass over to O'Reilly. She filled it to the top with a knowing look and a smirk.

"Let me guess," Jackson said. "There wasn't enough of Mr. Stockman to bury."

The boy's face went deathly pale, and he shook his head.

"Don't mean to be callous or anything," O'Reilly piped in. "But he was askin' for it, going after the gods with nothing but a shotgun. You got to have somethin' with a little more kick."

She sat up, always enthusiastic to show off her prized weapons. She unsheathed her scythe blades with a swish of leather and the high whine of metal against metal.

"These beauties," she said, "were passed down by the priestesses of my homeland when it was still green and the desert was only a nightmare far away."

The boy looked doubtful. "Swords? The gods would eat you before you ever got close enough to use those things."

O'Reilly scowled, indignant.

"Here we go again," Jackson muttered into her glass.

"How old are you, boy?" O'Reilly demanded.

"Thirteen."

She pointed to the etchings decorating the full arch of each blade. "Then you're old enough for what I'm about to tell you. You see these along here?"

The boy squinted. "I can't make it out…"

"It's a saying, old and worn, and it's never failed me yet. 'Send the enemy off to meet death with a farewell kiss of steel and a solid Irish blessing to go straight to hell.' A blessed blade is no common sword, I'll have you know, and the priestesses must be howling with fury back home to hear you say that. A god can't stand against a blessing slicing through its flesh. And I can get plenty close enough, boy, so mind your young tongue, why don't you?"

"Yes ma'am," he mumbled. His gaze dropped to Jackson's holster. "Does that have enough kick?"

Jackson studied him for a moment in utter silence, unmoving. Then she pulled a bullet from her belt and held it up. Clouds of the deepest, richest red swirled in the bullet's depths, streaked through with black lightning that snapped and sparked.

"You know what this is?" she asked.

"A Devil's Eye," he replied, voice soft with wonder as he reached out to touch it. "Made from the curse of a witch's blood."

Before his fingers made contact, Jackson snatched the bullet away. The boy frowned.

"But witches don't give their blood freely," he said. "How did you…?"

"All you need to know is that it makes gods bleed. And if a god can bleed, a god can die, just like any other fragile life out there. Got it?"

Jackson leaned on the bar again, shoulders hunched, closing the boy out. Conversation over. Too many questions made her uneasy. With a mind like that, knowledge was the kick he craved, the weapon he was looking for. The last thing she needed was some scrawny boy with whip-sharp curiosity to figure out she was the witch, taking her own blood to forge god-slaying bullets. Then she'd find herself pinned on the ground with the suddenly wide-awake folks of Seeker's Pass leering over her and draining her of every ounce of blood in her veins.

No. The boy definitely didn't need to know any of that.

But the boy seemed to be the only one in this dying town who harbored a lick of fight in his body. He remained at Jackson's shoulder and pulled himself up to his full height...which wasn't much. He hardly came up to her elbow standing there.

"I want to hire you," he said, his voice echoing in the silent saloon. "This is the only home I've got, and I'd like to keep it if I can. My farm was taken last summer by the gods. My parents, too. I got nowhere else to go."

Jackson kept staring straight ahead. "Move to the city then. That's what most folks are doin'."

Not that it makes much of a difference, she thought. The sands were crawling into the cities just as steadily as they were crawling into the half-rotten towns like this one, trembling at the edge of the world where mercy didn't exist anymore.

"If you've got the money," the boy replied, an undeniable bitterness biting through his words. "Which I don't. But I ain't runnin'. My parents died here, and I won't leave 'em."

Jackson turned to look at him now with a faint light of admiration in her eyes. O'Reilly nudged her with an elbow.

"He don't look like much, but he's got a fighting spirit," she whispered. "I like him."

Jackson tapped her cigar ash onto the floor, poured a fresh shot of whisky, and slid it over to the boy.

"What's your name?" she asked.

The boy pushed the drink back in refusal. "Spencer Perkins," he said.

She gestured to the handful of onlookers who had been alternately gaping and glaring at them for the entire conversation.

"Your friends don't seem to agree with you," Jackson said. "Seems like they could care less whether Seeker's Pass rots or not."

"They don't trust you. They think you'll take your cut and hightail it when the trouble comes."

"It's a decent concern. And so far, we haven't discussed payment. You said you don't have enough to get into the city, but you think you've got enough to pay me for my work?"

Spencer's bravado flickered, just for a moment, and he hesitated. He pulled a thin silver necklace from his pocket and placed it on the bar's counter. He spread it out gently to display the fine chain, slight as spider-silk, and the tiny pearls that winked in the lamplight.

"It ain't much, but…" He paused then added, his voice quieter this time, "It was my mother's."

Jackson didn't look at O'Reilly. Payment wasn't needed for O'Reilly to dive head first into a fight like this. But Jackson had pulled countless bullets from her veins and sent countless gods returning to the ravenous desert sands in her lifetime, and she was tired. Where one god died, three more sprang up to take its place. The fight never ended. And the desert continued to creep in. Steady as water, moving and rustling and eating away. Nothing slowed it down. It was in her hair, in her mouth, in her whisky. *All* the time.

Before Jackson could reply, the batwing doors squeaked open, accompanied by the familiar whispering footsteps of Imala. A collective hiss rose in the saloon, the first sound Seeker's Pass had managed to muster up together.

"No," the bartender said. He was a short, stooped man with wire-rimmed spectacles clouded by years of scratchy sand and wind. While Jackson had been sitting at the bar, he'd shown no interest in anyone or anything else besides wiping down his humble collection of shot glasses. But now that Imala stood in the doorway of the saloon, with no weapon and not a grain of sand anywhere on her…he was suddenly sharp and alive with anger.

"No," he repeated, waving his dishrag at her. "We don't serve your kind here."

Jackson pulled her duster back, presenting her six-shooter in all its glory. "And what kind would that be?"

The bartender faltered, his small wary eyes shifting from Imala to Jackson and back to Imala again.

"Sandspinners," he grumbled under his breath to Jackson. "You know they can't be trusted. They're no better than the gods."

"Ever met one?" Jackson asked.

"I…I've heard stories and…"

"Then I'd say you've got enough trouble on your hands without making an enemy of a spinner on top of it," she said, tapping her thumb pointedly against the butt of her gun. "Especially one who never travels alone."

There had been the rare occasion when Jackson resorted to violence against humans, though she didn't like to make it a habit. She'd much rather scare the stupid out of people instead of shooting them. The death grip some folks maintained on their small-minded and unfounded prejudices never ceased to baffle her. And when such pettiness put her friends in the line of fire, she had no tolerance for it.

The bartender dropped his gaze to the shot glasses before him.

"That's what I thought," Jackson said, easing her hand only an inch or two away from her six-shooter, but not so far she couldn't grab it if anyone else decided to take a disliking to Imala's arrival.

O'Reilly sheathed her blades and waved the now empty bottle at the bartender. "Why don't you get a fresh bottle of something nice for our friend to make up for it, hmm?"

The bartender nodded without looking up, rummaged around on the shelves behind him, and slid a bottle down the counter.

"On the house," he muttered.

Jackson waited and stared at him. Hard.

"With apologies," he added.

O'Reilly picked up the bottle and surveyed the label. "Unholy Temper. The man knows how to make a proper apology, I'll give him that."

Jackson maintained her steady stare for a full minute more, but the bartender never looked up again. Imala slipped into the open seat on Jackson's right. Idly, she placed her hand on the counter with a low hum. A dozen grains of sand picked up and swirled in a tiny vortex in front of her, spinning like a top. O'Reilly poured a drink and nudged it over. Imala stopped it with her palm, but the sand kept spinning, her concentration never broken.

Spencer came up to the bar and peered over the edge, watching the sand as it drifted in lazy circles.

"How does it look out there?" Jackson finally asked, still glaring at the bartender's back.

"We'll have trouble before nightfall," Imala replied. "And stop scaring him, Jackson. I don't care what he said."

"You never care what anyone says. But I do. How much trouble?"

Imala sent two grains of sand to chasing each other around the rim of her shot glass. One grain tumbled into the drink then bounced out again.

"Two storms. One close to bursting. The other small and far away."

O'Reilly's smile blossomed, partly from the effects of the Unholy Temper and partly from the promise of a fight.

"Just keeps getting better and better," she said. "Seeker's Pass is growing on me."

Jackson shot a dark look in her direction. "Are there any odds that scare you?"

O'Reilly snorted. "If there are, I haven't met them yet."

Spencer peeled a finger away from the bar's counter and pointed at the sand.

"How did you do that?"

Jackson, O'Reilly, and Imala turned as one to face Spencer. The bartender snapped his dishrag at him.

"Spencer, boy, run along. You'll get yourself killed, pestering bounty hunters with your ceaseless questions the way you do."

Spencer waved him off. "I'll get myself killed no matter where I go, Mr. Hale."

O'Reilly laughed and tipped her bottle in Spencer's direction. "Quick learner, that one."

Imala swept her hand over the counter, and the sand grains jumped into her palm, pouncing and tumbling over each other.

"The sands sing, Spencer," she said. "And I merely listen. That's all they want."

Spencer wrinkled his nose. "They don't sing."

"Oh yes, they do. You've heard how those sandstorms scream with power. You've heard them chatter as they scratch at the windows. And after I've listened to their song, I sing it back to them, and they dance for me."

"So you can control the whole desert then," Spencer said, his eyes lighting up. "You could stop the desert and the gods from taking anyone else."

Imala made a small sound of disagreement. "I wish it was that simple. As much as I can control the sand, I can't *stop* the sand. No one owns the desert but the desert itself. And I have tried. Believe me."

"Almost got yourself killed, too," Jackson grumbled.

Imala flashed a gentle smile in her direction. "But you were there to fix my mistakes, as always."

Jackson grunted in response.

Imala's fingers drifted over Spencer's necklace that still lay on the dark wood of the countertop, glittering like a thread of silver starlight. She opened her mouth to ask about it, but a gust of wind cut her off. It howled between the only two buildings of Seeker's Pass and swept into the saloon. A spray of sand grated over Jackson's face, skittered along the edges of O'Reilly's blades, and came to a stop in front of Imala, showering to the floor as if it had hit an invisible wall.

"A little early, aren't they?" O'Reilly said, sliding her blades from their sheaths. "Don't even bother waiting for sundown anymore."

"You should know by now," Jackson replied, clamping her cigar between her teeth and pulling her six-shooter from its holster. "The gods do whatever they damn well please."

Jackson, O'Reilly, and Imala pushed out of the batwing doors and into the street.

Only a few feet away, against the pale wash of the sky, was a massive churning ball of sand, spinning in place, a private world of storm for the gods alone. Flickers of the gods could be seen inside, shapes of their shadows—a rattlesnake tail, a scorpion claw, a human-like face—before the sand tumbled those faint glimpses out of sight again.

Jackson turned to find a second storm just beginning to form on the other side of town, a mere pinprick against the horizon, sucking in sand from the nearby desert until patches of hard-packed dirt and bare rock were exposed. It might be small now, seemingly inconsequential to the immediate trouble at hand, but she'd seen these storms explode in minutes, gods swarming out like cockroaches.

A flash of movement caught Jackson's eye. Spencer stood on the steps of the saloon, clinging to the hitching post against the tearing winds as bits of sand flew from his hair and his clothes in clouds of dust.

"We've never faced two storms at the same time before," O'Reilly said, shouting to be heard over the wind. "And here I thought this was only a sleepy little town in the middle of nowhere."

Jackson couldn't stop staring at Spencer, still holding onto that hitching post for all he was worth. That boy wasn't going to let go of this forsaken town until the gods pried his dead fingers from it.

A light touch at her elbow brought Jackson back to the present. Imala was studying her, dark eyes steady and concerned. The wind whipped Imala's black hair around her face, but otherwise, the sands didn't make contact with her the way it did for everyone and everything else, coating clothing and hair and skin in a layer of grit that never came off. Imala was at peace despite the chaos around her, untouched, unmarked as sand grains jumped and vibrated around her feet.

"You can sit this one out," Imala offered. "We won't blame you. It takes such a toll and…"

"It's like that for all of us," Jackson cut in. She paused then added, "Except maybe O'Reilly."

Imala said nothing. She had noticed Spencer as well, the only unarmed human who dared to be in the street with the gods so near. Jackson swore under her breath. She'd never turned anyone down when they asked for help against the gods. Few people had the power to do anything. But she did. She had it coursing through her veins, her very life's source.

She could feel Imala and O'Reilly staring at her. Waiting. Jackson swore again, louder this time, and marched up to Spencer until she towered above him.

"Get inside," she roared over the wind.

Spencer shielded his eyes against the sand, the sun, and the wind and peered up at her.

"Are you leaving?" he asked.

Jackson blinked, startled. "What?"

"I heard your friend, the Irish one with the blessed blades. She said you've never fought two sandstorms at once. And I can see it on your face. That's too many. Even for you."

Jackson ground her teeth together. She *should* run. That would be the smart thing to do. Hightail it like all of Seeker's Pass expected her to. Then again, she hated meeting people's expectations…

"Haven't backed down from a fight in my life," Jackson replied. "And neither has O'Reilly. Or Imala. We're not going anywhere."

The smile that transformed Spencer's dirt-stained face made Jackson's chest ache. He looked so young. Too young to be here with storms threatening to break. Spencer's fist shot out, the silver necklace dangling from his fingers.

"Don't know how you'll split it three ways though," he said. "Hadn't exactly thought that far ahead I guess."

Jackson tucked the necklace into Spencer's palm and pushed it to his chest. "Keep it," she said. "Carries more value for you anyway."

Spencer's smile wobbled just a little, and he nodded.

The winds fell away in that moment, and the sands trailed from windows and eaves like dry rain. Jackson jerked her thumb at the saloon.

"Get inside," she repeated. "Before I drag you in there myself. And don't come out for anything, understood?"

He muttered a quick "yes ma'am" before he hurried inside. Jackson returned to O'Reilly and Imala. She checked the bullets in her six-shooter, more of a ritual than a necessity since she always kept it loaded.

"Losin' your touch *and* goin' soft, old girl," O'Reilly said with a wry glance in Jackson's direction.

Jackson snapped the barrel into place. "Shut up."

The first sandstorm burst like a bubble in a shower of sand, and three gods tumbled out, black against the fiery gold of the desert. They uncurled and stretched, legs and limbs and scales scraping over the desert floor. Each bore a resemblance to part of the desert—a snake body, scorpion claws, spider legs—and each bore a human likeness as well, caught between two species, earning them the title of gods among men.

"So the cavalry has arrived at last," one god said, with a snake-like tail and a human torso. Charcoal black skin gleamed in the blazing white sunlight. The god smiled, and two perfect fangs flashed out. "It's nice to have a bit of a challenge every once in a while."

A rustling rumble began to grow at Jackson's back, but she didn't dare take her eyes off the first three gods who had emerged. She knew that sound though. The second sandstorm was expanding, hot and fast.

"If you leave now," another god said, this one with the long, dusty brown body of a scorpion and the head of a woman, "we'll give you a head start, just to be generous. You might survive, depending on how fast you run."

"Afraid we can't return the generous offer," Jackson said. "If you run now, we'll still kill you."

The gods hissed with laughter and seemed to swell against the sky as they shifted, fanning out around Seeker's Pass.

"Big talk for such tiny humans," the snake god replied. "We'll enjoy sucking the marrow from your bones and grinding you into the dirt. Just like every other weak human who has tried to stop us from wiping the earth clean and claiming it as ours."

O'Reilly lowered her head and grinned, feral and wild and hungry for the ensuing fight.

"You'll be the one pickin' your teeth with your own bones when we're through with you," she said. With that, she launched herself at the snake god, blades singing and slicing through the air.

Jackson bit back a curse at O'Reilly's early attack and switched her attention to the encroaching scorpion god hurtling toward O'Reilly's left shoulder. Jackson fired and clipped the scorpion god in the abdomen. Red tentacles of smoke curled out from the bullet wound and burst like a flower, crawling over the god's body. It writhed and shrieked with fury, twisting in the sand, claws snapping at the curse as it worked its way under the scorpion god's thick plates of armor and into the soft flesh beneath.

Imala turned her hands palm-down toward the earth and began to sing, a quiet melody that gained strength with every word. The sands twisted up in strings toward her hands, swaying back and forth to the rhythm until she had dozens of strings at her command like a puppeteer. With a guiding push, she sent the strings of sand out towards the third god, spider legs stomping against the desert floor as it charged toward her. The sand tangled in the god's legs and made it stumble before it regained its footing.

Imala sent a second assault of sand against the spider god, this one a swarm of sand darts, peppering the spider god until it shrieked and tunneled beneath the sand for shelter.

The second sandstorm burst apart, and three more gods tumbled out, bearing the bodies of lizards and the heads of humans, gliding over the desert floor towards them. Imala's voice climbed another octave, stronger, louder, soaring into the sky. More sand rose at her command in a jet of dust behind her. It curled forward like smoke and blinded the second wave of gods scrambling over each other to join the fight.

But the distraction lasted only a moment. The lizard gods tunneled below the sands and disappeared from sight. Jackson pulled up, watching the desert floor as it heaved and rippled in every direction. She kept her pistol trained on the ground, waiting for the first god to poke its head up. The saloon shuddered on its foundation as the gods burrowed underneath, making the building sway. Wood creaked and groaned in protest at being disturbed as it shifted then settled flat again. The handful of folk inside the saloon spilled out of the door and onto the sands, frantic for shelter that wouldn't threaten to crush them.

Jackson stepped forward, waving them back inside. A lizard god burst out of the sand like a daisy, mouth transformed to a wide open black hole, guzzling sand and humans alike before it whipped around.

"You lose, gunslinger," it said, then advanced on Jackson, slithering over the desert floor.

Imala brought her hands up sharp and fast. A wall of sand shot into the air, cutting the lizard god off from its attack on Jackson. So long as Imala could keep the sand wall strong, their backs were covered. She pulled and pushed, coaxed and teased the desert into life, bigger than anything Jackson had ever seen Imala work before. Spinning ribbons of sand ducked and twisted around Imala, Jackson, and O'Reilly, fending off blows from the gods like a shield. Lightning crackled and snapped in blinding flashes as curses and blessings flew amid the billowing sands.

Jackson could hardly see anything now as the storm grew, colliding and absorbing the storms of the gods. Imala trembled from the strain of controlling so much sand at once, but she put her head down, gritted her teeth, and held on. She wouldn't let herself slip, not now, when Jackson and O'Reilly needed her the most.

Jackson could just make out O'Reilly fighting off two gods, blades winking in the orange-red haze of sand. Pieces of scaled armor fell all around her as she cut and carved.

A scream pierced the battle, small and faint and so very human amid the war cries of the gods.

Jackson spun at the sound. Two gods ripped the saloon's roof clean off, shingles peeling away like flower petals in the storm. And Jackson knew there would be only one person left in that saloon...

Jackson took off running through the storm, firing over and over in desperation. There was simply too much distance between her and the saloon to make it before those gods would have Spencer. Curses coiled like snakes in the air, leaving a trail of red searing through the sands and biting into the gods' armored bodies.

O'Reilly sliced with her blessed blades, forging her way toward the saloon.

And Imala screamed with the full force of the sand flaring out around the entire battle in a halo before crashing in on top of them all.

The sands rushed away like a wave running out to meet the sea. Then the grains scrambled over each other and returned to settle at Imala's feet, barely kissing the toes of her moccasins.

Jackson lay to Imala's right, just before the saloon steps, cursed six-shooter across her chest. Finally at rest after so many years of giving her own blood to others.

O'Reilly lay to her left, her half-moon blades splayed out on either side like wings.

The saloon was in splinters, gone. Along with Spencer.

And the gods...the gods were nothing but massive skeletons on the desert floor, sand sifting from their bones.

Imala's legs trembled where she stood. She tipped forward almost as if to take a step, then dropped to the ground with a small sound of surprise as her body shivered with fatigue.

The three of them had never fought like that, with so much power, using up every scrap of energy they could summon in the heat of battle when they were exhausted and exhilarated at the same time.

But the gods didn't die like that either, not all at once as if...as if some common thread had been binding them together.

A wink of light in the sand caught Imala's attention. She crawled to it, fished it out.

Spencer's necklace came free, though tarnished slightly by the grating grains of sand caught in the delicate silver chain. She never did get around to asking him about it. But she'd seen Jackson give it back to him, refuse his payment. It meant something to him, something precious and rare in this cruel, harsh land.

Imala closed her fingers around the necklace, and the sand fell away from it. Maybe this was what they'd been looking for all along, Jackson, O'Reilly, and Imala, wandering the desert together, killing as many gods as they could, helping as many poor, tired souls as possible. But it was Spencer's bravery, the only one to stand up and speak for the entirety of his humble little hometown that had been the final piece they needed to end the cruel reign of the gods— Jackson's curses, O'Reilly's blessings, Imala's spinning...and Spencer's heart.

So much power all in one place, wrapped up and entwined as it had been in that storm, no one—human or god—could withstand such a blow. Only a spinner would survive, forged by the desert sands, protected by the desert sands.

Imala lifted her face to the sky and felt the desert sigh all around her, a bittersweet sound, filled with relief and sadness to match her own. The gods were dead, the thread tying them together broken at last. But her friends were gone, too. Jackson. O'Reilly. Spencer.

She was the last one left standing with the pale blue of the sky stretching above and the hazy soft orange of the desert stretching below in an endless expanse of color and heat.

A persistent tapping at Imala's right knee pulled her from her thoughts.

She looked down. Three grains of sand, one red as the devil, one black as night, and one pale as the moon, rattled with insistence. She scooped them into the palm of her hand, and they chased each other in dizzying circles.

Imala would never be alone, so long as she had the sands to keep her company.

RAILROAD

Matthew J. Hockey

August 1885 – Harker's Hill – Dunnswood County – Dakota Territory

CARSON DISMOUNTED HIS HORSE AND FLIPPED OPEN HIS FILIGREE POCKET watch. He'd timed the ride perfectly. It was exactly thirty minutes to midnight. The bluff above town afforded him an unrivalled view of the whole valley, dark at this time save for the fires burning in the isolated gold claims out in the pines.

He muzzled the horse and tied the reins to a tree; it had taken many months to train the animal to keep quiet once they were up there. He installed himself in the camouflaged blind that he'd built at the specified location between the lumber camp and the third loop of the river. He settled down to wait for exactly thirty minutes as per the instructions the previous Station Master had given him the day he landed.

He checked the straps on the satchel hidden in the hollow tree stump at the center of the blind. Once he had satisfied himself that they hadn't been tampered with, he concentrated on the vigil proper. The satchel was full of ladies' clothes for the next Station Master: a smock, winter coat, boots, and a bonnet. Buying them had been a great exercise in deception. He'd had to invent a sister out east as an excuse for the seamstress at Kim's general.

It was a town of tongues: tongues that gossiped, tongues that tattled, and tongues that told outright untruths. A bachelor, a bachelor living alone in a ranch house, a bachelor all alone in a ranch house without cattle, dogs, or any interest in the town's one prostitute, buying women's hosiery no less. God knows what they'd say about him.

He hoped they would fit her, whoever she was. The only things he knew about her were that she was a woman and that she had set off two minutes behind him. Now sixteen months later, he was still waiting for her to arrive.

He'd ridden the horse up onto that bluff every night without fail, always to the same spot, always at the same time. He hadn't missed one night in sixteen months. Sixteen months. Four hundred and eighty-five nights of rain, mud, wind, snow, stinging wasps and horse bites and all, so far, for nothing. Always the same flat silence. Always the same uninterrupted darkness.

The thirty-minute window closed for another night. He snapped the pocket watch closed. He mounted the horse, whipped it to a fair clip, and headed for his stead. He rode the first four miles before realizing he was not looking where he was going; the horse was guiding them through dense woods, over estuaries, and down steep ravines. He couldn't keep his eyes off the sky, off the stars.

He watched the stars whenever he got the chance; he had never seen anything so beautiful. Where he was from, he was lucky if he saw even one star through the clouds and the lights, yet there on the horse, in that moment, the sky was so full and so bright that there seemed to be barely a gap between the galaxies. As if space was vibrant and meaningful instead of the cold, dead emptiness he knew it to be. He held onto that thought. He held onto it until his fingers were blue.

He arrived home, stabled the horse, and hung his gun belt on the doornail. He checked every room of the house from the parlor up into the attic, then he checked them again. No intruders. No bogeyman under the bed. He shuttered the windows, drew the curtains, locked the doors, and let the fire die in the hearth. Even in the dark, he held his breath before taking the chest from its place in the earth wall of the cellar. He unlocked the chest with the key from the chain around his neck. Inside was a gunny sack, inside that a Smith and Wesson ammunition case, inside that a box of matches and his watch.

He struck a match, the last in the box, and used it to light a foul-smelling candle. He sat cradling his watch in the shifting light. It was a Casio digital with a black rubber strap and buckle. Its screen was gray and lifeless, its battery long since dead and irreplaceable in this timeframe. He would never throw it away, could never throw it away. It was the only tangible proof that he was not insane. He came to be with it at least once a day. On bad nights, he would come down every hour just to hold it and rub his thumbs across it. He had long since worn the decals to illegible hieroglyphs.

It was three o'clock in the morning when he went to bed.

Friday came and he made his weekly amble into town—'town' being a big word for what was essentially just a few buildings sprung up round a well and a crossroad. There was a clapboard stable, part horse-trader, part smithy, complete with a belching stack that painted the air rust red for miles around. There was a post office and telegraph center, Kim's general, and Tabatha T's mercantile. No sheriff. No mayor. No politics save for that which spilled out the doors of the saloon "The Diamond Hostelry." He didn't let himself go in there, not since the first time. He'd ended up drunk and holding long, fully coherent discussions on all sorts of scientific topics. It had taken a long time to rebuild himself as the harmless boob after that.

The town's children ran out to gawk at him as he rode in. They pointed and laughed as they always did. His horse didn't suit him; it was far too big for such a short man, and he had to jump to get off it. It was flighty and nervous even on the calmest of evenings, prone to biting if its impatient hoof stamps were ignored. That, in part, was the reason why he'd gotten it so cheaply from the stableman; its previous owner had been shot out of the saddle, and the experience had left an ugly brown powder mark on its temperament. He chose it precisely because they were so incompatible. He'd seen it bucking around the paddock like a dog with its ass afire and pointed. "Yessir, that's the one."

Like the frayed elbows of his shirt or the loose waist on his trousers, the horse was just another brush stroke to the impression he was trying to convey. Ask anyone in Harker's Hill, and they'd say he was a harmless, maybe even dull-witted, recluse.

He drew up outside Tabatha T's mercantile. The door had a few lovingly tended bullet holes; they were twenty-year souvenirs from the taking of some forgotten road agent who had plagued the valley. The road agent was dead, the triumphant lawmen were dead, and Tabatha T was dead longer still. These days the shop was run by a family of Germans who had never met the old crone but kept her name over the door. They had rather judiciously decided that Schneidermann-Adlersflügel might be hard for the locals to pronounce.

The sheer variety of goods inside always amazed him: .65 rifle ammunition butted up against imported European candies, sacks of coffee beans spilled onto a delicate photographic apparatus, the shop's trained bird hung talon-deep from strings of smoked sausage. Clocks, fuses, taxidermy, maps, naval charts, opiates, and children. Children. Children. Children. The German family could not stop having children. Though from the look of them, they were both pushing sixty.

"Good morning?" the storekeeper said. Carson wasn't sure if it was a greeting or a heart-felt question. The storekeeper had never really mastered inflection.

"Good. How's your wife?"

"She's just swell. Just swell. Somebody came in asking about you."

"About me?" He turned his back, pretending a sudden interest in a display of non-patented remedies, boxed cataplasms for helping women get through the monthlies.

"Ja. He asked for you by name. Wo ist Carson? Wo ist Carson? He was very insistent, sniffing around like a dog after a dead skunk." The shopkeeper came around the counter and kicked one of his daughters from where she was eavesdropping. She ran outside laughing.

"Did he look a good sort?" Carson piled his things on the countertop, and after a moment's tabulation, he added a box of .44 Russian to his haul as casually as he could.

"He smelled of witch-hazel and wore an outmoded hat. Between you and I, I think he is being a Pinkerton." The shopkeeper clapped and wriggled on the spot.

"Which would make you an outlaw, no?"

"I take it you didn't tell him anything? What I look like? Where I live?" He placed his money on the counter.

"Of course," the shopkeeper said. Carson's sigh of relief strangled in his throat. "I even drew him a map. He took a room in the Diamond, not slept there but once by all accounts."

Carson left the store, a paper bag gripped in one fist and the two dollars walking jerkily over the knuckles of the other. One of the shopkeeper's sons had joined the daughter on the duckboards out front. Carson waved the money in their direction, and they looked up from the dead rodent they were examining.

"You little'n's seen that new fella around, been asking questions on your pa?"

"We seen 'im," the freckled girl said, hands tucked into her dungarees.

"Two dollars says you can't follow him, find where he goes, who he visits with."

"Two dollars each?" the boy said, high color in his cheeks like scarlet fever that never went.

The girl slapped the boy quiet.

"Two dollars gets you four days. If'n you want us any longer than that, the price is one dollar a day," she said.

"One dollar up front. You get the other the first time you tell me something good." Carson told her. They shook and he knew from the girl's handshake that one day she was going to turn her pa's store into an empire.

The kids scattered and he rode home, taking a strange route and stopping every now and then to check his back-trail. A low down sick feeling started in his underparts and didn't show any sign of stopping.

The next day, he awoke to a hammering on his front door. He'd slept with his Schofield model 03 pistol next to him on the nightstand; he took it down and held it tight as he squatted with his ear against the keyhole. The knocks were coming from stomach height. He laughed, hid his gun in a sash at his belt, and opened up.

It was the oldest of the shopkeeper's daughters. She was carrying a baby of no more than a year with the same enthusiasm usually reserved for toting sacks of coal.

"Morning Mattie," he said.

"That ain't my name," the girl stepped inside. "It's Lizzy."

"I know that. Just a little joke of mine," he said. "You got here alright then?"

"Sure. Everybody knows the Carson place." She put on an arch, Germanic voice supposed to be her father. "You kinder better behave, or Mr. Carson will get you."

"Cute," he said. "You thirsty? I only got coffee."

"That'll do it." She looked away from him then, his purpose served, and set about changing the baby into fresh duds. He came back from the stove with two tarnished tin mugs. The girl drank a big gulp, and though it obviously burned her, she tried not to show it.

"We found your man," she said.

"What does he look like?" He put her dollar on the table.

"Like he don't eat none. Nor sleep neither. And what you call these?" She grinned and pointed to the lines that appeared from the sides of her nose down to her chin.

"Nasolabial creases," he said before quickly changing his mind. "Laugh lines."

"Yeah them. He had real deep ones of them. He weren't old though. Hair still black."

"Has he been back to his room?"

"Maybe. Not while we was watching. I got three of my brothers on it. There's a big rock out back, and if you stand on it, you can see right inside. His stuff's there, but he hasn't so much as glanced at it."

"What stuff?"

"I don't know. Bags. A… like what my ma calls her Valise. Keeps all her knickknacks in it from when she used to live in Germany."

"That's good work. Worth every cent. There'll be a bonus if you answer me this. If they aren't sleeping in their room, where are they sleeping?"

The baby cried; the girl picked it up and went to the door.

"Soon as I know, I'll come back for another dollar."

She set off on her long walk with the baby crying on her shoulder. After she had gone from view, he realized that he was sad she'd left. It was one of the few conversations he'd had that had lasted more than a few minutes.

Lizzy came back the day after. She didn't have the baby with her this time and had a smug smile on her face. She strode in with her hands on her hips, picked up the coins, and slid them into her bib pocket.

"He's bivouacked down in Werner's wood. Him and another fella… a nigger," the girl said, seeming to enjoy the special flavor of it.

"Don't say that word."

"Why not? That's what he is." The girl's brow creased up, and her lips pursed.

"No, he ain't. He's a person. Like you and me."

"But… you're white. I'm white."

"Only hateful and ignorant people use that word, and you aren't either." He ruffled her hair to show her no hard feelings. She brushed his hand away.

"I just thought I'd let you know is all. They're set up away from the road near the big lightning-struck oak."

He gave her another dollar, enough to buy all the candy in her father's store four times over. She walked as far as the doorway, then stood shuffling her feet. She was trying hard not to say something.

"Spit it," he said, it was like popping a balloon.

"I seen your book on the table and… well, I weren't snooping, I promise. I just wondered if maybe you needed somebody to show you how to read on account of you being backward is all."

"And I suppose that'd be you would it? Show me how to read."

"I read just fine. A missionary learned me how last year gone, and I didn't tell nobody because my brothers would have beat me, so I never got a chance to read nothing but the Bible." She took a huge gasp and waited.

"Let you in on a secret? I read just fine, too, and I got plenty of books that ain't the Bible."

"Show me," she said, almost mocking. He motioned her to a chair and picked the nearest heavy book off the table.

"*The Count of Monte Cristo* by Alexander Dumas. Chapter one. The arrival at Marseilles. On the twenty-fourth of February, 1815, the Marseilles port lookouts signaled that the three-master Pharaoh was coming up the harbor..." He tried to put the book down at the end of the paragraph, but she twirled her hand for him to keep on. And he did keep on. He kept on for hours, stopping only when it got time for him to leave for his vigil. She promised to be back the next day. He offered to walk her back to town, but she ran off hooting before he could get his boots on.

He felt eyes gaping on him as he waited in place, though whether they were real or his own paranoia, he couldn't tell. Either way, nothing happened.

The next day he made the effort to cook a proper breakfast; he rustled a few eggs from the coup out back and fried them on the skillet. They tasted so good that as soon as he had finished sopping up the last of the busted yolk, he went outside and rustled himself two more.

He boiled water and washed up his plates, and once he'd done that, he cleaned the big pile of dishes that had been gathering for months by the back door. Where before he had seen character in the unkempt corners of his house—the unmade bed, the cobwebs in the corners, the weeds growing up round the windows—now all he saw were faults to be corrected. He busied himself all morning and then partway into the afternoon. Sweeping dust into the yard, beating out rugs, and straightening furniture. When Lizzy arrived, he was up a ladder clearing an abandoned bird's nest from the eaves.

"Didn't your momma ever tell you that's bad luck?" she hollered behind him. He startled and had to grab the coving to keep from falling off the ladder.

"Didn't your momma ever tell you there ain't any such thing as luck?"

She had a few bits and pieces to report. The two men didn't have horses and were getting low on supplies; she surmised that they'd be making a trip into town within the next day or two.

"That's real fine. Have you managed to get a looksee in that room yet?"

"I'm fair shamed to admit I haven't. I do have a plan though. Lyle, the innkeeper's son, well, he's kind of sweet on me. He's two years younger, but I said I'd trade him a kiss on the cheek for ten minutes snooping."

"Lizzie, I don't want you doing something like that on my account."

"Well, I wouldn't say it was entire on your account. Lyle isn't bad to look at."

He rushed her through the rest of the report so he could read her the next part of the book. He'd made his front room out to look like Dantè's cell. It hadn't taken much effort; there was barely any furniture in there to begin with. The first reading had been stiff and awkward, but this one was flowing and theatrical—he paced up and down the room as he talked, flourishing his arms, and putting on different voices for the characters. Lizzy loved it. She laughed at the right parts, cried at the right parts, and toward the end, she took the book from his hands and stumbled over a few chapters. She read well, but she mangled many of the longer words and ended up throwing the book across the room in frustration.

His days went on like that. He'd tend the house and garden in the day, read in the afternoon, and then ride up onto the bluff at night. Here and there a tiny mention of the two men intruded on his routine. Inconsequential details mostly; the black man had the crown of his hat repaired, the white man went into town for a sack, nothing useful.

"Did you ever get into his room?" Carson asked.

"No. Lyle ended up welching on our agreement. I seen in the white man's bags though. They was dumped out in the street when he never came back for them. Empty. Always been empty. Still got the store ticket on one of them."

Weeks went by like that. They evolved a system for their readings. They'd each take a turn reading aloud; their turns lasted as long as they could go without stumbling or making a mistake. Then the other one would take over. It took a long time for her to realize that he was tripping on purpose, though once she had calmed down, she didn't really mind.

Sometimes she brought him a portion of whatever her family had been eating the day before. Sometimes he bought ice from the traveling traders and flavored it with wild strawberries. Sometimes she told him about her family and waited for him to say something about his. After a while she stopped that.

They finished *The Count of Monte Cristo*; they read *Robinson Crusoe, Oliver Twist, Gulliver's Travels*, and a lot of Jules Verne.

One day he decided to tell her a story; she didn't seem to notice that he didn't have a book in his hands.

"There is a kingdom far away…" He didn't know how else to say it.

"As far away as London?" She dangled her legs over the edge of the chair.

"Farther."

"Marseille?"

"Farther."

"Blefuscu?"

"Farther still," he said.

Her face glowed with awe.

"The kingdom had been ruined by war, smashed and burned and reduced to fields of black glass. From this ruin rose a king. A wise and benevolent king who said to his people, '*Whomsoever helps me to rebuild this land, who breaks his back in toil, with no more reward than food and shelter, whomsoever works as a slave in thrall to me shall own their share of this kingdom once it is built.*'

"And so it was. The people toiled. The people broke their backs. The people were as slaves. Hundreds of years. Until the kingdom was restored. A city the size of a continent, a city that stretched farther than the sharpest eye could see, a city that took three months to cross on foot. The city flourished, for a time.

"The original king did not live to see it—in his place his son's son's son. Another king. A bitter king. A dreadful king. A president-for-life. His kingdom, his city had been built by slaves, and to him, the people would always be slaves. He did not give them what was theirs. He broke the ancient promise his great, great, great grandfather made. He expanded the city, outwards as far as the sea, upwards as far as the sky. When there was no more room for his kingdom, he began to build a kingdom in the people's minds.

"The buildings were high as canyon sides, blocking out all but the noonday sun. One billion people lived a perpetual night, skins painted orange and pink and green by electric lights. There were too many people. The air became poison, the water was fouled, and there was never enough food for their bellies.

"The king built towers that peered into people's thoughts, pylons that shaped their dreams, their ideas. His experiments were wicked, his pleasures brutal, and for that, he was killed. When he died, the kingdom erupted in violence, torn in half by fighting, by fear. Those who had been loyal took control and killed thousands in the king's name. The rest cowered in their homes and waited to be collected, to be scooped up like chickens for the chop.

"There came a wise man, a sorcerer, a scientist. He took pity on the people and he built a Machine, a magic doorway to somewhere the king's men could not get them. It was very dangerous to go through. The door didn't always take them to where they thought it would. Those who did make it were condemned to wait on the other side, waiting for the next person to come through. Waiting for the king's men to build their own doorway perhaps. Waiting far away from home with no way of knowing if they would be alone forever."

"I don't like that story," she said standing up.

"Neither do I." He stayed sitting.

"Then why did you tell it?"

"I'm not sure."

After she went home, he climbed into the attic and picked through the books. He wanted to read her a book that hadn't even been written yet. He sat half the night in his chair trying to decide the next one. He couldn't pick between *A Connecticut Yankee in King Arthur's Court* and *Looking Backward*. He fell asleep right there with the horse blanket pulled over his lap.

It was the silence that woke him. The usual susurrus of soft night noises had stopped. The tiny thuds of moths battering their bodies against the house, the click and clatter of the bats that hunted them. Gentle padding footfalls moved around the house as though a deer had come up to crop at the grass. That's exactly what he thought it was until he tried to open a shutter. Five seconds. Ten. Fifteen. Another shutter rattled, another hinge groaned.

The Swiss clock struck four with a peal of tinny bells. A sharp breath sounded at the window, then came back as a nervous titter. Waves of blood crashed at his temples. His heartbeat rang through his chest as if it were hollow.

The intruder found the unlocked window. He boosted himself up and slithered belly-down over the sill into his kitchen. He was too eager. His outstretched foot knocked something metal on the counter. He stopped. Paused. Listening for movement upstairs. Carson forced himself to stay in his chair though he had a perverse urge to yell, "I'm in here!"

He let himself get adjusted to the dark and then crept through into the parlor. A black shape against the wall. A man. A tall man. They looked right at him and didn't see him. They walked for the stairs. He cocked the revolver. The sound was obscene in the silence. The man froze, arms locked into claws.

"I suppose you want me to explain everything," the man said with a sigh. "I—"

Carson shot him in the head. The flash of the gun left purple spots in his eyes. The smoke burned his nose. He started the fire in the hearth and threw the blanket over the ruin of the man's face; even through the sheet he could see that the head was the wrong shape. The man's arm twitched against the cabinet making the drawers' brass handles jingle back and forth. It took a long time to stop.

The man was barefoot, and his soles were black with dirt. He was wearing home-cured buckskin chaps, a checked work shirt, and a bag strapped to his back. There was nothing in his pockets, but the bag was full. He dumped it out on the floor. The things inside made his joints ache with fear: a shot filled sap, a roll of silver gaffer tape, a red rubber ball-gag, pruning shears, a straight razor, and smelling salts. They would have asked him when the next station was. He would have told them eventually.

His hands shook as he shoveled everything back into the bag; they were still shaking when he staggered into the stable. The horse smelled the gunpowder on his clothes and cowered away into the corner. He had to nuzzle his face against it and feed it handfuls of barley sugars before it would let itself be saddled. He rode about a mile too far, skirted round the end of the dairy pastures, and circled to the far side of Werner's wood. The wood was a three-way tangle of elms, pines, and oaks; the roots choked the earth, and none but the hardiest grasses grew up around their trunks.

He dismounted, tethered the horse to a low branch, and moved away slowly through the trees. It was a new moon, and he could barely see where he was going. He edged forward, always expecting a root or a heavy stone to send him scrambling into the bushes.

He smelled a whiff of smoke on the breeze: a campfire, burnt kindling, roast pork. It was only as he headed toward it that he realized how cold he was—he'd rushed out without any winter clothes on. An owl circled overhead, its cry made him flinch, and small animals screamed in their burrows.

The mud sucked at his boots as he squelched toward the boggy center of the wood. He kept low as he moved through the bottom of the dell, then back up the rolling hillock on the other side. The smell of fire grew stronger, and the dappled red light glowed on the underside of the canopy.

He lay down to look over the brow of the hill. The two killers made their camp in a bowl of earth sheltered from the wind by the carcass of a lightning-split oak. A black boy of no more than seventeen was sitting between two canvas tents. He was as close to the fire as he could get without burning himself, wrapped in a caribou skin with a trapper's hat tied to his head. He shivered violently and muttered to himself in a low voice. He was clearly struggling with a dilemma: sit in the cold or put another log on the fire and make himself more obvious from the road. The boy reached a decision. He dumped a log on the fire. The resulting swarm of sparks and popping knots covered Carson as he crept up behind the boy. As soon as he was in touching distance, he reached out and pressed the gun to the nape of the boy's neck.

The boy stopped shivering.

"That's some sick joke, Karl." He tried to turn, and Carson pushed his face back with the muzzle. It left a perfect circle of paler skin on his cheek. "If you kill me, they'll know we fucked up, and two more'll appear."

"If they were coming, they'd already be here. That's how it works."

"Tell that to Karl. He's the expert. He knows how it all works. I'm just the triggerman." The boy's voice had never broken.

"Bullshit. If you're the triggerman, what's he doing in my house?" He pressed the gun against the boy's eye. The boy's hand drew back from the knife he'd been inching towards.

"I'm sick. He figured you was soft. He got impatient." The boy coughed until his chin was slick with mucous. "He dead?"

"Yeah," he said. His elbow ached; the gun grew heavier by the second.

"Dumb bastard. I told him there was no way you were as soft as you look."

"Where's your Machine?"

"Don't have no Machine."

"You came in on a one-shot?"

"New company policy. Everybody one shots now. Too many people going off reservation, realizing they like it a lot better back here. If the company sends another team after them, what happens if they go AWOL? Do you send another team? At what point do you stop?"

"How were you supposed to get home?"

"Plan was—do for you. Wait for the bitch. Do for her. Use your Machine as our return ticket."

"I don't have one either. There isn't one in this frame."

"Not what the reader says." The boy pointed to the tent. Carson looked.

The boy spun on him and stabbed him with a long-tined fork. The blades went into his wrist, bent around the bone. He dropped the gun. It skittered away from him across the ground, and he groped for it left handed.

The boy kicked him in the guts, and he staggered back choking on nothing. He had time to raise his head when the boy tackled him to the ground. Arms pinned. Forearm across his throat. Tried to roll, tried to get arms free, tried to breathe. Couldn't. Couldn't. Couldn't. Dead air in his lungs. He felt the fever baking out of the boy's face.

Everything black and white. Everything shrinking. Down. Down. Down. Gone. He kicked his legs, clipped the fire, sparks flew. The boy's caribou skin caught, flames licked, the boy tried to shake it off without letting him go.

His vision came back in spots. The boy stood up, backed away, he squealed. All Carson could hear was the wind whistling in his ears.

He struggled to drag a few breaths in; his throat was swollen and bleeding. The boy couldn't get the fur off his back, the knot pulled tight at his neck, his screams turned to liquid now. The flames crawled all over him, his skin charred, sloughed off. He picked up the knife, cut through the knot, shrugged out of the burning fur.

Carson hit the boy with a rock. The boy fell. He hit the boy again. The boy tried to get up. He hit him again. Again. Again. Again. Until the boy stopped screaming. Until the rock was coated in bloody tufts of hair. Until he couldn't swing it anymore and he collapsed to the ground. He dragged himself away on his elbows and knees. Blood poured out of the holes in his arm, and he could barely breathe. He pushed his face into the earth and tried to make the pain go away. Tried to make the burning boy go away. Tried to make it all go away. It wouldn't.

Later when the boy's body had cooled, he wrapped it in the tattered remnants of a tent and made a litter of broken branches. He tied a rope around it and climbed up onto the horse's back. The horse shied away from the stench of burnt flesh; he didn't untie it from the tree until the body was secure. Once they got moving, the wind blew the smell away behind them.

He arrived home at sunrise. He drew level with the porch, dismounted, and hefted the flaking body over his shoulder. He carried the boy inside, into the trapped heat and stink of his parlor, over the other body, and down the stairs to the basement.

He dug a shallow grave in the mud floor and dropped the body into it. The sheet unraveled as it landed, and the boy's head lolled clear. His face looked like poorly carved wood, and his skull shone through in places.

He made certain that the horse blanket was belted to the other corpse before he took it to the cellar. The man was much heavier than the boy, stiff with rigor mortis. He couldn't lift him. He had to hook his hands under the armpits and drag him down the stairs backward, the bare feet thumping off every stone step. He rolled the body into the grave with his foot, and it landed with its head between the other's legs. Though he owed them nothing and knew that they wouldn't have paid him the same respect, he arranged them into a more dignified position before filling in the hole.

He cleaned the blood from his floor, then his clothes, then the horse, then himself. After that he collapsed into a chair and tried his hardest not to dream.

When he went out later to take the air, he found an envelope on the third step. It was blank and unsealed. Every dollar he'd given Lizzie was wrapped inside a note written in tiny, fragile script:

My brother saw what you done. I tried to talk him out of it, but he told.
She hadn't signed it.

He looked to the sky for a moment and then punched his hand through the rotten boards of his porch. He didn't go back inside until the bleeding had stopped. He carried the books from the attic in rough handfuls, looked them over one by one, and then tossed them onto the fire. He did not stay to watch them burn; instead, he walked out back and carried on walking. The smell of burning paper would not let him alone.

He beat the horse harder than he meant to on the way to his vigil. He whipped, slapped, and kicked it to a high gallop. He didn't realize he was doing it until he heard the sound of his open palm hitting smooth muscle. His hand was red, and the horse whinnied in pain. He hit it again. It ran in silence.

He came to the appointed place between the lumber camp and the third loop of the river. Steam rose from the horse's flanks, and white froth sprayed as it shook its head from side to side. He got down and the horse turned to face him. Whichever way he walked, it circled to keep its eyes on him. It would not show its back. He reached out to pat its nose, and it flinched away.

"Sorry," he said, upending his canteen into a shallow trough for the horse to drink from. The horse snorted warily and skittered away into the trees when it had finished. He chased it through the undergrowth, and it danced out of reach. He tried again and again, and each time the horse pulled out of his grasp. Finally, he sank his fingers into the horse's mane and held it still as he swung himself up.

A howl of hot air rushed past him, pulling leaves and dropped branches along the ground. A flash of blackness spread around him, thicker than shadow, a momentary darkness that hung in patches that looked solid enough to touch. He fell with foot tangled in the stirrup.

The horse reared up screaming and slammed down beside his head. Its hooves sparked on the stones. He rolled into a ball, and the horse crashed into the woods. If it wasn't for the woman's cries, he would have stayed that way all night.

She had landed by the side of the road. All he could see of her was a mass of auburn tangles run through with brambles and dropped pine needles. She wore combat fatigues and a gamekeeper's vest with a hundred zippered pockets. Jags of black electricity arced off her before earthing into the ground. The grass around her grew ten inches in an instant. It grew up around Carson's shoulders, shot purple buds, and died back to bare soil before he could so much as raise his hand to hack through it.

The woman babbled gibberish. Steam poured off her tongue and out of her eyes. She arched her back and then fell, arched and then fell. Jump sickness. The temporal equivalent of the bends. The worst case he'd ever seen. They'd sent her too quickly; things must have been getting even uglier at the other end.

"What's your name?" He held her hands to stop her scratching him.

"Name."

"Do you know where you are?"

"Are."

"Do you remember how you got here?"

"Here."

A dog barked in the woods. Followed by another. Another. Another. Bloodhounds.

"Shit," he said.

"Shit," she whispered unthinking.

He laid her down and looked for her things. A long black canvas bag had landed by the bowl of moss-coated tree. Though it had been there for a minute at most, it was covered in a week's worth of silver-scummed snail trails. He knew it would all be there. Even so, he looked. It had been so long since he had seen a Machine that his blood hummed.

Men's shouts rang from the wood. Chains clanked. Leather leashes creaked. The dogs barked frantically, tripping over each other to get to his scent.

He dragged the bag to where the woman lay, its weight ripping up the ground behind him. He sat her up, and she cried with the pain. He took the Machine out and fastened her into to the flexible metal roll-cage.

"No." She was momentarily lucid and fought out of the straps. "You go. I stay. That's the mission. I'm the Station Master now. I wait for next runner."

"There's no time. Listen." He pointed to the woods. Hoof beats and booted feet came slashing through the drifts of dead leaves. Her eyes grew large then contracted to the size of burnt match heads. She was gone again, into the depths of her pain.

He started the Machine with a few touches to the keypad. The coordinates were pre-programmed. He had no idea where he was sending her. Sending her on again so quickly and while she was already jumpsick… it was probably a death sentence. If she was strong, she might have a chance. The black flash of the jump sucked the air out of his lungs.

The horse emerged from the woods, lost and confused. It saw him and slid to a stop, as fearful of him as it would be of a cliff edge. He pulled himself up into the saddle before it could decide. Shots ripped out from the trees.

They ran.

Carson emerged from the smoke and cacophony of New York. He had a freshly tailored suit of a generous cut and a rakish hat that the shop-girl freely told him looked dashing. He was bound for the port and from there Europe. Maybe later Istanbul or Cairo. Before he left, he bought a leather-bound copy of *Uncle Tom's Cabin* from an upmarket store and wrapped it in exquisite paper. This he pressed into the hands of a bored US postal agent along with Lizzy's address and several hundred dollars. He had no way of knowing whether the book would get to her, but he chose to believe that it would.

Pixie Season

Seanan McGuire

My mama tried not to raise any fools—I can't speak for my father, never having met the man—but I'm not proud. I'm willing to stand up in front of whoever cares to listen and say that, at least in the beginning, the whole mess was partially my fault. That doesn't mean I'm taking the blame alone.

It had been a long, hot summer at the Lazy Daisy Ranch, and tempers were running as high as the temperature. Cattle ranching in Arizona is never easy, and when you're rationing water and the AC in the bunk house is broken again, it's only natural for folks to get a little snippy. I've been here long enough to know how to hunch my shoulders and wait for things to pass. It would've worked, too, if not for two small problems.

Someone was making messes in the stud barn. Nothing big—just knots in the rope and kicked-out slats in the stalls—but it was enough to keep us in busywork, and pretty well annoyed. And we had a new ranch hand.

Enter Celia.

Some folks seem to think being alive makes them an expert at everything there is, like getting born is an automatic graduation from the university of life. Celia Osborn was one of those. She walked big, she talked big, and she had a way of looking down her nose that made a person feel lower than a rattlesnake's belly. That wouldn't have been so bad—we've had troublesome folks around here before, and you can't afford to turn away willing help when you're trying to keep cattle fed through a dry summer—except that I seemed to be her "special project." Seemed like every time I turned around, she was there, taking an interest in whatever I'd been doing.

Still wouldn't have been so bad if she hadn't felt the need to correct me. And even *that* might not have got under my skin so much if she hadn't been *right* three-quarters of the time. Girl had no concept of social niceties, but she knew how to tie a knot and how to milk a hose for the last drop of water, and that was enough to make it clear Boss Jones wouldn't fire her any time soon.

By the time we hit August, I'd taken to avoiding her. Eight years at the ranch means I pretty much set my own chores. If she was on barn duty, I was fixing fences on the back range; if she was fixing fences, I was rooting out stumps or braiding ropes or plucking cactus spines out of the dogs. We got a lot of cactus-spiked dogs that summer—it was like they'd forgotten that saguaros sting and taken to running at them full-tilt.

Shuffling the chores didn't fully keep her from finding me, but frankly, any day where she didn't bother me before noon went down in my books as a good one. Of course, nothing works all the time. I was examining some holes in the wall of the stud barn—they looked like mouse holes, save for the suspicious lack of either droppings or tracks—when she clamped up behind me and demanded, "Dusty, what are you doing?"

"Looking at mouse holes, Miss Osborn." I turned to face her. She'd been exercising horses all morning. I knew she had because I'd assigned her chores myself, and no one had ever seen Celia skip out on something she'd been told to do. You couldn't tell it to look at her. She was fresh as a daisy, assuming daisies were brown and spiky and glaring at me.

"Why are you looking at mouse holes?"

"Because they're a nuisance, ma'am."

"Don't we have cats for that?"

"Well, ma'am, they don't seem to be doing much looking." I stood, dusting my hands against my jeans. "If the cats took an interest in the mouse holes, I suppose I wouldn't need to."

She hunkered down, transferring her glare to the holes. "I can't see where a few mice would be a problem for something as big as a bull."

"They get into the feed, nibble, and make messes. Some of the bulls are fair irritable; they hear too many things rustling in the dark, someone may get stomped on."

"Meaning me."

"I'd like to think you'd have enough sense to stay away from the stud bulls."

"You never know." She rose. "Stranger things have been known to happen."

"I suppose that's true, ma'am. You heading off?"

"I need to finish exercising the horses. I was waiting for the dust to settle before I took the second lot out." Her gaze was challenging, daring me to accuse her of neglecting her duty.

I knew better. Sometimes you get more work done by knowing when to take a break. "Enjoy, ma'am. I'm going to go start marking the dead cactus for this year."

Her expression sharpened—something I hadn't realized was possible. "Marking them? For what?"

"Some of those saguaro get pretty tall, and when they pass on, they fall over with no real respect for what might be standing in their way." I shrugged. "It's time to start figuring out which ones need to be taken down this year."

She stared at me before turning on her heel and stalking off without another word. I frowned after her. The look on her face hadn't just been confused—it had been angry, verging on outraged. Over cutting down a few dead cacti?

"Maybe she wanted the job herself," I said. Something behind me giggled, the sound as clear and crystal-pure as the first drops of rain falling during a seasonal storm. I whirled, too slow to see the source of the laughter, but fast enough to see faint eddies in the dust at the base of the nearest mouse hole. That was the confirmation I'd been hoping not to find.

We had pixies in the stud barn.

Pixies are the cockroaches of the supernatural world. You'll probably never have to deal with them if you keep things clean and looked after; they're not as invasive as gremlins or as random in where they pop up as poltergeists. Most folks never see a pixie in their life, no matter how much magic they live with. Back when I traveled with Mama and the circus, we dealt with pixies once every two or three years—one of the sibyls would forget to clean up her entrails, or the handlers would get behind in mucking out the menagerie, and there we'd be again, up to our necks in senseless pranks and endless acts of tiny vandalism. I hate the little bastards, have ever since the time they filled the trailer with tree frogs and left me trying to calm my baby brothers for the rest of the night.

Most people think of pixies as sweet little things that twinkle and shine and grant wishes, but like I said, most people go their whole lives without seeing a pixie. Pixies break things for the fun of breaking them, and while they're individually about as smart as grackles, they can be clever enough to present a real nuisance when they're in a big enough flock. They're a hive intelligence, like ants, but nowhere near as benign. They're also near impossible to get rid of once they've established themselves: they breed like rabbits and sting like wasps, and they're the last thing any functioning ranch needs to contend with.

I was not amused.

There's a lot of residual magic roaming around the Arizona desert. Coyote keeps a pretty close eye on the land, and when the moon is full and bright, someone who knows where to look is likely to see the saguaros dancing the night away like tall, elegant aristocrats. Add the European monsters and ghosts that followed the settlers, and the number of pixie infestations we get out here starts making a lot of sense.

I stayed in Arizona because I felt at home there. Mama knew it; that's why she was willing to leave me behind. The Lazy Daisy was strange enough to be a fit for my own eccentricities—but I'd never figured on a barn full of pixies. Boss Jones was a good man. He never fired somebody for doing their best, even when that stuck him with someone who didn't get as much done as he'd like, and he never questioned the superstitions that are part of running a healthy ranch.

But that was also the problem: he thought it was just superstition. He was one of those men who could see a woman ride her broom across the moon and dismiss it as swamp gas and beer. He had the sort of specialized blindness that only comes naturally to people who know, deep down, that it's safer not to see. He'd never believe me if I said we had pixies in the barn.

So the boss wasn't going to be any help, and we haven't had a working witch around the place since Astrid struck off to find the Fountain of Youth. A couple of the boys knew some parlor tricks, but they wouldn't know what to do with a pixie: there's a difference between catbone charms and *magic*. Pixies are the second sort, and that meant I'd be dealing with them on my own unless I wanted to put the boys in harm's way.

I got on with the day's chores, trying not to show how concerned I was. There's always something that needs doing. I was distracted enough that I made it all the way to dinner without tripping over Celia, and by the time I realized she'd settled next to me, it was too late to move gracefully. I kept shoveling eggs and salsa into my mouth, hoping she'd take the point and leave me alone. I needed to get back to the barn before moonrise if I wanted to lock the pixies out. If she didn't start talking, I might make it.

No such luck. She cleared her throat and when I didn't look at her, said, "Dusty. Did you find your mice?"

"No, ma'am, I can't say I did." I gave in to the inevitable and turned to face her.

Celia scowled. "Why do you call me 'ma'am' all the time?"

"Because it's polite."

"I have a name."

"You'd rather be called Miss Osborn?"

Her scowl deepened. "That wasn't what I meant."

"I know what you meant. But my mama would have my hide if she heard me calling someone I've only known a few months by their first name."

"You call me 'ma'am' because you're afraid of your mother?" She sounded faintly amused. Not a familiar emotion, coming from her.

"If you'd ever met her, you'd be afraid of her, too." I rose, collecting my plate, and said, "If you'll excuse me, ma'am, I have chores to finish. Enjoy your dinner."

I walked away and left her watching me, expression somewhere between unhappy and annoyed. I couldn't read that woman to save my soul; she might have approved. She might also have wanted me dead. I honestly had no idea, and as long as there were pixies in our barn, I didn't have time to worry about it. I just kept walking.

When dealing with a pixie infestation, first you need to check whether there are any local spirits you're trying to hang onto. Chasing pixies out of the kitchen can also get rid of the brownies, for example, and that won't sit well with them; clean up one problem, turn around to find that your ousted brownies have gone boggart and are making trouble. So it was sort of a relief that our pixies were where they were: the only spooks we have living with the stud bulls are a few ghost cats that have been around the ranch since before I got here. I spent a few hours in the early evening setting out bowls of spoiled milk and plates of fish bones, luring them away from their standard haunts with the ghosts of their favorite foods and then telling each of them what I needed. They can't talk—they're cats—but they seemed willing enough to move into the bunkhouse for a few days. So there was one problem down.

After taking care of the local spirits, it's time to set your pixie traps. I raided the kitchen for basil and rosemary and mixed them into the next morning's hay; nothing drives pixies out of a place faster than the smell of rosemary. The bulls gave me a healthy berth as I nailed horseshoes above each of the barn entrances, intending them to serve as warnings to the pixies—hang around here, those horseshoes said, and you're likely to find yourself stuffed into a cold iron cage and sold to some witch's kid to act as a nightlight. Then I went about the rest of my chores whistling and happy, sure we'd have a pixie-free barn before dawn. It couldn't be a very advanced infestation, or we'd have been seeing a lot more signs, so I was fairly sure those simple measures would do the trick.

They might have, if I hadn't come back from checking the perimeter fences to find that someone had swapped out all the hay while I was away. They'd also taken down the horseshoes, nailing yarrow branches to the inside of the windows. Yarrow is a fairy plant: putting it up in a place already contending with a pixie infestation is like dousing your sheep in barbecue sauce because you want the coyotes to stay away from them. I could already see the signs of the hive starting to spread. Leave it alone for a week and they'd have grass growing on the floor and branches sprouting from the shingles, and then I'd have to explain why the milk cows were throwing unicorn foals instead of good, basic calves when the spring came.

Not my idea of a good time—and not a safe thing to let happen. Magic is dangerous when it starts chaining like that. I yanked the yarrow branches down and poured iron ball bearings and salt over the mushrooms growing in the corner, then retreated to plan my next set of traps. If somebody was sabotaging my efforts to clear the hive out, I'd need to be subtle. Otherwise, anything I did would be taken down again the minute I turned my back, and it'd be a case of trying to fight a constant uphill battle, *without* actually getting rid of the damn things.

Stupid pixies. They hadn't even fully established themselves yet, and they were already starting to cause trouble. If they managed to get a complete hive set up and start really making mischief, well...

I didn't even want to think about it.

My second batch of traps was keyed to play into the barn décor. More iron ball bearings in the corners, yes, buried under a thin layer of dirt where they'd be harder to spot. Fresh salt licks made with blessed salt from the plains of Utah that I knew for a fact had been treated by a certified shadow priest who practiced veterinary medicine on the side—I'd been saving them for breeding season when the bulls would need to be especially virile, but now seemed like as good a time as any to break out a little extra ammunition. Anise and mustard seeds in the feed, where they'd wind up in the manure and get spread everywhere, no matter was done to try and stop it, and finally, finely ground mint around every doorway and window frame. The little bell-brained bastards wouldn't be able to *stand* the barn after the bulls had had a day or so to eat and digest. I was willing to wait if I had to.

The next day dawned with no signs the pixies had spread during the night; the sugar cubes I'd left on my windowsill were untouched, and it's rare to find a single pixie that won't go nuts over sugar, much less a whole hive. Pixies don't know how to practice self-restraint. I went out onto the range with the cactus clearing crew, heart light, sure that the problem was finally taken care of.

We spent the day chopping down dead saguaro, and I put all thoughts of trouble—the pixies, the person who'd sabotaged my traps, the fact that the ghost cats seemed a bit too comfortable in the bunkhouse and might not be willing to move back to the barn—out of my head as I helped shift the trunks into the pickups.

Saguaro can take a good amount of damage over the years, but eventually they die and decay where they stand, becoming a danger to fences, men, and livestock. I always feel bad chopping them down; they're the lords and ladies of these deserts, and it feels like they deserve a better funeral. But we burn what we cut, and that sends their ashes back into the desert, so maybe that's all the funeral they'd want. At the time, I'd never had the opportunity to actually ask a saguaro.

There was just one black spot on my day: Celia, who'd somehow managed to petition the boss to get herself added onto the cleanup crew. Once she'd requested the duty, I couldn't exactly deny her, but having her around took a lot of the pleasure out of the simplicity of working hard under a hot sun. She wasn't just efficient, she was cranky about it, hoisting chunks of cactus into the trucks and glaring at everyone around. I didn't see why she'd requested the job if she didn't want to do it, but that was her business, not mine.

I was taking a minute to pluck the cactus spines out of my sleeves when Joe came up to me, glancing over his shoulder, all anxiety and strain. Joe usually looks like that, has ever since he got turned into a human. I guess being raised as a jackrabbit encourages jumpiness, and with Astrid gone, he's just gotten worse; after all, no witch means no turning back into a man if something bunnies him up again.

"What's wrong, Joe?" I'll admit, I was expecting him to say he'd seen a snake. Or a spider. Or maybe an unusually large horsefly that he thought was the beginning of a swarm.

"Miss Osborn isn't wearing any gloves," he said, so fast the words all ran together.

All right. I hadn't been expecting that. "She took them off?"

"No!"

"She lost them?"

"No! She isn't wearing any! She hasn't been wearing any." He gave me a worried look, large brown eyes grave. "I'm afraid she's going to prick her finger on a thorn and get an infection and get gangrene and then die."

"Thanks, Joe," I said, clapping him on the shoulder. Hypochondriacs have nothing on a man who used to be a rabbit. He twitched but managed a worried smile, staying in the shadow of the truck as I walked toward Celia.

She was working by herself by that point, gathering the smaller chunks of cactus off the ground and loading them into a wheelbarrow. I frowned as I caught sight of her hands and realized that Joe, twitchy as he was, had been telling the truth; she wasn't wearing gloves. She was just scooping bits of cactus off the ground, expression dour but not pained, and dropping them as pretty as you please into her pile.

"Ma'am?" I said, stepping up behind her.

She dropped the chunk of cactus she was holding, whirling to face me. "I'm working as fast as I can," she said, instantly defensive.

I blinked. I'd been expecting irritation—having the foreman walk over when you're doing your job just fine can seem like micro-management, and that's something I try to avoid whenever I can—but there's a difference between that and actual hostility. "I didn't say you weren't, ma'am," I said slowly. "Joe just came to tell me you'd lost your gloves. We wouldn't want to get thorns rammed up under your skin, would we? Makes it hard to work." I kept my tone light, like I was just making conversation, but I was starting to worry. What kind of person clears cactus without gloves? Even I wouldn't do something that stupid, and I'm pretty well known around here for healing too fast to use common sense before grabbing hold of the barbed wire. Cactus thorns *sting*, and they're harder than hell to get loose once they've grabbed hold.

"He shouldn't worry, I'm fine," said Celia, holding her hands out toward me, palms up. I leaned in to study them and blinked. There were no thorns anywhere in her skin. I'd seen her touching the cactus bare-handed—and saguaro isn't a polite plant, it jams you with thorns just for looking at it funny—but you wouldn't have known it to look at her. "I know how to pick up cacti without getting hurt."

"Pardon me for saying so, ma'am, but I'd be grateful if you could teach *me* that trick," I said. "I get thorns jammed in my hands all the time." And feet, and less socially acceptable places. Running the range isn't a good way to stay smooth-skinned and cactus-free.

"It's an old family secret," she said.

"That's as may be," I allowed. "Still, you're making the men uncomfortable. Would you mind putting on your gloves, please? Just until we're finished here?"

She gave me a smothering glare but pulled her gloves on, going back to hoisting cactuswithout saying another word. I decided discretion was the better part of valor and walked back toward Joe; he'd need to be talked down before I got any more useful work out of him.

We were on our way back to the ranch, trucks loaded down with chopped cactus, before I realized what was really bothering me. Celia's hands had been untouched. I've seen stranger things; far be it from me to complain about one of my workmen being able to avoid injuring themselves. But her sleeves had also been clean. She was wearing a long-sleeved shirt like the rest of us, and there hadn't been any thorns lodged in the flannel. I can believe an "old family secret" would protect hands, but clothes? Something wasn't right there. Something was missing.

When I got back to the bunkhouse, there was a ghostly calico sleeping on my pillow, and the sugar I'd left on the windowsill was gone. Tiny footprints led from the saucer to the window, and someone had tied all my socks into a vast, helplessly snarled knot.

The pixies were spreading.

Unknotting my socks took the better part of two hours. By the time I had them unsnarled, the sun was down, the mess hall was finished serving dinner, and I had an audience of a dozen spectral felines watching me. A coyote howled somewhere outside, a long, mournful-sounding note of invitation—
Are you there? Can you hear me?

Now there was a thought. Coyote eyes aren't as cunning as human ones, but coyote ears and noses are better. Maybe that could help. Leaving my socks on the bed for the cats to sleep on, I climbed out the window and dropped to the ground, already starting to strip. When I was done, I pitched my clothes back through the window, leaving me standing naked in the night, looking out on a whole world full of possibilities.

I knelt, stretched, and rose on four weathered paws. The view changed during the shift between forms, color becoming black and white, perspective tilted by my new height and the stretch of my muzzle. The smells more than made up for the loss of color, shining sharp and almost tangible in the air, like something you could reach out and grasp hold of. Assuming you had thumbs, that is.

Tail low and nose to the ground, I trotted toward the barn.

The smell of the stud bulls was the first thing to hit me, strong and musky and dominant. I resisted the urge to squat and mark this as my territory. We had a deal of sorts, me and the bulls, an unspoken pact of non-aggression. As long as I didn't piss on what they considered their own, they wouldn't trample me into the dirt when I was in my human form. Most of the crew thought that was the only shape I had, but pain can bring on an involuntary shift. There are explanations I never want to give, and that was one of them.

Inside the barn, I could hear the bulls shifting uncomfortably, their hooves knocking hard against the ground. I kept sniffing, trying to filter their scents away, and was rewarded with the sharp, minty smell of pennyroyal. I followed the scent to the window and snarled when I saw the little leather posset someone had nailed there. There was a sweetness undercutting the mint: honey. Pennyroyal and honey over each window and door, all tucked into possets that lay almost flush to the wood, making them damned near impossible to see unless a body knew they were there. Someone was trying to *attract* the damn pixies.

I circled the barn twice, fixing the location of each posset in my mind before shifting back to human. Naked as the night I was born, I grabbed a ladder and dragged it with me as I pulled every one of the cursed things down, heaping them in a pile just outside the territory the bulls considered to be their own. Then I gave in to instinct and pissed on the whole damn mess, dousing it completely. I kicked dirt over it when I was done, then shifted back to coyote form and trotted for my bunk.

The cats were still in my bed when I got there. I hopped up among them, tucking my nose under my tail and trying to figure out what else I had smelled at the barn. Something was bothering me. I was almost asleep when I realized what it was.

Everyone at the ranch had reason to be at the barn at one point or another; there was no one whose scent *shouldn't* have been there. But Celia...

I had smelled her much too strongly. She was up to something.

I was still thinking of her when I drifted off to dreamland.

The next night was more of the same: more pennyroyal possets over the barn windows, more signs of pixie mischief around the farm. Half the sugar had gone missing from the mess, and the damn things had plucked two of the best laying hens half bald. No one was getting any sleep, kept up well into the night by the sound of distant giggles.

This couldn't go on.

When the third night was drawing near, the sun sinking low on the horizon, I was ready. I lurked around the back of the old outhouse, waiting for the sound of someone driving a nail. When I heard it—the steady, rhythmic pounding of a hammer—I bolted.

I came around the corner of the barn at a dead run, set on catching whoever it was had turned cruel or foolish enough to be trying to attract pixies, and nearly ran headlong into Celia. She shrieked. It was the first honestly surprised sound I'd ever heard that woman make, but there wasn't time to enjoy it. She made a little jerking motion with her right hand, and suddenly my entire face felt like it was on fire. I stumbled to a stop, raking my hand across my cheek, and came away with a palm full of blood and cactus spines.

The sight of the blood made the smell of it register, bringing all the other scents around me into a sudden, unpleasantly sharp relief. The blood; the cows stabled so close at hand, and the sheep in their pens a little way off, with their wooly white bellies and their thin, thin skin; the sharpness of the mint that clung all around the barn. Celia's perfume was an icepick in the mix, a spike of artificial violets and roses that made my head spin. My teeth were doing their best to get longer, pushing themselves out past the limits of the human norm. Blood does that to me.

"What the *hell* did you just do?" I demanded. My changing jaw made the word into something closer to a growl. I swiped my hand across my face again, clearing away more of the blood and another palm's-worth of cactus spines. The holes were closing, the blood slowing down. Thank the midsummer moon that I heal fast. Otherwise, every little scratch would be an exercise in self-control that I don't have the willpower for.

"What *are* you?" she asked, eyes going wide. She raised her right arm to chest-height, the underside toward me. She was wearing short sleeves, I realized, and I could see the bristling lines of thorns she was readying to fling in my direction.

I wiped my hand on my jeans and wiped my face again, counting backward from ten like Mama taught me. It was working, but slowly; it's hard to resist the urge to change when there's blood already in the air. "Ma'am, I think I'm within my rights to ask you the same thing."

"Are you some sort of...some sort of werewolf?" She kept her arm up, hand tensed back. I was starting to see what would happen if she twitched her wrist—I'd get another dose of thorns, and this one would be a lot more focused.

"No, ma'am, and I'll thank you not to call me that again. I don't really hold with werewolves. Too high up the food chain for me." I wiped the last of the blood and thorns on my jeans, adding, "I also wouldn't hit me again, if I were you. I've pretty much got control of myself, but I can't guarantee that's going to last if you go and hit me again. I'd really rather not find out what you are by trying to eat you."

"I doubt you could," she said, pride briefly winning the battle with frightened confusion.

"Do you want to find out the hard way?"

We stood there glaring at each other for a while. I knew pretty much what she was thinking; I've seen it before. There I was, scrawny Dusty Tucker, with blood drying on my cheeks, saying I wasn't a werewolf. Either she wasn't going to believe me and she'd run off to find herself a silver bullet—not that it'd do her a bit of good, but try telling people that when they're *sure* they know what they're doing—or she was going to back down and spill first, just to find out what I *was*. I was pretty sure she was going to do the latter. I look too harmless, even when I'm trying to force down a change in the middle of the day, to be anything a woman who can shoot thorns out of her arms needs to worry about.

Finally, she dropped her arm, the thorns sliding back into her skin and disappearing, hey-presto. They didn't even leave indentations behind. I was pretty sure that if I ran my hand along the place where they'd been, I wouldn't feel anything but skin. Her camouflage was perfect.

"Nice trick," I said, genuinely admiring. Most folks with built-in weaponry at least flinch when they have to retract it.

"I'm a saguaro dryad," she replied. There was a note of challenge in her tone, and a whole lot of wariness in her eyes. She was expecting some sort of argument, I'm sure; being something that far off the beaten path makes a body a little wary about telling people. For every person who accepts you, there's three more who won't, and some of them can be dangerous.

Well, if she wanted an argument, she wasn't going to get it from me. "Is that so?" I asked, admiringly. "Well, I'll be. That's one I'd never have guessed. Never met a saguaro dryad before. Oak and elder, yes, and one little lady that was a field of dandelions in her off time, but never a saguaro."

"You're not...you don't have a problem with that?"

"Ma'am, I'm a Tucker. We get sort of used to things being somewhat to the left of what's considered normal. It comes with the territory." I shrugged. "My mama drives a haunted truck for a circus that's owned and operated by a genuine retired muse. After you've grown up dealing with that, just about everything else seems like the soul of normalcy."

Celia's expression hardened somewhat, taking on a trace of its old arrogance. "Now you're making fun of me."

"No, ma'am, scout's honor." Not that I was ever a Girl Scout; we didn't stay in one place long enough for that, and anyway, Mama never liked me getting overly friendly with the townies—nor the townies getting overly friendly with her children, and that always started to happen eventually. "I left the circus and came here when I decided I wanted to do something with myself that meant staying in one place. Needed a territory of my own, you could say."

"And you are...?"

"I take after my daddy's side of the family, ma'am. I'm a werecoyote."

She stared at me for a moment, then started to laugh. The sound was buoyant, almost infectious, but I stood my ground and watched her calmly until her mirth finally died down and she managed to say, "You *can't* be a werecoyote. You're too *white*."

"Believe me, ma'am, I'm fully aware of the color of my skin. I've got too much English blood in me to tan—I don't even freckle in the sun. That doesn't change what my daddy was, or the fact that I'm his natural-born daughter." If there'd been any question in his mind when Mama sent him pictures of his blond-haired, blue-eyed baby girl, they'd died the day she sent him a picture of herself and my brothers sitting in the cab of the truck with a yellow-furred, blue-eyed coyote bitch. He wrote back telling her that he was glad to finally know he had a daughter, and that she wasn't to write him again. Teaching me to survive was up to Mama—and me.

"Well I never."

"If you're quite done making fun of me, ma'am, and you're not planning to shoot me full of thorns again, I'd be interested to know why you've been filling our stud barn up with pixies."

Celia blinked. "What? No. I've been trying to get *rid* of them. You're the one inviting the nasty little things in."

"I most certainly am not. I've been trying to get rid of them as well."

"Then why are you hanging pennyroyal all over the damn barn?"

"I'm not."

She stared at me. I stared at her. Finally, she passed judgment.

"Well, hell."

One of the ghost cats rubbed against my ankle, leaving the faintest feeling of static behind. I stooped to pet it, noting the way Celia's eyes followed the motion, not only of my hand, but of the cat itself. She could see it. That wasn't too much of a surprise—most supernatural creatures can see the ghost cats—but it was somewhat reassuring to know. People often didn't care to see what didn't relate to them.

I paused. "If you don't mind, ma'am, I have an idea," I said. "Can you turn all the way into a cactus?"

"Can you turn all the way into a coyote?" she snapped.

"Good," I said. "I have an idea."

There's things that turn invisible in the desert, so commonplace that they aren't worth seeing anymore. Saguaro cactus, for example. It takes years on years for them to reach their full, towering height, but it only took Celia a few seconds to melt from woman into thorny plant, her body melding seamlessly into the thick green skin and bristling thorns. I stripped quickly, concealing my clothing behind her before shrugging off my own humanity.

A cactus isn't much of a surprise out here. A coyote that doesn't run when someone comes walking by, now that can be more of a shock. I stretched out on the ground in front of Celia's trunk, putting my head on my paws and trying to look like part of the landscape. Coyotes don't normally do that sort of thing. Anyone seeing me would take me for a dog, or figure I was unwell, and either way, we'd have a little time.

I settled in to wait. I assume Celia did the same. It was hard to tell, with her being a cactus and all. The shadows grew long around us, slowly blending into the darkness dripping down from the sky. Night made itself known. Still we waited, until the scuff of a foot in the dust caught my attention. I forced my head to stay down, ears swiveling toward the sound.

Boss Jones came walking out of the shadows, a mint-scented sack slung over one shoulder, his eyes set on the stud barn.

I was on my feet in an instant, running for him with a snarl in my throat. He shouted and fell back. I slammed into his chest, shifting back toward human, so that he landed on the ground with a naked woman on top of him. He shouted. I snarled again, and he was still.

"What in the *hell* do you think you're doing?" I demanded, as Celia ran up behind me. *She* was fully clothed. It wasn't fair.

"Dusty, what the hell—" he began.

I snarled again. He went quiet. "Do you *know* how much damage pixies can do to livestock? *Do* you?"

"They're the reason you've had so much dead saguaro around here this season," said Celia. "The little bastards have to go."

"I didn't...they were supposed to bring in the tourists!" protested Jones. "They're exotic! Something for the kids!"

"And they'd make up for the rattlesnakes and the cactus and the scorpions?" I scoffed. "You're a fool, and when I tell the owners, you're a fool who'll be gone."

His eyes went wide. "I'll tell them! I'll tell them you're a dog!"

I smiled, showing all my teeth. "What, you think they don't already know?"

He whimpered. This time, the scent of urine was not canine in origin.

The owners were not thrilled to hear how their trust had been abused, and Boss Jones was sent packing, along with a sack full of his precious pixies. Some people deserve what life hands them. Celia celebrated the disappearance of the threat by spending three days dancing with her people in the high desert before returning to work like nothing had happened. She was still mulish and occasionally snappy, but we had an understanding now—one which seemed to extend to all the other saguaro in the desert. It's been months since I've had to pull a cactus spine out of my nose.

Like I said, my mama didn't raise no fools. And it would be a damn fool of a coyote who left a ranch where the pay was good, the cacti were friendly, and there was always a dance to be had on a full moon night.

THE MEN WITH NO FACES

Alexandra Christian

WHEN THE FIRST ONE DISAPPEARED, BLUE DIDN'T PAY IT MUCH MIND. It wasn't a surprise, after all. Life out here wasn't for the faint of heart. And especially not for those war-weary widows and calico queens that had followed Blue and Nellie out into the desert. She'd tried to warn them. Every woman who came to the desert came with her eyes wide open. Each one had her own reasons, but there were always a few who got homesick and skint out for the security of some boozy belvedere with loose fists and a slick tongue. That wasn't really Blue's problem. Like her old granny said, to each her own. But when Nellie, her friend and the closest thing to a daughter she'd ever known, vanished, Blue knew something was wrong.

"What we gon' do here, Nena?" Lotte's eyes were everywhere as they started into the town of Perdition. "This is a mean place."

"Hush, child," Blue hissed, steering the old gray stallion into the dusty road that split the town down the middle. "We don't want to call too much attention to ourselves." Not that it would make much difference either way. An old black woman and a little white girl riding into town together wasn't exactly everyday. She shouldn't have brought Lotte with her, but at twelve years old, the child could shoot straight, and she never hesitated. Blue liked that in a gunfighter. "I didn't ride twelve miles with my bohunkus stuffed in this saddle just to get shot."

"Do you think we'll find Nellie here, Nena?" Lotte asked.

"No way to tell. All we can do is look." Blue had to stare into the sun. Now was not the time to be sentimental.

Perdition was a grimy piece of Hell smack in the middle of the desert. Blue hadn't set foot on this road in near thirty years, but Nellie was the only real family she had, and Blue was damned if she was going to let her go so easy.

There was a line of buildings as they came into town: a restaurant, a general store, and a barber shop, and surgery. Her destination was farther down the street.

The hotel. Well, they called it a hotel. Puttin' on airs was another thing Blue had no time for. Just call it what it was: a whorehouse. The wooden façade dominated the landscape on the far side of the street. Years of dust devils had nearly peeled the paint off until you could barely read the name, Bareback Betty's. *Charming*, Blue thought. A snaggle-toothed saloon dove grinned down at them from the raggedy old sign out front, inviting them in.

Blue slid down from the saddle. Her boots scraped on the gravel, and the noise echoed off the meager buildings. Lotte started down behind her, but Blue stopped her with a gnarled hand. The town was unusually quiet for a Sunday morning. After all, there sure as shit wasn't any churchin' up going on in Perdition. Folks here tended to worship things more basic like violence and money. Out here, those were the only things that mattered. One invariably led to the other, and without them, the desert would devour you quick, bones and all.

"Stay with the horse," Blue hissed.

"No, Nena! I wanna go with you," Lotte said. Of course she did. Little Lotte had been hanging on to Blue's petticoat since the day she found her.

"Listen to what I'm tellin' you girl. Anybody come 'round that bend you don' like the looks of, you plug 'em." Lotte pulled the six-shooter out of the holster at her hip and clutched it to her chest the way an ordinary child might hold their favorite doll.

Blue straightened the ruined sunhat that sat askew on her head. A thin, gray braid trailed over her shoulder, and a few escaped tendrils tickled her sweaty forehead. She pushed them away from her face and steeled herself to walk into the saloon. Thirty years ago, she'd left Betty's and swore she would never be back.

The doors swung closed behind her, catching the hem of her dusty work dress. She almost stumbled, but she kept her head high. The mirror behind the bar blinded her with the glare, and her boots made a scraping sound across the dirty floor. It still smelled the same, that was for damn sure. A mix of turpentine, dust, and French perfume that could take your breath away with one good sniff. As Blue's eyes adjusted, she could make out the silhouettes of several men up at the bar. Strangely, there was almost no noise. No conversation. No hatchet-faced girl caterwauling over an out-of-tune piano. In fact, there wasn't a woman to be found in the place. Even the poker game in the corner was quiet.

"Women ain't 'llowed," the barkeep grumbled, as if plucking Blue's thought right out of her head. "Unless o' course you lookin' for work." He gave her a once-over with a greasy smirk as he scrubbed at a glass with a dirty cloth. Just the way he rubbed his palm over the butt of the glass was suggestive. "Yer a bit past prime, but all our girls have absconded."

"Skinned out like a bunch of scalded heifers," someone called from under a tired-looking bowler.

"What about baby-faced growler monkeys?" Blue asked.

The barkeep chuckled and tossed his towel aside. He leaned forward on the bar, staring holes into Blue. She knew he had his hand on his iron under that grubby old apron. "If yer talkin' 'bout Charlie Bishop, we ain't seen him in days neither."

Blue's heart was a still stone in the middle of her chest. She'd known that Nellie was sweet on that boy for months. They'd met at the general store last winter, and ever since there had been something between them. They were attracted like sparks to dry scrub. Blue didn't mind all that much. Charlie Bishop was one of those soft-spoken, intellectual types. Nose always in a book unless he was workin' for his daddy here at Betty's, slinging barrels of beer and tending the bar. Some said he was touched, and others thought he was a nancy-boy; Nellie didn't care.

"Think you best get on back to whatever hovel you come from," the barkeep said.

Every eye in the place had settled on her, but now was not the time to settle old scores. She heard a scraping noise behind her and detected movement out of the corner of her eye. Then the rough shuffle of boots behind her. The tip of her finger played on the trigger of the rifle in her hand. She let everything fall away except for the gentle pounding of her own heartbeat that mirrored the slow footsteps approaching.

"I know you," the voice behind said. "I know all 'bout you, Blue Tompkins. You got a lotta damn nerve comin' back here."

When he said her name, she recognized him immediately. "Alistair Bishop," she said. "You just tell me where Charlie and Nellie run off to, and I'll leave you in peace."

"You scared to face me, woman?" Bishop asked.

Blue turned, raising the long rifle as she did and forcing the man to take a step backward. He hadn't changed much since the last time she saw him, standing in this same spot. His posture had been a little straighter back then, and his eyes had lost some of the carefree gleam they'd once had, but Blue could see the boy she'd once loved lurking inside.

"I ain't never been 'fraid of no man in my life, Alistair. But I 'spect you knowed that already."

"True enough. But you know what they say 'bout bein' brave. It's just another word for foolish." At that, four men stood up behind Bishop with their irons in hand. "And you are mighty damn foolish for comin' back here, Blue."

"May hap be, but I ain't leavin' without Nellie." She nudged Alistair in the belly with the muzzle of the rifle. Her eyes were keen, and she could almost see his heart pounding in his chest. "So if you know where she's at, I suggest you bring her out here now."

"It don't look like you're in much of a position for suggestin'," one of the others said.

Blue smiled. Unlike her old lover, she wasn't a bit afraid. "Friend, I think you've mistaken me for a woman who won't put a bullet in yer boss's belly. You might kill me, but not before I drag old Alistair to Hell with me." She nudged him once more with the gun for emphasis. "So you either tell me where your son has taken my Nellie, or I swear to God I'll drop you right here, Alistair Bishop!"

"All right, Blue," Alistair said, putting his hands up and stepping back. "Ain't no need to get so agitated." He gave a nod and waved his stoolies away. "You always did get mad faster than any woman I ever saw."

"And that's high praise," Blue replied, lowering her rifle. "Considerin' how many women you seen."

He grinned, stepping into the golden light seeping through the slats of the doors behind Blue. "Look, Blue. Nellie ain't here. If she was, you know I'd tell you."

"Would you? Your daddy wasn't much for lettin' go of his money." The scar of an old brand on Blue's thigh, hidden under a layer of crumpled and worn petticoat, throbbed with a dull ache. "I know she was comin' here. Mayhap we just go upstairs and find her."

"Don't you get it?" the barkeep barked suddenly. "Nellie ain't here. None of 'em are!"

"What are you talkin' about?" Blue asked.

"There is a definite shortage of whores in this place, or ain't you noticed?" the barman went on. "The last one was gone this morning. In fact, I bet you won't find another woman in Perdition for miles. Unless they seen too many summers or too few. We figured they all slipped out to go live with you on the tommy farm outside of town." His words were met with chuckles from the others. Only Alistair wasn't laughing.

"Maybe we should just go on out to the tommy farm and round 'em up," another said.

"Bring 'em in like stray heifers!"

The crowd of men that had seemed so sullen when Blue first arrived were now starting to turn. The old woman wasn't afraid of much, but a room full of desperate men were apt to do most anything. Perhaps this had been a fool's errand after all.

"Nena! Nena, come quick!"

The whole place started at the girl's shouting and crowded to the windows. Blue jerked away from Alistair and pushed her way through the doors to where the girl stood pointing to the horizon. A cowboy, silhouetted against the bright, unforgiving sky, galloped toward the center of town. As he got closer, Blue could see that the man was barely hanging on to his saddle, gripping the apple tight. He didn't reach the hitching post before falling down in the street.

"Nena! It's Charlie Bishop!" Lotte said.

The man Blue had come to see was lying in the dirt, pouring sweat and red with fever. The boy looked like a heap of raw meat. His face was such a mess of blood, it was a wonder Blue could even tell who he was.

Alistair pushed through the crowd that had now oozed onto the porch of Betty's. "Charlie! What the hell happened?" Blue helped Alistair get the boy to a sitting position. His head lolled back and forth, like he couldn't focus on anyone. The barkeep handed Alistair a bottle of whiskey, and he waved it under the boy's nose. It seemed to bring him around a little, and he was able to take a sip or two before coughing and sputtering to life. They backed off as Charlie shook his head, trying to clear it. He peered up into first Blue's face, then his father's. It was as if he didn't recognize them at first, starting with a sharp gasp.

"Where are they?" he cried. "Let me go! Nellie…"

"Easy, boy," Alistair said. "Just take it easy for a minute."

"No!" he exclaimed, pulling away from his father. He tried to stand, but his legs wouldn't bear the weight, and he sat down hard. "No… Pa… we gotta go. We gotta get out of here!"

"What are you talkin' about, son? Where have you been?"

"No…Nellie…"

Blue knelt down, still gripping her rifle. "What about Nellie? Where is she?" she demanded.

"Me and Nellie, we was gonna leave. I give her Granny's diamond, and we was gonna go back east. But they took her! They took all the girls! They didn't get me. They didn't..." His head fell back, exhausted.

"Who?" Bishop asked. "What in hell are you talkin' about, boy?"

Charlie looked up at his daddy with a blank expression that made Blue's blood turn cold. It was an almost hopeless stare, like he was giving up to some devil that was lurking just behind him in the shadows. After a minute, he focused and took a watery breath. "The men with no faces."

Charlie Bishop had the look of a man whose mind was completely lost. Blue had seen that look a lot since the war. Whatever happened to that boy out in the canyon, it was bad enough that his mind had retreated. Maybe for all time. Funny, men were supposed to be so tough. In Blue's experience, they were anything but. They couldn't stand up to the ugly parts: pain, sorrow, loss. Blue herself had lived through slavery, a horror most men couldn't fathom. She often thought about her ma and pa and how much courage they must have had to keep getting up every day. Blue was a little thing when her pa had tucked her in that crate full of supplies bound for Kansas. She could still taste his tears when he hugged her tight, knowing he'd never see her again.

"Doc says he's going to be all right." Blue's memories dissipated when she heard Alistair's voice. He descended the stairs and emerged from the shadows, wiping his handkerchief over a sweaty forehead creased with worry.

"That's real good, Alistair," Blue replied.

He shook his head. "I can't make heads or tails of what he's goin' on about. I don't know if any of it's real or just some peyote hallucination he had in the desert."

"Did he say anything about Nellie?"

"He kept raving about some men with no faces hidin' out in Clearwater Canyon."

"Men with no faces?"

Alistair shrugged. "No idea what he's talkin' about. He kept goin' on about creatures with thin, white skin and no faces. Doc says it's probably the fever."

"No, it isn't." They turned to see Lotte sitting by the door. Her knees were pulled up under her chin, and her wide eyes darted here and there. The child was afraid, and that made Blue afraid. "I seen 'em."

ALEXANDRA CHRISTIAN | 57

"Seen what?" Blue asked. "Speak up, child!"

Lotte hesitated just a moment, staring from Blue to Alistair and back. "The Men with No Faces. I seen 'em outside my window. That night that Nellie disappeared. I remember it was so dark. There was barely any moonlight, and the wind was blowin' so hard the windows were rattlin' in the frame. A wolf howled down toward the canyon, and it woke me up. I got scared, and I called out for Nellie, but she didn't answer. So I got my rifle out from under the bed, went to the window, and looked out. I could hear 'em scratchin' around in the dirt around the fence. Prob'ly trying to get to my rabbits. I slowly opened up my window and peered out before I stuck the barrel through the crack. If there was wolves outside, I was gon' shoot 'em! But what I saw that night weren't no wolves. They were taller than any man I ever saw. Their skin was so white they looked like ghosts in the dark. And their faces… they didn't really have faces. Just a mouth… When one of 'em opened its mouth, I could see a thousand sharp, white teeth shining in the dark. When it come toward the window, I cried out. I just knew it could see me, but when it came closer, it didn't have any eyes. Just that wide mouth. I had to bite my cheek to keep my screams in, but it was right there. So close that I could have smelled its breath if there hadn't been a windowpane between us. I wanted to run away, but I was scared they would see me, so I just sat there still as the air before a storm!"

Anger bubbled up in Blue's belly. "And you didn't think to tell anybody about this 'til now?" Lotte winced, but Blue just tightened her fist.

"I thought it was a dream, Nena!"

Blue looked back at Alistair, expecting to see disbelief. The child's story was ridiculous. Monsters with no faces peeking in windows? Lotte had never been a child to make up stories. Before she could say a word, Alistair shoved past her and started down the corridor.

"Alistair! What are you doing?" Blue cried, following. "Alistair!"

He threw open the back door leading into the saloon. The crowd inside had shrank considerably since Charlie's abrupt return. Only the barkeep and a few others still sat there talking in hushed tones.

"I need as many men as I can get," Alistair said. "Ridin' out to Clearwater Canyon." Not a single one of them looked up from their whiskey. "Well come on then," he said. "Jensen! Sam!"

The two turned and stared at Bishop as if he'd taken leave of his senses right along with Charlie. "I don't know, Alistair," Sam started. "After what your boy said…"

"Maybe we should just go to the sheriff, Al," Jensen said.

"We don't have time for that!" Alistair said. "It's only a half day's ride out to Clearwater Canyon. If we wait for the sheriff to come in from Silver City, it's going to be a week before we get there!" He turned and offered Blue a sorrowful expression. "The girls could be dead by then!"

"So what?" that nasty barkeep snarled. "Just a bunch'a whores anyway. There's wagons full come through here every day. Admittedly, none as fine as that Nellie…"

Something in Blue snapped. Before Alistair could stop her, she was over the bar with her pistol against his forehead. "You listen here, string bean. Nellie's the closest thing I got to a daughter, and you call her a whore once more, I'm gonna put a hole in your brain big enough to drive a locomotive through."

"You sure 'bout that, bitch? They hang black whores in this county for threats…"

Blue was cool as she let the pistol go off right by his ear. "Ask me if I'm scared." He flinched at the click of the hammer pulling back once more. "The memory of your brains splattered all over that mirror will be enough to carry me through to St. Peter."

"All right now," Alistair said, stepping between them. "Just take it easy, everyone."

"Maybe Sid's right," Jensen said, knocking back another shot. "If what your boy says is true, we'd be plumb crazy to go out into the desert lookin' for those things."

"Especially not over eight wh—I mean, girls," Sam added, looking away from Blue.

Blue stepped back from behind the bar, shaking her head. "Damn cowards," she murmured.

"You implyin' we're cowards?" Sid the barkeep demanded.

"No. I'm sayin' it real plain." She shoved Alistair out of the way and started toward the door, calling for Lotte. She paused at the door, not looking back. "I'm headin' for Clearwater Canyon. Anybody else comin' with me better have their own irons."

The sun was low in the sky when Blue and Lotte started out toward the canyon. Both women had packed enough firepower to take down the devil himself if he should show up. Blue suspected whatever these things were, they weren't going to give up Nellie without a fight. She looked over at Lotte and smiled to herself. She'd tried to leave the child behind at the settlement with the others, but the girl wouldn't have it. She'd been insistent. *"You the only mama I ever had, Nena. I ain't lettin' you go out there alone!"*

And they were alone.

As Blue looked out across the desolate plain, looking like an ocean of fire in the failing light, she had never felt more alone in her whole life.

Prob'ly shoulda waited until first light.

Blue pulled up on the reins of her horse, stopping short when she heard the voices carried on the wind. She looked back over her shoulder to see two figures silhouetted against the gray and galloping toward them. Blue's eyes might be old, but she would recognize the long, lean form of Alistair Bishop anywhere.

"Thought y'all was too scared to come out chasin' demons," Blue said as they approached. She groaned when she recognized Sid the barkeep perched beside him. His smug grin had been replaced by a stern line, but his eyes were wide. Blue wasn't sure which he was more afraid of: the creatures or the thought that someone might think he was scared. He gave a grunt of recognition.

"The way I see it, those things out there nearly killed my boy. I can't let that pass," Alistair said. He hesitated, looking away from Blue toward the canyon. Blue nodded and spurred the horse, galloping toward the horizon.

They rode in silence for hours, it seemed. Lotte and Sid galloped ahead, but Blue and Alistair rode beside one another. The air between them was heavy with things better left unspoken. So much had happened in the years since Blue had run away from Perdition, taking Nellie with her and retreating into the desert. She stole a glance in his direction, hoping he didn't see. Even after all this time, she could see the shade of the boy she'd loved so long ago.

"It'll be gettin' dark soon," Alistair said, his voice jerking Blue from her memories. "Might want to make camp."

Blue nodded. "I figure these things move around easier at night. If we can make for the canyon before the sun goes down, we can hide out and wait for first light. Catch 'em while they're weakest."

"How many do you think there are?"

"No idea. But it must be quite a few if they can snatch all them girls. Plus Nellie." Blue paused, unsure what to say. She'd been too long in the desert, and talking wasn't high on her list of priorities. "Thank you for comin' with me,

Alistair," she said finally, and nodded toward Sid. "How'd you get him to come with you?"

"I told him if we got out of this alive, I'd give him Betty's."

Blue's eyes went wide in disbelief. "What are you talkin' about, Alistair? Your daddy left you that place!"

"And a whole lot of misery to go with it. Truth is, Blue, I don't blame you for runnin' away like you did. My daddy… and me too… we treated you terrible."

"Now Alistair, this is not the time to go dredgin' up old bones…"

"I should have stood up to him, Blue. And I shouldn't have let you go that night. I was a coward, and I've never forgiven myself."

Blue nodded, staring off into the darkness. She didn't want to look him in the eye. There was just too much to say, she guessed. "But you did all right. Your boy turned out just fine," she said finally.

"True enough," he replied. "I never wanted to be a bully like my daddy was. 'Course, Charlie's ma deserved better than me." Before Blue could respond, Sid began shouting from where he and Lotte had stopped at the trailhead that led down into the valley below.

"Alistair! You better get up here quick!" Blue kicked at the horse's flanks and galloped toward where they stood. Before they could reach the trailhead, the horse pulled up short, nearly throwing Blue from the saddle. "Whoa," she soothed, holding tight to the reins.

Blood was everywhere, so deep Blue could smell it. It left the sand soaked red. The horses backed up, trying to keep their hooves out of the ghoulish muck that pooled around them. It was fairly fresh, but already flies had started to swarm in. Laying by the trail farther down was an unrecognizable mass. Sid slid down from his saddle and crept toward it with his gun drawn. Lotte started to follow, but Blue reached out and took the girl's arm. "Stay here."

Blue dismounted and followed the trail of blood to where Alistair and Sid knelt. The smell of the thing almost knocked her down as she approached. An odor like rotting meat and sun-baked shit emanated from the bloody mass on the ground. It looked as if it might have been human at some point, but by now, it most definitely was not. The flesh was gray, tinged with shades of pink and purple. The thing was small, about the size of an infant, but misshapen. It had bulbous protrusions where its limbs should have been, and its head was too large. There were no eyes, only that gaping mouth that Charlie had described, filled with teeth.

"What in hell is that?" Sid asked, pulling his bandana over his nose to keep the stench at bay. "Some kind of demon?"

Blue shook her head. "Surely even the devil couldn't make somethin' like that."

"What is it?" Lotte called from where she was still hanging back.

"You stay there, child!" Blue said.

"Think maybe we oughta go back?" Alistair said, using his hat to fan away the flies.

"And leave Nellie behind?"

Sid stood up, kicking dirt over the carcass. "Look, it's gon' be pitch black out here soon, and from the looks of that thing, your Nellie's already dead. And we will be too if we keep on!"

Blue was about to call Sid out as a coward when a scream sounded from off in the distance. It echoed off the walls of the canyon below them and across the barren plain. "My God..." Blue whispered. The scream came again, this time louder than before. In the springtime, back on the plantation, Blue had heard screams like that when her daddy used to slaughter lambs in the barn. "What in Jesus's name was that?"

"The coyotes that are gonna rip us to shreds in the dark if these... whatevers don't get us first!" Sid exclaimed.

"That wasn't a coyote," Alistair said, stalking back to his horse. "The way I see it, we'll never make it back to town before nightfall anyway. We'll just keep toward the canyon and make camp someplace safe."

Sid's eyes were wide, staring at them in utter disbelief. "You're both crazy." He mounted up and turned his horse back toward Perdition. "I'm headin' back now while I still can. Ain't no whore worth this."

"Wait!" Alistair called. "You can't go back alone!" But it was too late. Sid was gone before his dust settled.

Clearwater Canyon was a deep gouge in the desert that stretched for miles in both directions. The trail leading down into the canyon was a labyrinth of razor-sharp rock with a network of caves that had been carved out by the rushing waters. The walls on either side were so steep and narrow that one could easily lose their way. Only desperate outlaws ever tried to traverse the trail, and none ever came back to tell the tale.

Blue guessed they were desperate.

There was no more talk as they headed toward the canyon under the darkening sky. A few stars were peeking out, and it made Blue nervous. They would have to find a place to hide out until morning. She should have listened to Alistair before and waited until first light to come out here looking. Then again, Blue wasn't sure Nellie had that kind of time. If it even still mattered.

They approached the mouth of the canyon slowly with Blue keeping Lotte between them. Once more she kicked herself for allowing the child to come along. What had she been thinking? They hadn't heard any more of those screams, but the smell of the dead thing at the trailhead stayed with them.

Blue heard something behind and turned to see Alistair striking a match. "What are you doing?"

"We're gonna need some kind of light here in just a few. I figure a makeshift torch might do us some good."

"Still scared of the dark, I see," Blue teased.

He gave a grunt of amusement and lit the torch. Suddenly the trail was illuminated. The rising walls of the canyon around them were slick, glistening in places with what looked like condensation. There was also green lichen covering the jagged stones. The air was close, hot and stifling. The death-smell was stronger. It mixed with the coppery smell of fresh blood and dirt. Blue could taste it with every breath, and it turned her stomach.

"What in God's name is going on here?" Alistair whispered.

"God ain't got nothin' to do with this," Blue said.

"Maybe we should turn around and make camp farther out."

"Nena!"

Blue pulled up short as Lotte slid down from her saddle and ran toward a small grotto carved into the canyon wall up ahead. More of the green lichen grew there, covering the place like a curtain. "There's something in there!" Lotte said.

Blue and Alistair jumped down from their horses, reaching for the girl. "Don't touch it!" Blue shouted, but it was too late. As soon as Lotte touched the plant, it began to coil around her wrist like a vine.

"What's happening?" Lotte shrieked. She tried to shake her arm free of the vine, but it held on fast. "Nena!"

Blue ran to the girl, grabbing her around the waist and pulling. The vine was nearly to her shoulder and more tendrils were beginning to reach for her even as she struggled. Blue tugged, and the strange lichen seemed to pull back, as if it were trying to pull Lotte into the nest with it. "Alistair! Help me!" He rushed over and tried using his pistol to beat and tear at the tendrils. Lotte screamed as the tendrils hung on tighter. They were growing fast now, emitting some kind of hissing noise as they slid across both arms and around her throat. They silenced her screams in seconds, growing into her mouth. "It isn't working!" Blue shouted, almost in tears as she kept pulling on the girl. "You have to help me! Please!"

Alistair touched the flame of his torch to one of the tendrils, and it shrieked, receding just a little. He did it again, this time igniting the lichen at the base near the rock face. Almost immediately the lichen blackened and shrank, falling away from Lotte's struggling arms until she fell into Blue's. She sputtered and gasped for air.

"There, child. You breathe slow now." Blue cradled the child against her bosom while she wept, rocking her as if she might still be that foundling baby. "Thank you, Alistair..." she puffed. "What in Hell was that thing?"

But he didn't answer. His eyes were fixed on the contents of the grotto that the lichen had been protecting. Hidden in the shadows was what looked like a slimy cluster of egg sacs. A milky substance that glistened in the torchlight dripped from the near-transparent derma of the eggs. Alistair reached out, running a fingertip along its surface. When nothing reached out to grab him, he pulled one of the eggs free of the cluster.

"Don't touch it!" Blue scolded, rushing to her feet. She leaned over his shoulder as he turned the jelly-like egg over in his palm. The surface had purple veins that ran through it, but Blue could clearly see something inside. Very much like the something they'd found on the trail, but much smaller.

"What the hell is it?"

"I don't know, but I think we've made a terrible mistake coming here." She pointed above them, and Alistair stepped back, raising the torch. Overhead they could see hundreds of grottos containing thousands of those egg sacs. "We need to get out of here. Now."

Screams sounded in the canyon, much louder than what they'd heard on the trail. This time the noise was an ear-splitting blade that brought them all to their knees. Their horses neighed and reared before fleeing back toward the trail. Alistair dropped the egg-thing and went for his pistol. The egg shattered at Blue's feet. She could see the thing inside. Its eyes opened, and it made a weak squeal as if answering the screams of whatever was coming through the caves for them. It began to crawl toward Blue, and she watched with morbid fascination.

"Step back!" Lotte pushed Blue out of the way and stomped on the thing with her heavy boot heel. It splattered in a mess of black blood, staining Lotte's petticoat. "Let's go!"

There was another scream, but this time it was coming from behind. They turned to see a half dozen man-sized creatures. They moved like a swarm of bees, oozing over the desert floor and crawling down from the canyon above. They were as Lotte described, tall and thin with milk-white skin. Where their faces should have been, there was only a wide mouth that blossomed like a flower as they screamed, showing rows of jagged teeth. One of them carried the pulpy remains of what could only be Sid.

Lotte pulled her six shooters and fired at them. The first shot bounced off the rock face, but the second one caught the one carrying Sid in the gut. It fell forward with a gurgling shriek and began crawling toward Lotte. Blue pulled the long rifle from the scabbard at her back and pushed Lotte behind her. She picked them off with ease, sending the creatures flying back against the canyon wall.

"They're getting up, Nena!" Lotte shouted.

Before Blue could respond, she heard Alistair groan behind her. Two of the creatures had descended on him from the cavern above. He was quick and kicked hard at one. It grabbed his foot, forcing him backward until he sat down hard on the ground, his torch rolling away from him. The creatures closed in, grabbing him up by his arms as if they meant to pull him apart. The creatures hissed and shrieked, their gaping mouths opening and snapping down as Alistair held them back. Shots echoed in the canyon as Blue shot them with startling precision. But it was of little use. As soon as they fell, others would get up, their bullets having almost no effect.

"We have to get out of here," Alistair said. "We're outnumbered."

"But we still haven't found Nellie!" Blue hissed, firing again as the creature closest to them tried to get up.

"This place is a giant hive! A nest! Those things are protecting something, Blue, and whatever it is, I don't want to stick around long enough to find out!"

"Follow me!" Lotte yelled as she ran by them. She was holding Alistair's torch in one hand and a stick of dynamite in the other. Blue and Alistair followed, running as fast as they could along the canyon floor. They could hear the creatures screaming behind them. Blue was afraid to look behind, knowing they were gaining.

"We'll never outrun them," Alistair shouted.

"We don't have to outrun them," Lotte said, pushing them into a cave as she lit the stick of dynamite with Alistair's torch. "We just have to get out of the way." Lotte smiled as she peeked around the wall of the cave and threw the dynamite as hard as she could. They got down just as the dynamite blew. When the dust cleared, the canyon was silent again.

"That was damn good thinkin', girl," Alistair said, clapping Lotte on the back.

"When the horses broke free, my saddlebag fell down," Lotte said, holding up the leather bag.

"Come on," Blue said. "Let's get out of here."

"You keep that dynamite close, girl," Alistair added.

"How you reckon we're supposed to get out of here?" Blue said, feeling her way along the walls. "We certainly can't go back the way we came."

"Prob'ly comes out somewhere on the other side. These hills are full of secret places dug out by outlaws."

"We could be walkin' ourselves into a trap."

They continued down the narrow corridor, going deeper into the canyon. Strange noises echoed around them, but fortunately no screams of those faceless creatures. The thought that this whole thing might be a trap began to weigh heavier on Blue. If this cave didn't come out someplace, they were likely done for. Alistair's torch wouldn't last forever. The air was already close and fetid. Soon they might not be able to breathe. The ever-present stench of blood and decay was strongest here, almost gagging them with every breath. Maybe that was what those things did: just trapped their prey and waited for them to die.

"Nena! Mr. Bishop! Down here!" Lotte waved them through to where she stood at the end of the twisting corridor. "It opens up!"

When they emerged into the heart of the cave, the source of the stench was revealed. All eight of the whores from Betty's were piled in a haphazard sort of cairn in the center of the room. They looked like broken toys discarded by a spoiled child. The bodies were emaciated and pale, as if something had sucked the life right out of them. Lotte broke, crying out and dropping the torch to hide in Blue's bosom.

"There, child. It's all right now. They're gone on to Heaven now." Yes, Blue believed in a higher power. After what she'd seen today, how could she not?

Alistair knelt down looking at the piled corpses as if taking inventory. "There's no blood. None at all," he said. "Those things must have sucked them dry."

"Nena," Lotte whimpered, wiping her eyes. "Do you think that's what happened to Nellie?"

"I…" For once, Blue was speechless. She didn't want to lie, but all she could think was yes, that is what very likely happened to Nellie. And could happen to them all if they didn't get out of here fast. She peered around the room, desperately searching for a crack or crevice that might lead to escape.

"Little Lotte. Is that you?"

Blue froze. Her blood ran cold as she recognized the voice. It was thin and more of a whisper, but she knew it. It was Nellie. All three turned to see the girl stumbling toward them. She was white as the sheets Blue used to hang out to dry in the sun. Her red hair had gone dull and whipped around her face in a disheveled halo.

"Nellie!" Lotte shouted. "Is it really you?"

"I knew you'd come for me," Nellie said. There were tears glistening in her eyes. "You and Blue…I knew it was just a matter of time."

Lotte broke away from Blue and ran to Nellie. "Oh Nellie! I missed you!" Lotte cried. "We thought you were dead!"

"Of course not," she said. Her voice was so weak, almost a whisper. "I hid… for days I waited. After Charlie…" With that, the girl began to weep into her hands. They were stained with blood. Blue could see it under her fingernails and caked in Charlie Bishop's ring. "I tried to help him."

"Charlie's all right, child," Blue said. "He made it back to Perdition…"

Nellie shook her head. "No… no no no…" she cried.

Alistair managed to catch her just as she fell, swooning into oblivion. "Come on," he said. "This way. I think I see a way out." Blue gasped as the earth beneath their feet shuddered. Those screams, those all too familiar screams, echoed in the corridor behind them. Evidently the creatures had recovered. Or more of them were coming. "Let's go!"

The three companions and Nellie made for a narrow crevice at the end of the tunnel. Moonlight peeked through the small crack in the cave wall. It would be just large enough for them to crawl through. The ground shuddered once more as two of the faceless creatures rushed into the cavern. They screeched as if calling for others before running toward them. Blue took Nellie from Alistair, pushing her and Lotte through first and then herself. Alistair was last, lighting several more sticks of dynamite and throwing them into the pit behind them.

"Run!" Alistair shouted, shoving the women ahead of him. They barely cleared the mouth of the cave before the dynamite exploded, throwing them forward. Rocks and debris whipped at their faces as the narrow opening from which they'd crawled collapsed, burying the cavern.

It was what the old schoolmaster had called a Herculean task to keep Nellie away from Charlie Bishop when they got back to town. Since they'd left the canyon two days previous, the girl had been chompin' at the bit to get over to the surgery, but the doctor kept putting her off. She cried and carried on that she couldn't live one more second without Charlie's arms around her. To the doc's credit, he insisted that she get well first. Blue still thought she looked a little pale, but on the morning of the third day, she couldn't hold Nellie back any longer.

"He's been mostly out of it since he came home. But I think he's going to be all right." Blue smiled and gave Nellie a reassuring pat on the arm as she led her up the stairs. "Especially now that you're here."

"Thank you, kindly. I promise I won't get him excited," Nellie said with a wink. Blue smiled and embraced the girl once more. "I'm so glad you're back home now, Nellie-girl. That was a close call."

"Everything's all right now," Nellie said, stroking the old woman's hair.

"You the only family I got," Blue said. "I just don't think I could take it if anythin' ever happened to you."

Nellie shushed her. "You don't have to worry, Mama Blue. I'll always be here."

Blue nodded and let go, waving her toward Charlie's bed. "You go on, child. He's been waitin' for you."

Charlie lay in a feverish stupor, breathing lightly. Nellie knelt beside the bed, taking his hand and pressing it to her cheek. "Oh, Charlie. I never meant for you to get hurt this way," she whispered as she pulled back the blanket to examine his wounds.

"He looks some better today," Blue said. "The doctor said his fever's gone down and the dressing looks real good."

Nellie leaned forward and kissed his cheek. Then she did the oddest thing. She began licking the tiny wounds at Charlie's throat and cheek. He whimpered in his sleep, almost recoiling from the girl's touch. Nellie pulled back, offering Blue a toothy grin that she wasn't sure she liked. It was too wide. Too sharp.

"You just hush now, love. It's all right. I'm here now."

LOST WORDS

David B. Coe

THE DAY BEGAN NORMAL ENOUGH, GIVEN HOW IT ENDED. I DIDN'T PUT much trust in the Fates—they were about as dependable as a dowsing rod in west Texas—and yet a person'd think that there'd at least be a warning in the stars when things started tromping off to Hades. But no. I was in my spot before dawn, out front as usual, staring up at the constellations, and there weren't nothing.

Business started slow. I sat in my rocker on the porch, Demetrius beside me, my Henry repeater resting on my thighs. The eastern sky lit up, casting reds and golds on the buttes, ridges, and crags this side of El Paso. Lizards scuttled over the dirt, and a coyote slunk through the brush, watching me, watching Demetrius watch him.

It was a good hour or two past sunup when I got my first nibble of the day. I was tracking a hawk across a cloudless blue sky when Dem lifted his head and gave a low growl. That usually meant company.

Two of them topped the rise: a grizzled man and a kid barely old enough to shave, who might have been his grandson. Or his boy, I suppose. Maybe Gramps married lucky. Not for me to judge.

The old man rode a bay. Impressive, big. The kid was on a ragged pinto. If I'd thought they were in the market for a new horse for the lad, I'd have been on my feet already, a grin on my lips, hand raised in greeting. But that bay was the only thing about them that said they had means. The rest was dust and tatters and hard times. I kept my seat, eyed the hawk again.

Dem rumbled another warning.

"Easy, boy."

He thumped his tail.

The old man reined to a halt a few yards short of the porch and climbed off his horse. He muttered something to the kid, who swung himself down as well.

"Good morning," the man said, smiling a smile I didn't believe.

I nodded, spat. But by then, I knew. The kid's eyes were glassy, and the jolt of his dismount brought a wince. Scrutinizing him, I noticed the swolled cheek and the way he held his jaw, like the slightest whisper might bring him to tears.

"Tooth problem?"

The man nodded. "Wisdoms come in. He can't barely chew." He gave the Musaeum a once-over, his expression like curdled milk. I'd seen that look on other faces, and I bit my lip so as not to laugh. Not that I blamed him. I knew how the place seemed. Worn wood, a single grimed window, a crooked door on rusted hinges, barely bigger than the average shithouse. My regulars saw the place different, but strangers? Sometimes it was all I could do to keep 'em from riding off without even a word.

"Sign's wrong," the man said.

I was used to this, too.

"Pardon?"

"Your sign. Ain't no 'a' in 'museum.'"

"Sign's all right. Spelled it that way once."

He shrugged, gaze still on the building, skepticism still creasing his leathered forehead. "Can you help us?"

"Sure can. We'll get you set up right away."

"It don't look like much."

"There's more to it than you might think. Let's get the boy inside."

"You got a dentist?"

"I'm the dentist."

He squinted and pulled his head back a touch, like a snake rearing to strike.

"I'm a lot like the building: more to me than looks tell."

That sour face had tipped over into a full-blown frown. "Maybe we ought to push on."

"Your choice. But you might want to ask the boy what he thinks." I didn't wait for Gramps. "Boy, you want to ride on, search for another dentist? Or you want me to help you now?"

The pinto whinnied and stomped—it didn't take more than a little tickle from me—and the kid actually flinched.

"Please, PawPaw," he said, the words thick. "I can't ride no more. Just let him try."

Sera opened the door and joined me on the porch, respectable in white. "Why don't you come on inside, hon," she said, shining a smile the boy's way. "We'll get you fixed up just as quick as you please."

"Hold on," PawPaw said, wary like a twice-bluffed poker player. "What's all this gonna cost me?"

"You can have it done for a song," I said.

"A song."

"Keep scowling like that and you're gonna pull a muscle."

Sera slapped my arm.

"Doesn't have to be a song. You don't strike me as the type to write poetry, but I could be wrong."

"This a joke?" he asked, serious as could be.

"It's not, but that'll do, too. If you know one, and if I ain't heard it."

"Look, mister . . ."

"Call me Tole."

"Mister Tole, I'm not playin' games, and I'm not in the mood for any who is. My boy here is in pain, and I'm tryin' to get him fixed up. We've got work to get done, and he ain't worth a horse's fart to me like this. You understand?"

Another low growl rumbled in Dem's chest. I didn't say a word to ease his mind.

Sera reached for my arm again, this time to give it a squeeze. She didn't want me goin' off on the poor man, at least not before we had whatever goods he might give us. I opened my hand, letting her see it was all right. First customers of the day—I had no intention of scaring them off.

"First of all," I said, easy as a morning sky, "it's just Tole. Not Mister Tole. Second, I don't play games. Least aways, not about payment. I want a song, or a poem, or a story, or a joke. Something I ain't heard before. Preferably something you made up. Give me that, and we'll fix the boy and be squared away. If you prefer to pay in cash, you can, but that price is gonna be steep. Steeper, anyway."

He eyed me, flicked a glance to Sera, then stared at me some more. "You're serious."

"As can be."

"Well, that's . . . I ain't never . . . Well, all right then." He scratched the back of his neck, embarrassed all of a sudden. Bashful. It wasn't that uncommon, really. Folks made stuff up all the time. Fine words, jokes that were laugh-worthy, songs that could set a toe to tapping or bring a tear to a grown man's eye. But often times they were embarrassed to share. People might cuss a blue streak, or make asses of themselves spouting nonsense about things they were ignorant of, and think nothing of it. But ask them to repeat a few words with any value at all, and they fold up like a rose in a cold rain. "All right then," he said again. He laughed, nervous as a boy working up the courage for his first kiss.

Sera and I just watched him. Even the kid turned his way, pain forgotten for the moment.

"This is a . . . well, this is a poem, actually. Wrote it a long time ago." He spared the boy a quick grin. "For your grandma."

Sera nodded encouragement.

"Whenever you're ready," I said.

He laughed again, took off his hat, and ran a finger over the rim, his eyes avoiding ours.

> "Sunset colors in a velvet sky,
> Golden glow in sapphire eyes;
> Skin so white, like sweetest cream,
> Lips like rubies, in a treasured dream;
>
> By flowing waters, by and by,
> Where geese do call and rivers sigh;
> I search for words, fair and true,
> To declare unto God my love for you."

On it went for another four verses, none of them much better than those. I'd heard worse, of course. Long as I've been collecting, a person would expect as much. But I'd certainly heard better. Still, we'd struck a bargain, and it was new if nothing else.

Grandpa finished in a sort of daze, a faint smile on his lips. "Been years since I spoke that poem. Years and years."

"That really yours, PawPaw?" the kid asked, sounding impressed.

The man lifted his gaze at that. "Yeah, it's mine all right."

"Say it again."

He opened his mouth, only to close it an instant later. He blinked. "I . . . I can't remember it now. Had it a minute ago, but . . . It's like it's gone."

"No matter," I said. "Payment's been made. Sera, can you escort our young friend inside?"

"I sure can." She beckoned to the boy with a waggle of her fingers. "What's your name, hon?"

"Um, Thomas, ma'am."

"That's a fine name for a strong lad like you. Let's get you settled. This ain't gonna hurt one bit."

That was a lie. He'd be all right in time, and a fair bit better off than he was now. The kid had some hurt in his future, though. He probably knew as much. But Sera's ebon eyes and diamond smile had charmed men a whole lot more sophisticated than this boy. Poor Thomas didn't stand a chance.

He stepped onto the porch and let Sera lead him into the Musaeum. Grandpa remained where he was, confusion clouding his face.

"I can't remember it," he said again, more to himself than any of us.

"I'm gonna see to the boy," I told him. "You just wait out here." I waved a hand at my chair. "Feel free to avail yourself of the rocker. We won't be too long."

Inside, the building had made itself a full-blown dental establishment, complete with chair, instrument table, and sink. The boy reclined in the chair, and Sera was clattering my tools onto a silver pan. I didn't waste time on chatter. Seeing all that I was going to put in his mouth, the boy had gone white as a full moon. I ethered him, wrestled the teeth out, and left him in the chair to wake, Sera by his side.

I told grandpa that everything had gone just right, and gave him the teeth—some folks are sentimental about such things. He still muttered to himself, wondering where his poem had gone. But he thanked me, and when the boy could walk, groggy though he was, the two of them rode off.

Sera went back inside, I settled into the rocker, and Dem dropped down beside me, chin resting on his paws, expression forlorn as only a dog's can be.

"Boy's better off," I said. "And the man himself said he hadn't spoke the poem in forever. It's not like he's gonna miss it."

Dem gave me look I didn't much want at that moment and closed his eyes.

I guess I dozed off, because the next thing I knew, the Musaeum bustled with voices and noise. Women laughed. Lamper pounded out songs on our out-of-tune piano, and Zeno clinked bottles and glasses behind the bar.

I knew who was coming before I spotted him kicking up stones and dust on the path leading from town. He raised a hand and grinned. Demetrius woke and lifted his head, but then went back to sleeping. Dennis was a regular.

People told me he was better than Lamper. "You oughta hire that boy," they said. "He's got a sweet voice and light fingers, and he writes his own songs, 'stead of playin' the same old standards all the time."

Maybe they were right. Problem was, then I'd be paying him instead of him paying me, and I didn't want that.

"Afternoon, Tole," Dennis called, when he was in shouting distance.

I poked my hat up with a finger. "Dennis."

He was a good-looking boy, baby-faced, with feathered wheat hair and eyes the color of a summer sky. Didn't strike me as the kind of man who had to pay for loving, no matter the price. But Sera said he was on the shy side, and not knowing much about it, and not interested to know more, I didn't question her. Sure did have a spring in his step, though. Probably the highlight of his week.

He peered past me, gaze hungry and filled with anticipation. "Clara around?"

"Ain't she always?"

He lifted a shoulder, still hoping to spot her at the door.

I called for Sera.

A few seconds later, she appeared in the doorway, her hair done up, a red lace dress hugging her curves, black stockings and high-heeled shoes making her look like she belonged in Paris, France, and not here in the middle of lizard central.

"Good day, Dennis," she drawled, eyeing him through her lashes.

He turned red as a beet. "Miss Sera. You're lookin' fine today."

"You're sweet."

"Tell Clara that he's here," I said.

"I will." She flashed another smile his way. "She was hopin' you'd come callin' today. She's missed you."

The boy beamed like a lighthouse.

Sera went back inside, leaving him and me alone.

"What you got for me today, son?"

His whole bearing changed. His gaze slid away, and he fidgeted with his hat again. "Well, Tole, I was wantin' to talk to you about that. I was hopin' maybe you'd let me pay with cash this one time."

"You know I can't do that. Rules of the house."

"Please. I'm runnin' out of songs. People back in town are startin' to complain because I play too many popular numbers. They like *my* songs. *I* like *my* songs. And I can't hardly remember any of 'em anymore."

"Guess you need to be writing more then, don't you?"

"Quick as I write 'em, you take 'em."

I leaned forward, stared hard at the lad until his glance met mine. "I don't take them," I said, my voice dropping low. "You use them to pay for a service. You don't like my rates, you don't have to come here. You know that."

"Well, sure I do, Tole. And I'm not . . . I don't want you angry with me. But I like Clara, and her and me, we got plans. So, yeah, I come here to call on her—"

"Clara works for me. As long as you see her, you pay the price. If that price is too steep, then you can take your business elsewhere. I'll understand. No hard feelins."

Happy as he'd looked before, that was how pitiful he looked now. "I don't want to go anywhere else," he said, the words coming out as barely more than a whisper.

"Well, good. We're glad to have you here. Now how about that song?"

He nodded. I thought he might cry. But he took a breath and started to sing. It was a ballad—for all I knew he'd written it for Clara. The verses were pretty enough, but it was the refrain that caught my ear.

"With night fallin' o'er the desert, and wolves howling the wind,
I choose a star, and make a wish for a dawn not long from now,
When all the world unfolds before us, a life we can begin,
Your hand in mine, my name in yours, our love upon a cloud."

The boy had talent, and no denying. He was a jewel in this forsaken land. That was how I justified it, to Sera and to myself. Clara joined me on the porch while he sang. She wore white lace, her dark hair down, satin shoes on bare feet, as demure as a girl could be, a counterpoint to Sera. Her eyes were the same color as Dennis's, her features as delicate, almost like they was made for each other. Which I suppose they were.

When he finished, she clapped. The smile that touched his lips was almost enough to make me forget what I'd seen in his face moments before.

"Good day, Clara," he said, breathless.

"That was beautiful, Dennis. Will you sing me another later?"

He looked my way.

"It's all right," I said. "I won't be listenin'."

"Well, then, I just might."

She spun a little circle, like a child too excited to speak, then held out a hand for him.

As they hurried past me into the building, I sat back in my chair and scratched Dem's head. "You two have fun," I called after them, pulling my hat low and pretending like I was going back to sleep.

It was late afternoon when Dennis finally left. I should have been cross— too much time for one song—but truth was I felt a little bad and so I didn't fuss at him as he left, or the girls after. Still I didn't expect I'd make any more sales the rest of the day, and I wasn't happy.

It's funny. Sometimes the best deals are the ones we don't see coming.

She arrived as the sun angled low over the mountains, shading valleys in purple and blue, stretching shadows across the scrub. She sat a dappled gray, her hair white beneath her broad-rimmed hat, her green eyes as bright and fresh as new spring leaves. She wore chaps and a duster that was as ageless as she was. As she clicked her tongue at her mount and swung herself out of the saddle, I glanced back at the Musaeum.

It was a general store now. She needed supplies, I guess: food, ammo, maybe something of a feminine nature. Sera appeared at the door in a plain gingham dress.

I stood, and Dem scrabbled to his feet as well, ears raised, tail swaying in a tentative wag.

"Evenin'," she said in a voice like gravel underfoot.

Maybe she needed tobacco.

"Good evening."

She approached slowly, scanning the building, the scrub around it. "Still open?"

"Always open. Something in particular you're tryin' to find?"

"This and that. I'll know it when I see it."

"Well, come on in and look around."

Her smile was more leery than friendly, but she didn't hesitate. Sera opened the door for her, and she stepped past both of us into the store. I noticed she carried a six shooter on her belt.

I circled behind the counter and watched her. Sera remained at the door. The woman orbited, picking up an occasional item, turning it over in her hands, and returning it to its shelf. After a few minutes of this, she sauntered to the front of the store, empty-handed.

"There's no prices on anything."

"That's right."

Her smile didn't reach her emerald greens. "That mean it's all free?"

I laughed. "We operate on a sort of barter system."

"Barter."

"No cash. You pick out what you want and you pay with a song, a poem, a story. You got anything like that?"

"I've got stories. Twenty years in the saddle, you bet I've got stories. Question is, what are you gonna do with them?"

"If there'd been prices like you were lookin' for, would you have asked me what I was gonna do with the money you gave me?" I didn't give her time to answer. "Of course not. We keep the stories for as long as we can. We enjoy them. Some time later, we let 'em go."

For the first time since arriving, she seemed unsure of herself.

"You write poems?" I asked, gentling my voice. "Maybe make up songs as you ride?"

"No, nothing like that."

I waited, knowing she had to have something. Everyone does. There ain't a person alive who don't create. Words, tunes, images. Hell, an astute thought given voice with eloquence can sustain a man for days.

"How 'bout a recipe? Something you make on the trail that no one else knows?"

She shook her head again. "Beans, mostly. Sometimes a jackrabbit on a spit. Fancier fare doesn't sit right with me. At least not out here."

"Maybe a drawing, or some other—"

"I have a journal," she said. "I can read you something from that."

I smiled. "Perfect."

She nodded, turned on her heel, and left the store. Sera cast a glance my way, her expression flat.

The woman returned a minute or two later carrying a worn, leather-bound volume. She entered the shop again, stared first at me and then at Sera. At last she held out the journal.

"No!" Sera said, as if the woman had reached for a hot pan.

I warned her with a glare, pivoted to the woman. "Better you read us a page or two. Wherever you like. Just open it up and start."

She flicked another gaze at both of us, shy like Thomas's grandpa, reluctant as Dennis. But she opened the journal, cleared her throat, and began.

"As I ride, I am aware of rhythms, cadence, song, dance. The beat of hooves, the sway of my body in the saddle, the whisper of the Rio Grande. Warblers trill, unseen and secretive, and wrens answer, more bold than their cousins. As afternoon deepens, coyotes yip and yodel.

"Melody lures and embraces, teases and sustains. It is ubiquitous. Some speak of the loneliness of the trail. In towns, I am asked why a woman, well read and sophisticated, would choose solitude over companionship, open land over hearth and home, risk and uncertainty over the protections I might be afforded by ceding my autonomy to a husband. How, I am asked, could I exchange the culture of 'normal' life for something so empty and primitive? I want to laugh. I would not know where to begin my explanation, and so I offer none…"

I finally stopped her after five pages. I wanted more. Sera did, too. I could tell. The woman's rough voice was as comfortable as old boots, as hypnotic as a waterfall.

But fair's fair. I didn't imagine she'd be buying much, and I wouldn't take more than was my due. I could see, as she turned the pages in her journal, that the ones she'd read were now blank. I don't know if she noticed or not. She didn't say a word about it. When I told her she could stop, she closed the cover, tucked the journal under her arm, and browsed the store.

A few over-ripe apples, some jerky, a pouch of tobacco, and an old issue of the El Paso *Times*: that's what she got for her trouble. I threw in an extra apple, some bread, and a small flask of Tennessee whiskey, just because. As I say, fair's fair.

She was out the door and back in the saddle with plenty of daylight to spare. I watched her go from the door.

Sera lingered by the counter.

"Wound up being a good day," she said, breaking a long silence.

"I guess it did."

I faced her. The Musaeum had changed back to its usual form. Dusty shelves lined every wall, floor to ceiling, all of them overflowing with scrolls and sheaves of parchment, volumes frayed and new, drawings, paintings, and daguerreotypes—portraits and landscapes both.

New pages—the poem, song, and journal entry we'd added today—rested at the top of a haphazard pile on the standing desk, which was no more ordered than the shelves. I should have fixed up the place. It needed cleaning bad enough, and I'd been meaning to for a long time. But something stopped me. Maybe I knew what was coming.

I went back outside and fell into the rocker. The chair creaked. So did the porch. Demetrius lifted his head again but didn't tap his tail. Maybe he knew, too.

Sera let me be. She could read my moods and probably figured I'd come around before long. Any other evening, she would have been right.

I sat until the sun dipped below the western horizon, watching a riot of color burn down low in the sky. The instant the sun vanished, I felt a frisson of power at my back, vibrating like a plucked string on a lyre.

"Tole." Sera's voice, taut as a telegraph wire.

I stood, turned. My rifle leaned next to the door. I left it there and walked inside. Sera still stood by the counter, as if she hadn't moved since I went out. Three other women stood near her. Tall, olive-skinned, with shimmering black hair that hung to their waists, and eyes as dark as pitch. They were identical, and beautiful, and as remote as stars. They wore robes clasped at the neck with golden brooches, each jewel more valuable than everything I had.

"Ptolemy." Hearing my true name spoke in the cold, clear voice of the first one, Melete, sent shivers through me. And not in a good way.

"Long has it been since last we saw you," Mneme said.

Aoidi's gaze raked over me. "You look old." She had always been the most capricious of the three.

"You haven't changed, any of you," I said, trying to sound like I wasn't surprised to see them. On some level I wasn't. But my voice shook anyway.

"We never do."

"Time cannot touch us."

"Nor mortals. Not even one with your talents, meager though they are."

Aoidi smiled, joined an instant later by her sisters. Strains of a tune I'd never heard echoed in my mind. A verse took form in my thoughts. I had no talent for either music or poetry, but these three could fire even my imagination.

Melete studied Sera, appraising her like she was livestock. "You know us, Serapeum?"

Mneme regarded her as well. "Perhaps she has heard our names."

Mischief glimmered in Aoidi's dark eyes. "Or perhaps he has kept her in the dark, lest she flee this place."

Sera lifted her chin. "I know who you are." She sounded less scared than I had. "You're the Muses."

"She does know. I am Melete, which means Practice, in your tongue."

"I am Mneme. Memory."

"Song. But I prefer Aoidi."

"What is it you want with us?" I asked. "Why are you here?"

Frowns twisted their perfect faces.

"Rude."

"He speaks from fear."

"And well he should."

I wanted to deny it. No man likes having his courage questioned. But they were right. I was afraid. Of them, of why they might have come, of what they might do. No one in his right mind seeks the attention of goddesses.

"You're welcome here," I said, trying to mollify them. "Always, of course. But it's been a long time, and I wasn't expecting—"

Melete cut me off with a flick of her fingers. "We come with grievances. You have violated ancient law."

"You have broken with custom and tradition," Mneme said, "to the detriment of all."

"We will have satisfaction." Aoidi drew herself up to her full height. "Or you will suffer the consequences of your trespass."

"But I haven't—"

"The name of your establishment is an affront, and a presumption."

"It dishonors the true Musaeum."

"You, of all men, should know better."

"The Musaeum was mine," I said, none too wisely. "Its purpose—"

"Its purpose did not belong to you."

"Ever."

"You created it for us. You dedicated it to us. If it belonged to anyone, it belonged to the three of us."

Aoidi took a step in my direction. It was all I could do not to cower and back away.

"But you know this, as well," she went on. "Unlike us, you are much changed, Ptolemy, and not for the better or wiser. You take and you cheat, and you turn art—"

"And knowledge—"

"And memory—"

"Into commodity, which they were never meant to be."

I couldn't deny it, not without lying. And lying to these three was as tricky as it was foolish.

"Is it Tole who's changed?" Sera asked, surprising me, and also the Muses, judging by their expressions. "Or is it all of us? This world isn't the same as the one that honored you with the Library."

The Three glared at her until Sera dropped her gaze, her cheeks robbed of color.

"There is some truth in what she says," Melete admitted, her tone grudging.

"The ideal of Alexandria has faded with the centuries," Mneme said, the words heavy. "It pains us, and yet it is undeniable."

Only Aoidi seemed unbowed. "All the more reason for us to remain vigilant. The world can change. Mortals can change. But we remain constant. We preserve what is deserving, be it song or thought or principle. The Musaeum has long since fallen, but its mission will not be lost."

"Exactly," I said. "That's what I have in mind with this place."

"This place is an appendage."

"An echo."

"An abomination. And yet it serves a greater good."

I didn't like the sound of that at all. "What greater good?"

"Your methods have grown questionable."

"You have lost your way."

Aoidi made a vague gesture with her hand, encompassing the entire room and all it held. "But still your harvest has been impressive. We would take what you have collected and reposit it where it belongs."

"No!" I croaked the word, unable to draw breath, my heart frozen in my chest. I looked from one to the next, searching their faces for any hint of mercy. "Please. I've worked so hard for all of these. They're everything to me."

They considered me the way parents would a misbehaving child.

"This is our decree."

"In keeping with what we have always been, and what you once were."

"The moment you began to think of these things as your own, they became something other than what they are supposed to be."

My knees buckled. I reached for the desk, held onto it as I sank to the floor.

"Wait," Sera said. "You might not like his methods, but he always trades for what he brings in. He never takes a thing."

"Your point?" Melete asked.

"What does he get?" Sera's gesture recalled Aoidi's. "You're going to take all of this. But he's worked for it, earned it. So what does he get?"

"Another presumption! You ask us to treat knowledge as a good, just as he has."

"That is not who we are. You would have us barter, and thus make us less than what we have always been."

"He has violated laws that span millennia. He is fortunate that we choose to spare his life. You are fortunate as well. Do not test us further, mortal."

Sera started to say more, but I caught her eye and shook my head. She was a fine negotiator, but she was out of her depth with these three. Just as I was.

"Still," Melete said. "We might make a small concession."

"Acknowledgement of a task well accomplished and a goal that lives on."

"Yes," Aoidi said. "We will take what is here, but we will also permit you to continue your trade, provided those who give do so freely and you agree that all you collect will be given over to the common good."

Sera huffed a dry laugh. "So, in other words, you're willing to tolerate him treating all this as a commodity, as long as he gives it all to you."

"So long as we keep him from accruing art and knowledge as he would wealth, it is not a commodity."

Mneme nodded. "In this way, he can continue to honor the tradition of which he was so vital a part, knowing he does so with our blessing."

"But he has to change the name," Aoidi said. "This is not the Musaeum. There is only the One, and it burned long ago."

Melete shared a look with her sisters. "Those are our conditions."

"They offer balance between what we were and what your world has become."

"Agree, and you can continue to gather what you love. Refuse, and you will be nothing."

The Muses didn't wait for me to answer, knowing what I would say, understanding that I couldn't resist. They grasped each other's hands.

"Farewell, Ptolemy, Serapeum. Heed us."

"Remember what we have told you."

"And do not think to cross us. Either of you."

A wind swept through the building, raising dust and grit until I had to shield my eyes. It lasted several seconds and then died away, as sudden as it had come, leaving us in the dark. Alone.

Sera knelt in front of me, a shadow among shadows. But she found my hand with hers. Her fingers were warm. Mine must have been cold as snow.

"You all right?"

I nodded, only to realize she couldn't see me. "I suppose so."

I stood, groped over my desk for a candle and a match. Finding them, I struck a flame to the wick and raised the candle to see.

The shelves were empty. All of them. There wasn't a shred of paper left in the place. Everything was gone. And I remembered none of it. Not a word.

"Damn," I whispered.

Sera stood. "Could have been worse."

There was no arguing the point. We were alive. My eyes stung, and I could barely swallow past the fist in my throat.

"We start again tomorrow," Sera said. When I didn't answer, she leaned forward, forcing me to meet her gaze. "Tole? We start again tomorrow. You hear?"

"Right," I managed to say. "Tomorrow."

"Dennis will be back. You know he will. And there'll be others, too. There always are."

Yes, it was true. I took a breath. Another. We'd be all right. There would be grandpas again, and journal writers.

"We'll need a new name," she said.

I wanted to argue. I wanted to shout to the hills that the Musaeum was mine and would be forever. I could call it whatever I damn well pleased. But I knew better.

Do not think to cross us . . .

I shook my head. "I can't think of one now."

"That's all right. We don't have to decide tonight."

"Tomorrow?"

She smiled. "Yes. We'll come up with a name. We'll find more poems, more songs and paintings. Who knows what the Fates might bring us. You'll see."

I scanned the shelves again. Wood and dust and not a thing more. But Sera was right. The world wasn't about to run out of stories.

BOOTS OF CLAY

A STORY OF THE DEVIL'S WEST

Laura Anne Gilman

IN HIS DREAMING, THEY STILL LIVED IN THE VILLAGE HE HAD BEEN BORN in, family to every side, and when he woke each morning, it was with the cold knowledge that all of that was gone.

Gershon swung his knees over the side of his bed, feeling cool wood under his feet, the scratch of rough wool blanket under his palms. One of the other beds in the cabin was empty, the other two still holding blanket-covered lumps. "I thank you, living and eternal one, who has returned my soul into me with compassion. Blessed art thou, who led us from fear and into this day, this Territory."

He thrust his feet into boots now, rather than the shoes he had grown up with, and they made a solid, still-unfamiliar noise on the doorframe. He reached up to touch the mezuzah as he passed, the battered tin casing a familiar reassurance.

This much, they had been allowed to bring with them.

Outside, the sun had risen over the treetops, filling the sky with light. He had gone to bed late, the stars thick-spread overhead and the howls of beasts in the distance all a reminder of Adonai's glory, but the expanse of blue sky overhead always surprised him, reminding him of the vastness of this land.

This strange, still-strange land.

The right to settle here had cost them seven chickens—bright-eyed, brown-and-cream feathered—and two cows born on the way from Pennsylvania, plus a bull calf come next spring in payment to the native tribe who lived there first, but the water of the creek was sweet, and the lands gentle and free from rocks. Even the forest seemed kind, although the last settlement, an hour's walk south, had warned them to use caution if they entered the woods.

"Their gods live there," Isaac had repeated, when the village was only an encampment of wagons turned inward, the men sleeping outside, starting awake at every unfamiliar sound. "And bears."

"I fear neither bears nor heathen gods," Yakob had returned, and the two had fallen into discourse on the nature of gods that might live in a forest, and if a correlation might be drawn between the tribes of this land and the tribes of ancient Judah, and if so, might they also be brought to understand Yahweh.

Gershon had left them to it; he had no Talmudic bent, no desire for an afternoon spent negotiating arguments that had little application to the moment, and he knew, of experience, that they would argue the matter until they had long ago forgotten the original question. They still, he assumed, had come to no conclusion.

But in the meanwhile, the wagons were dismantled, homes built, and a village had grown.

The community of Shaaré Tikvah was now seven months old. Through the grace of God and careful planning, they had lost only one calf and Yosef Elder's three fingers to the cold, and now the wooden slats of the wagons made a pasture fence, and the blankets rested on beds under rude but water-tight roofs, made with the aid of Strong Knee's people.

He still had trouble thinking of this as home, but others had adjusted more easily.

"Good day, Gershon!" Miriam called, and he lifted a hand to acknowledge his cousin, her two young ones clinging to her skirts, but kept walking. His thoughts were too unsettled for prayer.

They had paid—everything they had—to come to this land, chasing a dream. They had been warned that this was a harsh land, but how could it be harsher than what they had left? At least here, they were promised, there was no Church, no auto-da-fé for those who refused to renounce their faith. The Territory worked on a simple principle, they had been told: give no offense. And if the wild folk of the Territory were heathens who worshipped idols and animals, if the creature who kept the peace here was called the devil by those who knew no better? The unknown was better than remaining like sheep to be slaughtered by the known.

Strong Knee had sent his people the morning after they arrived, unable to go farther, unwilling to leave this respite of open valley and fresh water. His warriors had eyed them carefully, circling around the small, clustered camp, and then disappeared, returning mid-day with venison and maize, skin blankets, and carved wooden toys for the children.

"You run from pain," Strong Knee had said. "You need run no farther."

They owed more than chickens and cows to their new neighbors. But how could one repay what was not a debt?

The first warning had come two weeks before. Two of Strong Knee's warriors had gone missing, their ponies returning, lathered and wild-eyed. Yosef Younger, Ham, and Abner had gone with the party to search for them, but returned empty handed, without explanation.

Men died. This was fact. But to disappear in such a way?

"It may be that another tribe took them." Horsehair Boy had been one of the warriors to look them over that first morning, and become a regular visitor to Shaaré Tikvah, often sitting quietly while they prayed on the Sabbath, willingly fetching water or making fire as needed. The elders thought he might be willing to learn, but Gershon thought he merely found them curious, the way he might watch a new bird in the trees to better understand its song.

The natives spoke of their own gods, of the winds that carried medicine, the myths they spoke of as though of relatives only recently deceased. They had no interest in the prayers or beliefs of their neighbors. And yet, there was a familiarity to their faith that made the folk of Shaaré Tikvah ease their shoulders a little, speak less softly, sleep more deeply in the night.

Then one of the native camp's fields was ravaged, something churning dirt, trampling the soft green sprouts, and the young woman who had been on guard against night-grazers left with a headache and a lump on the back of her head.

Shaaré Tikvah's fields, smaller, closer to their homes, were left untouched, but within their walls there was murmuring, worries.

They knew, firsthand, that this was how it began.

Two days later, an empty storage hut was torched, the thatch burning bright into the dawn.

In the days after, the children of Shaaré Tikvah were kept closer to the houses, sheltered by the young women who carried hazel staffs, thick as a thumb, in unaccustomed but determined hands. An older boy, just past his mitzvot, perched on a roof with a ram's horn to hand from sun rise to set. At night, they barred doors and waited, sleep restless, riddled with memories.

And the men argued late into those nights, thoughtful, but heated.

"We have the right to call for aid. When we came here, we were promised that."

"From the devil?" Anton scoffed, frowning his disapproval.

"They call him that from ignorance," Yosef Elder said. "He is the power in this land, and we have given no offense, to be at risk."

"We are not at risk. Our neighbors are. It is their problem, not ours."

"If they are at risk, do you think we will not be, soon? They have no claim on the Master of the Territory, and we are far from others, far from this devil. He cannot protect us from enemies at our front gate."

Not in time, they meant. Not before their homes could burn, their belongings splintered and destroyed again. Everything they had built, gone.

"And how do you say we protect ourselves, then? Prayer? Or have you some secret training with guns or knives, to be our *militares*?"

They had been forbidden weapons back home; forbidden any means to defend themselves. The handful of muskets they carried along the journey were used for hunting deer now, and they had only a few bullets left. The women carried staffs, and the younger men had begun learning the bow and arrow, but they were not competent hunters, yet.

"We must distance ourselves from the village. Show that we are no danger, no risk to whoever threaten them."

"Abandon those who aided us?"

"This is their problem, not ours."

And thus it went, for nearly a week, until erev shabbat came, and the rebbe placed one weathered hand on the table between them. "We have eaten at their tables, slept under their roofs. They are our neighbors." Once the rebbe spoke, discussion continued, but the matter had been decided. Shaaré Tikvah would stand with Strong Knee's people. But how? They were farmers and scholars, not warriors.

Gershon had leaned back in his chair and watched the candles flicker.

Miriam and her younglings and the noise of the settlement now behind him, there was peace. Birds chirped and trilled overhead, the grasses sighed at his feet, the sky arched over him with the blue promise of Yahweh's lovingkindness. He could see Strong Knee's village in the distance, half a day's walk beyond, across the creek that served both.

That peace was an illusion.

Two nights after the rebbe's words, something destroyed the men's sweating lodge at the edge of Strong Knee's village, knocking an entire wall and half the roof down, as though a great wind had swept through, although none inside were harmed. Ham, who had a keen eye, had gone to look and found sign of metal hooks attached to the shattered remains.

Not a beast, then, nor an angry spirit or bitter wind, but men.

And from the works of men, there could be protection.

Gershon had gone to sleep that night and woken with the madness of a plan.

Now, he touched his fingertips to his tālēt, feeling the fringe move gently. A prayer rose to his throat, but he stifled it, holding back the words. The creek rushed at his feet, the banks smooth with mud. It might not be enough; it would have to be enough. Shedding his jacket and his narrow-brimmed hat and placing them on the grass behind him, he rolled up the sleeves of his shirt, picked up the rough-carved wooden shovel he'd carried from the village, and began to work.

It took him the rest of the day to gather the clay, mounding it in the sun to dry so he could clean it of impurities, then slaking it down again with river water. Living water, fresh and running; for this, rainwater gathered in buckets would not do.

The sons of Deer Walking appeared, as though drawn to see what the white man was doing, bringing him dried grasses and dung, watching with curiosity as he blended them into the clay, nose wrinkled at the sun-warmed smell. He had been raised with books and inks, not beasts, and while it was not unpleasant, it plagued the senses.

"You are making...a doll?" The older boy soon became bored and wandered off, but the smaller son, a bright-eyed child of seven, moved closer, fascinated by the figure taking shape under Gershon's hands. "A ceremony doll?"

"Of a sort." He had visited as well, his scholar's mind always eager to learn, and had some sense of the ceremonies their people observed, with dancing and cries and brightly colored cloths; it had reminded him of Purim.

"You are a…." The boy struggled to find a word in English. "A mystery-man?"

Gershon did not recognize the term, but the tone the boy used suggested meaning. "I am no hakham," he responded. "Not like our rebbe. I am merely a shaliah."

"Shal-leelah?"

"A go-between," he said, his fingers deep in the sticky clay, thumbs forming eyeholes and a mouth, bringing the excess clay back to form rudimentary ears. "One with authority to ask for things. To arrange things."

He had not asked for the role, but the weight of it had eased him, in the early days of their leaving. He could bargain, negotiate, ease the way. It was not the same, but it was something.

The boy scrunched his face, then nodded once, with confidence beyond his years. "A medicine worker. What do you do now?"

"It needs to dry in the sun."

"The sun is almost gone."

"And so it will wait until tomorrow. And you should be getting home for your chores, or else get no dinner."

The boy grinned at him and took off, curiosity faded in the light of more immediate concerns.

Alone, Gershon considered his creation. Tall as himself, which was to say not tall at all, but broader in the shoulder, with heavy hips and arms that hung graceless at his sides, the face a smear of features, the cheekbones high and wide, the ears lopsided, the mouth a shadowed, lipless hole.

Gershon returned to the riverbank the next afternoon, heart in his mouth that something might have happened to the figure, that it might have cracked in the sun, or someone damaged it, beast or man. Instead, he found Deer Walking's youngest son sitting cross-legged next to it, as though playing sticks with a friend.

The boy looked up when Gershon approached, the morning sun finding red in the blackness of his hair, his eyes bright with anticipation.

"May I watch?"

He was a child. A child should not be exposed to such things.

And yet, he was interested and eager to learn. Gershon could not bring himself to refuse such a student.

"Move back and remain silent."

The clay was warm and rough-dried to the touch, giving only slightly when he pressed a thumb into it.

Prying the half-dried mouth open slightly wider, Gershon reached into his pocket, and took out a tightly-rolled scrap of paper, carefully torn from one of the rebbe's books, fresh letters inked in the blank space.

This was no thing he should do, a reach he should not dare. And yet, the rebbe had tasked him with this; as shaliah, he could bind others to terms, could make agreements for his people.

His hand shook as he placed the tiny scroll into the figure's mouth and pressed the hole closed.

"My name is Gershon ben Adão, of Shaaré Tikvah of the Territory. I have been tasked with ensuring the protection of our synagogue from those who would harm it, and those who have given us friendship and shelter. Adon Olam, if you find these goals to be worthy, grant life to this, most humble figure of mud and dung. Ain Soph, who caused Creation in your wisdom, grant spirit to this flesh, that it may protect your children, all born of Adam, though they know it not."

"You give it life?"

"Not I. I merely ask."

The boy nodded, more serious than a grandfather. "The winds will bring it life, and it will protect us?"

Horsehair Boy spoke of the winds thus as well, in tones of respect and caution. Gershon shrugged, stepping back from the figure, his fingertips touching the fringe of his tālēt, words of prayer gathering behind his lips.

The golem's eyes remained empty, its mouth pressed shut, its limbs clay without breath.

"Your will be done," Gershon said, and placed his hand on the boy's shoulder. "Walk me back to your village?" Because children had not been attacked did not mean they would not, but it would injure the boy's pride to suggest he needed a white man's escort home.

On the riverbank, the wind shifted in the grass, and two fish splashed against each other in the creek. And when Gershon returned that evening to return the clay to the river, the figure was gone.

That night, he ate his meal with the rebbe's family. The old man was pensive, a single lamp on the table between them, the remains of dinner cleared away, his wife the rebbetizin shushing their daughter as they moved about in the kitchen.

"Why now? What here?"

The rebbe turned his hands palm up, a familiar gesture of acceptance, resignation. "Who are we to question Yahweh?"

"Who are we *not* to question Yahweh?"

That made the rebbe smile. "And did he not answer?"

No, Gershon thought, looking down into his tea. *Not the question I am asking.*

A runner came a day later, in the hour before dawn. He waited, panting slightly, while the men finished morning prayers. Unlike others, the runner did not exhibit impatience, but waited until ritual was satisfied and the rebbe came to speak with him.

"Sweeps Water would show you a thing, if you would come to see it."

Even in a hurry, Gershon thought, *they were polite.* It was oddly unnerving to those used to being ordered about, forcing them to question the intent behind every request, sifting through words offered sideways to see where the sword waited. Offer no offense, they had been told, as though their very existence had not been considered offense enough, nearly two thousand years now.

"We will come," the rebbe said.

By "we," the rebbe had meant Gershon, who was younger and stronger and could walk more swiftly, and three of his choosing. Even so, the sun was well-risen by the time they came to where Strong Knee and the medicine man, Sweeps Water, stood in the debris, his ink-marked eyes narrowed, knees half-bent as though caught between a crouch and rising. Behind them, a young man Gershon did not recognize waited, his eyes more lightly marked, hair clubbed back to show a scar along his neck, livid and raw. An arrow, stung across flesh and half-healed. One of those restless young men, proving their worth by raiding other towns.

But this had been no raid.

They stood on the bank above the creek, the village too-quiet behind them, as though those within all held their breath. Even the dogs, rawboned and yellow-coated, lay still outside the doorways, waiting for humans to set things right.

"We heard them come, past moonset." Sweeps Water did not rise, but he was clearly addressing the newcomers. Abner and Ham shifted uncomfortably behind him, and Old Yosef coughed politely, waiting for the native to face them. Gershon did not bother.

"And they did this?"

"No. But you knew that already."

Sweeps Water did rise and turn, then. His skin was smooth, save for a cut through one eyebrow, but his hair grayed in thick streaks where it was tucked behind his ears, and the bare arm that gestured around them was corded with lean muscle and scar tissue. Gershon let his gaze follow the gesture, and wished he hadn't. What they had taken for debris was bone, flesh intact save where it had been severed, more like a deer's haunch than a human limb.

Once seen, it could not be unseen: too many parts to be even three or five men. Seven at least, perhaps more.

Ham gagged, bile rising and splattering on the ground as though he'd never seen dead flesh before. Abner muttered at him, shoving a kerchief at his mouth, then looked to Old Yosef, whose expression had not changed.

Old Yosef had served in the army when he was young; he had seen men die before.

"We heard them come, and we readied our arrows and our staffs. If this was to be a raid, we would meet it as warriors. But they did not enter the village. And then the screaming began." Sweeps Water looked at him then, and rather than the fear or rage he had expected, Gershon saw only exhaustion and sorrow.

Something acrid burned in Gershon's stomach. "Your village was not harmed?"

"None within came to harm," Strong Knee agreed, but his voice did not say this was a good thing.

"There is blood in the bones now," the young man said, and Sweeps Water shot him a glance that clearly told him he spoke out of turn. The young man did not care. "Spirits linger where the bones are blooded. And we do not know their families, to bind and release them."

"A thing destroyed them," Sweeps Water said to the men of Shaaré Tikvah. "You know of this thing."

Gershon forced himself to look at the remains of what had been men, once. "I do not know for certain." He had seen nothing, could say nothing for certain. The figure had been gone, but that did not mean it had walked on its own. "I asked our god for aid, to protect us. And our neighbors."

They had asked before. Endlessly, before, and the only answer had been in broken bones and burnt homes, in suspicion in the eyes of neighbors.

A muscle jerked in Sweeps Water's jaw, and something in his eyes changed. Gershon did not look away. "If in doing so, we have given offense in some way…"

The air stilled between them. He could offer no more chickens, no more calves, reminded once again how precarious their lives were, even here. Forever at the mercy of those who had no reason to choose mercy. Strong Knee had allowed them to build here, but Gershon had done more.

Would this home, too, be taken from them?

"The thing of clay you shaped. The creature of the bones and dirt."

Gershon swallowed, feeling the men behind him still once again, for different reasons this time. "Yes."

Sweeps Water studied him. "You worked medicine for us."

He had not; he had only petitioned Yahweh. But Gershon merely nodded. What did the details matter? They had meant to help, had meant to share what little they had with those who had given them everything. He had not thought it would be unwelcome.

"This one was correct: the bones are blooded, and we do not know their names."

Gershon heard what was said: They could not honor those who had come against them. This land was beautiful, but it was strange, the people it made were strange, and his fingers touched the fringe under his vest, his lips moving in silent prayer that he might be given better understanding.

"This is gratitude?" Ham burst out, and Gershon turned to snap at him to be silent, but old Yosef's elbow landed in Ham's ribs first.

"Be silent, fool," Old Yosef told him in the language they no longer used in this place, the syllables odd under the weight of open sky and heavy pine, and as though summoned by it, Gershon felt the regard of something silent, measuring and thoughtful.

"It watches us," Sweeps Water said, and both Strong Knee and the young man at his side tensed: they had not felt it, either. Gershon did not look at the men behind him, afraid to break Sweeps Water's gaze, afraid to see what watched them from the shadow of the pines, hands wet with the blood of men.

"It is a guardian," Gershon said, searching for a word that would explain and finding none. "It will not harm you."

The other man's eyes narrowed, the dark markings around them only emphasizing his expression of—not doubt, but consideration. "So long as we do not harm you."

To live unharmed, unmolested, unthreatened. All they had looked for, coming to this new land. So many times before, they had called for help and been unanswered. Here, in this place, Yahweh had answered. Gershon felt the weight of what watched on his skin, and his fingers fell away from his fringe. "I think… it did not see a difference between us."

But there was. A vast gap, that all the good will in the world could not bridge.

Sweeps Water closed his eyes, his stern expression not slackening, but softening, slightly. As though he also felt what Gershon felt, both the weight and the gap.

In Strong Knee's face there was no suspicion, no anger; only sadness, and waiting.

"These grounds will need be cleansed." There was a command in those words, and a request, and Gershon bowed his head before them both, the acrid taste in his mouth softened by the faint mint of hope.

Two days later, Gershon returned to the creek bed. His shoulders and elbows ached, and his skin was bruised from kneeling, his tālēt fringe smudged with ash and soot from the offerings they had burned. It had been a small satisfaction when he saw how certain things rested comfortably against each other as they burned, rather than knocking each other aside.

Perhaps he was wishful; perhaps it was a sign. He was no mystic, to tell such things. But he clung to it, nonetheless.

Ashes into the ground and ashes into the wind. He would not compare it to the burnt offerings made at the Temple, in better days of better men, and yet he could not help but remember how the wind had swirled, dust sparkling in the morning light. Strong Knee's people were satisfied, Sweeps Water's eyes less shadowed.

But there was one thing left yet to be done. A thing only he could do.

"Bo elaiki anokhi yatzartikha. Come to the one who shaped you."

He waited, and it came to him, shoulders rounded by weight, hands restless, but face implacably still, eyes dull and feet a dry shuffle. It came to him, misshapen by man's hands but glorious within. "Thank you," Gershon said, then reached into its hollow pit of a mouth, and with two fingers removed the scrap of paper from within.

The youngest son of Deer Walking found him there, hours later. The boy dropped to a crouch, small hands touching the lumps of clay where they had dried and cracked on the riverbank, as though something sloughed them off on its way back into the water.

"They argue, over the fire," the boy said. "Over what you did."

"I know." Gershon had not gone to the village; none of Shaaré Tikvah had, waiting once more to be welcomed, before they would presume.

"Sweeps Water spoke with the winds. For three nights. He has never spent that long with the winds before, and when he came out, his eyes were like an eagle's."

Gershon had no idea what that meant.

"It's gone now, isn't it? The thing you called."

The clay seemed to mock him, inert in a child's hands. "Yes."

"Many are angry. But Sweeps Water said that," and he was clearly repeating words he had overheard, "only fools refuse a hand that lifts them from the ground, or shields them from a blow. And that this guardian… we might have need of it, again."

Gershon cast his eyes down, a prayer of relief releasing from his heart. "Then we will ask, again."

The boy considered that, thoughtful. "And if the answer is not yes?"

Gershon could only shrug, helpless before the Power that shaped them as the clay was helpless before him. "As Adonai and the winds will it," he said.

TRICKSTER'S CHOICE

Jo Gerrard

"LADIES AND GENTLEMEN, BOYS AND GIRLS, COME AND FEAST YOUR EYES on the doubly unbelievable! Not just a beast in human form, but a li-ving, brea-thing, *double* myth. Just two bits and you can step inside to see this horr-i-fy-ing crea-ture with your very own eyes!"

They shuffle in, wide-eyed rubes clutching each other or the toys they've won at the games, those lucky enough to be so favored by fate or an easy carnie. I can see them through the sheers, carrying dust along with their curiosity. Rhianne hustles them in; she'll hustle them out. I sit on the converted workbench, nearly as naked as the day I was born, a fine piece of sheer over my crossed legs, and wait for Rhianne to finish the familiar spiel, for the drapery serving as curtains to fall. And then sit there for several heartbeats longer. Got to give them what they paid for, after all, a look at my tits before my little trick.

The change is simple at first. My ears elongate toward the top of my head. Antlers break through my skin with a fine mist of blood as the crowd gasps, and my jaw begins to shrink toward my neck and narrow. The distance between my eyes widens; dun and white fur sprouts all over my body.

I grab the sheer when the pain rises from zero to "the gods aren't listening" and flip it up to cover me from antler-tips to mid-thigh. I never quite black out, but I never remember the change.

At last I shake off the sheer, still sitting on top of the workbench, my long ears on either side of a four-point rack, of which I'm rather proud. Scattered chuckles or outright thunderstorms of laughter follow. On rare occasions someone faints, though I blame the heat trapped in the tent from the sun and the dozens of bodies passing through rather than overexcitement or fear. I'm not exactly threatening. I use my powerful hind legs to hop from one end of the table to the other before jumping off and darting through the gap in the rear curtain.

No one ever complains they didn't get their money's worth. I'm the double unbelievable all right: were-jackalope. And I play this show three times a night, except during full moons, wherever we're stopped.

What can I say? It's a living.

Rhianne counted the night's take, her deft hands half a shade darker than the copper coins she moved in arcane patterns. I burnished my nails, watching her. Pedro's sharp knock on our wagon door announced him like a desert squall. Which was good, because he never waited for an invitation to enter; I half-figured he hoped to catch us canoodling one of these days.

"A good night, then?" I asked, watching the reflection of his florid face in the piece of silver-lined glass serving as my mirror, worried his scowl might shatter the glass. Silver-inflicted wounds take forever to heal.

He grunted. "Not so good," he said, with a glare for Rhianne, who kept counting, undisturbed by the interruption. "The police just left the box office. There are complaints against you."

He leaned against Rhianne's table. She subtly moved our funds away from his hands; he already had his share of our take, but no sense taking chances. She wouldn't have worried about any of the other freaks.

"Their preacher swears we've a Wilding among us. Namely, you."

He watched my reaction, hard eyes narrowed. I rolled my eyes, shifted away from him in my chair.

"That's ridiculous and you know it," I said, fully aware he knew no such thing. "But we don't want to bring you no trouble. We can scout ahead while the rest of you stay."

I heard Rhianne's soft sigh. Pedro shook his head. I closed my eyes and counted while he spoke.

"We hain't enough food or water to move on, and we've got three wagons down thanks to that last river crossing." Two axles to be repaired and a cracked wheel. Rhianne was an occasional strong woman and all-time wainwright. "So either you show them how 'the trick' is done or they take our goods and only run us out of town if we're lucky. Or we give you over to be strung up and hope they don't burn down the show to be sure they've got 'the wickedness' out." He leaned over my shoulder, leered at my reflection. "I suggest you show them 'the trick.'"

He left, slamming the wagon door behind him before I had a chance to answer. I scrubbed my hands over my face like I could wash away the sick flash of panic his words carried. Fear, like fleas on a dog.

"We've been in Bluestown before, haven't we?" Pedro was a lecher, but the life I had now was miles and away better than anything I'd known since...well, since ever, really.

"Places change," Rhianne said, pushing a stack of bits my way and leaning back to light a cigarillo. "What are we going to do?"

"I don't know." Some places, the preacher wasn't so honest and could be bought off with coin or flesh. I'd heard talk around the chuck wagon, though, and this town had a woman with hellfire and brimstone right up to her eyeballs and the determination to drive out sin. Pedro had got us a pass from her because we were a mid-winter show and the people were gasping for entertainment like a fish on land gasps for water. I couldn't slip away in the night and leave Rhianne alone with Pedro, neither. Couldn't leave Rhianne, period.

But revealing myself as a Wilding, even here in the western desert I'd always called home, was beyond foolish. Nobody'd forgot the way the forty-niners woke the mountains, sent magic tearing through the world, ripping everything open like the end of days. We Wildings had been here before and since, but there was no telling history to people who'd decided *different* was *dangerous*. And dangerous had to be cut, hanged, or burned out, full stop.

Rhianne's work-callused hand covered mine, warm copper over cool sunstone. I looked up at her, though I felt like my throat was stoppered up good and solid with a cork.

"We'll work something out."

I nodded, sure she could see the turmoil in my eyes. Feeling the cork sink deeper because I could see love and confidence in hers. A thought occurred to me, a tale of star-crossed lovers and an oddly detailed ritual whispered among my mother's people after the children were abed. A might-be, a could-be, a devastating possibility.

A way out. A way to stay with Rhianne, to stay in Pedro's good graces, to stay *alive*. But mostly not to lose Rhianne, the one truly good thing I'd ever found in almost thirty years of living.

She cocked her head, studied me. "You've thought of something?"

"Maybe. I need some herbs from Cook, though. Some of those nails you bought at the last stop." I hesitated. "Sharpened silver. A snare rigged to catch, not kill. And your drum. I'll need to dance."

Wheedling the necessary herbs from Luis, the cook, wasn't too difficult. He came from bayou country, and I'd figured correctly that he'd spent most of his take on spices from home. The nails weren't too tough, either; Rhianne had stored them with the rest of her kit in the heavy trunk in our wagon. She was good with snares, too, I knew that much, good with her hands in trapping as she was in so many other things.

The problem was the silver. I didn't need much, just a coin would do, as long as it was sharp enough to break skin. Rhianne recalled the way a train's rolling wheel could crush a penny, which gave me the idea of a brick and one of Giselle the stunt rider's still-shod horses. We lost three silver to the effort, but the fourth nicked Rhianne's thumb when she went to pick it up.

None of us were much pleased at the ruination of silver coins, but needs must when the devil drives.

We thanked Giselle and went back to our quarters to wait for full moonset, which wasn't going to happen for another three or four hours. We filled the time with each other, and then Rhianne napped.

I couldn't sleep, but I kept her company on our narrow bed anyway.

Just like I knew when the full moon was about to rise, I knew when the thumbnail-waning moon had set; I nudged Rhianne. She sat up.

"We need whiskey."

I grimaced. "You know I won't touch the stuff." Old stories about the best way to catch the jackalope side of me. Nonsense tales at best, though alcohol calls who it catches.

"Okay, then *I* need whiskey." Rhianne hardly drank, and I couldn't begrudge her. So I pulled myself out of bed and let her fetch her drink while I carefully wrapped my supplies in the bit of sheer from the act. Rhianne was going to have to support us both for a little while, until I felt up to joining the dance again.

If this worked. If I didn't kill myself trying.

We walked out into the desert a ways, through scrub and across stone. Our hands bent toward each other, not actually touching, not even out here where only the stars and the sagebrush and any passing animals could see us.

When I was satisfied we were far enough away, but not so far I couldn't see the dark bulk of the Big Top blocking the stars on the horizon, I spread out the sheer and its contents while Rhianne set three snares before unwrapping her drum and smoothing her hand over its skin the way I always imagined she'd caress a fussy infant. She started to tap the thin horsehide with her thumb and pinkie, her broad palm initially muffling the sound.

Like a heartbeat rising up in the dark womb of the desert.

I let my hips sway, my feet take measured steps on the sheer, and wound two of the nails into my hair so they stood up right where my antlers would have been. The iron scratched at my scalp but didn't quite pierce the skin, even as my movements shifted broader and my feet led me in a circle.

The silver coin with its fierce edge rested inside a bowl with Luis' spices and some flash paper I'd tried using in the act once, until I'd decided singed whiskers weren't a good look.

Fire and fatal silver would be at the heart of my salvation. Or undoing.

Rhianne's fingers picked up a quicker rhythm. My feet carried me along the edge of the sheer, faster now over the coarse fabric and the uneven ground, the scent of crushed sage rising each time I set a foot down. The stars were a thousand scattered mirrors above, reflecting my own light back at me.

I whipped around like old Haku, Pedro's dervish, a prayer to the Mothers and any other god who might hear me in my heart and radiating off my skin like sweat, my feet moving in evermore intricate steps and the only clear word in my head a *please.*

Please.

The head of one of the nails bound in my lashing hair caught me just below my eye, drawing a crescent of blood. I pulled out the match, struck it across the tip of my thumbnail and tossed it into the bowl.

Everything stopped.

Rhianne's drumming, the scent of the sage, the stars suddenly frozen without a twinkle in the deep distant sky. Even the plume of smoke from the paper, normally as there-and-gone-again as the nitrocellulose itself, lingered heavy and gray just inside the rim of the bowl.

I dropped to my knees, panting; a trickle of something heavy, watered down by sweat, fell from my cheek to stain the sheer.

There shouldn't have been enough light for me to see the two coyotes, a mated pair, push their way through the nearby scrub. Two screech-owls, almost as tall, landed on the earth nearby, their wings ruffling silently to their sides. Two dust-colored jackrabbits hopped up and settled catty-corner to the coyotes, their long, notched ears twisting in the stillness. Two puma slunk out of the darkness and settled, their fangs bared and dark with blood.

They watched me. I watched them.

A sudden urge to laugh welled up; laugh or cry or scream, I didn't know which. Dual-spirits, like me, they belonged to each other and within themselves. If I did what I intended, for the first time in my life, I would be almost singular.

Singular sounded like freedom, like an eternity of captivity. Sage and cold cream and silk and dust and the sky closing in around me until the stars were a thousand thousand bright points of pain. But Rhianne, always Rhianne, and the low hum of her voice and the soft strength of her body and the deep throb of drum and lust and blood.

I reached out to the bowl, feeling the smoke warm and viscous and smooth before touching the grit of the ash beneath. I curled my fingers, bringing them to my mouth. Paused. Opened eyes I hadn't consciously closed.

My eight witnesses sat still in a half-circle just outside the boundary of the sheer.

I touched the ashes not to my lips, but to the cut still bleeding beneath my eye. Rubbed them in, trying not to grimace at the pain. Reached back into the bowl. Fished up the silver coin. Held its distorted shape up against the ineffable blackness of the sky between the stars.

"Oh."

I barely breathed the exclamation, yet sound returned: the thumping of my heart in the rhythm of Rhianne's drum, the desert wind soughing through the brush. The small sounds of my companions. The pop and sizzle of the short-burning paper, extended to a solar wind, cacophonous and angry.

In that moment, I could have released the coin and created a new moon. Devastated the earth with new magnetism and tides and to hell with everything. I could have destroyed everything I'd ever known or ever might know. The strange lingering remnants of the pre-cataclysm West. The carnival. The coyotes and the owls and the jackrabbits and the puma.

Rhianne.

I let go the illusion, the power, dropped the coin back onto my palm, nothing but silver remaining. The carefully created sharp edge dimpled my fingers but didn't cut through my skin. I tightened my grip. Dipped my hand back in the bowl, into the faintly swirling dark smoke, into the black heart of ash beneath. Brought my coated fingers to my mouth this time. Touched my tongue to the ash and the silken warmth of the smoke.

I chose.

The world started again when I retched. The witnesses, spooked, turned tail and ran. I retched again, dropping my hands to the ground and cutting my palm on the would-be moon. And again, some grotesque parody of birth knotted in the center of my chest, something sharp like antlers caught in my throat. Again, and Rhianne held my shoulders while I tried to draw in another breath around whatever was crushing my windpipe; she grabbed and *pulled* as my diaphragm contracted *again* and the silken bundle slid out onto the ruined sheer, trailing something behind it that I never wanted to feel or taste again.

We wouldn't need the snare. I couldn't breathe until I used the silver as a makeshift knife to slice away the birthing caul and the tiny head broke loose, nostrils flaring even as I wiped them clean. We sucked in one heavy wet breath together, and I passed out.

I came to with Rhianne leaning over me, the palest slice of pink and gold lighting her face, and my Wilding tucked in the crook of her arm like a baby. The pale ochre of its horns stood out around the warm copper of her bicep. My Wilding's nose twitched as she watched us with those wide, knowing rabbit eyes.

Rhianne sat back on her heels, then pulled me up to a sitting position. I gripped her ribs, laid my head on her bosom, and sobbed like a baby.

When I quieted, stroking the clean, soft fur of my Wilding's stomach, she spoke.

"If they see you in two places at once, that should set their fears to rest."

I nodded, and sighed.

"I hope it's enough," I rasped, "and we can get away with 'a magician never reveals her tricks'."

I spat blood, let Rhianne draw us both to our feet. Held my hands out for the jackalope; Rhianne passed her over without comment. We gathered everything up from the desert floor and headed back; across the scrub we could hear Pedro's shouting over the soft murmur of our home coming back to life.

WOLVES HOWLING IN THE NIGHT

Faith Hunter

1879

*Author's Note: This is a story from the world of Jane Yellowrock.
This short story takes place in 1879 in Arizona.
Ayatas and Etsi are around forty years old.*

AYATAS TOUCHED HIS HORSE'S FLANK WITH A HEEL AND GUIDED HIM CLOSER
to the mount ridden by Etsi, his Everhart woman. They had been on the trail
for days in the summer heat, with limited water, only enough for them and
their mounts to drink sparingly. They had run out of even that twelve miles
on the south side of Eagle Tail Mount and Dry Wash, which lived up to its
name. The summer sun had baked the land dry. If they did not reach the town
of Agua Caliente by nightfall, their plight would become desperate, yet Etsi
still laughed, saying she smelled ripe, her scent as strong on the air as his own.

The town they hoped to reach had abundant water, enough to have a bakery,
saloons, a laundry, a livery, a feed and seed shop, a half dozen seamstresses, a school
run by a woman from back east, and two dry goods stores. The newsletter they had
read when they shared a campfire with a wagon train said that an inn was being
built in Agua Caliente, "*with a bathhouse,*" as Etsi kept reminding him, a bathhouse
with hot water that rose from the ground, from hot springs. Etsi would get a hot
tub-bath with soap, as her own people, the *yunega,* the white men, bathed.

He would wash out back with the other people of color—the Mexicans,
Africans, and Indians. Though Ayatas might prefer to bathe in the Gila River,
near the town, if *Indian* meant Apache or Pah-Ute. The *Tsalagi* and western
tribes did not make peace together, and fighting would anger Etsi. His redheaded woman's temper was hot like fire, and he had ached the few times she
had turned her anger toward him.

Tonight, Etsi would sleep in a real bed, and Ayatas would bed down with
the horses or out in the night, under the stars, knowing that if she called him
with her magic, he would hear the sound of her summons on the wind.

Beneath him, the horse stepped higher and his head came up, moving better than the tired beast had all day. "I smell smoke," Ayatas said. "And water."

"Hallelujah and praise the Lord," Etsi said, her voice hoarse. She tied the small pouch of *dalonige'i* into her skirt to hide it. White men traded for gold, gave news for gold, stole land for gold, killed for gold. She was wise to keep it out of sight.

Together, as the sun slid into the scarlet west, they studied the town from a small rise. Aqua Caliente was mostly low adobe houses and buildings, a few stone-built ones, and some dried brick buildings, all flat-roofed and mud colored. Wood smoke billowed in low waves down the main street, curling and mixing with the dust clouds. Horses and mules, saddled or loaded with packs, stood tied to hitching posts here and there. A scrawny, short-legged dog trotted down the street, her teats dragging on the dirt. A wagon rolled out of town. A Mexican woman with a white head scarf and dark skirts carried a heavy bundle into an alley and disappeared. The sound of a piano plinking and men singing echoed down the street.

They let the horses have their heads, and the tired animals moved down toward the town. The noise got louder. Dogs barked. Chickens ran across the main road and under a bakery. There was much shouting from laborers, still working in the town, using the last light in the cool of evening. He spotted stonemasons, bricklayers, adobe plasterers, and tile layers constructing the inn that would make the town great and bring in more white people. And drive out more tribal people and people of color. The walls were rising, arches appearing where windows and doors would go. Heavy beams were in place to hold the roof. The wind spun and changed direction, bringing the smell of the town to them.

The horses found a spill of water and a clay-lined pool outside the bathhouse. The puddle stank of soap, white men, and sulfur, but the mounts drank with desperation. "Son of a witch on a switch," Etsi muttered. "I forgot how noisy and stinky towns are." The stench of outhouses, saloons, fires burning, and food cooking was overpowering after so long in the wild.

"White men always stink," he said, keeping his own thirst at bay until he could get Etsi and the horses to safety.

"Yes. Well. Don't forget," Etsi said, her tone telling him more than she knew, speaking of pain and long-held anger. "It's only a game we play to keep you safe."

Ayatas grunted. The game claimed that he was her servant instead of her man. That he worked for gold instead searching for his dreams. But Ayatas would pretend many things to keep Etsi, which meant My Love in the tongue of The People, safe. His red-haired woman, who had gone by many names as they traveled, was possessed of a fiery nature, changeable as the wind, and was constantly searching out danger. She had been born Salandre Everhart, but when she ran away with him, she had changed her name to *Igohidv Adonvdo*, or Forever Heart, in *Tsalagi*. Now, after many years of travel and adventures, his fire woman used a different name in each town, but she was always and forever his Everhart woman, and Etsi.

He pulled the horses away before they could take in enough to grow sick and jumped back into the sheepskin saddle. The mounts knew they would be fed now and trotted on into the town and up to the sheriff's office. The man with the badge waited, his guns in clear view, an old hunting rifle in his arms, and a six-gun at his hip. They reined in the mounts in front of the man, and Etsi slid from the saddle to the ground. She groaned with pain on landing in the dusty street, knees stiff from all day in the heat, on horseback. Ayatas landed behind her, silent.

"Good evening, Sheriff," she said, approaching him and smoothing her skirts. His Everhart woman did not offer her hand, but the sheriff looked pointedly at her left hand, and the thin gold band that could be seen beneath her dirty gloves. "I'm Mrs. Everhart, reporter for the *Arizona Daily Star*, out of Tucson."

"A woman reporter?" The sheriff spat, the sink of tobacco strong on the air. He transferred his sharp gaze to Ayatas. "Women can't work for newspapers. That your young buck? He don't look like Apache or Ute."

"He is Cherokee, from back east," Etsi said with asperity, "and he's my guide. And women most certainly *can* be reporters. Watch your tongue, young man. You may be sheriff, but you are not above manners."

Etsi was no longer a girl, but a woman now, sharp tongued and stern, and she knew how to stop young men from showing disrespect. They had been together since 1860, and she had grown more fiery with each passing year.

The sheriff laughed, the sound like sand scouring rock in a low wind, and when he spoke, it was with a tone of insult and amusement. "*Manners.* Yes, ma'am. I'll mind my *manners.*" Before Etsi could respond he added, "You looking to take the baths and find a bed, Old Missus Smith can help you. Your *guide'll* have to sleep in the stables with the other animals or outside the city. We don't risk our scalps letting Injuns stay inside after sundown."

"You have nothing to *fear* from my guide, Sheriff."

"I ain't afeard a no redskin."

"Hmmm." Her tone suggested that he lied. The sheriff's eyes narrowed. Etsi continued, "I'm sure he'd rather be as far from the white man as he can get. If you'll direct me to the boardinghouse and the baths and point my guide to the livery?"

The man with the tin star on his chest gave directions. Etsi turned to Ayatas and gave him six small coins, saying things she did not need to say, to appease the sheriff and to fulfill their roles. "Aya, take the horses to the livery and purchase their care. See if they will also feed you and let you sleep there. If not, go to the back door of the bakery and buy some dinner, and then bed down outside the gates."

Ayatas took the coins and nodded his head. "Yes, ma'am. Thank you, ma'am." Gathering the reins, he led the mounts down the street, following the scent of manure and hay more so than the lawman's directions. With his predator's senses, he could feel several pairs of eyes on him as he walked, so he kept his shoulders slumped and his head down as befit the station of servant instead of the warrior and skinwalker he was, a beaten man instead of a man of much power and magic. It galled him. But the world was not kind to people of color.

He had spent much of his youth in the Blue Holly Clan house, under the thumb of his *uni lisi*, grandmother of many children, in the Indian Land of the Western Cherokee. He had hated being with the women in the summer or winter houses, but with no father, and with the obstinacy of the grandmother, he had no one to take him in among the older men. Until his uni lisi taught him to shift into an animal when he was fifteen and he had learned to dance. Then he had many offers to join the hunters and many offers of marriage from the women, but he had refused them all. He had changed his name to *Ayatas Nvgitsvle*, or Fire Wind, for the raging fires he saw in his dreams.

"Pride," *Uni lisi* had said. "Foolish and stubborn pride."

"Dreams," he had responded. "Dreams of fire and wind and magic," such as his people had long ago lost to the white man. And he had left the Indian Land.

At the livery, the white man and his two half-white sons sold him two stalls and enough feed for three days. They helped him to brush down the mounts, check their feet, and untangle their wind-tossed manes. One of the boys was good with animals, discovering a swollen place on the cannon bone of Etsi's mount. The older man applied an herbal liniment and wrapped the limb. Ayatas gave the boy great praise. White men needed praise to feel worthy. *Tsalagi* warriors needed no such words to know their worth.

The man and his sons gave him permission to sleep in the hayloft, sold him a meal of dried meat and cold beans, and sent Ayatas to the back of the bathhouse as he had suspected. His bath consisted of a bucket of water he poured over himself, a sliver of soap in hand. It cost a penny, but the water was clean and pure and still hot from the springs.

As he dried off, Ayatas heard two white men talking within the men's private room of the bathhouse. They talked about a bird that was to be sold. He thought nothing of it, except that the dove would be in need of cleansing, which he thought was strange. Etsi would likely understand and would explain it all to him, and perhaps in the telling, she would find a good story to write for the newspapers back east. Smelling much better, dressed in his clean canvas pants, wool socks, and cotton shirt, Ayatas bedded down in the small loft. Tonight he slept on layered sleep rolls and blankets and his serape, atop fresh hay. His pillow was his scarf, his gun and skinwalker necklace by his hand.

He slept well until about three a.m. when a noise woke him, the squeal and creak of a buckboard with a wheel that rubbed, needing a wheelwright. Above the rubbing he heard a woman's muffled sobs. The sound of a ringing slap. The woman fell silent.

Ayatas rose and secured his clothing, hiding his weapons, tying his moccasins. He crept down from the loft to the stall where his own mount slept, standing, head low, and to the window that looked out onto the street. A wagon rolled by, a white man driving, two white men, a Mexican, and a black man in the bed. A woman was propped on a feed sack, her hands tied, her mouth tied with a gag. In the bright light of the moon, he could see that she had been beaten. Some of her clothing had been torn away.

Abuse of women was a foreign thing among the *Tsalagi*. Had a man tried that on *uni lisi* or *elisi*, the women would have removed the parts that made him a man and put him to work in the fields. But Ayatas knew that white men were often cruel to women.

The buckboard rolled on, and Ayatas thought on what he should do. His Everhart woman would have intervened, even at the risk to her own life, believing that her magic could protect her from anything. It was hard to keep her safe from her own actions, but he could not keep this from her even to keep her safe.

Ayatas secured his long hair, rolled out the window, and landed silently on the dirt. Keeping to the shadows, he followed the buckboard to the biggest saloon. Etsi had taught him to read and write, and the sign over the door read Peacock Saloon. The words Faro and Dancehall were beneath it. Faro was a card game. Dancehall meant that women danced with men and then pleasured them for money, though the women seldom got to keep much of their earnings. It was a hard life, and the women died young and sickly. And ... the women were called soiled doves. Ayatas recalled the conversation between the men in the bathhouse, the words about a bird that was to be sold and the dove that would be in need of cleansing. Were these men selling the woman to the saloon owner? Slavery was now illegal, but women were often kept as sex slaves, and the law did nothing to stop it. Ayatas remembered the sheriff and his insulting tone to Etsi.

The buckboard stopped in the street. Ayatas climbed the rickety stairs of a building nearby and crawled across the flat roof to the next building, and then to the Peacock. He heard the sound of coins clinking. Gold made a dull sound, silver clinking sharply. The woman was crying behind her gag, making a single sound over and over. He thought it might be, "No, no, no..."

He spotted an open shutter on the back wall of the saloon and dropped from the roof to the ground. There was no glass here to bar the way or to stop a breeze from cooling. Ayatas raced to the window and vaulted inside, landing on the wood floor in the dark. Silent. The smell of alcohol assaulted his nostrils, a sneeze threatened, but he forced the urge away, staying crouched, allowing his eyes to adjust. Gray shapes resolved out of the dark—large whiskey and beer barrels, a side of smoked hog hanging from a hook overhead, bags of flour and cornmeal. He was in a storage room. Still stealthy, he moved through the room and out the door to find himself behind the bar in the saloon's main room, the barkeep asleep on a blanket on the floor, snoring.

Ayatas crawled to the opening and studied the main room of the saloon, which was lit with two lamps, one on either side. A piano was on one wall. Roughhewn round tables made from broken wagon wheels with boards atop them were everywhere. Stools and a few chairs were scattered. A small stage took up the space beneath the stairs to the upper floor. On it stood a man, part Mexican, wearing a fancy suit and two guns on his hips. There was an air of ownership about him, the saloon owner, surely. He watched as the two white men carried the bound woman up the stairs. She was kicking, fighting, screaming behind the gag. Ayatas could not help her. He remained in place, watching, learning the room the woman was placed in—room seven at the hall's end. The white men carried her in and shut the door. The sound of blows and muffled crying followed.

The other men were each poured a shot of whisky by the saloon owner, who said, "Turner, you sure—"

"I'm sure." Turner was slim with a curling blond mustache and blond hair slicked back. His clothing was expensive, his boots shiny. He pulled two cigars, offering one to the saloon owner, and snipped off the ends with a small silver clipper. The two men lit their cigars from a taper placed in the flame of the nearest lamp.

"If you want her back," the saloon owner said, "I'll make sure she comes away a more contrite and pliable female. The women sold through this house are valued up north and eager to pleasure a man."

Turner said, "I've had enough of her sass. And her money's mine now, so I don't need her. According to the sheriff, law's on my side."

Turner was the man who had held the buckboard reins. Ayatas studied him the way he studied prey when he was jaguar. Turner had delicate hands, un-calloused with rounded nails. He was dressed in city clothing, the kind Ayatas had seen in San Francisco, worn by the wealthy. This man had taken his wife's property, her gold, and had sold her into abuse.

The saloon owner was part Mexican, a handsome man with a pockmarked face. He had grown wealthy on the labor of women slaves. Ayatas had heard the words himself. He would tell his Everhart woman. They would decide what to do.

Ayatas stayed for an hour, listening to the men talk. Long enough to learn the name of the stolen ranch. Carleton's Buckeye Springs Ranch. When the men left, Ayatas tried to get into room seven, but the door was locked and he did not have a key. So he disappeared into the shadows, following the buckboard to the ranch. It was only three miles away, a short run.

Dawn came quickly, and Ayatas had already checked the horses when the liveryman and his sons arrived. The sore place on the leg of Etsi's mount was better, the heat pulled out by the liniment. Their piss smelled healthy, and their eyes were bright despite the days with low water rations. The liveryman began shoveling out the stalls, giving the horses hay, feed, and fresh water. Knowing that the mounts were cared for, Ayatas wrapped his scarf around his waist to help hide the weapon he wore strapped to his leg and went in search of the inn. His Everhart woman was still asleep, so he left word with the small Mexican child who came to the door, and sought out the bakery. He approached the back door and knocked.

A large woman came to the door and looked him over, head to foot. Her skin was white; her lips were full and fleshy. She smelled of wood smoke, sweat, and sourdough, and she mopped her face with an apron she pulled up. It was already warm in the desert air, and the heat in the room where she toiled was stifling from the wood-burning stove and oven. She dropped the apron and heaved a breath. "Not Apache. Not Ute. What are you?"

"I am a man."

The white woman blew out a breath. "A traveling storyteller, full of comedy. What tribe, injun?"

"*Tsalagi* or *Chelokay*. Cherokee as you might say the tribal name."

"Long as you ain't Apache, I don't care who you are. Apache killed my father when we first came out west." She waited, as if to give him time to think and speak. Ayatas shrugged with his shoulders as the whites did. White men had claimed and invaded lands that belonged to others. The people who lived there had fought back. People on both sides died. The white man was winning that war. There was nothing else to say, and the white woman would not understand his reasoning. Those who grieved seldom did.

"You want food?" she asked gruffly. "I got fresh loaves coming out of the oven shortly. Fifty cents for a fresh wheat loaf. Yesterday's bread is half that, and I got one left. Dime for a square of cornmeal." She held out her fingers in a square to show him the size. "I can toast the bread, and I got eggs I can skillet-cook, mix 'em up with yesterday's beans, five cents for three."

"Your prices are low."

"I charge three times that for the ranch hands." She pulled off her kerchief and finger combed the sweat-damp hair. It was gray and wet with sweat. She leaned against the jamb of the door, resting. "Ranch hands pay more for my cooking. People like you eat cheap."

People like him. Nonwhites, so long they were not Apache. Or perhaps men who had bathed and were not drunk. Ayatas tilted his head, wanting clarification. "You charge more to feed a white man?"

"Cowboys are always drunk and causing trouble, so they pay more. You have a problem with that, I can charge *you* more."

"No." Ayatas waved one hand between them, as if to wave away the smoke of a fire. "Cornmeal bread and three eggs with beans. Yesterday's please." He pulled the necessary change from a pocket that held little and gave the coins to the baker.

"Coming up."

"Thank you, baker of bread."

"Name's Mrs. Lamont." She shut the door in his face.

Ayatas sat on the stoop to wait and to think about women and their power in the world. They were often weak because of childbirth and because of the blood they shed each month to bring life. But when they were no longer burdened with children, they were stronger than any man. The baker, Mrs. Lamont, ran the only place for many miles where the men of the land could go to buy bread. The baker would be a woman with influence and power in the town, even though the male leaders would not know it. His mother and his grandmother had been such women of power. He had been gone from Indian Territory many years. He did not know if they still lived.

The door opened and Mrs. Lamont handed him a tin plate wrapped in a frayed cloth. Ayatas took the offered food and bowed his head. "Thank you, Mrs. Lamont."

"Leave the cloth on the hook by the door and the plate on the step when you're done. The chickens'll peck it clean." She shut the door, and Ayatas sat back on the stoop. He ate with his fingers, and the food was delicious, filled with salt and spices and red peppers. When he was done, he wiped his hands clean on the cloth, hung it on the hook, and placed the pan on the stoop. As soon as he did, four laying hens and a small rooster raced out from beneath the house and attacked it, pecking at each other as often as at his leavings.

Hunger satisfied, Ayatas decided to look over the town. It was the biggest place he and his fire woman had been to since they went to San Francisco. He had been lost there. Surrounded by wealth and filth, amazing things to buy, countless new things to eat, many different ways to live, and dead men lying in the streets. He never wanted to go back. He and Etsi stuck to the smaller settlements where she could gather information and send it to the newspaper that paid her half pennies for the words she sent in. The stone and adobe town of Agua Caliente was small and cleaner than most places white men lived. Someone here knew how to build a decent latrine, and the abundance of hot water meant clean people and clean clothing. The hot springs meant wealth would come.

A prospector riding a mule, leading a heavily laden donkey, passed him at a slow walk, tin pans tied to the pack on long tethers, clanking softly. A woman wearing a starched blouse beneath a well-mended waistcoat and full skirts swept by him, carrying a satchel. A cowhand lay in a pool of vomit in a small alley, his pockets turned out. Three children passed, faces clean, clothes mostly so, metal lunch tins dangling, heading for school. He passed the church, its shutters closed; the saloons, which stank of piss, alcohol, and vomit; the site of the inn, walls rising as stonemasons and bricklayers were already at work, trying to get as much of the day's construction completed as they could before it became too hot to labor. They would sleep in the heat and return to work in the cool of evening.

He had the layout of the town in his mind, a mental map that told him where the wealth was, where the power was, and where the poor and the victims were. He returned to the inn and sat in the street to wait, as was expected of people of his race. Fortunately, a small screwbean mesquite tree had grown up, and it cast some shade.

"Are you sleeping, Aya?"

"Dreaming of you, my *Igohidv Adonvdo*." Ayatas didn't open his eyes, but let a small smile cross his face.

"And if I had not been alone and you had been overheard?"

"The white men in this town would have dropped me into tar and then rolled me in the feathers of Mrs. Lamont's chickens. I would have shifted into my jaguar to heal. And then I would have killed them all." He opened his eyes and smiled up at her. Her face was no longer as taut as when he first met her, her eyes not quite so brilliant blue, her hair not so fiery, but she was the most beautiful woman he had ever seen. Though she always wore a hat, her face was tanned and lines fanned out from her eyes. She smelled clean again, and her hair was down in a long braid. "Beautiful woman, such torture would have been worth this single vision," he murmured.

"Oh, pish." But she blushed like the girl he remembered. "Come. Walk with me. What have you discovered? The wind told me you have been out and about for half the night."

Her magic was the power of the air, and it would have told her. Ayatas stood, his body long and lean, lithe as the day he left the tribal lands. He took his place a little behind her, his hands behind his back. Etsi wore her dark blue dress and matching short jacket with a white shirt. She carried a matching dark blue parasol and wore a wide brimmed hat against the sun. Her gloves had been washed overnight and were nearly white again. Her leather shoes scuffed the earth, and her skirts swung with the motion of her strong legs. She smelled of the blue flowers she loved, lavender.

Etsi said that barring accident, she was likely to live to one hundred years of age, which meant that if he could keep her safe, they might be together for many years. While he … Skinwalkers never aged. He still looked like a young man of less than twenty years.

Speaking softly, he told her about the men at the baths. About the captive woman and her vile husband. Described the Peacock Saloon and the location of room seven. He shared about Mrs. Lamont. About the workers and the inn. Described the ranch and the town to her.

"Dreadful," she murmured when he was done. "But it will make a wonderful story."

His Everhart woman sent in stories of the Wild West to the newspapers of the east, using the name E.V.R. Hart, stories that were a strange mixture of truth and lies and were called fiction. When the newspapers published her stories, Etsi made much money. E.V.R. Hart had been approached by a publisher about writing a novel set in the Wild West, and she had begun the story. His best memories were the two of them at the fire at night, while she read the day's words aloud.

"Did you hear the name of the rancher's wife?" she asked.

"He called her Amandine. His name was Jessup Turner."

"Interesting names for the owner of *Carleton's* Buckeye Springs Ranch. I postulate that Amandine's father owned the ranch, and when he died, he willed it to his daughter. And when she married, the husband assumed ownership. Let's take a walk out toward the ranch before the sun is too hot so that I might visit my dear old friend Amandine. Then perhaps I'll stop by Mrs. Lamont's bakery and ask some questions."

"Perhaps," Ayatas said, amused.

"You have your gun?"

"It is strapped to my leg inside my pants, hidden beneath my shirt and scarf." Ayatas wore his shirt outside his pants in the *Tsalagi* warrior way, tied with a scarf that could double as a turban, and could be tied about his neck when he shifted shape, so he might carry his clothing to dress in when he shifted back. Today, he wore boots, which they had purchased in San Francisco, but his moccasins were tied in his scarf, and his skinwalker necklace was tied around his neck, strung with the teeth and bones of predators. Should he need to shift, to fight or heal, he could choose from among several big cats, a gray wolf, and a young boar. He preferred the jaguar. The cats were strong and swift, though rare in the desert. As they walked, the heat continued to rise, and sweat trickled down his spine and darkened Etsi's clothes.

<hr />

It was near ten a.m. when they reached Carleton's Buckeye Springs Ranch. The house was long and lean, with thick adobe and stone walls and narrow windows that kept out the heat. There were arches in the Spanish style around the wrap-around tiled porch and plants in large clay pots. He called to the house, and when the door was opened, he stepped into the shade and passed the small child the business card of his Everhart woman. The card summoned a small, pretty, dark-skinned woman in an apron who told them that Mr. Turner was out on the range.

Etsi pulled on her magic.

A small dry whirlwind sprang up, bright and hot, and entered the house. A moment later Etsi's words and magic had convinced the housekeeper that she was an expected visitor. The girl told Etsi a tale of woe about the troubles of the ranch as she let them into the coolness to wait.

A man took a fast horse to find Mr. Turner while the maid brought tea to the study where Etsi insisted she be allowed to wait. Ayatas was given a metal cup of water and sat on the cool floor in front of the closed study door, the place a man of his color and race would be expected to wait. In reality, he was his Everhart woman's lookout and guard while she searched the office and desk for important papers and evidence of Amandine's past.

A little over an hour later, he heard horse hooves coming at speed. He scratched on the door. Etsi opened it a crack and said, "This man is a rascal and a scoundrel. I think he'll make a wonderful story for back east. I'm ready to bring him down," she said.

"You will be cautious," he murmured as the sound of boots rang on the front tile stoop.

"I most certainly will not."

Ayatas sighed. Etsi made a harrumphing sound and closed the door. Moments later, the man who had sold his wife entered and stomped to the back of the house to wash up and to use foul language to the pretty housekeeper. And to hit her. Ayatas placed his hand on the hilt of his knife, ready to help the woman, but Turner slammed a door and stomped toward the study, Etsi's business card in his hand. The white man ignored him as trash. It galled Ayatas when fools though him unworthy of notice, but it was a useful tool.

The door opened, and Turner started to speak, but Etsi demanded, "You will tell me where my dear friend Amandine is, Mr. Jessup Turner, and you will tell me this instant."

"Who the bloody blazes are you, and what kind of woman works for a newspaper?" He spun the card across the room.

Ayatas caught the door with one hand and slid inside, into the shadows behind a chair. The door closed softly on its own. The room was dim, but his eyes had adjusted. Turner's eyes had not or he would not be still standing in the room. Several strands of Etsi's hair had come free from her bun and from beneath her hat, and they spun in the wrath of her magics, a slow tornado about her head.

A cool breeze blew through the room, carrying the smell and tingle of power. "Amandine and I graduated together from San Francisco Girls' High School in 1865. Now that I am out of mourning for my dear departed husband," her voice trembled as if she had begun to cry, "I was invited to visit her and her father at their ranch, to do a story on the daily life of a young female rancher. And as my publisher's own daughter went to school with us, he was most eager to send me. As of our last correspondence, all was arranged. However, I arrive and poor Mr. Carleton is dead and buried, and Amandine is both married and missing, all in a matter of two months." She lifted a hand as if to wipe away a tear. "All my … *wealth* is no protection against the vicissitudes of life and fate." The power of compulsion surged through the room. "You *must* tell me what has happened," she finished.

Ayatas smiled into the shadows. She had told the man that her whereabouts were known to the wealthy back east, and that she had wealth of her own, yet was foolish enough to travel into dangerous territory. His fire woman appeared to be in need of protection. A victim. Which she was not nor ever would be.

"My dear Mrs. Everhart, my heart breaks to tell you that my father-in-law died only last month after a horse fell on him. It was most unexpected and sad for us all. Yet yesterday's news has proven much worse. Please be seated." He indicated the leather sofa where Etsi had been sitting, and when she sat again, he sat beside her and took her hand. Ayatas gripped his knife at the man's presumption, though Etsi did not indicate that she needed his help.

"There is no good nor kind way to speak the news," Turner said. "Amandine and her personal servant rode out into the desert to bring me a picnic dinner yesterday. She never returned. I and all of my men have been out searching for her, all night and all day. All we found was a dead horse and a place of struggle. I fear a mountain lion or a small band of Ute or Apache may have taken her."

"Oh. Oh no! What did the sheriff say to the attack? We saw him in town last night. He wasn't leading a search? This is truly dreadful. You must tell me more!"

Ayatas smiled and listened as the man wove a tale of lies, and what his fire woman called seduction—his words leading her to trust when there was nothing to trust at all. As they talked, Ayatas slipped from the room and learned the layout of the house. He found the room where Turner slept. He found the location of the ranch's gun collection. He discovered that the housemaid was covered in bruises and cried softly in a tiny crevice of a room at the back of the house. He controlled his rage. Wrath would help no one.

It was the hottest part of day when Turner offered Etsi a small repast and left the room to order a bowl of fresh greens, a loaf of bread, and a bottle of wine be brought to the study. Ayatas slipped inside, and Etsi whispered, "He thinks I am a fool, to be drugged." Her expression was stern, and he knew she feared the food would contain the mushroom peyote or opium.

"You have never been a fool, my fire woman." Quickly he ducked back out and into the shadows. Turner and the housemaid came and went, leaving the door open. Turner continued his seduction, but Etsi ate little, drank only water and, as soon as the meal was over, insisted that she and her guide would walk back to town. Turner countered, equally insistent, that he drive them back. Etsi agreed.

The buckboard was brought around, and Turner helped Etsi up to the seat. They rode back to town on the bench seat. Ayatas sat on the back of the wagon, staring into the distance, planning how he would kill the man who sought to woo his woman.

"Is she still in room seven?"

Ayatas dropped his chin in the *Tsalagi* way. The scent of Turner's wife had come out of the window, along with the scent of opium. She had been drugged. The two of them would free her before the sun set. And kill her husband by morning.

"Where is the sheriff?" Etsi asked, her voice low so that Mrs. Smith, if she came back from her errand early, would not know that she had a man in her room.

"The sheriff and the dead man are at the ranch."

"Ayatas," she protested, laughter in her voice. "*Dead man. Really.* Here. Help me into the boots."

"They drink and play cards," Ayatas said, inserting the boot hooks in the leather loops. "In the morning, they will tell you that the ranch hands found what was left of the body and brought it in. They think you will not know the difference between the bones of a deer and the bones of a woman if there is no head."

"Of course. Women are uniformly stupid and gullible. And when not, then easily bruised and forced. Pull." She stood and Ayatas lifted the metal hooks against her weight until her left foot slipped in and then the right, snug. Etsi was dressed in dark gray and black, men's breeches and riding boots, shirt and black scarf over her hair and face. She wore a small gun at her waist and a knife at her thigh. He had taught her to fight. She was not a warrior, but she was capable. And she had magic.

"Is Mrs. Lamont still at the bakery?" Two hours past, they had talked to Mrs. Lamont, telling her the story of Amandine. The baker did not want to believe that Turner sold his wife to the saloon, the sheriff assisting, claiming that no white man would do such a thing. But she had been convinced and would help with the rescue and then care for Amandine through the night.

He dropped his head in agreement again, but this time his fire woman gripped his chin and pulled him to her. "What we do is good." Her kiss was heated, and she laughed low in her throat. Long minutes later, they were sprawled on the narrow bed, her shirt unbuttoned and his discarded. She whispered, "We'll be late if we keep this up."

"I do not care," he growled.

She smiled and trailed her finger across his brow and down his cheek. "We will save her and fix things and then we will leave this place for the wild lands. Just us two beneath the stars, the wolves howling in the night."

"You will write your story while I hunt."

"And we will indulge ourselves beneath the moon."

"You are my fire woman."

"You are my beautiful man." She drew his long black braid through her fingers and kissed him before standing. "Work before pleasure."

In the heat of day, they had prepared for the night, gathering a ladder, ropes, a blanket, and medical supplies. Their horses were saddled, needing only the girths tightened to be ready for a fast race out of town.

At the back of the saloon, they waited for dusk to fall and Mrs. Lamont to take action. They did not expect the noise that followed.

Women screamed, shouted, and guns were fired. Men shouted. Footsteps thundered. Etsi's eyes went wide. "Go!" she whispered.

Ayatas raised the ladder to the window of number seven and ground the legs into the dirt to secure it. He raced for the window of the storeroom. Dove inside. His last sight of his woman was her rounded form climbing the ladder.

He came up in the dark and raised the scarf over his face to hide his identity. Pulled his knife and his six shooter. He raced from the storeroom into the saloon. And he nearly stopped dead.

Mrs. Lamont and Mrs. Smith stood shoulder to shoulder with the school teacher and a man in a black robe. A priest. The women held guns on the saloon owner and three other men. "Shoot them! Shoot them!" the owner shouted. But the men with him could not decide what to do.

The priest shouted, "You have dishonored women! Repent!"

Ayatas raced up the stairs, his moccasins silent, his passage unnoticed by any but Mrs. Lamont. The gray-haired woman tilted her head at him, shouldered her shotgun, and shouted at the saloon owner, "We've heard that your doves are here against their wills! Drugged! Abused!"

Ayatas reached the far room and turned the knob. It was locked, and he had no key. He tightened his grip on the darkened bronze knob and drew on his skinwalker strength. The lock broke inside with a harsh snap. He put a shoulder to the door and slipped into the dark.

Amandine was deeply drugged, tied to the bed, her breaths shallow, her face bruised and streaked with tears. Her scent was sick and broken. But he knew a woman could survive many horrible things and become strong again. His mother had survived, and no one called her victim.

Etsi had cut the bonds on the woman and used the ropes to tie the blanket over her. Together they lifted Amandine up and over his shoulder. Etsi adjusted both their scarves so no hair and only their eyes would show. Ayatas drew his weapon with his free hand. Etsi drew her gun and the knife at her thigh. She raced from the room and down the stairs. He followed into the bright lights and the shouting and the sound of gunfire.

Halfway down, the saloon owner spotted them and raised his gun to fire. Etsi paused, aimed, and shot him. The saloon owner stumbled, screaming, a spot of blood on his chest beginning to spread. The smooth action, the lack of twice-thinking her actions, brought fierce happiness to Ayatas. But the owner was not dead. He lifted his gun again and this time aimed at the women gathered in front of him. He fired.

Mrs. Smith fell. Mrs. Lamont raised her shotgun and fired. His head blew back, blood and brains hitting the wall behind him. The saloon owner dropped. The other three men raced away.

Ayatas and Etsi carried Amandine into the early night. Hoof beats galloped away, one sounding lame already. "They'll go for the sheriff and the ranch," Etsi said. "Let's get Amandine to safety." They took her to the bakery. No one was there, but the door was open. Gently, Ayatas placed the unconscious woman on the small bed in the corner.

"We owe you."

Etsi whirled, aiming at the door. But it was, Mrs. Lamont. Etsi dropped the weapon.

"We all knew there were too many young women disappearing, most as they passed through. The sheriff blamed it on Apache, or panthers, or jaguars. Once a raiding party of Comanche, though Agua Caliente is a mighty long ways from their territory. And no young men disappeared. We—the women—knew something was wrong. But we didn't know what to do, not until you came."

"You'll care for her?" Etsi asked.

"All of them." Mrs. Lamont sat in the only chair, beside Amandine. "There's five other young women. Been abused something awful. We'll take care of them. Give them a place to stay."

"The sheriff?" Etsi asked.

"Oh. I have a feeling he'll disappear." Her tone was cunning, her expression amused. "Mrs. Smith is securing his rooms and the jail cell, making certain it's all locked up. One of us will stay there all night. If he ever shows up again, the sheriff's out of a job. But you, well, you best hurry if you want to … finish your night's work."

"Thank you," Etsi said. "We couldn't have done this without you."

"And we *wouldn't* have done it without *you*."

Ayatas and Etsi sped to the livery and within seconds were trotting out of town, warming up the horses. As soon as they safely could, they gave the mounts their heads and leaned forward, across the saddle horns, into the night wind.

They passed a man leading a horse. It was limping. Ayatas wanted to shoot the man for abusing the animal. Perhaps on the way back. They passed a second horse, this one lying on the ground, grunting with pain. His leg was broken. They rode past. Ayatas would come back and put the animal out of its misery. They ran for half a mile and walked the animals for half a mile. The lights of the ranch house came into view.

Ayatas and Etsi slowed their mounts. The horses were sweating and blowing, and Ayatas worried about the cannon bone on Etsi's mount, but it wasn't limping, not yet. Perhaps they hadn't damaged the horse. Through the night air came the sound of shouting and then silence. "The other rider got here just now." Etsi sounded sad. "They'll all ride in together, too many for just us to stop. And I doubt the town's women will have the gumption to face down a well-armed group of men."

But Ayatas knew men. The sheriff and Turner would not wait for the ranch hands to gather. They would believe that the two of them could handle the town's women. He slid from his mount and gave the reins to Etsi. "Take the mounts into the brush. I will shift into jaguar. I will herd the horses as they leave the ranch. Spook them. I will take one, you the other."

She looped the reins to her saddle. "Be careful."

"I most certainly will not," he quoted her.

Etsi laughed like the young girl he fell in love with nearly two decades before. She led the horses into the brush. Ayatas stripped off his clothing and tied it in his scarf, securing the weapons so they would be at hand when he shifted back. Naked, he tied the scarf around his neck, leaving the fetish necklace in place, pulling the heavy bundle uncomfortably tight. Then he sat and called upon the snake in the center of all things, calling upon the life-force of the jaguar in the bones of the fierce beast. He was not moon-called, but it was easier to shift into another shape when *gauwatlvyi* was full. It was only two days to *Guyequoni*—the Ripe Corn Moon of the month the white man called July. His shift was fast and painless.

Ayatas raced to the middle of the street when horses came at a run. Tilted his ear tabs, finding their speed and location with his cat-ears. He squatted, leaving fresh piss in the middle of the street. Then he leaped thirty feet to the top of a pile of boulders and crouched. Waiting. As the horses passed at a hard run, bright silver-green in his cat-night-vision, he growled, the sound rising. He screamed out his big-cat roar, a chuff of territory claiming, a roar of sound.

The horses screamed and leaped to the side, shying as they passed over his piss. One tucked his head and began to buck. The other raced off the road. The man on the bucking horse cursed, lost his stirrups, and then the horn. He was tossed high. He landed. The cursing stopped. The horse bucked its way into the night. The man on the ground groaned.

The wind began to rush, fiery with magic. In the distance, Ayatas heard a man scream.

Ayatas trotted to the man on the ground. It was the sheriff. Ayatas hungered after his shift. It took energy to feed his shape-changing magic. He sniffed the man. He bled. He was injured prey. Ayatas leaned and blew on the sheriff's face. The man screamed. Ayatas chuffed again. The sheriff screamed and tried to pull his gun. Ayatas bounded and caught the man in his claws. Flipped him over. Pounced on his chest. The man screamed again. Ayatas chuffed with laughter.

"Stop playing with your food, Aya," Etsi said.

Hungrily, Ayatas tore into the sheriff's throat and ate. The man died, bleeding out on the dirt, gasping wetly for breath. Ayatas sank his fangs into the sheriff's liver. He ate enough to appease the cramping in his own belly. He ripped out part of a lung and both kidneys, eating voraciously. Had he eaten of a human while in human form, he would have endangered his skinwalker energies, but as predator cat, he was free from such fears.

Full, he strolled away, leaving many tracks in the blood and in the dirt of the road. In the darkness, he shifted back to human form and dressed. All the attack had taken perhaps ten minutes in the white man's time.

He and his Everhart woman rode on to the ranch and alerted the ranch hands, who were gathering their gear in preparation to follow their boss into town. "Hello the house!" she called as they neared the bunkhouse. "There's a dead man in the road!"

At dawn, a very tired Ayatas and Etsi were in the saloon, sitting at a table in the dark beneath the stairs, sharing a pot of coffee. Etsi was writing her story, a sheaf of paper at her elbow, with pen and inkwell. They were watching and listening to what his Everhart woman called a *ruckus*.

The two dead men were lying on tables pushed together in the center of the saloon. The rest of the space was taken up by men, drinking and arguing and staying as far away from the women as they could. Because the women were angry and the men were rightfully afraid. The women were being led by Mrs. Smith, formidable even when wounded. All carried loaded weapons.

A mob of armed angry women was a frightful thing to observe, unless one had been raised under the heel of *uni lisi* and *elisi*. Nothing was more frightening than those two in a rage. Ayatas sipped his coffee. It had been served in his own tin cup, to keep his filth from contaminating the cups used by the whites. Ayatas found it amusing and thought that before he left, he might shift into jaguar again and piss into all the cups.

The hands from Carleton's Buckeye Springs Ranch were all drunk. Other ranchers from the surrounding area stomped the horse manure off their boots and entered. The men were all business and worried about the safety of their stock and children, most likely in that order. The undertaker, aware of his audience, measured the bodies for caskets. The doctor (who cut hair and shaved men at the bathhouse) was studying the wounds. He stood and tucked his thumbs into his vest lapels and pronounced, "These men are dead! The new owner of Carleton's died by a broken neck. The sheriff died by a broken leg that left him game to a …" He raised his voice. "To a marauding mountain lion."

"We need to track down that mountain lion and shoot it," a stranger said.

"No!" Mrs. Lamont shouted. The room quieted. "No one will be leaving this saloon until justice is served."

Amandine walked slowly into the saloon, and the place went as silent as the dead men. She stood straight, her bruises purpled and scarlet. She looked around the room as the other women moved to cover the exits with their bodies and their guns.

"You all know me," Amandine said. "You know that I was married fast to a man who appeared to be all that was ever in a girl's dreams. Then my father died, and it was proved to me that man I thought loved me was a flimflam man. Now he is dead. According to my father's will, the ranch is mine. Is that understood?"

The men around her nodded. Two men edged toward the doors.

"My husband sold me two nights past to Ramon Vicente, the owner of the saloon." Several of the men in the group drew weapons. Several others leaned in to study her face. "He and two of my former ranch hands abused my body and my person. Vicente is dead. The ranch hands who abused me are Jimmy Jon Akers and Slim Tubbers."

The two men bolted. Mrs. Lamont raised her shotgun and coldcocked one. The other was tripped. One woman sat on him, another beat his head against the floor. A third kicked his side so hard the snap of broken ribs could be heard across the room. Etsi laughed. She was taking notes as fast as her pen could flow across the paper.

"I have witnesses. I call the reporter, Mrs. Everhart, and the baker, Mrs. Lamont, to speak to the truth of my statement."

Etsi stood and told the story of the night Amandine had been brought into town, telling it as if she had been the witness. She told about finding Amandine and setting her free. About riding out to the ranch. His forever woman was a wonderful storyteller.

"The two men tried to get away," Etsi said. "You saw them. They abused the body of a woman. Where I come from that means either a neutering or a hanging."

Ayatas did not think the men would neuter the rapists. But one did pull out a length of rope and start braiding.

Satisfied, Etsi motioned for him to follow, and they left the saloon.

That night, under the stars, Etsi read him the story called "Savior of the Doves." It was wonderful. And then she fell into his arms on their layered bedrolls and they loved together beneath the nearly full moon, as they always had, as they always would. If he could keep his Everhart woman safe.

TO HEAR A HOWLING HERD

Gunnar De Winter

QUIETSPRING HUNG IN THE NOTHINGNESS.

He let the sensorsuit enter his mind.

Once upon a time, his people put their ears to the ground of the prairie on Old Earth to locate bison. Now they hunted for the spacetime ripples that announced a herd of rays.

Something slid through him, over him, past him. A faint flicker of movement. A bashful beacon.

Quietspring tugged the rope attaching him to the front craft of the caravan. He was reeled in.

A pair of strong hands peeled away the tight black suit that encased him. Vision returned when the opaque face cover was removed.

"Well, son?"

"Twenty-five, thirty-six."

"Excellent, that's our heading." The pat on his shoulder reverberated through Quietspring's entire body. His father, Ironlung, was a big man, working in the high gravity engine rooms. "How many?"

Quietspring lifted his bony shoulders. "Many far away, or a few close by." Ironlung rubbed his chin. He was one of the few men who still had to shave, an ancestral trait that occasionally popped up. "Go tell the chief." He winked. "See you for dinner." Heavy footsteps clanged on the metal walkways as Ironlung returned to the engines, the dungeons that held the dark matter in place.

Quietspring made his way to the bridge. His footsteps were soundless.

Gravitydancer was there. Of course she was there. She would take over the caravan when her father deemed her ready. Quietspring swallowed. "Chief Stareye?"

The small man turned. His dark leathery skin was creased and taut at the same time. "Ah, Quietspring, I trust you've got good news?"

"Yes. There's a group at twenty-five, thirty-six." He snuck a glance at Gravitydancer. She was almost as reedy as he was. Every generation seemed to become taller and thinner, elongated almost. Her large eyes were black holes that relentlessly sucked in Quietspring's thoughts.

"Good, we need to restock and refuel. As does the rest of the fleet."

The caravans were the scouts, the explorers chasing the rays before they could retreat beyond known space. It was an endless hunt. Humans needed the rays to enable their travel through hyperspace to the closest star systems, but by travelling through space, they scared away the rays. In fact, the whole human exodus was a giant expanding bubble. The rays at the edge were pushed farther and farther. And humanity had no choice but to follow. One jump at a time. Until they found a new home that would embrace them. In the meantime, humanity had learned to harvest the emptiness via the rays.

Sometimes Quietspring wondered if the bubble could collapse.

Stareye scrutinized the holographic radar display. "Hmm, they're not yet in sight of the ship sensors." He turned to Quietspring. "Excellent job, young man, you're very sensitive."

"Thank you, Chief."

"I'll go and talk to the hunters, tell them to prepare. Gravitydancer, you've got the ship."

"Yes, Chief." On the bridge, formality still stood its ground.

Quietspring stepped up the raised inner circle, the front of which was lined by a glass wall full of three-dimensional figures, floating numbers, and colorful trajectories.

"Why so gloomy, Quietspring?"

"Huh? What do you mean?"

"Every time you come here to announce that you've spotted… felt a herd, you seem despondent."

Quietspring stared at the ever-changing glass graffiti. He felt a soft, smooth hand on his. For a brief moment, his steady pulse galloped. He sighed.

"It's just that… I don't like it."

"Like what?"

"The hunting, the killing."

She withdrew her hand, leaving a mysterious coldness in its wake. "We have no choice. We need the cysts. It's the only way we can contain the dark matter, the only way to travel between the stars and find a new home."

"Yes, I know." Quietspring folded his hands behind his back, where they exchanged memories of Gravitydancer's touch. "But we're killing innocent creatures to do so. And the ceremony in their honor after the hunt is a sad excuse for... well, an excuse."

"We honor their spirit, we cause them no pain, and we ensure the survival of humanity. Like it or not, this is our way of life now. This is the only way of life now."

"How do you know we cause them no pain?"

She looked at him, slightly puzzled. "They've got no nervous system or anything like it."

"I suppose."

He didn't tell her about the howls. He hadn't told anyone about the howls.

Quietspring stood in the nothingness.

This time, he was firmly anchored on the scout shuttle. The sensorsuit's tendrils crept into his consciousness. He wasn't looking for rays now. After all, they were right there for anyone to see. Elongated lozenges the size of the entire caravan. Almost translucent milky white. Flapping their wings as they glided through space. Inside the milk, dark globs of treasure.

He felt the rays, felt the waves they caused in spacetime course through him. But he had different quarry now. Other hunters, seeking to steal their prey. Scavengers, looking to perpetuate their selfish way of life. He was the alarm.

"All systems check. All hunters confirm." The voice of Spaceripper, pack leader, sounded in the darkness of Quietspring's world.

A wave of "confirms" followed.

Quietspring felt the hunters rush past, each one of them seated in their small torpedo-shaped spacebike.

"Batwing formation."

Spaceripper's bike led the way. Red stripes on a dull gray background, one for each successful hunt. The others gathered around it and arranged themselves in neat pyramids with the tips pointing to their victim. Spaceripper had chosen a ray that lingered at the back of the herd. Large. Old. The front of the herd sped up. *How many eons of life will we attack when we strike this old one?* He signaled Spaceripper. "They know we're here." A trickle of bile crawled up his throat. He swallowed it down, hoping the guilt would follow suit.

"On we go, hunters."

As one, the pyramids lunged.

Energy weapons or long range beams weren't the most effective weapons against the rays. Short range kinetic projectiles did the trick. Bows and arrows. In space. Sometimes, young dogs had to relearn old tricks.

The target? A small red light at the front of the ray, faintly pulsating. A heartbeat, perhaps. Or a plea for mercy.

"Outer left wing, detach. Outer right wing, detach. Inner wings, maintain."

The formation spread its wings.

"Outer wings, circle."

The predators prepared to strike.

"Inner wings, target sides."

"Target acquired."

"Target acquired."

"Inner wings, engage."

The prey slowed, weighed down by the harpoons in its wings.

"Outer wings, engage."

Quietspring wriggled uncomfortably in the sensorsuit. *Wait, wait, I can hear it, I can feel it. Wait.* His voice did not find its way out.

The prey faced its predators. The ray had almost stopped moving. The outer wing squadrons fired their harpoons and flew over the ray, drawing it up as they went. The bullseye stretched out before Spaceripper, enticing him.

"Engage," Spaceripper grunted as he fired.

A howl entered Quietspring's mind. A scream that wasn't his own freed itself.

Then, darkness. True darkness.

Quietspring lay in the nothingness.

Naked. Unsuited.

A burst of light.

"Wh…"

"Whoa, calm down, son. Calm down."

A strong hand softly propped up the pillow under Quietspring's head.

Reality came into focus.

"What happened?" A stammer more than a question.

His father's bulk hung over him. Behind it, he could see Gravitydancer, who did her best to wipe the concern from her face, but failed.

"Welcome back, son. How are you feeling?"

Besides the odd taste in his mouth, he was just tired. "Tastes like red," he mumbled.

"What's that?"

"What happened?"

"You tell us. Spaceripper struck and you suddenly started screaming." An involuntary shiver ran across Ironlung's broad back. "The scout came rushing back, but you had already fainted before it entered the vehicle carrier."

Gravitydancer had moved to the other side of the hospice bed. "That scream, it wasn't... It wasn't you."

"I don't know. I'm tired."

His father nodded. "Hint taken." With a gentle demeanor that seemed out of place for a man of his size, Ironlung shepherded Gravitydancer out of the room. Just before she left, she turned her head. "See you at the ceremony later, right?"

How could he resist those big eyes that longed for loving obedience?

"Of course."

He leaned back on the pillow and closed his eyes.

A throat was cleared. Strong. Manly.

Quietspring opened his eyes and was surprised to see Spaceripper. Somehow, the boundless bravado that hung around the muscular hunter seemed to waver. "How are you?"

"Fine. Tired."

"What happened out there?"

Quietspring shrugged.

"I'm not stupid. You started to scream the moment I struck. Can't be coincidence."

"I'm not sure. Even before you struck, there were... voices. No, not voices. Feelings. Awareness within my awareness, if that makes any sense."

Spaceripper frowned. An odd and unusual expression for someone who appeared to have the gift to take everything in stride.

"Sorry I can't be clearer," said Quietspring.

"You should tell the chief."

Quietspring nodded.

Spaceripper turned to leave. "You know," he said, facing away, "I don't enjoy killing, Quietspring. But it's the only way, and if it has to be done, I'd rather make sure that it's done quickly and efficiently."

The caravans were collections of crafts attached to each other via flexible carboplast tubes. Massive, segmented beasts crawling through the universe. The powwow craft sat stately in the middle of the beast and outsized all other segments. It was there that ceremonies were held and social events organized. Like white blood cells attracted to a virus, everyone who wasn't performing essential tasks gathered to listen to Chief Stareye honoring the ray.

Even Quietspring joined the group standing around the holographic bonfire. Gravitydancer quickly spotted him and snuck away from her father's side.

"Are you alright?" A soft touch on his arm, panacea.

"Yes. Thanks." He hesitated. "I need to talk to your father."

"He'll finish soon." She grinned. "Look at him, he enjoys all this ritual stuff." Stareye wore the war bonnet that supposedly belonged to his Old Earth ancestors and, with full conviction, chanted words whose meaning had long been swallowed by time. The chant ended with a loud triplet of "A-oums" formed by hundreds of mouths. Smaller green-blue bonfires flickered into life. People gathered around them in small groups. They talked, shared food, and enjoyed each other's company. There was little time for that in the caravan, so each opportunity was treasured.

Gravitydancer took Quietspring's hand and dragged him along. "Let's go talk."

She sat down next to her father and pulled Quietspring down alongside her. "Dad, Quietspring wants to talk." No formality between father and daughter in the powwow craft.

Chief Stareye turned his flustered face to Quietspring. "Ah yes, I heard what happened. I would have come to see you myself, but preparations…"

"I understand, Chief."

"Well then, what is it that you want to talk about?"

"It's about what happened."

Quietspring hesitated.

"Yes? Go on."

"This might sound strange, but I think the rays tried to reach out. I think I can hear them. Feel them." The conversation in the small group halted, but Quietspring was fired up by sudden passion. "We've been wrong this whole time. They are aware and they feel pain."

"Stop right there." Stareye held up his hand. "You've gone through an ordeal. You should rest and allow your thoughts to calm." Approving mumbles circled the conversational partners.

Quietspring readied himself to mount a counterattack, but Gravitydancer tugged him away. "You're right, Dad. I'll make sure he reaches his bed." Snickers and innuendo danced around each other.

When they had left the powwow craft, Quietspring snapped, "You don't believe me either?"

Gravitydancer bit back, "I heard the scream. It wasn't you. Maybe Father believes you as well. He simply can't allow you to make such claims without support. Believe me, there are those would like to claim the title 'chief' for themselves."

"Now what? Stay quiet and continue the killing?"

"Maybe I can help." Distracted by their own bickering, they had missed Spaceripper following them. The hunter's smile was that of a mischievous cat. "Let's fly."

Quietspring sat in the nothingness.

Sniffing, tasting.

Loosely tied to the scoutship piloted by Spaceripper, he scoured the universe for waves. A scared herd was too fast to keep up with, but hopefully the rays had settled down by now.

He tried to calm the storms in his mind. He was a senser. A feeler. His breathing deepened, slowed. Quietspring sank into the cosmos.

Spacetime quivered.

There.

"Minus six, eleven."

"Got it. Hold on." Spaceripper set course to the herd.

"Stay in range of the comm beams, guys." Gravitydancer was alone on the bridge. She'd dismissed the officer keeping watch to allow him to join the powwow. The gathering should last long enough to buy the trio time for Quietspring to try and make contact.

True to his name, Spaceripper tore through the void.

"Slow down," Quietspring said when they came upon the herd. "Don't spook them."

The scoutship dropped speed.

"Stop here."

"Aye aye."

Quietspring sat down on top of the spacecraft. This time he wouldn't have to attune himself to listen or feel. No, this time, he had to shout.

He could feel the slow and steady waves emanating from the rays. He had to find a way to push back.

Reach within.

Push back.

To stop the killing.

Push back.

To end the pain.

Push back.

To silence the suffering.

Push back.

To see new horizons.

Push back.

Something emerged from a hidden place within himself, from the unknown depths beneath the surface waters of his thoughts. A bubble of emotion, feeling, sensing, burst through the mental shallows. Quietspring's mind screamed for attention.

The herd stumbled. The rays' movements staggered with confusion. With languid motions, they turned towards the scoutship.

"Guys, something's happening here. We've picked up other ships heading toward us. Everybody's being jostled back to their stations."

"Something's happening here, too," whispered Spaceripper. "I think Quietspring made contact."

"Good, then we can try again later. Right now, you really need to come back. They don't look friendly." A brief moment of silence. "Spaceripper, we might need your skills."

The rays were closing in, inspecting the tiny louse that shouted.

"Heard that, Quietspring? We've got to go. We'll be back."

Quietspring was vaguely aware of Spaceripper's words, but the inquisitive emanations probing the edges of his mind demanded most of his attention. He couldn't leave. He wouldn't leave.

"Quietspring? Do you hear me? Quietspring?"

"Guys, get back here now. It's a scavenger group. They must have followed us since the hunt. Bastards took advantage of the ceremony to try and get their hands on the new cysts. Damn. Come back. Now!"

"On our way." Spaceripper turned the scoutship and fired up the engines.

Quietspring felt the lurch of the sudden acceleration. *No no no. They're here, they're trying to make contact. I'm so close.*

He forced his throat and tongue into action. "Can't go. Not now."

"You heard what's happening. We've got to go back before the scavengers reach the caravan. A single pair of hands can mean the difference between victory and defeat."

"You are needed. You go back." *My hands are useless anyway.*

"What do you mean?"

Quietspring untethered himself and pushed off. "Don't worry. I'll find my way."

"Quietspring, what are you doing! Stop!"

A ray came swooping down, more agile and elegant than its size seemed to warrant.

I hear you. The ray filled Quietspring's vision.

Closer. Closer still.

The last thing Quietspring saw was Spaceripper's ship rallying back to the fleet, to the pack that needed the warrior's help.

The ray swallowed the tiny human floating in front of it.

Quietspring floated in the nothingness.

But he was not alone.

There was something—someone?—else beside him, around him. He couldn't breathe. He didn't have to.

He remembered…

He remembered hitting the ray and sinking into it.

He remembered the panic when the viscous goo breached the supposedly impenetrable suit and clogged the oxygen ducts.

He remembered how his breath became a prisoner of his lungs, unable to escape.

He remembered how the goo snuck into his body.

Then, welcome and curiosity. Two minds sniffing at each other, trying to understand, to see, to find common ground.

There were waves and images. Exchanges. Slowly, Quietspring's brain began to make sense of it, assisted by the sensorsuit's extensive sensory capacities. Seeking patterns, real or illusory, was one of humanity's greatest abilities. A gift and a curse.

He felt the herds roam through space, being nourished by spacetime itself.

He felt how humanity's exodus had drawn the rays, inquisitive creatures as they were.

He felt how humanity lusted for the cysts and began harvesting them.

He felt the deaths, the confusion, the frustration at the inability to communicate.

He understood that the rays could manipulate the cysts more deftly than humans.

He understood that the rays could travel between the stars.

He understood that they could share this ability.

He understood that it would take healing and reconciliation.

Something niggled at the back of his mind. Of its mind. Of their mind.

His friends. His family. They were in trouble.

Quietspring/ray extended their shared senses. He/they perceived turmoil. Ripples of high energy. *Weapons*.

Gravitydancer!

The caravan needed help. The scavengers, usually a baseship and smaller raiders, were no longer interested in finding suitable planets after generations of failing to do so. Instead, they stalked the caravans and usurped the spoils of their labor. Scavengers struck hard; scavengers struck fast. If main fleet reinforcements were sent at all, they would be too late. The distance between the caravans and the rest of humanity was simply too large.

Waves crashed into him/them. The herd was growing restless. The rays were aware of humanity closing in and wanted to move on.

But they need our help!

Quietspring tried to convey the intimacy of the caravan, the bond between its members.

They, too, are a herd.

They, too, seek to live in peace.

The ray, *his* ray, remembered it. Felt it. Understood it.

Ripples in spacetime moved back and forth. Waves interfered. Constructively. Neutrally. Destructively. Arguments flowed. Discussion reverberated.

Quietspring was amazed at the complexity of the interactions. The rays were so much more than the caravans could have ever guessed. His sadness at the senseless killing crept out.

We never knew.

I'm so sorry.

The dance of waves subsided.

The rays circled each other slowly, wings flapping in synchrony. Quietspring/ray was in the middle. Pulsations bounced through his/their body. It was the most beautiful thing his mind had ever perceived.

The circling ended.

As one, the herd moved.

Quietspring swam in the nothingness.

The void of space had become his turf. He/ray marched through space, riding unseen waves. Its/their brethren were with them.

A pinprick just moments ago, the caravan became more detailed with every flap of their wings.

Wave echoes painted a picture of strife and struggle.

Some caravan craft had been punctured and vomited materials. Small agile scavenger raiders—all hooks and edges—harassed the lumbering collection of ships. The hunters did their best to mount a counter-initiative. A red spacebike dove into the fray with reckless abandon, the pilot's skill so great the scavengers couldn't lock their weapons onto the small ship.

Spaceripper!

The herd was skittish. The waves from the turmoil were frantic, aggressive.

Occupied by the struggle, none of the combatants had noticed the rays yet.

Quietspring/ray felt the reluctance of the other rays.

Scavenger beams ripped into the caravan. Connector tubes were severed. People poured out. Death swung its scythe. The caravan's segments moved as someone on the bridge began to shuffle the connected ships' configuration in order to minimize damage and casualties.

A flash. A short-lived spherical explosion.

An engine room blew.

Father!

The herd fought its own instincts to do something it had never done before. Engage.

As the massive beasts barreled onto the battlefield, the fighters finally took note. For a moment, both sides of the conflict froze.

A moment was all Quietspring/ray/herd needed.

Scavengers were slapped through space by the rays' giant wings. Concentrated bursts of spacetime waves ripped apart the peskier flies of the bunch. The scavenger baseship turned and tried to flee, but was torn asunder by a marvelously synchronized move from a ray trio.

The caravan's remaining hunters regrouped and established a spacesword attack formation. At the tip of the sword, a scuffed spacebike with red streaks. The spacesword did not strike.

Spaceripper held off his hunters.

Quietspring/ray moved closer cautiously. Eagerness met trepidation in an uneasy truce.

When the ray's front tip almost touched Spaceripper's spacebike, it curled upwards.

Quietspring knew how to draw the attention of a warrior. Just show him his target.

The ray's body rolled back while Quietspring swam through it, toward the pulsating red dot that would hopefully hypnotize Spaceripper long enough to draw his attention.

Don't shoot, Spaceripper, don't shoot. Steady your hunter's heart.

The spacebike held on to its harpoons.

Quietspring looked at Spaceripper and waved. He had to smile at the big man's open mouth. Finally, he saw Spaceripper grab hold of the radio.

A small ship detached from the caravan's vehicle carrier. *You can let go.* Quietspring detached from his ray. The sensorsuit, despite the goo's incursion, shielded him from space long enough to be picked up.

Gravitydancer and Spaceripper were waiting on the bridge.

She hugged him. "Oh, Quietspring." Spaceripper put a hand on his shoulder. Quietspring looked around. "Dad?"

Gravitydancer's lips trembled. "I'm sorry."

"Chief?"

She swallowed.

Quietspring took her hand. "I'm sorry."

Their heads touched. Shared grief eased the pain.

Spaceripper engulfed them in a massive hug. "They will be remembered."

A few moments later, the hunter said, "But what about those rays?"

Quietspring told his tale, and the rays' tale. They could unite, cooperate. It could be a new dawn. Man and ray together, cruising the stars.

Outside, the rays grazed on spacetime.

Gravitydancer moved to the holo-display. There were still some sparks and leaks, but it was functional enough. She watched the herd. "Could it really?"

Quietspring nodded. "Trust me."

A thoughtful look crossed Gravitydancer's face. "Okay, let's try this."

Quietspring danced in the nothingness.

His ray danced with him. Bonds formed quickly between ray and rider. Quietspring had become a pilot of a living spaceship. In fact, he was no longer the only one. A young girl, sensitive as Quietspring was, swam next to him in her own baby ray. Shared sensations, shared minds, shared space.

The rays were magnificent. And so much more mutable than they seemed. They could engulf entire spaceships and take them along for a ride. They could even be turned into spaceships themselves. Spaceripper was leading the effort to sculpt one of the larger ray's insides to make it suitable for large scale human populations.

Word had reached the main fleet by now. For the first time in the exodus, the bubble of expansion came to a halt. All along its edge, contact was made. Hunter and prey turned into cooperators. There was dissent, but the sense of discovery quashed it without too much trouble.

Quietspring could already picture it. The bubble would start growing again soon. Faster than it ever had. So fast that it might divide into many bubbles. Some would continue the search for a new home. Others might continue to explore the prairie of stars, to seek the frontier.

Quietspring would be one of the latter.

Being one with the ray was bliss. He felt less and less inclined to leave it and kept spending more and more time with it.

A burst of waves came directly at him, modulated by the goo. With the help of his ray, he unscrambled them.

"Quietspring, come home. Your daughter and I are waiting."

Gravitydancer and his newborn child were the only thing that could make him leave his union.

For now.

CALLIOPE STARK:
BONE TREE BOUNTY HUNTER

Edmund R. Schubert

IT WAS HALF PAST HIGH NOON WHEN CALLIOPE STARK STRODE INTO THE largest saloon in Blackwater, Utah, her right hand clutching a wanted poster, her left hand resting atop the weathered wooden grips of her Colt Peacemaker. On her other hip was holstered a Colt Dragoon, the other star in a lead-spewing cast of characters that featured a sawed-off shotgun slung high between her shoulder blades, an 1858 Remington six-shooter under her long skirt (strapped to the outside of her left thigh, just above her knee), and twin Derringers, one inside each of her dusty black boots.

The abundance of guns was an insurance policy because when it came time to feed her bone tree, there wasn't much margin for error. And it was well past time to feed that tree. She could feel it; her bones were as brittle as old glass, and her body ached as if she'd been thrown from a horse and landed flat on her back—fifteen or twenty times. She'd waited too long, and she was paying for it.

So it was time for Calliope to kill someone. Quickly. Her one hard and fast rule was that if she had to kill someone, it had to be someone who deserved to die. Someone who *needed* to die. Hence the wanted poster.

"Anyone know the whereabouts of this man?" She thrust the wrinkled brown poster into the air, holding it high overhead. "I'll give ten percent of the reward to the first person who tells me where I can find Dan Hatcher. That's a hundred dollars for nothing more than a few words."

A murmur spread through the room, a wounded dove of disbelief, fluttering from lip to lip, from man to man. In other words, the usual bullshit she heard every time she showed up in a new town.

"A woman bounty hunter?"

"A woman bounty hunter?"

"A woman bounty hunter?"

In all her twenty-seven years on Earth, that was the one thing that rankled her most. She dropped the wanted poster, drew her Colts, and cocked them, saying, "I swear on the grave of every asshole in this room, the next man who says, 'A woman bounty hunter,' gets a bullet."

A long-haired trapper in a fringed buckskin jacket turned from the bar to face her, a shot-glass of whisky between two filthy fingers. "A *lady* bounty hunter?"

Calliope wouldn't kill someone for something as petty as being called a woman bounty hunter. It did piss her off, but being pissed off was a lousy reason to kill. Calliope did, however, need people to believe that she was not to be trifled with, that she would kill anyone who crossed her. Respect and its overgrown little brother fear were the currencies of the West. Being a woman meant working twice as hard for half the pay. So she pivoted to the whiskey-drinking trapper and shot him in the thigh. He collapsed in a cursing heap, the whiskey glass landing unbroken next to him and rolling in a slow, resonant circle.

The bartender whipped a shotgun from beneath the mahogany bar and pointed it at her. "He didn't say '*woman* bounty hunter.'"

"That's why I only shot him in the leg," Calliope replied. "And if someone's defense for being an asshole rests on semantics, I'll shoot them twice: once between the eyes and once between the legs. Not necessarily in that order."

Before the bartender could react, Calliope shot him, too, grazing his shoulder, drawing blood but damaging his pride more than his body. As his shotgun clattered to the floor, the red-faced man howled. "What in hell did you do that for?"

Calliope sneered. "You said, 'woman bounty hunter.' I told you what would happen."

A fiery, piercing pain shot up her spine. Damn bone tree. When it lacked sustenance, it broadcast its hunger pangs in crippling waves.

Calliope looked from the bartender to the long-haired trapper and back to the bartender. Both of them were bleeding, wounded, and disarmed. It would be so easy to finish either of them off. Get what she needed and be done with it.

So easy.

But neither of them *needed* to die. They were annoying, yes. But nothing more.

Damn it. The only thing worse than having emotions was having a conscience.

She bent over and retrieved the wanted poster from the floor, wincing at how much it hurt to straighten back up. "Let's try this again. Anyone know where I can find Dan Hatcher? I know he recently shot up this shit-hole town. Where'd he get to next?"

One of the saloon's whores piped up, saying, "Where'd he get to? More like where *didn't* he get to? That man is everywhere. T'ain't natural."

"What the hell's that supposed to mean?" Calliope asked.

Nearly twenty men developed an intense interest in the drink in their hand or the cards on the table in front of them.

Good Lord, Calliope thought. *They're more afraid of Dan Hatcher, who's not even in the room, than they are of me and my guns, right here, right now. That means he's done nasty shit to these people. Real nasty.*

Calliope preferred to get confirmation before she killed someone. Now she had it; these folk's fear spoke volumes. The bone tree needed to be fed and watered, and Calliope needed to be the one who killed the person whose blood and bones she scattered around the tree. But that was it. The tree didn't care whose blood and bones she brought—it wasn't sentient or anything batshit crazy like that. But Calliope *did* care who she killed. She considered it her greatest weakness—her greatest vulnerability.

She scanned the saloon for threats. You never knew when someone would try something stupid, and the odds went up exponentially if people were scared. And these folks were plenty scared.

But no one looked twitchy—no one's hands went underneath a table or inside of a jacket—so she holstered her Colts, turned, and exited through the swinging doors. Experience had taught her that the sooner she left after shooting someone, the better. *Sling some well-placed lead and get the hell out,* was her philosophy. *The stories they'll make up about you are always twice as good as the ones you'd tell about yourself.*

Calliope headed for the sheriff's office and jailhouse. If you were new in town, the saloon was the place to go to make a memorable first impression. But the jailhouse was where you went if you wanted reliable information.

As Calliope stepped off the saloon's front porch, a dozen men on horseback stampeded through town, headed for the jailhouse, and it only took one glance to know they were trouble. Only two groups that size rode that hard for the jailhouse, and this wasn't the group that wore badges.

Calliope studied them as they galloped by, assessing them. They were a peculiar sight for three reasons: first, the men did none of the usual whooping, hollering, and random gun-shooting that a gang that size normally delighted in. With the exception of the thundering of the horse's hooves, they were virtually silent.

Second, one of them was a black man, and black and white generally didn't ride together.

And third, their leader was a freckle-faced, redheaded young man who couldn't have been more than eighteen years old. Calliope had seen gangs led by eighteen-year-olds before, and they were invariably the most undisciplined bunch imaginable. But this crew was more like an orchestra on horseback: finely-tuned and under the guidance of a young man who was in control of their every movement.

Normally Calliope enjoyed a good orchestra, but this group set her instincts on edge.

As soon as the gang passed by, Calliope jigged across the manure-filled street, holding up her skirt as she side-stepped the multitude of steaming brown piles. It wasn't the fastest way to cross the street, but she'd be damned if she was going to dip her boots or skirt in shit.

With that bit of street-dancing accomplished, she edged her way down the row of wooden storefronts, getting as close to the red-brick jailhouse as possible. This had the potential to get messy. Cattle slaughterhouse messy.

That was lucky; it meant that if she played her cards right, bounty money aside, she might not need Dan Hatcher at all.

As she drew closer, she calculated how best to play things: clueless brunette or frisky sex kitten. Both had advantages, but she concluded that men as disciplined as these would have no patience for cluelessness. Sex kitten it was then. She undid the top two buttons of her blouse. Discipline was no match for breasts.

Most of the gang dismounted and filed one at a time into the jailhouse, but two of them took positions outside the door. One noticed Calliope's approach, so she adopted a flirtatious demeanor.

"Hello, boys," she said with a toss of her head and her hip.

Both men raised their rifles and aimed them at her. "Turn around and walk the other way," ordered the taller of the two.

Calliope noted that both men carried Spencer Repeaters, rifles favored by Union soldiers during the Recent Unpleasantness Between the States. That explained their discipline; despite being dressed like cowboys, they were ex-military. She'd need to proceed with caution. The Spencer Repeater fired a rimfire cartridge the size of a .56 caliber musketball, combining the raw power of a musket with the speed of a lever-action rifle.

On the other hand, she knew that soldiers, more than anyone else, were suckers for a sex kitten. She removed her silver-plated hair comb and let her hair down, slipping the comb into her skirt's pocket with her left hand while twirling a strand of her shoulder-length auburn hair around the middle finger of her right.

She also adopted a light Southern accent. If she were lucky, they wouldn't notice it hadn't been there a second ago. If these truly were ex-Union-soldiers, distracting them with sex while irritating them with Southerness ought to do the job quite nicely.

"Now, now, fellas," she sung, slipping deeper into her role. "I'm only here to visit my cousin. Won't be in your way the teensiest bit."

The taller soldier placed his thumb on the rifle's hammer and made a show of cocking it. He didn't say a word.

Calliope continued ambling toward him. She needed to get herself into position next to the jailhouse's four-foot by four-foot paned window.

The shorter soldier, who Calliope realized wasn't that short at all, the other one was just that tall, lowered his rifle and said, "You got a death wish, lady? Man said walk the other way."

With her peripheral vision, Calliope glanced through the enormous, multi-paned window, assessing the situation inside. Within the jailhouse, the redheaded gang leader stood with his back to the window, pistol pointed at a deputy who was failing miserably in his effort to look unafraid. The redhead had three of his men with him; Calliope assumed the rest were in the back, liberating a comrade or two.

Calliope took one more step toward the soldier pointing his Spencer at her. It was a calculated risk. The problem was, sometimes she sucked at math. The soldier fired. Half a second too late, Calliope threw herself sideways. The massive bullet tore through her left shoulder, and her already brittle bones exploded into shrapnel, shredding everything.

Calliope crashed through the window, landing awkwardly on the wooden floor, her mangled shoulder erupting into a ball of fire. Calliope did the only thing she knew to: she swallowed the pain. Then she turned her awkward landing into a roll and came to her feet immediately next to the redheaded gang leader, drawing her Colt Dragoon with her right hand. Her left arm hung limp and lifeless at her side.

"Drop your gun," she said, placing the barrel of her pistol against the redhead's cheek. "Tell your men to do the same."

The young man made a show of raising his hands overhead. Calliope noticed that he didn't actually obey her command, holding his gun with one outstretched hand.

"Darling," said the redhead, "you have no idea what kind of trouble you're sticking your pretty little neck into."

His eyes drifted down her partially unbuttoned blouse, then up to the ugly red scar around her throat.

"Interesting," he said. "I see we both have experience sticking our necks places where they don't belong." With the index finger of his free hand, he lifted the handkerchief tied around his neck and revealed a nearly identical scar. "Mine's special, though. Like nothing you've ever seen."

"Aw cripes, Joey, not again," said one of the soldier cowboys. "I'm not gonna shoot you again."

The redhead—Joey—replied, "What can I tell you? As an infant I was nursed on rattle snake milk. Damn hard to find the nipple on a rattle snake, let me tell you. So you can shoot me, or I can shoot you. I'll be happy either way."

The soldier turned his pistol on Joey, his face an odd mix of trepidation and... something. Something Calliope couldn't identify. Contempt? Not quite. Disdain?

But before she could sort it out, the soldier fired his gun.

Ka-blam!

The soldier's shot hit Joey square in the chest. Blood flowed freely, like moonshine from an overturned jug. Calliope reflexively stepped back. She didn't know what she'd expected, but it sure as hell wasn't this.

In the same moment that Calliope recoiled, Joey staggered back a step or two, his arms spread wide like Christ on a crucifix. The pose seemed mostly deliberate.

As soon as Joey had his feet set, he smiled. "That wasn't altogether unpleasant."

The soldier must have been expecting this because no sooner had the redhead spoken than two more shots rang out in rapid succession.

Blam! Blam!

A second hole appeared in Joey's chest just to the left of the first one. A third followed in almost exactly the same spot. For a moment, Joey simply stood there bleeding. He took a deep breath. Held it. Exhaled. Slowly. Then he turned to face Calliope and pulled open his shirt, displaying the three bullet holes.

And Calliope knew her suspicions about him had been right. About what he was.

He leaned in close, wide-eyed, whispered in her ear, "Wanna know a secret?"

Joey rocked back on his heel and looked her in the eye before continuing in a conspiratorial whisper. "Hurts like hell, but I can't let the boys see. Gotta keep up impressions, you know? Important thing here is that it won't kill me the way it would you or them." He paused, immensely pleased with himself. "The way that shoulder of yours is bleeding, you'll be lucky to survive the night. But me? A few days from now I'll have three scars and a great tale to tell while we're drinking tequila around the campfire."

No, there could be no doubt. This eighteen-year old menace had been hung from a bone tree. Just like her. *Well, probably not* just *like me,* she mused with a certain amount of bitterness. *He probably hadn't done it voluntarily, in place of his faithless lover.*

Calliope looked at the redhead with disdain. "You are one sick individual to enjoy pain as much as you do. Beyond sick. Deranged."

Joey's eyes grew wide, feigning shock with the over-the-top exaggeration of a circus clown. "How can you say such a terrible thing?"

Calliope frowned. She was liking this clown less and less with each passing minute. "Three bullets? When one would make the point? Even your own man is tired of shooting you. How many times would he have to shoot you without you dying before the novelty wore off?" She shook her head. "Just sick."

"No," Joey said with a smile. "A great diversionary tactic."

He gestured with his eyes to something behind her, and Calliope pivoted just in time to see the butt end of a rifle crash into her forehead.

She dove headfirst into a lake of inky blackness…

Calliope awoke lying on a bunk, locked into one of the jail cells. Her shoulder hurt like hell, but it had been neatly bandaged. Her forehead hurt only slightly less than her shoulder. As brittle as she was, she thought the rifle butt might have actually cracked her skull. She tried to touch her face to see how bad it was, only to discover her wrists and ankles were shackled.

She also noticed a black cowboy locked in the neighboring cell.

The cowboy said, "Joey wasn't sure if you'd bleed out. He'll be happy to see you alive."

"Who the hell are you?" Calliope asked, even as she realized the cowboy was right about how much blood she'd lost. On top of everything else, she was lightheaded and weak. What she needed most now was water.

She could also tell that her shoulder was beginning to knit. Her wounds healed faster because of the bone tree. She was glad the bandage was in place to hide the wound as it healed; that would help avoid questions she'd rather not answer.

She sat up and what little blood remained in her system rushed straight to her head. The inky black lake swirled, trying to reclaim her.

"Who am I?" the cowboy said, grinning and nodding. He had the most beautiful smile. "Just a guy who rode into town at the wrong time. Some other black fella murdered one of the locals, and apparently all black men are guilty of one black man's crimes. So they threw me in here." He paused for a second, then added, "How are you feeling?"

Calliope's instincts told her not to trust him. "You part of the redhead's gang?"

Still grinning, the cowboy shook his head. "Just a black man in the wrong place at the wrong time."

"Then how did you know their leader's name is Joey?"

"Because I heard his men say it. 'Do I really gotta shoot you again, Joey? Don't make me do this, Joey.' I heard it all. Including the gun shot and the breaking window when you first showed up. You seem to be doing well, all things considered. That shoulder healing okay?"

"Heard all that from back here, did you?"

Calliope fished her silver hair comb out of her pocket, shackles clanking. She inhaled deeply, slowly, and cleared her head. Her body hurt like hell, but there was nothing to do but push through.

Cowboy nodded. "I heard everything. Got good ears."

Calliope pulled the left-most tooth out of her hair comb, revealing a tube with a metal tang protruding from the end.

Cowboy made a funny face. "What the devil is that?"

"So you were in your cell the whole time?" Calliope repeated. "Didn't see a thing?"

"No, I told you, I—"

Calliope inserted the end with the tang into her left leg-shackle's keyhole and unlocked it, then the one on the right.

The cowboy stepped back, eyes growing wide.

"So how did you know his hair is red?"

"Whose hair?" the cowboy asked, distracted by the small miracle in Calliope's hand.

Calliope repeated the process on her wrists and was loose.

"Joey's. I asked if you were part of the redhead's gang. If you couldn't see him, how did you know his hair is red?"

The cowboy grinned but hesitated. Only a fraction of a second, but it was one fraction too long.

"I, ah, I assumed. Why would you ask about some flunky? It had to be their leader."

It was a reasonable answer. Without the hesitation...

Calliope put the skeleton key back into its slot in the comb, then pulled out a different tooth, this one from the middle. It was larger than the first and had no tang. Calliope worked it back and forth, trying to pick the lock of her jail cell.

Cowboy sauntered over and put his hands through the bars that separated their cells, leaning his elbows on the cross-section. "That's a hell of a hair piece you got there, young miss."

Calliope's eyes remained focused on the lock. "You know what I love about men," she said. "So many sexist morons. Not all of them, mind you. But enough that sometimes it actually makes things easier." She stopped working the lock long enough to gesture to her silver-plated comb. "They'd never let a man take something like this into a jail cell, but make it shiny and wear it in your hair and men think you're adorable. Morons."

The door's lock was tougher to pick than Calliope expected. She needed a break. She needed a minute to clear her mind.

She also had a theory she wanted to test.

"I made this myself," she said, taking a step toward the cowboy so he could better see her creation. "It's not actually silver, just silver plated. It's something new called titanium. It's lighter and stronger than silver. My father was an inventor. Had all sorts of interesting things in his workshop."

"Did he teach you how to make this gadget?"

Calliope snorted. "Funny." After a second, she added, "He said I was too girly to learn about inventing. My poor little feminine brain would never comprehend it all. But I watched him—how he approached his theories, how he used his tools." She raised the comb, gazing at it as if mesmerized by its sheen. "When he saw this… saw what I had done…"

"Real proud, was he?"

"He beat me for touching his tools and took the comb. I stole it back that same night and ran away. Only seen him once since."

The cowboy shook his head in slow dismay. "When was that?"

"March 24th," she said. "In the Year of Our Lord, Eighteen Hundred and None of Your God Damn Business."

That brought the conversation to a train wreck of a halt—which wasn't the plan at all, but it was okay. The memory had made her angry, leaving her mind unfocused. Diverted.

She hadn't sought this path, but she'd take it. She stalked back to the door and let her fingers work by feel, not trying to guide them, not trying to think. Her fingers had done this often enough that what she needed most was to get out of her own way.

The lock clicked. The door opened. Calliope put the pieces of the hair comb back together, twisted her auburn locks into a loose bun, and used the comb to pin it. The weight on top of her head was comforting. She walked toward the exit.

"Take me with you," pleaded the cowboy.

"I'm tempted," Calliope replied. "You lie real pretty. Not real well, but real pretty."

The cowboy hung his head. For a long, ponderous moment, Calliope wasn't sure he'd try again to convince her to release him.

When he lifted his head, he looked vaguely embarrassed. "I was supposed to be watching Joey's back. When you got the drop on him, he blamed me, so he threw me in this cell the same time he threw you in yours. Sprang the two guys we came to town for and left me to rot."

Calliope's eyebrows drew together. "I came crashing in through the window, and he expects you to anticipate that?"

"Joey don't tolerate excuses. Said he'd be back tomorrow to see if you survived. Something about sacrificing you to a tree. If you're gone and I'm still here, who you think he's gonna sacrifice?"

"Not my problem," Calliope said. "I'd say you've earned that, riding with a man like Joey."

"He's the only one who'll *let* me ride with him," the cowboy said. "You of all people have to know what it's like to be an outsider. To be rejected, never accepted."

"What's that supposed to mean?"

The cowboy locked eyes with her, and his omnipresent grin vanished. His eyes were hard, but his voice softened. "You know exactly what I mean. A woman trying to make it in a man's world. Can't be any easier than a black man trying to make it in the white world. We ain't so different, you and me."

Calliope's heart melted, just a little. She wanted to punch him for making her feel this way. She hated getting emotional.

"You got a name?" she said.

"Thomas Marshburn. They call me Swamp."

Calliope raised an eyebrow as she drew her comb out of her hair and prepared to pick the lock to the cowboy's cell. "Why Swamp?"

"It's like Marsh, only smellier." He pointed behind her. "The key to the door is hanging on the hook, right there on the wall behind you."

Calliope looked over her shoulder. "That would be easier, wouldn't it?"

The cowboy drawled, "Sure 'nuff."

Calliope turned back to the cowboy, key in hand. "Okay then, Thomas, tell me one thing: You willing to help me take down Joey and his gang?"

Cowboy grinned his beautiful grin and nodded. "Sure 'nuff."

That told Calliope everything she needed to know. Thomas Marshburn grinned entirely too much for his own good.

Calliope was relieved to find her gray appaloosa, Fred, right where she'd left him, tied to the hitching post outside the saloon. She dipped her head into the water trough where Fred stood, drinking long and deep. The water was warm, funky, and full of things that would make her stomach churn if she thought too much about it. She pushed those thoughts aside. With all the blood she'd lost, she didn't have much choice. Human blood and bones were what the tree required—and her life and health were irrevocably tied to that of the tree—but water helped heal Calliope's wounds faster. Sometimes she felt like she was turning into a damn tree herself.

The sun was setting, a welcome break from the heat of the day and a small bit of good luck she could add to the luck that her horse hadn't been stolen and that she hadn't had to hunt too far for water. Aside from getting her face smashed in with a rifle butt and her shoulder shot and shattered, she might be the luckiest woman in town.

A jolt of electric pain screamed from the base of her skull, running across her shoulders and down her arms, leaving her hands feeling like they were swarming with fire ants. The tree was still hungry, still unfed.

Calliope wished she had been as lucky with her guns. She'd thoroughly searched the sheriff's office before she and Thomas walked out, hoping to find her Colts and her sawed-off shotgun. But who ever had stripped her of her guns had apparently kept them. That's precisely why she kept secret spares.

But Calliope really liked those Colts, the Peacemaker in particular. Now she was down to twin two-shot Derringers in her boots and the Remington under her skirt. And, of course, the hair comb. It was more tool than weapon, but she had once stabbed a man in the throat with it, so it had a variety of uses.

Calliope climbed the three wooden steps to the porch outside the saloon. "Grab a bite to eat?" She gestured with her head toward the saloon's well-lit interior. "Or we could head out of town. Go someplace quiet where we can build a fire and plan our next move."

Thomas grinned his gorgeous grin. "I could stand some grub."

So Joey and his gang were waiting inside. She'd need to find a way to keep the locals from getting caught in the crossfire.

Inside, she and Thomas took a seat at a small round table near the piano.

"What's worth eating in this place?" Calliope asked the pianist.

"Usually got a pot of stew going in the kitchen," the man replied, eyes never leaving the black and white keys. "That never killed nobody."

"Why don't you go fetch us some," she said, and he skittered away faster than a lizard on a hot rock. She didn't expect to see him again.

Calliope noticed a collection of wooden signs nailed to the wall and chose one to use as a target, selecting a square, white-washed sign with ornamental script that read: *Dr. Scott's Medicine Show.* She had heard of the good doctor, a snake oil salesman traveling the major and minor towns of Utah.

Calliope took off both boots.

"What in the world are you doing?" Thomas asked.

Calliope shook the twin Derringers out of her boots and laid them on the table in front of her, then returned her boots to her feet.

"Practicing."

She picked up one of the over-under Derringers and took aim at the white, wooden sign, squeezing off two quick rounds.

With the first shot, the bar fell silent. With the second, a few folks—including all the whores—got up and left. Whores always knew when trouble was getting ready to rear its head.

Calliope strolled over to the sign to see precisely where her bullets had struck. One had hit within an inch of the 'o' in 'Show,' right where she'd been aiming. But the second was above it, to the right of the 'D' in 'Dr.'

She studied the saloon's patrons. Some of these folks were slow to take a hint; some had no intention of taking one. She returned to her original position at the table, reloaded two more bullets into the Derringer, aimed, and fired again. More people left the saloon.

"I don't miss by much. Know why?"

"Because you're good?"

"Because I practice every goddamn day, rain or shine, light or dark. You think someone just whips out a gun and hits their target because they're naturally gifted?"

Calliope re-inspected the white sign, finding one bullet hole barely to the left of the 'o,' the other one nearly through the center. It had nicked the edge, breaking the line. Technically a bulls-eye, but she'd have been happier if it'd been 100% within.

Calliope turned from the sign and scoped out the cadre men still in the saloon. Lots of customers had left. In fact, aside from the bloody-shouldered bartender—who'd been studiously wiping the same beer mug for five minutes—all of the remaining men sat facing her. About a dozen men, all with hands inside of jackets and underneath tables.

A lot of men who needed to die.

Now that the room had thinned out, she observed that one of those men had her Peacemaker and her Dragoon. It was the ridiculously tall soldier who had shot her outside the jailhouse. She wouldn't have recognized most of Joey's gang, but this guy she remembered. This guy she would kill extra dead.

Still seated at her table, Calliope palmed the second Derringer, removed her hair comb, and re-did her hair into an oversized bun around the Derringer. Then she stood again and scanned the room. The only thing missing was their leader.

She shouted, "Where is he?"

"What are you doing in Blackwater, anyway," demanded a voice from the second-floor balcony. "This is my town. I own it. I eat it. I shit it out any time the mood strikes me." Joey had an arm around one of the saloon's whores.

The wounded bartender called out loudly, "She's a bounty hunter."

"A woman bounty hunter?" said Joey incredulously.

"A woman bounty hunter?" echoed three or four of the others.

The bartender flinched as laughter flitted around the room.

Calliope's body tensed. There it was again, that damn vicious dove, hopping and fluttering from lip to lip, from man to man. She despised it more than words could express. Except this time she couldn't just draw her guns to put people in their place. If she so much as touched a gun, a dozen would instantly be aimed at her. And while she wouldn't die, no matter how many times she was shot, she didn't care to endure that much pain just to prove a point.

Ignoring the pain already flaring in her hips and back and legs and neck, Calliope made a somewhat awkward show of sauntering over to the tall soldier with her Dragoon and Peacemaker. She raised her left leg, planting her foot on the chair next to him and tugging her skirt up toward her knee. The too-tall soldier leaned back to get a better view.

Predictable. He'd get an eye full, all right. Of the business end of her Remington. She would shoot him through his lecherous eyeball and reclaim her Colts before anyone could so much as—

Marshburn jumped from his chair. He shouted, "She's got a gun."

Calliope froze. Raised both hands high in the air.

"No gun," she said, slowly turning to face her accuser.

Thomas aimed a dark finger at her, eyes darting back and forth between Calliope and Joey. "She's got keys in her hairpiece and Derringers inside her boots. I'll bet good money she's got a pistol under that skirt, too."

Calliope turned to face Joey, her black boot sliding off the rickety chair. Pistols emerged from inside of jackets and underneath tables.

Joey looked down from on high, and Calliope realized he had his flunkies arranged in a perfect crescent around her. No chance of getting them to inadvertently shoot each other.

The redhead said, "Nice work, Swamp. Learn anything else useful? Is she bone tree born?"

"Hard to say," answered the black cowboy. "Shoulder appeared to be healing even before I bandaged it, but she seems sluggish and in a lot more pain that I'd have expected. I asked her a couple of times how she felt, but she kept changing the subject."

"You're going to be the first one to die, you know," Calliope said coldly, eyes hard.

"Seriously?" Joey said, gesturing to Swamp. "You thought he was helping you?" He laughed. "Of course you did, sweetheart. He let you catch him in a small lie; that way if you didn't trust him right off, you'd think you had him figured out."

Calliope looked from Thomas to Joey and back to Thomas again.

"No, not him," she said, whipping her hair comb out of her hair and throwing it at the too-tall soldier. "*Him!*"

In a perfect world, the teeth of the comb would have caught the overly tall soldier in the throat and ended him. But Calliope didn't live in a perfect world, and she had never practiced throwing the comb, so while every eye in the room tracked the flight of the shining comb over the soldier's head, she shook out the bun on top of her head and grabbed her second Derringer from its hiding place.

The comb hit the wall, then the floor. It landed with a clank. The soldiers looked at each other and laughed.

When the laughter died down, their attention returned to Calliope to find she'd crossed the floor and put herself directly between Joey's men and Thomas Marshburn.

"Don't shoot," Joey barked. "You'll hit Swamp!"

"You've all seen what I can do with this," Calliope said, pointing her Derringer at Thomas. "Anyone have any doubts I can put a bullet through his forehead from ten paces?"

"It's not loaded," said one of the soldiers. "She emptied her guns shooting at that stupid Medicine Show sign."

Calliope fired once, shooting out the mirror over the bar to prove him wrong, hoping she didn't come to regret spending the bullet. "You saw exactly what I wanted you to. Any more stupid questions?"

Calliope gazed at Thomas with contempt. "You have to be the worst poker player I ever met. Are you aware that you grin like an idiot every time you lie? It's a beautiful smile, but it gives you away like the sunrise at the beginning of a new day. Stunning, but impossible to miss."

She cocked the Derringer a second time.

"Please," Thomas said. "What I said about being an outsider. About you and me fighting similar battles. I told you the truth."

Damn it, damn it, damn it. Damn it. That was probably the *only* thing he had said that was true. Her heart softened, so she punched him in the face. Thomas went down and had the sense to stay there.

Calliope remembered she needed him as a human shield and yanked upright again.

"I'll give you one thing, sweetheart," Joey said. "You managed to do something no one has ever done before: you surprised me. Let me see if I can return the favor. I got someone that I hear you been looking for."

Joey strode to the edge of the balcony and gestured to one of his men. "He look familiar?"

Calliope followed his gaze to… yes, yes he did. It was the outlaw from her wanted poster: Dan Hatcher.

"How about him, over there?" Joey pointed to a second man, behind and to the left of the first. Another Dan Hatcher.

Two of them?

"Twins," Joey said gleefully.

That explained why the locals thought he was everywhere.

Joey continued. "I don't need them both. I'll trade you one Hatcher—worth $1,000 dollars, from what I hear—for my man, there, Swamp. You take your pick: whichever one you'd like."

"But boss—" One of the Hatcher twins stepped forward.

"Shut up, Danny boy," barked Joey. "No one's talking to you."

"I'm Dan," said the other. "He's Stan."

Joey spread his arms and shrugged. "You see? I can't tell them apart. They even *smell* the same to me. You'll be doing me a favor taking one of 'em off my hands."

Calliope placed the barrel of her Derringer just below Thomas's ear. "If you like this asshole so much, I think I'll hold on to him, thanks."

Joey stopped smiling. "A Mexican stand-off? Really? Those are *always* fun."

"You have a strange idea of fun."

Joey stood up straight and tall, spreading his arms wide. "I need somebody to shoot me! I haven't been shot in hours."

Calliope wasn't falling for that again.

"Come on, damn you," Joey screamed, spittle flying from his lips. "Somebody shoot me!"

The boy was insane.

Or was he? Was that what he *wanted* her to think?

Screw this. She was playing chess with a lunatic and she didn't even like chess. To make matters worse, she was playing his game his way. If she wanted a different outcome, she'd have to play by different rules. Hell, she'd have to play an entirely different game.

She sighed, accepting the inevitable. With this many guns and this much testosterone, did she really think she was getting out of here without a gun fight?

At least she still had that metaphorical ace up her sleeve. And she didn't need to kill Joey, which was lucky, since she couldn't kill him anymore than he could kill her. The only way to truly kill someone who'd been hung from a bone tree was to kill their bone tree, and she had no idea where Joey's tree was. She assumed he kept it a closely guarded secret, just like she guarded the location of her own. No, right now Calliope just needed to slow him down. Cut his legs out from under him.

It was a calculated risk. This time she paused and did the math in her head, just in case.

Twelve bullets in her two Colts, assuming they were fully loaded. That seemed like a safe assumption. Plus one in her Derringer.

She wasn't going to waste a bullet on Joey, and she didn't think she'd need to shoot Thomas. He was a liar, but he seemed otherwise harmless.

That meant she had thirteen bullets for twelve men. One to spare. Good thing she had a literal ace up her skirt to go along with the metaphorical one up her sleeve.

She shoved Swamp to one side and strode toward the absurdly tall soldier, shooting him in the throat with the last bullet in her Derringer. His neck exploded in a spray of blood. The whole plan hinged on that one shot; without it, she was screwed. With it, she at least stood a chance.

She continued straight for her Colts even as the rest of the gang opened fire. The room was instantly transformed into a smoke-filled, high-pitched killing zone as guns blazed and ear drums screamed. She could see little and hear even less. And the odor was biting and caustic; she could taste the gunpowder on the edges of her tongue.

She threw the empty Derringer at one of the Hatchers to make him duck, make him stop shooting for a second. A bullet caught her in the bicep of her throwing arm. She counted her blessings that it only tore muscle and didn't shatter bone.

A second bullet hit her in the side, shattering a rib. Her vision momentarily whited out from the pain, but it passed as quickly as it came. Calliope knelt and retrieved her Colts, testing their heft. She could tell by their weight that both were fully loaded, so she cocked the Dragoon and shot whichever Hatcher she'd thrown her Derringer at.

No sooner had Hatcher number one fallen than she saw a muzzle flash through the smoke and fired toward it. No more flashes followed, and she assumed she'd hit her target.

The smoke grew thicker. Calliope headed where she thought she remembered seeing Hatcher number two. She was almost on top of him when they simultaneously spotted each other. Both fired into each other's chests, and only Calliope stood afterward.

Calliope was going into shock; her body ceased feeling pain. It would catch up with her again later, much worse. But that was a problem for later. Right now she had four down and seven to go.

Two men came at her as she stood over the second Hatcher. She raised both guns and shot both men. One of them managed to shoot the Dragoon out of her hand before dying, but it landed at her feet and she grabbed it again and moved on.

The smoke came to life then, snaking on its own. For a moment she wondered what strange magic was afoot. Then she noticed a breeze playing with her hair. Her ears were ringing too much to have heard it, but stray bullets must have shot out the saloon's windows. As the breeze shifted the smoke, visibility cleared enough to spot someone coming up on her left. She shot him in the throat, too. She liked throat shots; if the bullet went high, it hit the head; low, it hit the chest.

She got lucky again when someone shot her in the right wrist. Bones shattered and her hand dangled at an impossible angle, barely attached by a few tendons. But the hand that was nearly shot off was the one holding her Dragoon. She'd fired five of its six bullets, so losing it only cost her one. She still had five bullets in her Peacemaker, and the Peacemaker was in her good hand.

She had *all* the luck.

The last four men rushed at her together, thinking she couldn't kill them all before they got to her. Calliope proved them wrong, but not before getting shot five more times herself.

Her body was still in shock, so she only registered the general impact of the bullets, not where she'd been hit. She just knew her body twitched repeatedly like an epileptic marionette.

Calliope dropped to one knee when another man came at her, surprising her, messing up her math. It wasn't Joey and it wasn't Swamp. She must have missed when she shot at the muzzle-flash in the smoke. Luckily, she had that last bullet.

She fired true this time. She wobbled. Her head swam.

Smoke began to clear, and Joey's voice came out of the darkness. From somewhere in the room, he shouted, "Damn, woman. You're good."

But Calliope couldn't tell where he was; her ears were ringing too much to pinpoint him. She fell to her side, still in shock. The pain hadn't caught up with her yet, but she'd lost so much blood that her body was struggling to function at all.

Is this it? she wondered. *Do I lay here in a room full of men I killed, not able to feed a single one of them to that stupid fucking tree?*

Thomas appeared in front of her, pistol in hand.

"Get out here, Joey," he shouted. At this point if you were alive, you were shouting. Everyone's ear drums were blown. Calliope laughed, which hurt like hell.

"I *am* here," Joey shouted, appearing out of the smoke. "What are you gonna do?"

Thomas smiled. "Same thing we talked about before. The experiments I planned for back in the jail. Never thought she'd escape so damn fast."

Calliope looked at Thomas, puzzled. Her hearing cleared a little.

"Be careful," Joey half-yelled. "She's shot up pretty good, but she's still got her gun."

"She's out of bullets. I counted."

Thomas glanced around the room, surveying the carnage. "You've messed things up for us quite thoroughly, young miss. The boy has amazing abilities, true, but he's still just a boy. I guide him and steer him, but sometimes we need other men. Now I'm going to have to start all over, build a whole new gang. You have no idea how much time and effort it took to get them to follow Joey without realizing he was taking orders from me."

Calliope stared at him, hoping he could feel her hate.

"At least I still have you," Thomas said, finding his silver lining. "I've always wanted to know how much punishment the boy's body could withstand. Test his limits. But I've been afraid to push him too far too fast."

"What the hell are you talking about?" Calliope said thinly, afraid she already knew the answer. She gasped for air like a trout tossed on the bank of a river.

Thomas smiled. "For every person who enjoys experiencing pain, there needs to be someone who equally enjoys inflicting it. Otherwise the pain has no meaning. I need to know what Joey's limits are if I'm ever going to unlock his full potential."

Thomas pointed his gun at Calliope's midsection and fired all six bullets, shredding her abdomen. Smoke curled around the muzzle of his pistol. His lips were moving, but Calliope heard none of it. She did, however, feel every single bit of it. The shock had worn off—or been blown away by the barrage of bullets—and the pain was indescribable. She realized she was screaming and had been screaming for as long as Thomas had been shooting, unable to hear her own screams but feeling every fiery shred of it because she suddenly felt *everything*, screaming until her throat was raw. Thrashing on the floor, she felt absolutely everything.

Including the Remington holstered just above her knee.

In the chaos and carnage, she'd forgotten about the Remington. She focused her mind on it, focused all of her rage on it, and reached down and jerked the weapon from beneath her skirt. She wanted to tell Thomas to fuck off before she killed him, but she knew his ears were ringing as much as hers.

Screw it, she decided, and said it anyway.

"You know what, *Swamp*. It's not about black or white. It's not about male or female. It's about honor, and you have none whatsoever."

Then she fired five bullets straight up into the surprised-looking man looming over her. Five bullets might have been overkill, but she was pissed. That was an emotion she could embrace.

Thomas fell down dead.

He would never get up again.

Joey screamed, his face twisted in rage. Calliope fired her last bullet into that twisted face, right into the bridge of his nose, blowing out the back of his skull. He might like pain, but she doubted he'd like that very much.

He fell to the ground.

Unlike Thomas, eventually Joey would get back up again. But not any time soon. From the way he twitched like a bolt of lightning was coursing through his body, she didn't think he'd be getting up again for a very long time. She'd never seen a body react that way. But then she'd never shot a man in the face who'd been hung from a bone tree either.

Calliope lay on the ground, in unbelievable pain but feeling immensely pleased with herself. She'd accomplished far more than she'd set out to. Not only had she cut the legs out from under Joey, but she had destroyed the brains of his operation. Turned out Joey was no chess master; he was just a lunatic who had a lot of trouble dying. She wondered if he'd been driven insane by too much pain or if he'd simply snapped when he woke up dead at the end of a noose.

Either way, with a bullet in his face and no Thomas pulling his strings, Joey was unlikely to pose much of a threat to anyone for a very, *very* long time.

Now Calliope just needed a little time herself—to get accustomed to the new level of pain—and then she'd drag her sorry ass outside to that water trough. As nasty as that water was, a deep, long drink would help a whole lot. Then she'd drain all of these soldiers' blood and grind their bones so she could feed her tree.

But she'd get there, eventually. She'd swallow the pain, like she always did, and she would do what needed doing. Like she always did.

Once she got that tree fed and watered, she'd be right as rain. Nice clean rain, as opposed to the sludge she knew waited for her in the horse trough.

On the other hand, she did have two Hatchers. She'd collect the bounty on one Hatcher in one town, and then again in another town with the other one. It would be months before anyone noticed.

She was one hell of a lucky bone tree bounty hunter.

She just needed to lay here for a while and hurt. Then she'd get to work. But for a minute, for one sky-blue minute, she'd just lie here and rest, watching the smoke swirling overhead.

And as she did, a little voice in the back of her head spoke up, wondering what the hell ever happened to her sawed-off shotgun…

CARDS AND STEEL HEARTS

Pamela Jeffs

IT'S HARD GOING, THIS MIDDAY FLIGHT ACROSS THE YELLOW, WINDSWEPT prairie. My throat is dry and my fingers are seized on my horse's reins. I'm exposed out here, but I can't afford to stop. The Hawk Riders are hunting for me—the ones who killed my parents and my tribe because they wanted what was not theirs to own. I can still feel the warmth of my mother's blood leaking through my fingers, still see the image of my father lying face down in the dirt. I want my revenge, but right now something greater is at stake. I need to get to the Allies, cousins to my mother's people. They will protect me—and the treasure I carry.

Kohana's stride is even beneath me until it is suddenly not. He falters, and next thing I know, I am laid out flat on my back. I get to my feet, brushing dirt and grass from my buckskin dress and leggings. I wince. My palms are stinging, grazed where they caught a thorn bush on the way down. I flick my hands, the pain eases. I walk over to Kohana.

He's expired.

His body lays stretched out as if he is still running. Front legs straight, rear bent, and his nose pointed into the wind. The breeze catches the black and white feathers entwined in his mane. I curse at the luck fate has handed me.

My bone-handled knife slips easily from my belt. I kneel down and dig the point of it into the muscle crease of Kohana's chest. Pushing down, his blood wells thickly around the blade. It drips onto the grass, looking more black than red. The knife then slides deeper, and in slicing down, I am rewarded with a metallic *clink*. The blade has found what I am searching for—Kohana's heart. I pull the knife free and push my fist into the wound. My fingers extend and burrow into the warm flesh. I feel the smooth metal orb, and I pull it free.

I turn it over in my hand. Seeing it makes my grief surge again. Here, I hold my parents' legacy: their hopes and dreams for an Indian nation not ruled by white men. It is a weapon, this steel heart. A weapon my father designed for the people even though he was not born of them. He used the technology of his own people, those who live amongst the stars, to build the metal heart. But I can see the stamp of my mother's artistry in the balanced lines of the steel.

Always my parents had worked as a team—my mother the artist, my father the inventor. Their combined efforts were a celebration of art and life.

I look for the display of digital numbers I know to be on the underside of the orb. They are there, glimmering green beneath the streaks of Kohana's blood. Four zeros. I, of all people, should have known better. I should never have let his time wind down. If only the attack on my camp had not been so swift, and I not so hard-pressed to escape, I would have remembered to press the small button beneath his chin to reset his heart.

A keening cry from above draws my attention to the skies. Black pinpricks mar the stretch of watercolor blue. Hawk Riders. No time to lose. I reach into the leather satchel slung over my shoulder. Spare arrowheads clink against my firestones. My fingers travel over the prairie turnips and packets of pemmican I had grabbed during my hurried escape. They finally fall on the buffalo hide string-tie bag in the bottom. I pull it out.

I place Kohana's heart on the ground and loosen the string. I tip the bag over and a small wooden box falls out. It is made from a strange white timber, not of this world my mother once told me. The design is simple, low in height with a sliding lid. On top, the image of a star is burnt into the timber. My father's mark, He Who Came from the Stars. I open it and reveal a small stack of thin leather cards, an image painted on the face of each one. Coyote. Wolf. Buffalo. I shuffle through them, searching for the one that will help me most now. Finally, I find it. She who is the Bald Eagle named Kimimela.

I wipe my sleeve across the steel heart. Kohana's blood smears away to reveal the card slot pressed into the metal. Next to it are two small buttons. One green, one red. I, myself, have only ever had occasion to press the green one. I press it now and then flip the card in my hand over and slide it in. Kimimela's painted eagle eye seems to wink at me before disappearing into the orb.

There is a click and a whir. Next to me, Kohana's body begins to fold in upon itself. His legs double back, his head neatly flattens and his barrel chest disappears. Soon he is a leather card with a picture of a horse drawn on the front. I pick him up and put him back into the box.

The steel heart in my hand begins to shudder. The digital numbers on the side begin to flip, faster than my eye can register. They stop at 9999— as many minutes as to last for seven days. Then an alarm sounds, a low, continuous note. I drop the heart and scuttle to one side. A bright light flashes, and Kimimela burgeons into existence.

She is larger than a real eagle, large enough to carry me on her back. She shakes the impossible length of her bronze wings, unfurling them like draping sheets of canvas. Her bright eagle eyes catch mine. "Wichahpi," she says, naming me. "Star Girl. Time to fly."

I climb up her side and seat myself between her wings. Her back is broader than a mustang's, and I feel the difference in the stretch of my leg muscles. I lock my arms around her glistening white-feathered neck. She calls out a long, piercing cry, and then we are airborne.

The rush of air is deafening, loud and electric all at the same time. The ground falls away beneath us, expanding to reveal the far-reaching prairie that ripples like a golden sea from horizon to horizon.

In the distance, the serpentine sweep of river marks the border of my people's lands. Beyond it, gray smoke rises gently against the sky—there lie the tribal camps of our cousins.

Not far now.

But, suddenly Kimimela veers right. My legs tighten around her to keep my seat. A dark brown shadow edged with razor claws sweeps by in a gust of air. I see the outline of a man's back sitting upon it. I glance around.

Hawk Riders. Five of them.

Kimimela's cry is a shriek of fury. She banks left as two hawks bear down on her flank. She spins in the air, her claws raking down the side of one. Blood sprays across the blue backdrop of sky, and the hawk crumples. The man on her back cries out before falling to his death.

Another hawk swoops by. This time I hear the laughter of the rider on her back. A whip hangs loose in his hand. His wrist twitches, and the end of it curls around Kimimela's foot. Her wings falter as she is jerked violently sideways. My hands slip from her neck, and I am suddenly dangling precariously by my legs. I grasp the knuckle joint of her wing and pull myself up. She cries out, and I understand her predicament. With me on her back, her fighting prowess is crippled. I do not begrudge her decision as she twists her way out of the whip and then dips out of the sky. This fight will be better fought on the ground.

Her claws clutch up loose grass and clumps of earth as she lands. I slide off her, feet first, reaching back for my tomahawk as I do. Its weight is comforting in my hand. Kimimela turns and curls her body around me, standing guard at my back. I smell her sweat, a mixture of warm feathers and sun-heated skin. I watch as the four remaining Hawk Riders land in a circle around us.

Their hawks are huge, easily twice the size of Kimimela. Their fierce eyes are black pools ringed with gold. They jostle on their clawed feet, their leather and iron harnesses jangle.

The riders dismount. They are white men, dressed in the leather boots, chaps, and wide-brimmed hats typical of the outlaw gunslingers that terrorize the skies. The one with the whip now carries it coiled at his side; the others have guns slung low on their hips. I recognize these men. My gut begins to roil. They are the ones who attacked my camp.

"Well, looky here, Boss," says the man with the whip. "It's the lil' Indian girl we been looking for."

I understand the white men's words; my father taught me well. And I don't like the man's tone. I don't like that he called me little. I am fifteen summers old. Old enough to hunt buffalo with my father, old enough to kill a man. I shift my grip on my tomahawk. Kimimela shuffles behind me. The prairie is silent around us except for the chirruping of grasshoppers.

One of the gunslingers, the tallest one with the dark beard takes a step closer. His gaze falls on Kimimela. "That's not a natural beastie you got there, girlie. Definitely got to have a steel heart, I'd say."

The other men begin to mutter and shift. I can see the greed in their eyes, their eagerness to possess the heart, and perhaps to possess me. I will not let that happen.

The leader smiles; his teeth are yellow and broken. "Hand it over."

"Come and get it," I reply.

My words are followed by the sharp crack of the whip. I feel the lick of plaited leather fall across my forearm. It slithers away just as fast, leaving in its place a line of blood. I turn toward the man holding the whip. His leering grin is no more attractive than the leader's. All of a sudden I am acutely aware of the sun's heat on my forehead, the hot, dry prairie breeze in my nostrils. Of Kimimela, and my mother's cousins too far away to help me now.

I lunge toward the whip man and, before he can blink, my tomahawk has split his skull. It cracks like a melon, the features of his face lost in a sheet of hot blood. Kimimela is attacking the next man, but he is fast. His gun is clear of its holster, but his grip on it is uncertain. The weapon tumbles into the grass. He ducks to retrieve it. I have no time to see what happens next.

The leader grabs me from behind. I let my joints go slack, and I slither free of his grip. I turn and swipe at him with my tomahawk, but he dodges to the side. I follow and suddenly find myself looking down the barrel of his gun.

"Get up," he growls. "And lose the tomahawk."

I do, letting my weapon slide to the ground. I glance about. The fight is over before it has started. Kimimela is captured. Her bright head is held beneath the talons of one of the hawks, pushed hard into the trampled earth. Her wings are spread out awkwardly across the grass, their surface tattered and marred with streaks of blood. She calls out to me, and I feel as if I have failed her.

I look back at the leader. His weathered face is stern. The gun he holds has not moved. "Get me the heart," he says.

I nod and tip my chin over to Kimimela. "I will need to go to her."

The leader nods and moves to position himself behind me. His gun stays aimed on me, but is now pointed at the back of my skull. "Walk," he says. "And no funny business."

My heart breaks when I get to Kimimela. I kneel by her side. Her eagle eye swivels up to meet mine. Its brightness captures the light of the sun overhead. The hawk's talons have torn at the flesh on her face and neck. Her lush feathers are coated in her black-red blood. I place my hand on her shoulder, wishing I could somehow warn her of what is about to come.

"Now." The leader shoves the barrel of his gun hard against my skull.

My head jerks forward, making my teeth clatter. I turn and glare at him. "My knife."

He tips his chin up in consent. I reach down and close my fingers over the bone hilt. I lift it. Kimimela's eye follows the line of the blade as it crosses her field of view. Her gaze snaps back to mine. Now, she understands.

I place my free hand on her polished beak. She blinks, and then keens a soft cry. "Fly free," I whisper.

Her end is not painless, but it is quick. I draw the blade across her neck. The pupil of her eye widens, her back arches, her claws scrabble at the earth, and then she falls still.

There is a moment of silence, but then I feel the press of the gun barrel again. The leader's voice is harsh. "The heart," he says. "Now."

I don't bother looking at him. Instead, I pull aside Kimimela's lax wing and plunge my knife into her feathered chest. The blade crunches past her breastbone and into her body cavity. I feel the warm rush of her blood coat my hand. I push deeper. The metallic *clink* follows. I remove the knife and push my fist into the opening. Kimimela's heart is closer to the surface than Kohana's was. I pull it free with a slurping sound.

I lift the gruesome prize, holding it high for the men to see. My fist, arm, and the heart are coated in dark blood. I smell the iron in it and hear the buzzing of the flies already gathering to drink.

The leader reaches around and takes the heart from my hand. His skin is rough against my fingers. He wipes at the blood. The heart emerges, colored in patches of silver and red. "We got our prize, boys!" he says.

His grin is filled with triumph.

His attention is not on me.

Stupid man.

I flip the bloodied blade in my hand. Next thing, it is buried in his throat.

His cry is short and sharp, quickly fading to a gurgle as he falls to his knees. He is dead in moments. As his grip weakens, the heart tumbles from one hand, and his gun slips from the other. I scrabble to get the weapon, but a gunshot from one of the other men sends it skipping away from me. Instead, I reach for and succeed in retrieving the heart. I twist on my heel and get to my feet. I stop, looking at the remaining two men. One is wearing a red bandana, the other a faded yellow one. Both have their guns aimed at my heart. Yellow Bandana has his gaze leveled at my breasts.

"That's a mighty silly thing you've gone and did," says Red Bandana. He is younger than the other man, but seems to hold the authority.

"Let me at her. I'll teach her a lesson," says Yellow Bandana.

A look of disgust crosses Red Bandana's face. I can see he doesn't like the other man. "Give me the heart, girl," he says. "Show me how to use it, and I'll let you live."

He will let me live? I almost laugh out loud. "Come closer then," I say.

Red Bandana moves cautiously. He reminds me of a coyote—sly, wary and clever. In moments, he is standing before me, his gun still held steady. Up close, he is handsome for a gunslinger with his smooth, clean skin and neat, well-tended clothes.

"Show me," he says.

I turn the heart over in my hand. The green numbers are flipping over. 8199...8198...8197... My thumb traces the line of the card slot and brushes over the green and red buttons.

The red button.

The answer to my problems.

"Put the card in the slot," I say. "Press the red button."

"Card?" asks Red Bandana.

I pull the wooden box out from the satchel still slung across my chest. I open the lid. The Coyote card tops the deck. A good omen, he is the trickster. I pick him up. "A card like this."

"So you slot in the card and press the button?"

"Yes. The red one. The green one will destroy the heart."

The man nods. "And when you want the heart back, you kill the beastie and cut it out?"

His lack of humanity disgusts me. "Yes."

"And where do yon cards come from? How can I get more?"

I am inspired by the Coyote's trickster nature. "Make them. Leather and paint. Easy to do." The idea is not so far from the truth, but enough for it to be a lie.

Red Bandana smiles, and with that simple gesture, I understand he does not intend to keep his word. Given the information, I suppose he feels he has no reason to.

He moves quicker than I expect, does not even hesitate as he pulls the trigger. I hear his gun fire, see the smoke bloom out of his gun barrel, and then I feel the searing bullet tear though my chest.

I feel it hit my heart.

I hear the metallic sounding *clink*.

The bullet stops dead.

I look down at my chest. Blood, more black than red, stains the front of my dress. I look back up at Red Bandana. He looks confused. It's my turn to smile. "Not all creatures with steel hearts are obvious," I say.

Then, I press the red button.

It is the first time the weapon has ever been used against humans. My father had planned to do it next summer—to go and stand at the center of the gunslinger's town and use the heart to make the place fold. But his untimely death saw the chance taken from him. Time to even the score. I take a breath and brace myself.

The heart's alarm sounds. I place it on the ground and step back. The sound grows increasing louder. Stupidly, Red Bandana reaches down and snatches it up.

Then—the alarm stops.

A flash of light, brighter than the sun overhead, suddenly illuminates the prairie. My smile widens as I stand in the blaze, protected from what is happening by virtue of the steel heart that beats in my chest—the heart my parents made for me, so they could have a child when nature failed them in that quest.

The light fades. Red Bandana stands frozen. His eyes move wildly, but he has no control over his body. Slowly, he begins to flatten. His arms fold in on himself, his face becomes flat. I can see he wants to scream, but it is too late for that. Behind him, Yellow Bandana suddenly falls sideways. He too begins to flatten, arms, legs, and torso losing dimension. Kimimela's body follows, as do the four hawks, all jerking as they try to fight the process.

Soon, I am standing alone on the prairie. Scattered on the grass are nine leather cards, an image painted on each one. One is Kimimela, her eagle eye winking at me. Four hold pictures of hawks, and the other four, images of white men—one holding a coiled whip, another sporting a dark beard. One wears a red bandana, the other a yellow.

I reach down and pick up Kimimela's heart. It is one of only two that exist, the twin being the one in my chest. Both are weapons that can create life as easily as they can take it away. I reach up and press the button beneath my chin. The steel heart in my chest resets. I bend down and begin to collect the cards lying on the grass. The ones of the men will help to light my fire tonight. But the hawks I will keep. Once re-trained, they will prove useful.

My thoughts turn to the Allies—of how I will join them, and together rid the lands of all white men. I will finish what my parents started. I place the cards in the box, holding back the one of Kimimela. I slip it into the steel heart and watch as she burgeons into life.

BLOODSILVER

A.E. Decker

THE BAY'S SIDES RIPPLED WITH ONLY A SLIGHT SIGH OF PROTEST AS RIDER Bell flung her tooled leather saddle over his back. "Good boy." She gave him a pat before leading him out of Myer's Livery Stable and into the dusty yellow expanse of Sutton Street. A notion struck her as she was hitching him to the post beside the watering trough in front of her house.

"S'pose I'd better wake up Dead Guy, huh?" she said, stroking The Bay's nose. "He'll want to know where we're headin'."

The livemetal disk flashed in the sunlight as she hauled it out of her shirt by its leather cord. Her fingers tingled; the disk was always cool to the touch, even on days her spit evaporated before it hit the ground. Rider nicked her thumb on her knife, squeezed out a bead of blood, and swirled it over the disk. The shiny surface absorbed the red wetness like dry sand sucking up the drippings from a canteen. She never had to wipe it clean.

Dead Guy didn't always show himself the same way. Sometimes he rose up out of her shadow or spun himself into existence from a passing gust of wind. None of that today: a mad hot day with a glaringly blue sky, not a breeze stirring. Today he just appeared: blink, and there he was, resting his long forearms against The Bay's saddle.

"What's up, Rider?" he asked, his black hair ever-whipping in a gale that blew solely for him. One eye glowed like a thundercloud before the lightning forked down; a crescent scar sealed the other. Black hat and black boots and black trousers. Black shirt, a laced-up red vest only a couple shades off black, and a long black duster. Brown gloves, though. Rider often wondered if that was an oversight or Dead Guy's strange brand of humor.

He'd had a name when he was alive, but Rider never used it.

"Rumors of Skeleton Dancers at Bondee Camp," she told him.

Molly Bindle sashayed down the wooden sidewalk wearing a new hat. Whoops of laughter erupted inside the Hellbell Saloon as Abe Jabbot and Darly Firth burst through the swinging door. They staggered across Sutton, kicking up dust, smug as a pair of tomcats. Probably just spent the night wasting all the earnings from their arcsilver mine on faro, whiskey, and ladies of negotiable virtue.

Dead Guy rubbed his chin. "Where'd you hear this?"

"Miles Bronson."

Snorting, he rolled away from her, lounging against The Bay's side. "Miles Bronson is a son of a bitch," he said to the sky.

"I ain't arguing with you," said Rider. Everyone in Camlock had seen Mrs. Bronson with an eye all swollen up like a plum behind its mask of powder.

"Miles Bronson would steal the last tooth from his granny's gums to turn a profit."

"I still ain't arguing with you." Rider worked the pump. The first trickle of rusty brown coughed out. She pumped it clear then held her canteen under the spigot's mouth.

"Miles Bronson—"

"Bronson got no reason to come crying to me without cause," said Rider. He'd wept right there in her parlor, tears cutting slug-tracks through the layers of dust caked into his pores. "He knows I don't look kindly on him."

"There is that," admitted Dead Guy.

"And why make up something unlikely as the Dancers leaving Rattling Sky Mountain?" Canteen filled, she hefted her saddlebag, already loaded with biscuits and jerky. "It's a Shadowmarshal's duty to investigate supernatural doings." He wouldn't miss the emphasis on "duty." Nor would he forget that every self-important male in Camlock ached to see her slip up and neglect it.

No reply. She glanced over at him. Dead Guy was still observing the sky, arms folded over his chest. "Ain't you gonna call up Dead Horse?" she asked.

That wrung a wince out of him. "His name," said Dead Guy, "is Huntsman. Why can't you ever remember?"

She snorted. "Why bother? It's not like it's gonna answer when I call."

"I'd find your logic unassailable if you'd ever tried calling him."

"Pah." She clomped up her porch steps, stepped into her house, and took her Arbiter down from its rack over the door. Her seven-chambered Lucky Cat already rested in its hip holster, loaded with dewdrops—arcsilver bullets. Neither dewdrops nor regular bullets would bring down a Skeleton Dancer. If they got nasty, she'd have to rely on the flaked obsidian knife in her boot, and even more on Dead Guy, to bring her out alive. But skreekers haunted the plains: spiteful wisps of things long dead, clinging to existence through sheer hatred of the living. Those arcsilver could banish.

She emerged blinking into the sunlight, giving her door a little push to be sure the latch caught. At the base of the porch steps, Dead Guy sat atop Dead Horse. Thin tendrils of mist rose from Dead Horse's hooves as it stood, patient as a chunk of steel-gray rock. The Bay kept a body's breadth of distance between them, but at least didn't seem inclined to kick up a fuss beyond what was fitting for a gelding of sixteen years. Nodding approval, Rider slung the Arbiter over her back and mounted.

"Let's ride," she said.

Rider recalled the desert full of life. As a girl, she'd spent hours catching skittery purple lizards with yellow streaks painted down their backbones, but she saw fewer of them these days. The cactus owls, round handfuls of chalk-and-tobacco-colored feathers, came less and less often to the area around Camlock and she hadn't heard a whooping kite give its *ooweeoo* cry overhead since she'd grown to be a woman. She wasn't so old, not even three double-handfuls of years, that things should've changed so bad in her lifetime.

"There was a whole carpet of redbird brush down in that gulch last year," she noted. "Now look at it. Just raggedy shreds."

"Yep," said Dead Guy.

"You could at least turn your head, being how it's on your blind side."

"I saw it as we rode up."

"Well, here I was thinking it would interest you a little more." She folded a leg to rest on the saddle afore her. "What could kill off a whole patch of redbird brush in a year? Stuff grows like bristles on a hog's back."

"There's death in the desert," Dead Guy replied.

"Hm." Rider drummed her fingers on her saddle, watching as he rode past, hair whipping in his private gale. "If it comes to choosin', the world belongs to the living."

"You think?"

"Sorry, partner. That's just how it is."

Midday came. The sky rained down heat, and the cracked ochre earth radiated it all back upward, hot as a baked stone. White foam mottled The Bay's flanks. Rider took off her hat to mop her brow, her eyes squinting up tight as babies' fists under the sun's remorseless glare. Ahead, a tangle of mesquite cast a patchwork shadow over the dusty ground. "Let's stop," she called to Dead Guy.

Leisurely, he turned Dead Horse around, circling to her side. "Need a breather?"

Rider scowled, particularly at Dead Horse, still sleek and unwearied. "Maybe you and that spook-horse can go on without a break, but us flesh-folk ain't so lucky."

He held up a hand. "Just teasing."

"Pah." She'd have wagered her boots he didn't enjoy the heat any more than she did. He didn't show it in sweat the way she did, but the sun's rays seemed to pass right through him, thinning him down like watered soup. She turned The Bay toward the patch of shade, and he pricked up his ears and picked up his pace. But, fifty paces from the stand of trees, his hooves inexplicably slowed. His nostrils flared.

"What's up, buddy?" Rider leaned forward to rub his shoulder, all the while keeping a wary eye out. It wasn't like The Bay to dally when he knew a rest was in store.

No animals. No tracks. Only a hawk hanging black and seemingly motionless in the blue expanse of the sky. The Bay wouldn't spook at a hawk—a desert guinea, yes, but she'd hear their throaty chirps gurgling out of the mesquite branches if any were perched up there.

The mesquites. Rider stood in her stirrups, craning her neck for a better look. "Their leaves look awful brown."

Dead Guy's mouth tightened. Hooking the reins over his saddle horn, he dismounted. After a moment, Rider followed suit. Grit crunched under their boots, crunched under The Bay's hooves as he tossed his head and stamped, a sad contrast to the stoic Dead Horse.

"Easy," Rider soothed. She cast another glance around the clearing, shook her head. "Don't see nothing, but I'll check the scry-crystal, just in—"

An icy jolt shot through the vein pulsing at the back of her knee, right above the top of her boot. Her thigh muscles knotted into one giant cramp as a dead-woodchuck stink filled her nostrils.

"Son of a bitch!" She staggered as a clammy hand with many thin, flexible fingers wrapped up her leg and began levering itself out of the sand.

"My baby," grated a voice. "They smashed his head against the wall. Help! My baby!" A distorted woman-shape pulled itself out of the ground, its face horribly elongated, jaw rattling against its breastbone, eyes pulsing out of their sockets.

Skinning her Lucky Cat, Rider sighted along the barrel. But beside her, The Bay reared. Forgetting his sixteen years, his lack of stones, and that stiff hind leg he played up when he felt lazy, he knocked her flat and bolted off across the path they'd already cut through the desert.

"Shi—" cried Rider, getting a mouthful of sand for her trouble.

Dead Guy flexed his hand. A trickle of liquid metal flowed out of his sleeve, coated his wrist, engulfed his fingers, poured itself into the shape of a gleaming blade. One swift downward jab skewered the skreeker. It gargled once, like a handful of pebbles swilling around inside a tin can filled with spit, then flashed in on itself and vanished.

Rider shoved off against the ground, swatting sand from her trousers. "I musta taken shelter by these mesquite near a hundred times. Never seen a skreeker here before." She dug in her pocket, brought out a quartz crystal, two inches long. Its tip glowed yellow. She jabbed it into the sand where the skreeker had appeared, and something like a rotted tater with a huge wailing mouth and two bulbous eyes maggot-wriggled up out of the ground. She shot it.

"That was the baby," said Dead Guy as it imploded. His livemetal blade flowed back up his sleeve.

"Was." Rider chambered a new shot, holstered the Cat, and slammed her fists onto her hips. The distant silhouette of The Bay skimmed across the desert, still going a fair clip. "Goddamn horse."

"What now?"

Rider thumbed back her hat. She had the Cat and the Arbiter and the ammo on her belt. She picked up the canteen The Bay had slung loose when he bolted, and it glugged, still half-full.

She corked it. "We ride double."

Three hours later, Dead Horse still hadn't tired of snaking its head back to snap at her leg. She kicked its nose as it came 'round again.

"Quit that," said Dead Guy.

"You talking to it or me?" Rider shifted, picturing the bruises blossoming on her rump come tomorrow.

"Either." He yanked the reins as Dead Horse tried to bite again and lifted a finger to trace a spot along the horizon where the land sloped downwards, forming a natural, shallow basin. Three sand-colored lumps and one roughly square stone structure sat in a semi-circle against the wall of the steepest slope. "Bondee."

"What's left of it, anyways." Rider reached for her binoculars, remembered The Bay'd run off with them, cursed, and settled for cupping her hands to her eyes and squinting. "Don't see any Dancers."

"Don't hear them either."

True, the Dancers kicked up a heap of noise. Rattling Sky Mountain earned its name from their antics on its peak. The air all around Bondee hung still as a held breath.

"I assume we intend to take a look around regardless," said Dead Guy.

"Come this far."

Another hour's ride into the afternoon's stretching shadows brought them to Bondee. Dead Guy guided Dead Horse to the middle of the abandoned camp, next to the old stone supply house where the stub of an ancient live oak jutted up out of the ground. A whole troop of soldiers must've used it as their hitching post; pale lines encircled the trunk where the bark had been rubbed off, like the marks of the hangman's noose.

Dead Guy dismounted. Rider went to follow, and Dead Horse's muscles bunched in that split instant where she hung suspended between hide and earth. She guessed its plans right before it corkscrewed its rear off the ground in an almighty heave. Sixteen years since last she'd been bucked. Felt the same. The sky passed at an odd tilt above her head before she whomped onto her back. The Arbiter, caught between her and the hard-packed ground, grunted and popped.

"Goddamn!" Rider rolled over quickly, even in her anger grateful it hadn't gone off. Dewdrops generally caused little harm to living flesh, but she didn't fancy taking chances at such close range.

"Bad Huntsman." Dead Guy swatted Dead Horse's flank, and it returned to standing like a carving of a horse. "You okay? What's the damage?" he asked over his shoulder as he tied up the damned beast.

Rider shook her head. The Arbiter breech-loaded; she tried to break it and peer down the barrel, but it jammed. Swearing, she slung it over her back. "Good thing I prob'ly won't need it." She tried to convince herself the smug expression on Dead Horse's face was her imagination, without much success. "I'll take it to Mr. Claggan tomorrow. Bronson can pay the bill for sending us on this wild jackass chase."

Dead Guy's lips quirked. "Let's have a look around, fellow jackass," he said, tugging his hat to shadow his face.

Nothing in the stone supply house but dust, rotted sacking, and a hairy brown tarantula. The first of the old clay quarter houses had so collapsed in on itself that Rider could barely squeeze her thin body past the fallen debris blocking the entrance. Only rubble inside. The second—the one that smacked right up against the basin wall—

The instant Rider stepped through the doorway, she knew something was off.

"Someone's been in here recently," said Dead Guy, bent near in half to avoid banging his head. He ran a hand along a thick pine branch, still smelling of sap, braced against the angle of a wall to reinforce the ceiling.

"And not Dancers neither," said Rider, finding a boot print pressed into the dirt floor. A fresh print, its outline unblurred by settled dust, pointing deeper into the room. A faint breeze tugged her hair. Tracking it to its source, she pulled down a tattered sheet of canvas tacked to the back wall. Behind it, a ragged black hole gaped, exhaling a breath of stone and darkness into her face.

"Well," she said.

Dead Guy's livemetal flowed over his hand, coating it like a second glove. Rider lit a candle. Mutely, they stepped into the tunnel.

Her sweat iced on her skin. Too big a drop too quick, just for getting out of the sun. Darkness settled in, thick as liquefied velvet. Sound came to her all hollow and echoing, like she'd stuck her head underwater. *Tap, tap, tap, tap* went her footsteps. The noise reminded her of the undertaker at work. She set her jaw as the tunnel narrowed. Her coat snagged against its rough-hewn sides. *Someone's chopped this out recently*, she thought, and no sooner thought it than the candlelight caught the glimpse of metal half-buried in a furrow of the wall. The head of a pickax, four broken inches of shaft still attached. Rider gave it an experimental tug, but it was wedged too deep to shift.

"Someone's gone to a heap of trouble to dig this tunnel," she said to Dead Guy, cramped up behind her. The walls caught her words and echoed them, sent them slithering up and down the tunnel, adding a sibilant hiss they hadn't possessed when they left her mouth.

"The only thing anyone would mine for around Camlock is arcsilver," he replied, and the echo returned his voice in the rumbling growl of an angered cat.

Rider ran her fingers along the embedded pick, trying to fit the two contrary pieces together. Arcsilver. Many experienced prospectors claimed the Camlock mines were almost tapped out. Then—after a few drinks and in lowered tones—they'd speak of rich veins just waiting to be claimed beneath Rattling Sky Mountain. No one cared to brave the Dancers, however. But Bondee? No one'd ever discovered arcsilver around Bondee.

As she puzzled, a new smell mingled with the sluggish air. A vivid recollection rose to her mind of the day she'd lifted a floorboard to find a sand rat decomposing beneath, its guts half melted into sludge, maggots squirming in its eye sockets. The stench flowed into her nostrils and ran down the back of her throat until it took all her grit not to spew it back out. She lifted the candle. The passage widened ahead. There, a sour, yellow-gray mist was flooding the tunnel floor.

"Skreekers." She drew the Cat.

"Rider," said Dead Guy, quietly in her ear. "I can't use my blade here. The tunnel's too narrow."

She tapped a finger against the Cat's barrel, tempted to stand her ground. She was Shadowmarshal, and how many skreekers could there be? The smell intensified, coating her tongue with its vile essence. The mist thickened into a fog swimming with vaguely human shapes. Sallow tendrils licked her boot's toes. Discretion won. "Back up," she commanded.

The fog exploded into a hundred starving faces, two hundred groping hands. Each lipless mouth opened to form an unending screech of hatred. Rider staggered back as the skreekers engulfed her, tearing her skin and clothes with stinking, clawed hands. The candle dropped from her hand. Its flame flickered twice and died on the wick. No matter; the skreekers cast their own, nauseous light. The wizened, yellow face of an ancient woman thrust into hers, nosetip to nosetip. A mad, half-second's eternity of staring into rolling, piss-colored eyes, then the skreeker's lips yawed open, the thin skin around them stretching like a snake's. Its eyeteeth lengthened into fangs.

Rider fired the Cat and the ancient horror imploded, gone—along with one of her arcsilver bullets. Six shots before she'd have to reload, presuming she could reach her bullet pouch before the skreekers tore her apart.

Dead Guy screamed in her ear, hoarse and hollow. Rider's chest knotted into a fist, recognizing the sound of agony. She'd thought nothing alive or dead could harm him. Pulse pounding in her temples, she whirled, shoulders scraping on rock, and found him wearing a sickly yellow cloak of skreekers. They'd flowed right past her to reach him. One tore at his neck, and wet silver trickled out. The skreeker clamped itself to the wound, sucking greedily.

Rider fired and it vanished. Another swarmed in to take its place. Claws scraped her face. She fired again. Again. Cold boiled up her legs as one grabbed her. Another shot freed her. Three dewdrops left and still the yellow fog seethed and screeched.

Gathering his livemetal up into a short, thick blade, Dead Guy jabbed at the skreekers. Not as efficient or elegant as the sword, but he cleared enough space that she could see him, bleeding drops of silver, leeched of color, leeched of essence. The disk around her neck scraped her breastbone, dry and virtually weightless.

Rider pushed her way to him, sacrificing another shot. Turning to face the skreekers still foaming out of the tunnel's depths, she took the Arbiter from her back. "Stay well behind me," she commanded Dead Guy. The damaged rifle could well misfire, and tattered as he was, she didn't want to risk hitting him.

Skreekers before her, almost a solid sheet of yellow, distorted faces that hated and hungered. Setting her jaw, Rider aimed the Arbiter and pulled the trigger.

Alternating flares of red and black throbbed behind her eyeballs. The world swum at a distance, waiting to hurt her when she returned. She'd dipped her right arm in hot tar. No, not tar, splinters, a thousand burning splinters all digging into her arm and shoulder and cheek—

"Steady." Dead Guy's voice, the words cool against her skin. Rider jerked back to reality, and the world walloped her over the head.

"What happened?" she rasped. Sitting up, she pressed all ten fingers into her scalp. Her right shoulder spasmed. Dirt gritted under her rump, something hard against her back. The storehouse wall. The dry air tasted open and clean.

"Shh." Dead Guy took hold of her wrist. "Your rifle exploded. Killed a bunch of skreekers, but there's plenty more. I dragged you out while they were stunned." He carefully tucked her arm into a sling he'd fashioned out of her bandana. The back of her neck pulled at the weight.

Rider turned her head for a look. Not so bad, she judged, examining the torn skin. No broken bones, best she could tell. Her wits cleared further as she breathed untainted air. "We better smoke it back to town," she said, already planning. Round up a posse armed with plenty of arcsilver, return, and clean the skreekers out of Bondee before they came to Camlock in search of fresher prey. Bracing against the storehouse wall, she levered herself upright. An ankle twinged, threatening to collapse underneath her, and her head dipped and spun, but she gritted her teeth and heaved.

Halfway to her feet, a scream she wished she could take back hearing for the rest of her days split the silence. It started her heart pounding so hard it damn near shot out her mouth. Instinctively, her hand flew to her holster and tangled in the sling.

"Huntsman. Oh, God." Dead Guy peeked 'round the corner of the storehouse, looked towards the live oak nub at the camp's center, and jerked quickly back, his mouth a clenched line. "We have to leave. Now."

The scream came again, shriller and more desperate. Rider hesitated. Dead Guy caught her under her good shoulder and shoved. "He's not alive," he said, urging her along, away from the screams and wisps of putrid odor that fouled the good dry air. "I might be able to call him up again even if—"

Rider stole a glance back. Beside the stump, Dead Horse reared, forelegs beating at the yellow-smoke figures clawing him, tearing bits of him away. They dragged him down again. Silver droplets spattered the ground, and the skreekers huddled like cats, lapping greedily.

Rider's lips clamped. She faced away. Let Dead Guy keep hoping as long as he was able.

They moved as one across the darkening plains, his arm across her shoulders, all energy focused into keeping their four legs going. They passed over a ridge, and Bondee disappeared behind them. The screams faded, more slowly than she would've liked, and at length sunk into silence.

"I need a rest," said Rider, breath hitching in her chest. An invisible hand kept squeezing her head: pressure, release, pressure, release. Aching from crown to tailbone, and worse, her sore ankle throbbed, puffed up against the inside of her boot.

Dead Guy eased her down into the shelter of a clump of leaping-blossom brush. Its yellow flowers drooped, spotted and wrinkled, instead of popping off their stems into her lap. Dying, like everything in the desert. She reckoned she might have discovered why.

"Could you spare a drop of blood?" asked Dead Guy, crouching before her.

"Might be possible." Pulling the disk out of her shirt, she rubbed it over the still-seeping wounds on her right shoulder. Dead Guy arched his neck, a soundless sigh escaping his lips. A subtle tension went out of his face as his skin gained color. She no longer expected to see shadows of things moving through him.

"Thank you." He touched her right boot. "When did that happen?"

"Damned if I can remember." She moved her foot gingerly, wincing. "Going to make getting back to Camlock tricky."

Cocking an ear to the wind, he stood. "At least I haven't heard any skreekers for a bit. Maybe they're not following. I'll take a look, then try to call up Huntsman."

She nodded. "I'll bind up my ankle and check the crystal."

His boots crunched off over the sand. Rider wrapped her good hand into a shaking fist, nails biting into her palm. Not even Dead Horse deserved that end.

Then, deliberately, she opened her hand, shook out her fingers, and reached for the Cat. She thumbed each bullet home, spun the chamber, and settled the pistol back in its holster. She tried working her boot off her gimpy foot, but flares of bruised colors erupted in her head and she gave it up. Instead, she took the scry-crystal from her pocket to check for signs of yellow.

Its tip glowed red.

Rider gaped. Then flung herself to her feet, ignoring her sore body's protests. Dead Guy, find Dead Guy. He couldn't have gone far; she didn't dare call out. Red tip, danger, red tip, that meant—

Clack.

Too late. Rider bent to unsheathe her obsidian knife, twisting her body across herself, left hand to right boot, as a whole clattering of sounds echoed over the desert. Rattles and clicks, dull, hollow thumps, and the crisp, incessant jangling of tiny bells, like a load of crockery pushed down a hill. Their angular black silhouettes painted a sharp contrast against the cherry red sunset as they came over the crest of the ridge.

Bondee behind her, Skeleton Dancers in front. Rider held herself tall and raised the obsidian knife as they surrounded her, the sky still bright enough to illuminate every detail. Bones of men, bones of beasts, bones of creatures that walked the world before the first footfalls of men, all held together with tough strips of knotted sinew. They rattled and champed at her, eyeless skulls painted with stripes of vermillion and ochre, cerulean spirals and jagged black zigzags.

Beads and feathers and oddly worked bits of clay dangled from their joints, adding to the endless clatter and creak of ancient bone knocking against bone.

Cut the sinews holding them together and they'd fall apart. Rider laughed inside her head. Sinew wouldn't part without a heap of sawing, and here she was, one-handed, lame, and shaky from blood loss. She darted forward anyway, knife aimed at bone, and a hand like a bundle of fire-hardened twigs caught her wrist. Another grabbed her collar. Her hat fell off, and her hair, sweat-damped into strings, flopped over her face. The third hand gripped her injured shoulder, forcing a gargle of pain from her throat. Trapped. Forced onto her knees, *crunch*, down in the dry dirt. Bone fingers gnarled in her hair.

The Dancers parted ranks. An imposing figure creaked forward, cocking its skull to gaze down at her with empty eye sockets. Seven feet tall, if an inch. No man had ever worn these bones, though it was roughly man-shaped. Two fangs, like those of a mountain lion, protruded down past its lower jaw. A curving red line streaked the yellowed bone of what had once been its left cheek. Under one arm, it carried a curious object, resembling a leather melon with pipes and tubes jutting out from it. One pipe, long and flexible, curled up under the Dancer's ribcage, ascending its spine to terminate at the base of its skull, attached to its vertebrae by carefully tied sinew.

The Dancer squeezed the melon bag. A hiss of air. Vibration. "You steal the bones of the earth."

Wheezy, sibilant, but perfectly intelligible. Rider gaped at the device in mute amazement before the words sucker-punched her below the ribs. "I ain't stolen nothing!"

A length of bone pointed at the sack of dewdrops hanging from her belt.

"I bought 'em," said Rider. "I'm no thief."

They threw her to the ground. Bone hands clamped down, hard enough she could barely wriggle. The chief stepped aside to allow a smaller Dancer through, its bones gone brown and brittle with age. One hand held a raw arcsilver knife.

She'd heard the stories. When the Dancers caught someone, they skinned him alive. Took off all the fat, the muscle, discarded the guts, scraped his bones clean. Then reassembled him, patiently tying all the delicate bits with thin sinew, and a new Skeleton Dancer would rise to join the rattling throng.

Rider didn't fancy finding out for herself if the stories were true. She flailed, bit, and bucked, managing to kick the skull right off the neck of a Dancer holding her left leg. But two more took its place before she could twist free. The arcsilver knife approached her right eye.

And then a metal even brighter than arcsilver caught every last glint of the dying sunlight. "Release her," said Dead Guy, stepping into the circle of bones, his livemetal blade poised to strike.

The Dancers drew back. The vise-like grips of those holding Rider down eased a fraction. "'Bout time you got here," she called. "These sonabitches called me a thief."

"The blood of the earth, you hold," came the wheezy voice of the talking device. The Dancer chief stepped forward again. Its fingers stroked the air before Dead Guy's livemetal blade reverently.

"Let her up," said Dead Guy. His lightning-eye held the chief's sockets. After a moment, the chief retreated a step. He clicked two fingers, and the pressure eased off Rider entirely. She struggled to her feet, cuffing the Dancers that didn't back off far enough to suit her.

"Dancers at Bondee. Bronson ain't entirely a lying bastard," she said between her teeth.

Bronson. The image of the broken pickax returned. Could it be Bronson's? Come to recollect, he had bought a new one recently.

"Bone thieves," wheezed the chief. "Take the earth's bones. Those that pass, rest not."

"Do you understand any of that?" Dead Guy asked in an undertone. He'd lowered his livemetal blade, but still held it at ready.

"They call arcsilver 'the earth's bones.'" Hands on hips, she tilted back her head to stare into the chief's eye sockets. "What's it to you?"

"We guard the earth's bones so those that pass may rest. When the bones are taken, those that pass sleep not. They eat the bone thieves instead."

"Those that pass." Rider pulled a dewdrop out of her pouch, held it cupped in one hand, cool and light, sparkling like mist in a spider's web. Ever since the discovery of that first arcsilver deposit in Keffren County ten years ago, a whole rush of folk had arrived, more and more every year, all alike in greed. And she, Shadowmarshal, sheriff's daughter, had watched the plains wither over the course of her years, always blaming the skreekers that haunted the land.

She closed her hand over the dewdrop. "You're sayin' arcsilver absorbs the spirits of the dead? And if there's not enough arcsilver, they become skreekers instead?"

"Blood of the earth to bone of the earth." The chief pointed to Dead Guy's livemetal blade. "Blood. It weakens over time, hardens into bone. Bone drinks the spirits of those that pass, turns back into blood. Endless circle."

"It bound itself to me when I was alive," mused Dead Guy, lifting his livemetal blade. "Then, when Huntsman—" He swallowed. "When Huntsman and I were gunned down, I didn't die, exactly. I merged with it." He tipped back his hat. Moonlight softened the angles of his face. "So perhaps one day I'll turn into arcsilver and absorb other people's spirits. It's not eternal, then. That's a comfort."

"Comfort, hell," said Rider. "What about those skreekers? They're killing everything around Bondee—"

She kicked herself for a fool. "That tunnel. It connects to caverns beneath Rattling Sky Mountain. Bronson must've gone mad with greed, hearing the old-timers talk about how there are still rich deposits there."

"So he dug a secret way in to elude the Dancers and started removing the last bits of ore that were keeping the dead at peace," said Dead Guy.

One of the Dancers perched on the crest of the ridge stirred. Lifting two slats of wood that dangled from its waist, it clapped them together. All at once the Dancers went to rattling and clattering, their naked jaws snapping, joints creaking.

A wisp of ghastly stench floated over the rise. The sky to the south turned sallow.

"The skreekers." Dead Guy bit his lip. "Nothing left for them out here. They'll be drawn to Camlock like vultures to carrion."

Rider whirled. "You!" She advanced on the chief. "If I promise to stop the mining, will you help?"

"Return the bones of the earth, we help," agreed the chief. He held out a huge hand, the lattice-work of his palm turned upward. On a hunch, Rider touched a finger to her wound and smeared a drop of clinging blood across a bone. The long fingers folded over it. "A pledge," the voice device wheezed. He rattled his jaw, and a skeleton horse trotted up as inhuman screams echoed over the ridge.

"Go." Dead Guy gave her a push. "It's your duty to protect the living. Evacuate Camlock. Tell everyone to leave the arcsilver and head north."

She'd already thrown one leg over the bone horse's back. She hesitated. "And you?"

"You need time," he said, and it was if a cloud passed over his lightning eye. "We can buy it."

Sitting smack against the bone horse's bare vertebrae made for the most uncomfortable ride of Rider's life, but she allowed the creature was fast with no heavy flesh to weary it. She'd covered almost half the distance to Camlock when the disk resting on her chest flared, so sharp and sudden a sensation she couldn't tell if she'd been frozen or burned.

Jostled, jolting, naught but her sense of balance preventing her from being flung over the bone horse's neck, she reached into her shirt and withdrew the disk. The moonlight revealed a circle of tarnished black. Just the barest "s" curl of a shine remained at the center. Rider traced it with her thumb. Her eyes prickled. Nose got snotty.

"Turn back," she said.

The bone horse paid no heed, legs eating up the distance to Camlock.

"Turn back." Letting the disk fall back inside her shirt, she hooked a finger into the sinews binding its neck together and pulled. This time it minded her. Flinging up its skull, it pivoted. She pressed a hand to her chest, clamping the disk to her skin all the while they raced back towards Bondee.

A maelstrom of yellow mist hung over the ridge, marking the spot. Skreekers, screaming like starved carrion birds. "Faster, dammit," she cried, and the horse redoubled its speed. Its hooves crunched scattered bones littering the ground. Even as she rode by, a circling trio of skreekers tugged a Dancer apart, broke its bones, and cast them to the earth. Ahead, a curtain of maddened skreekers swirled around a central point. She knew who stood at the eye of that storm. A flash of silver cut through the greasy yellow cloud, and she caught a glimpse of him: a fading shadow bleeding silver.

"Jace!" She leapt off the horse. Stupid, that: her ankle turned, she damn near pitched over and fell on her fool face. Several skreekers, perhaps sensing that her living flesh might be tastier than the Dancers' dry bones, poured over to investigate.

Skinning the Cat, she shot three. She heard Jace's cry, harsh as the rasp of metal against stone, whatever words he flung at her unintelligible.

More skreekers. The Dancers fought with raw arcsilver knives and precision, and the skreekers tore them apart. The skreekers vanished in the wake of Jace's livemetal blade, but it swung less and less vigorously. She shot again. Only three dewdrops left in the chamber.

She fired them. Tossed the Cat aside and drew her obsidian knife.

"Rider," cried Jace, down on one knee. "Rider!"

She wondered if he meant to tell her obsidian was no good against skreekers. Damn fool. She knew that. She had no intention of using it against them.

Working her right arm out of its sling, she pulled back her sleeve, turning her wrist so the soft white underside showed. Slashed. Took the disk from around her neck and pushed it into the wound.

At first, the blood welling up around the disk drowned it in red. Then the dull, silver metal started sucking it in, almost faster than she could bleed. Rider lifted her head as Jace began to glow. His livemetal blade traced dazzling arcs through the night air. A moment later, she wasn't just watching, but swinging along with him. Skreeker after skreeker vanished under the edge of their livemetal blade, no time to even scream.

She was distantly aware when her legs turned into jelly, no longer able to support her. That was okay. She let that part of her sink to the sand. As long as she kept the disk pressed to her arm, everything would be well.

Another flash of silver. The last skreeker vanished. She was breaking apart or coming back together; she couldn't tell which. The world pulsed softly in her ears, a muted murmur, soothing as a lullaby. Good. She'd appreciate a nap.

A hand touched her shoulder, her cheek, lifted her drooping head. "Damn fool."

She cracked open her lids to Jace's face, edges sharp and distinct, more real than the sound of her own heartbeat. Another head poked over his shoulder, steel gray and too long to be human. It appraised her, then let out a disdainful snort.

"Aw, hell," said Rider. "I thought that damned thing was dead for good." She lolled back against Jace's arm as Dead Horse tossed its mane.

"You gave me enough blood to revive him. Rider." He shook her a little. "You were supposed to warn Camlock. Why'd you come back?"

Rider considered, staring past his head with its ever-waving hair to the spread of stars littering the black sky. Pah. What did reason matter in the end? "I'll be dead too someday," she said.

"Not today," he muttered. He squeezed her arm, hard enough to numb her fingers as he pried the disk away from the wound. She tried to protest, but her lips refused to form words. "Dammit, Rider, you're bleeding to death. Camlock's too far—"

A bony hand shoved him away. The Dancer chief bent over her. In one hand, he held a length of sinew, in the other a knife.

"So, I went to Bondee, Mr. Bronson." Rider settled deeper into her comfortable chair on her front porch, her right foot propped on a stool. Around back, The Bay whinnied, wanting his dinner. After his stunt in the desert, she figured the fool horse could cool his heels for another quarter hour.

Bronson rubbed his tongue over his lips. "You searched Bondee good and thorough then, Miz Bell?"

"Yes, Mr. Bronson, I found your tunnel. I killed the skreekers you woke." She leaned forward, made her voice low and quiet. "I'll keep quiet for Mrs. Bronson's sake. You've shamed her enough. But I'm having it blasted shut tomorrow, you hear?"

His weasel-face puckered. "Miz Bell—"

"You got no right to dig round Bondee. I could have the law on you. Heed my warning," she put force on the word, "and never go near it again."

His shoulders slumped. "Fair enough, Miz Bell. Thankee for all you've done." His boots thudded off her porch. Thirty yards up Sutton Street, he paused, then sidled into Myer's Livery Stable.

Jace rose up out of Rider's shadow. "Low-down snake. He meant for you to die at Bondee—after killing enough skreekers so he could continue mining, of course."

"Yep," agreed Rider, folding her left arm behind her head. Bronson emerged from the stable, leading a rangy chestnut horse. He mounted up and rode off down the street.

"Heading due south," said Jace.

"Yep." Well, she'd warned him. Sure, he'd find his tunnel still open at Bondee. He'd also find the Dancers waiting, eager to replace the numbers they'd lost in last night's battle. "Perhaps it's only just."

"Sometimes you scare me, Rider Bell." Jace propped his elbows against the back of her chair. "How's your arm?"

She turned it over on her lap. Sinews crossed the deep gash over her wrist, like many minute bridges. She'd heal, but it would leave a deep scar tracking a ravine across the underside of her forearm. Jace traced a finger along the crimson zigzags and small blue whorls the chief had decorated it with.

She clasped his hand. "It's just swell."

How she'd like to sit here, enjoying the shade of her porch on this hot blue day. Just listen to the jaunty music from the saloons and the clip-clop of horses trotting down the street, Jace's comforting presence beside her. Perhaps drink a cool glass of whiskey and lemonade.

Sighing, she let the dream dissipate. No time for loafing, Rider Bell, Shadowmarshal of Camlock. She heaved her foot off the stool. Jace put an arm around her shoulders. Leaning against him, she set off to speak to the mayor about closing the arcsilver mines.

VOLUNTEERED

B.S. Donovan

"THAT MAKE YOU FEEL ANY BETTER?" I ASKED.

Karl spat out a shot glass worth of blood, phlegm, and half a tooth.

"Can't blame a man for trying," he mumbled through lips just starting to swell.

"Sure I can. Can't blame a man for shooting you in the head, you try it again," I answered. "Now turn facing forward."

Karl was not one for hiding his feelings. He was gauging me, guessing if I was bluffing. He'd been expressive with the Collier family, too, lining them up against the plascrete wall of their prefab shack before putting slugs through their heads. Mother, father, daughters, all of 'em. I belted Karl across the other side of his face in an attempt at symmetry. The result was more spit and blood, but no tooth. So much for my artistic skills, or my fighting skills for that matter, considering the man was bound and tied. But to drive the message home, I put the pointy end of my AES-K rifle, safety off, to the middle of his forehead. Truth is, rifle is technically wrong, there is no bore, no bullet, only a phased plasma nozzle.

It's not that pointy either.

Karl backed off and turned facing the front of the vehicle. The better part of valor, I guess. *The better part of valor,* I thought to myself. A phrase that comes from Shakespeare, I figured I was assigning a lot more cultural credit to the murderer than I should. Karl's restraints made it hard for him to gain any leverage on me. It was only when I was reaching down to tighten the bolt holding his bindings to the floor that he figured he'd have a chance. Not a great chance. That's why he lost a tooth.

I'd volunteered to take my prisoner, full name Karl James Hagen II, from Survey Junction to Accord City, the capital of Accord, the planet. From there, I escort him off world to Cannonade for trial.

Accord is in the Halo of the Milky Way. In more technically correct yet less Shakespearean terms, Accord is above the axilla of the Scutum-Crux arm of our galaxy. Axilla, from the Latin, originally used to describe the place where a bird's wing attaches to the body. It currently means—more appropriately when describing Accord—"armpit" of the galaxy. Similarly, the "Halo" of the galaxy is about as misleading as axilla, and makes it sound like there's a warm glow surrounding Accord. Truth is, the Halo is the interstellar equivalent of the Mohave, only more barren. Imagine the disc of our galaxy like a spinning starfish. The Halo is the stuff above and below the flat sides, the place where you think there are no stars. Turns out there are, just so few you never notice. It is where only the desperate or the dogmatic come, and then mostly to escape reality, responsibility, or the law.

Accord City, where Karl and I were just now riding in a self-driving car, was too small and remote to have our own courthouse, but it had the only spaceport on planet. If you could call it that. Like so many of the adjectives I have used to characterize my backyard, the terms are all too grand when compared to the reality. The spaceport was a walled flat span of bare rock where the Frontier Schooners touched down.

Karl sat in front of me in the two-seater. That is, until he decided to test if I was still awake. I was. And he was spitting blood and teeth because of it.

"Lockup's on Main," I said.

"Changing course for Accord Library at 1037 Main," the nav-system in the car responded.

"You gonna book me at the library?" Karl asked incredulously. "That's too ironic. Backwater burg."

"Been booked already, Karl. Just some iron bars around you till the shuttle comes," I said.

The jail shared a building with the library. Backwater burg, it was, which I have established. But it was my backwater burg, and only I can cast aspersions. Accord aspired to be a mining planet, mostly populated by surveyors and prospectors, with a handful of small businesses supporting them. No major veins had been discovered yet, just lots of hopes, dreams, and no small amount of desperation. Government was minimal, except for volunteer law enforcement comprised of, well, me.

The vehicle negotiated the back streets and rolled to a silent stop behind a short Jenga-pile of prefab, modular blocks, long room-sized cinder blocks with windows. The library was in front, the offices up top, the lockup in the back. Gray-blue light shone through the windows.

A woman—slender, late thirties—stood in the doorway behind a sliding screen door. I knew most of the people on the planet, but she was new. The streak of gray in her brown hair probably bothered her more than it did me. She wore a slug thrower on her hip. Truth is, someone else would notice the slug thrower. I noticed the hip. I was expecting a new librarian, so I wasn't worried when I saw a stranger standing there. Now that I'd seen her all of four seconds, I already imagined we'd be best of friends. I have an active imagination. She opened the screen door. I rolled down the window.

"You Conrad?" she asked.

"Yeah, you Maya?"

"Got you the room there." She nodded and pointed inside.

One door, plascrete walls, a sad lighting tube. I slid the door up and backed out of the car, rifle pointed at Karl.

"Out," I said.

The younger man pulled himself up and out of the cramped transport. He was fitter than you'd expect in the 0.7 g's of local gravity. Likely implants or growth injections. His hands were tethered through a hook at his waist to his ankles, which were bound barely wide enough to shuffle.

"Anyone in the library?" I asked Maya.

"A guy sleeping in a chair between the stacks. That count?"

"It might. You know who it is?"

"Don't know everyone in town yet. Some bum in a poncho."

"Anyone out on Main?" I asked.

"You just drove in. Did you see anyone?" she said, sounding a bit testy. Just my type. I imagined veritable minutes of romantic courtship, wine, candles. Accord was a genetically limited pool, and Maya was the new girl in the classroom.

"Drove the back way. Don't want it advertised I got Karl Hagen locked up in the library."

"He really kill that prospector family?" she asked.

"Yeah. Got an eyewitness, some security footage. All in this evidence pack."

I patted the messenger bag I had across my back. I needed to get it, Karl, and me on the schooner at 05:30 tomorrow. It was 17:00 now.

Maya said, "I didn't know those prospectors, the Collier family. But I know Nancy Collier's brother Jim. He's here in Accord."

"As long as he stays out of the way, I don't really care where he is."

Maya nodded and shrugged. Agreement or disinterest, it wasn't clear.

"I'm more worried about Karl's friends. He's the only one we caught," I added.

Maya looked uncomfortable at that. She said, "I'm starting to regret having the lockup back here. I'm supposed to be a library administrator, not a jailer."

"What did you expect in the frontier colonies?"

"I don't know what I expected, but I don't like what I got," she answered.

Maya's sentiment rang true. For all too many, Accord was a long shot. Moving here was a gamble. Just look at the Colliers.

I shook my rifle at Karl and jerked my chin at the cell. He shuffled off through the door past Maya into the building. He stopped just outside the cell, looking toward the stacks in the library. Between the stacks was the guy in the poncho. He was reclining in a chair, hands in his lap, feet crossed, hat pulled halfway down his face.

Turning toward Maya, Karl said, "You picked the wrong team, lady."

"What's he talking about?" she asked me.

Karl went on. "You think my boys are going to let him take me? I make you a deal. You let me go, and I promise not to do to you what I'm thinking right now."

Karl surveyed Maya's body with lecherous intent. She paled, her face scrunched like she'd drunk ipecac. I was none too happy about how he was treating the new girl, and I wanted to make an impression, so I kicked Karl's legs at the knees and slammed the butt of the AES-K across the base of his skull. See, I'm not above Neanderthal displays of physical dominance. I expected him to go down easy. Instead, he just went to his knees and looked daggers at me. Not for the first time, I was glad he was in restraints. In a fair fight… well, in a fair fight I wouldn't have fought fairly.

Maya stepped to my side and held onto my bicep. Note to self, Neanderthal methods effective. My fantasy relationship progressed to long evenings in hot tubs followed by drinks on the deck. Karl stood awkwardly and stepped through the door to the cell. He curled his lips around his bloody broken teeth. Maya pulled a datapad from her pocket and tapped. The door slid shut. The top half of his face was visible through the slot window.

"He really have friends still on the loose?" she asked.

"Is there a garage for the car?" I asked. "I'd rather it was out of sight."

"Yeah, I'll send the instructions to the vehicle AI."

She tapped at the datapad again. The car drove off toward the garage.

"You avoided my question," she said.

"Yeah."

"Then call in more deputies."

"No other deputies. Volunteers are all out looking for the rest of them."

"Shit."

A woman of eloquence. I think I was in love.

Maya shooed out the bum in the poncho and locked up. I pulled up a plastic chair and set myself down outside Karl's door.

"What they pay you, lawman?" Karl asked, his voice muffled by the door.

"What do you care?"

"I figure you get a lot, like hazard pay. You risk your life."

After a pause, I said, "I volunteer."

"What?" he laughed genuinely. "You do all this for free?"

"It's the benefits," I said.

"What, they got good dental?"

"Yeah, I get to break teeth, yours in fact. Today was a good day. Windfall profits. More to come."

Karl laughed again, surprisingly amiably.

"You like to crack heads. I can respect that," he said.

"Some heads," I conceded.

I watched Karl nod knowingly through the slot window.

"Seriously, though. How much you make?"

"Enough," I answered.

Truth is, volunteer means volunteer. Some say volunteering speaks to my generosity as a person. I know differently. I have a business repairing prospector sensors. It's enough. Never wanted to prospect myself though. Too much risk. So I volunteered as a deputy.

I never claimed to be a genius.

Karl added, "Until, one day you get a plasma blast to the back. Your momma would be disappointed. You're not using your head."

"I never claimed to be a genius," I said.

Deja vu.

"What's your price?" he asked.

He didn't beat around the bush. I had to grant him that.

"You can't afford me," I answered.

"You know why we took that prospector family out?"

Maya's ears perked up at this. I shook my head slowly.

"They found it," he said.

Unconsciously, the fingers of my hand gripped the AES-K tightly, my knuckles white. I'd been waiting for this.

He continued, "You not going to ask me what they found?"

I counted to five as I inhaled, five exhale. It keeps me calm.

"A major vein. No claim yet, though. And that means me and the boys are rich. We could use someone in the law that likes to bash heads."

I stood up and walked toward the door and put my face up to his. If there wasn't a door between us, it'd have been mighty uncomfortable. Maya was watching the exchange like a tennis match.

"I'm going to tell you this just one time," I said and paused for effect. "I want to bring you in alive. I really do."

My eye picked up a memory of the twitch I spent so long in anger management therapy to lose.

I continued, "I do like bashing heads. Don't really mind killing either. Gives me a sense of justice, killing the likes of you. Calms my hands. But I don't have to bring you in alive."

I patted the evidence bag.

"The evidence in here is enough to put away the rest of your boys. And I can easily claim you tried to attack me. In fact, you did."

Karl suddenly didn't look so cocky.

"But I can think of a price."

Karl grinned ear to ear, the kind that said he knew it, he just knew it.

"Every man does," he said. "Every man does."

"I want the Colliers back."

Karl's smile faded.

"I see a big payoff in keeping you alive for a while longer. But I'm not married to it. There are other benefits that I could live with. This plasma rifle can slice through this door like it was paper. Cut you clean in half. So let me give you some advice. Don't open your mouth, and I won't show you how that works. "

Karl sat down. Part of me was disappointed. Maya backed away. Maybe too much Neanderthal. Aw, our first fight. I imagined the steamy make up.

Accord's red sun set, dropping the twenty or so piles of prefab blocks we called a city into darkness. With it, the temperature fell and a cool mist rose. Maya took turns watching Karl. I went to the front and looked out at the muddy divot we called Main Street. I could see the homeless bum rummaging through trash, and I mentally named him Poncho.

Hours passed. Maya went out to get some food. She'd be back in ten. Around then, I saw another man talking to Poncho. The new guy took off down the street at a run. Karl was sitting comfortably on his cot, smiling down into his folded hands.

"What are you smiling at?" I asked.

He pointed to his mouth, his eyebrows raised.

"Yes, you can speak."

"I like having friends."

"You knew Poncho," I concluded.

Karl just nodded.

There was a knock at the back.

Through the door I heard, "Open up, Conrad. It's me, Maya."

I opened the door to an AES-K, pointy end aimed toward my head. A brawny prospector in flannel and denim was at the other end of it. I know I already explained that it wasn't really pointy, but when it's pointed *at* you, it looks pointy.

"Don't even think it," he said.

Dammit, I didn't see Maya turning against me. I didn't think our first fight was so serious.

From behind him, Maya said, "This is Jim, Nancy Collier's brother."

Not Karl's friends, then. Angry, revenge-driven victims I could deal with.

"Nice to meet you, Jim," I said. "Not too fond of your weapon etiquette, though."

"You step aside so I can end this murderer, and I'd be happy to mend my ways."

"Jim, I'll do that. But listen to me first."

"Drop the weapon and step aside," he said.

"Fine," I said, and put the rifle down. "But listen here. Nancy found a vein." I stepped aside.

Jim didn't end Karl.

"She what?" he asked.

"You heard me right, Jim. A big one, too. Karl told me."

"And you believed him?"

"Why else would he kill them all? Karl and his crew have always been bad, but they never killed anyone. Think about it. He needs to stay on planet, so he can stake a claim to your sister's fortune. If I can get him and this evidence off planet, then we can contest any claim. They get nothing."

Jim's kind and chubby face contorted with hate, pain, and hate again.

"He killed Nancy and the kids!"

I looked questioningly at Maya behind Jim. She stared with sudden and intense fascination at her own shoes. That gray streak in her hair was starting to bother me.

"Jim," I said. "You're right. He has to pay. But if we don't transport him to Cannonade, Karl's gang keeps it all."

"I don't want the money."

"Okay," I said, stepping forward again, my hands up. "But what's going to happen when they get rich and own half the planet?"

Jim looked at me like he was seeing me for the first time.

"Jim, don't let the rest of them get away with it. They all gotta pay."

Reason seemed to return to his eyes.

"Put the rifle down, Jim. You're making me nervous."

Jim's shoulders slumped. I maneuvered the pointy end away from my forehead, gently pulled the AES-K out of his hand, and set it down.

"You thought you could get rid of your problem?" I asked Maya.

"Something like that. Don't hold it against me."

Yeah, not liking that gray hair at all. I fantasized about throwing all her things at our love nest onto Main Street and changing the locks on the doors. Probably the fastest mental love affair in Accord history. Nearly ended in a gunfight, too.

"Don't hold your breath," I answered. "We're going to have some company, soon."

Maya and Jim both looked up at me questioningly.

"Poncho told Karl's friends."

They both deflated again.

"Jim, Maya, listen. The shuttle leaves at 05:30. All we have to do is bring this murderer alongside the landing pad. It's a long shot, but I've got a plan for the rest."

It didn't take much to convince Jim. Turns out Karl convinced Maya. He made the mistake of leering at her one time too many.

At 05:15, Maya and Jim were already gone. I opened the cell. The sky was starting to lighten with the early signs of dawn.

"Out," I said. "On your knees."

I cranked his restraints tighter, picked up my AES-K, and gestured for him to stand. I tapped Maya's datapad, and the car came like a dog to a whistle.

"Front seat again. Don't think I won't take you down if I have to."

Karl dragged his feet, glancing around, looking for his gang.

"No one here to come get you. Feeling lonely?" I asked.

Karl smirked through his blood-browned and broken teeth. He sat down in the front seat. I locked his restraints to the floor. This time I wasn't giving him a chance to attack me. You live, you learn. Or you survive and remember, anyway.

The car wasn't armored, but it was faster than walking. I splashed mud on the windows. I bet that Karl's gang wasn't willing to shoot it up if they didn't know who was who. Even if they had IR sensors, they still would only know that there were two of us.

I gave instructions to the nav-system, and we pulled out onto Main Street. The journey down the street was filled with light and sound, but lacked detail. The wind picked up and howled around the vehicle as we passed between the taller buildings.

One star in the sky grew brighter, the Frontier Schooner's engines burning in descent. They'd switch to air displacement soon. The street curved slightly. Still pretty far from the landing zone. Normally a five-minute ride, it already felt like an eternity.

The rumbling of the descending shuttle rose in our ears. The sun was brightening, making the colors more vivid. The green of the trees was bluer than Earth, the sky redder. The street was empty, even with the rare event of the shuttle arriving. Word must have spread through the town.

We reached the stretch of security wall surrounding the landing pad, the entrance about fifty yards away. The roar of the shuttle was deafening in its crescendo. The trees shook nearly out of their roots. And then, the car stopped with a thunk.

"Road obstruction," the nav bleeped.

Karl tilted his head at me and said, "Still time to take the money and run, lawman."

"What money?" I asked.

I cracked the wall-side window open and glanced at the wheels. A small boulder was deposited in the muddy wheel divot.

"Dammit!" I said.

"My boys are out there, lawman. You know we're not going to lose this stake for anyone or anything. Take the deal."

"Never actually heard any deal," I answered.

The rushing air suddenly stopped, whirring of engines fading. I stepped out on the security wall side of the street and kicked at the rock. The front half of the wheel disappeared, vaporized in a flash of plasma. Other loud reports were followed by thuds in the dirt.

I jumped back and did a mental inventory of the sounds. One plasma rifle. The rest slug throwers. Both could kill me, but one was more definitive. I returned fire, not really aiming, avoiding buildings and the people inside. I shot five times, two kitty-corner to the right of the still-closed shuttle pad gate, two left, one up on the roof straight across. I figured there were five men. The shots I took communicated where they were and numbered them.

I dove back in the car and pushed Karl against the window toward the shooters. Karl looked a little less fearless with all the blasts. I pressed the AES-K against his ribs.

"I told you I don't mind killing," I said, my voice sounding calmer than I felt. Then to his gang I yelled, "You shoot and I guarantee Karl Hagen dies!"

Maybe it was the calm in my voice that convinced him.

"Everyone stop!" Karl yelled. In the silence left by the engines, his voice was clear as a bell.

"You okay, boss?" came a voice from the street.

"Yeah, you got him dead to rights. We just gotta convince him. Make him a present."

The man who talked to Poncho last night stepped into the street carrying a messenger bag like the one I slung across my shoulder, only bigger and heavier.

He swung it like an Olympic hammer thrower and tossed it in front of the vehicle.

"That's all for you, lawman. All you gotta do is walk away," Karl said.

"What's in it?" I asked.

"Take a look."

"Half a dozen men just shot off my car wheel!"

"Take me with you then. I'm your hostage, right? They won't shoot you when you got your gun pointed at my kidneys."

"Prisoner, not hostage," I corrected.

"Semantics," he said.

Fifty cent word for a two-bit gangster. My opinion of his education increased. My opinion of him as a human was unchanged.

"Tell them to come out, where I can see them."

Karl cracked a smile again. The one that said the price is right. I let him go ahead and think that. I was aiming higher.

"Everyone out on the street. Point your guns at the mud. I mean everyone!"

Through the muddy glass, I saw a half dozen apparitions step out onto the street.

"Guns on the ground," I said.

Karl looked at me incredulously.

"You want out of this, you tell your men to put their guns down," I continued.

"They'll holster them."

I paused, thinking about it. Nodded.

"Holster those guns!" he yelled.

They did. I reached down to release his tether from the floor, thought about it, and paused.

"This is a familiar moment, Karl. Last time, you tried to choke me."

"I feel I've grown as a person since then. Just like this budding friendship," Karl said between his wrecked teeth.

I kept the AES-K against his kidney and released the tether. I backed out first, and then he did. Holding him by the scruff of the neck, I kept him between me and his men.

"Have them come in from the flanks."

"Kelly, Bolo. Join Ted. Don't bunch up," he said.

They moved in.

We walked to the overstuffed messenger bag. Karl and I crouched down. He pointed down at the bag and tilted his head back at me, eyebrows raised. I nodded, yes, so he opened it. Inside was about thirty pounds of ore. I'd seen enough to know it was the real thing. A million credits worth. In a pile of mud. In the middle of Main Street. Mine if I wanted it.

"Pick it up," I said.

"Now that's the smartest thing you've said all day. Good to see we've had a meeting of the minds."

"We need to get off this street."

"I tell you what, lawman... Conrad. You just back up to that landing pad entrance behind us. You know, and I know, you can't bring any weapons in there. They'll shoot you as dead as charity in the Halo. We back up to the landing pad together. Only you board by yourself. I walk away."

Karl handed me the bag over his shoulder. We backed up slowly. From the opposite side of the wall, a safety alarm bleeped a warning, and we could hear the shuttle doors opening. The gate slid wide. Karl was having trouble with his leg bindings. Or maybe he was just dragging his feet. We reached the threshold.

"No guns past here, lawman," he said. "Time to throw that thing away."

The split second it took for me to toss my weapon to the ground was the longest I ever experienced. As Karl saw the weapon go down, he cried out, "NOW!" and dove face first into the mud. Firearms came up from holsters. Across the street the other AES-K was leveled at me. With Karl in the mud, there was nothing between me and my maker but a prayer and good timing. I tried to follow him into the mud just as a plasma bolt split Bolo in half. A slug took Kelly in the arm.

Jim Collier called out from up the street, "You going to pay!"

Jim fired his AES-K again, but Karl's men were hidden by the buildings. Maya ducked away between a pair of prefab residences with her slug thrower. Her good looks had mysteriously returned in that moment. I took the opportunity they'd created for me to sling the bag of ore, grab Karl by the neck, and haul him across the threshold to the landing pad.

The weapons fire set the Frontier Schooner into defense mode. Underslung plasma turrets popped out from the shuttle and whirred online.

"No!" Karl called out and shoved me back. He slipped and fell in the mud. His boys pointed their weapons at me. And the shuttle behind me. Where the spaceship-mounted plasma guns had just whirred up to life.

The sound was deafening.

There was nothing left of Karl's gang to identify except DNA embedded in the walls.

Karl and I were detained, roughly, by shuttle security. They stunned us, beat us, and nearly ripped my shoulder from its socket. Can't blame them. When they saw my badge, papers, evidence bag, and prisoner, they were very apologetic.

On the trip to Cannonade, I visited Karl in his cell every day. We even got to talking.

"You know Karl, I like breaking heads and smashing teeth. It just doesn't keep me up at night when the teeth are yours," I said.

Karl nodded sagely and asked, "You ever consider taking the money?"

"Oh, that speaks to how greedy I am, I suppose."

"You're not that greedy, you mean."

"Oh no, greedier. I figured I could lay hands on the ore no matter what. This way, I enjoy watching your whole gang vaporized, see you hang, *and* I get the money. You don't think I'm going to turn this much ore over to the courts, do you?"

So yeah, I volunteered.

THE STRANGER IN THE GLASS

Dave Beynon

I RETCHED AND SPAT, TRYING TO CLEANSE MY MOUTH OF A FOUL TASTE that was entirely metaphysical.

"It's bad," I said, giving the horses a free rein. They took it, and the wagon rumbled forward, shifting and lurching in the ruts. "I know it's there in the village. I'm just not sure where."

Hale raised his hand and swept it toward the spire of the church.

"S'over there…Thereabouts, anyway." He leaned back and pulled the wide brim of his hat over his eyes. "Haven't got a good fix. Sun's too high. Too hot. Tonight though…after it cools off a spell…tonight we'll sniff it out…"

It was always impossible to tell if Hale was sleeping or just resting his eyes. It didn't matter. I'd been his apprentice long enough to know not to disturb him. He was gathering his strength for what was to come. Experience had shown me he would need it.

I coaxed the horses toward the stable. It stood next to the smithy and across the square from the inn. A broad, dark man in a leather apron walked out from the forge to meet me.

"Good day," he said. "My name is Lorne. I mind the stable when Vince is away. Are you stabling your horses?"

"Yes," I said, fishing around for our coin bag in the box behind the seat. "We will also need a place to set up to ply our trade."

Lorne's bushy eyebrows lowered, and for the first time, he seemed to notice Hale beside me. "Would this be your master then? Is he a dead man?"

"He is my master, and he's very much alive. He is resting."

"Hmmm. He rests deep, he does. What manner of trade? You needn't waste your time setting up if it's a trade we can manage ourselves."

I nodded and bowed contritely, just as Hale had taught me. The good will of the locals was paramount for success. "My master Hale is a glassman of great renown."

"Never heard of him," said Lorne. "Glassman? Bottles, jars, and such?"

"If you like." I nodded, reaching back into the box. Next to the coin bag, my fingers found what they were looking for. "We also do this."

Lorne's eyes grew wide. He watched the sunlight play across the globe in my hand. Gossamer strands of glass stretching like spun sugar across the span of the inside of the globe danced and glittered, capturing the smith's eyes. A grudging smile crept across his lips.

"It might seem unmanly of me," he said, "but that is a thing of absolute beauty. What my wife would say if I were to bring home such a thing as that."

"Perhaps some barter might be in order. I take it we might set up somewhere to practice our trade. You have no artists of glass?"

"No," he said, eying the globe. "No one here abouts can do such as that. Set up there, next to my smithy."

Hale slept right through the afternoon while I built the three-sectioned kiln from the blocks in our wagon and set up our stands. I stabled the horses, secured a room at the inn, and purchased wood and charcoal from Lorne, promising a glass globe for his wife as part of the bargain. Villagers came and went. Some asked me what I was building and the sort of work we did. Each time I was asked, I walked to the wagon and fished out the globe.

"This," I told them, "is what we do." The more practical side of me always added, "We also make bottles, jars, and the like."

Not a one was especially interested in bottles, jars and the like.

In late afternoon, just as I was unloading the specially shaped bricks that comprised the kiln's glory hole, the village pastor strode across the square. His robes were wrinkled, his hair disheveled, and his eyes red-rimmed. He held a prayer book in one hand and his holy crook in the other.

"Young fellow," he said, waving his hand as if he was harried by gnats. "You have no business here. Whatever you are building, take it down immediately. We need no strangers in our town. Be gone by sundown. I'll go have a word with the mayor, so you'd best make ready to depart."

I placed my bricks before the kiln.

"Sir," I said, starting toward the wagon to retrieve our magic glass ball. "I've paid good coin for a room at the inn. I understand that our trade is one no one in this village does. I'm assured that we are taking work from no one. We are glassblowers, sir. We make bottles, jars, and such. We also make these…"

As I reached into the box behind the wagon's seat to retrieve the globe, a hard, calloused hand grabbed my wrist. With his other hand, Hale pushed up his hat and nodded to the pastor.

"G'afternoon," Hale said. "May the blessings of the day be upon you, Pastor."

The pastor looked from me to Hale to the kiln, then back to Hale. "And... to you, good sir. As I was telling your boy—"

"'Prentice," said Hale.

"I...I beg your pardon?"

"Ain't my boy, Pastor. He's my 'prentice. He's Tod. My name's Hale. And you'd be?"

"Pastor Ranklin. As I was telling your boy...your...apprentice, you simply cannot stay here tonight. The innkeeper will return your coin, and Lorne will help you disassemble that...that thing."

Hale rose to his feet and hopped off the wagon. He twisted his neck, and all of us heard the crack of vertebrae lining themselves up like good little soldiers. He took off his hat and bowed his head.

"Listen here, holy man," Hale said. "I got a whole lot a respect for a man who dedicates his life to his flock, but when somethin' goes wrong with one of your sheep, it's a mistake to run off the only fella who knows how to help."

Pastor Ranklin raised his chin. "I have no idea what you're speaking of, my good man. Now, if you'd just—"

"It's a little girl, innit?" Hale said. "It's almost always a little girl."

Pastor Ranklin took a step back.

"Do you want the globe?" I asked, reaching into the box.

"Nah," said Hale. "We're past trinkets, Tod. This is the part where the good pastor starts to remember somethin' he heard when he was at the preacher college out east long ago." I looked at Pastor Ranklin and saw his brow furrowed, his eyes narrowed. "You're recallin' a little somethin' you'd all but forgotten, ain't ya, holy man?"

"I...I sent a letter to the Bishop a week and a half ago. Did he send you?"

Hale looked at me and sighed.

"Your Bishop and the church, they don't have much love for folks like me. Like I told you, I got nothin' but respect for the job you do, but all the prayin' in the world ain't gonna help that little girl. If the Bishop ever sends a response, he'll like as not tell ya to drown the girl or set her aflame. Now that straight out ain't right. I think we can all agree on that."

Pastor Ranklin had gone a ghastly shade of white. "But you're...you're..."

"What I am is here to help. And we—Tod and I—we mean to see it done. I'd like it to be with your help. Never hurts to have a holy man about, but Tod and me have a big burlap sack we can put you in 'til we're done. Wouldn't be the first time. Your choice, really."

The preacher looked about, checking to see if any of the townsfolk had noticed the interchange between himself and this flamboyantly dressed stranger. I looked about, too, and saw a number of curtains pulled back and the odd slightly ajar door.

"Your flock," I asked, "the townsfolk...do they know?"

"Some do," Pastor Ranklin said, looking at his toes. "We've been able to keep it the thing of rumors, but it has grown so bad...in the night...once the sun sets, it gets worse. Much, much worse."

Hale nodded, pulling his wide-brimmed hat back onto his head. "Where's the girl? I reckon she's somewhere abouts the church or maybe that big house over there." He tilted his head in the direction of a stately home with columns of freshly whitewashed wood.

The pastor lowered his voice. "It is a...sensitive matter. The mayor's daughter...It is a source of great embarrassment."

"Embarrassment? Why in the hell—beggin' your pardon in advance, Pastor—would the mayor have cause to be embarrassed?"

Pastor Ranklin flushed. "Well, the...condition of his daughter, of course."

"Condition?" Hale, ever the showman, spread his arms wide. He knew full well the audience was populated by more than just those of us in the square. More curtains shifted, and every door creaked open just a crack. "You say that like this is somehow that little girl's fault. Is that what you're thinking underneath that little skullcap on your head? Well, listen to me and listen good: ain't none of her fault at all. Ain't the fault of her family nor anybody in her house. Ain't nobody's fault. It weren't invited here, if that's what you're thinkin'. No sir. There's no reason. Ain't never any reason. Just happens now and again. And when it happens—if you're lucky—there's someone like me or young Tod here who might just be able to lend a hand." Hale lowered his hands to his hips and looked around, his gaze hitting every exposed patch of window and every sliver of open door. His eyes finally settled on Pastor Ranklin. "So tell me again, Pastor, just who's to blame for what you all been hearin' coming from the big house by the church these last few nights?"

"No one." The pastor shuffled from foot to foot as he whispered the words.

Hale cupped a calloused hand to his ear and leaned forward. "I really weren't askin' for me," he said. "How's about you tell it loud and strong so's all of them can maybe hear it from you. Who's to blame, Pastor?"

The pastor cleared his throat and responded in the voice he reserved for sermons and such.

"No one is to blame for what has happened here," he said.

Hale placed his hand on Pastor Ranklin's shoulder.

"Nicely done," he said. "It's good for them to hear it from you. Me? I'm nobody. Once we're done here, Tod and me, we move on. But you? You're the man they turn to. You're...what's the word...oh yeah. Permanent. That's you. Permanent. These folks'll be lookin' to you long after we're just a bad memory. It's best it looks like you have all the answers. Especially with somethin' like this."

Hale took a step back and smiled.

"That said, you given any more thought to that burlap bag I mentioned earlier?"

All agreed that the burlap bag could stay secure in the wagon. Given the choice, most holy men opt to help. The pastor wrung his hands and looked towards the mayor's house.

"Would you...would you like to see the child now?"

Hale gauged the sun on its trek toward the horizon, glanced at the big white house, and shook his head. Turning to face the inn, Hale adjusted his hat and strode away.

"I'm awful hungry," he said. "Tod, them kilns got fires stoked?"

"Not yet," I said, tilting my head toward the pastor. "I got a little interrupted."

"I don't pay you to be interrupted, Tod. We need a powerful heat, and to have that, the kilns need fire. Best get to it."

"You know, I'm hungry, too," I told him. "Working all day tends to build a hunger in a fellow. Just in case you've forgotten."

"Best hurry, then. Else I mightn't leave ya nothin' but crumbs. Pastor Ranklin, let me buy you a drink. You can fill me in on what's what while my 'prentice does his work."

I finished the last of my assembly. Lorne gave me a few coals from his forge to get my kilns fired. I fed the fires with wood and charcoal, then slid the stones of the glory hole into place.

Lorne accompanied me to the inn. Hale sat at a table with the pastor and another man. That man was dressed in quality clothing, and there was nary a hint of sweat or shit on anything he wore. Here was the mayor.

"Well, if it ain't my 'prentice Tod gracin' us with his presence. What's the matter, run out of daylight?"

"Something like that," I said. "There's about a half hour before sunset, I'd say. Any food left for us?"

A pot of stew sat cold in the center of the table along with some crusts of bread. I spooned some into bowls for Lorne and myself.

"Tod," Hale said, "this here's the mayor. It's his daughter's been afflicted. Eight years old."

"How long has she been presenting symptoms?" I asked.

"Afflicted near a month."

I whistled. "That's a long time. What do you figure?"

"Won't know 'til I see her. But I don't want to see her 'til it's good and dark."

The mayor glanced toward his house through the inn's single window and turned pale. "Why would you wait?" he asked, then his voice dropped. "It's so much worse after dark."

Hale sniffed. "After dark's the only time I got an even chance of getting all of it. Trust me on this. You want me to get all of it."

I looked up from my bowl and caught the pastor's eye.

"I was wondering, sir, if you might have a jar of ink to spare. I've been watering mine for the past two weeks, and it's mighty thin."

Pastor Ranklin leaned across the table. "If you and this…gentleman can help us with our…our problem, then I think I could convince the mayor to give you a barrel of ink."

"Much obliged," I said, "but a jar is all I'll need."

As I chased the last remnants of broth around the bottom of my bowl with a crust of bread, Hale cleared his throat.

"Tod," he said. "Once you're done, you'd best tend to those fires. I want the crucible filled and ready to go. Could be quick, could be a long haul. Might be this is your night."

I sat up taller.

"My turn?"

"We'll see," said Hale. "Let's get the lay of the land afore we go makin' any decisions."

I pushed my bowl to the center of the table and headed to the door. Lorne tagged along. The smith knew how to make a fire hot, and a second set of hands are always welcomed. We stoked all three sections of the kiln, and as we were closing up the glory hole, Lorne's curiosity got the better of him.

"In the inn," he said, "you asked the pastor for some ink."

"That's right. The ink I have barely stains the page."

"So…you know your letters?"

I told him I did, then went to the wagon and pulled out the leather-bound journal I kept. I opened it and leafed through the pages so he could see my writings and sketches. His eyes grew wide, more at the pictures than the words, I figure. I showed him the last few entries and their faded, watered-down strokes.

"How is it," he asked, "that a glassblower's apprentice has the way of words and letters?"

"I haven't always been a glassblower's apprentice."

Hale, Pastor Ranklin, and the mayor spilled through the tavern's doors. Hale walked about the kilns and racks and nodded with satisfaction. He turned his attention to the west. The curve of the sun had just crept below the horizon, staining the sky with an ominous streak of crimson.

"Might be a sky like that portents well for sailors," Hale said with a shrug. "Too bad we ain't sailors."

Hale hunkered down next to one of the wagon's wheels and pulled his hat down over his eyes. The pastor and mayor looked at me in disbelief, but I just shook my head. It wasn't time, and I told them so. To avoid conversation I busied myself, fiddling with the blowpipes and the tongs. I have to admit that was only part of it. I could feel it building, that presence in the mayor's house. It felt like ash in the back of my throat, and there was a thrum like the beating of a partridge's wings that unsettled me to my core, but the villagers couldn't feel it. Not the way I could. Once the purple had faded from the sunset and we were in full dark, Hale rose to his feet so abruptly that he gave all of us a start.

"Torches," he said to no one in particular. "Here, here, here, here and here." With every *here*, Hale ground his heel into the dirt to indicate where he wanted them planted. Lorne and I took the torches I'd placed by the wagon and set them. Hale checked that everything was positioned how he wanted it, then paused. "Tod. If it's you tonight, is everything where you'll need it? Would you move anything?"

I looked over our set up. "It's just as you've taught me, Hale. Everything is in easy reach. I think we're good."

"Then let's go see the little girl. Mayor, lead the way."

Inside the house, we were greeted by a serving girl and the mayor's wife. Both women were disheveled, and their postures spoke of a weariness that went deeper than the physical. The mayor's wife was weeping, and I noted that the serving girl's cheeks bore streaks of fresh run tears. As was usually the case, the women of the house were the ones carrying most of the physical and emotional cost of the affliction. My gender, it shames me to admit, tends to find excuses to vacate when the going gets too rough, and that's an option most mothers just can't abide. They remain and almost always pay a heavy toll.

"Who are these men?" the mayor's wife asked as Hale tipped his hat.

"We're here to help, ma'am," Hale said, "if we're able. Tod, can you feel it?"

"I can," I told him. "This one is frightfully strong."

Hale strode down the hallway toward a closed door. The serving girl moved to stop Hale.

"Miss," I said, gently taking her by the arm, "I assure you, we are here to help. We've seen this before, and we know the hell—pardoning my language, of course, but there's no other word for it—that you and the girl's mother have suffered through this past month. If you could please take your lady into some quiet corner of the house, I promise you, we'll do all that we can."

When I had first apprenticed with Hale, he told me, "Don't never promise nothin'. Tell them you'll do as you can, but don't give false hope. Tell them there's a chance, sure, but don't ever give false hope. 'Cause, pure and simple, sometimes there just ain't any hope to be had." I'd been with Hale long enough to know the truth of those words. I'd seen the lost causes firsthand.

Watching the two women as they hurried away, I prayed this wasn't one of those times.

Hale opened the door at the end of the hall. With his left hand, he motioned for the rest of us to follow.

Oil lanterns hung from hooks in the four corners of what was usually the salon where the mayor received guests. All of the stately furniture was gone and faded spots on the walls spoke to paintings recently removed. The windows were boarded shut. The room was bare, save for the bed in the middle of the room and a small table standing next to it. On the table was a tray with a wooden bowl containing some pale broth.

Walking into the room past the heavy oak door, I paused to look at deep gouges in the wood at the top and bottom corners.

"Sometimes…" Pastor Ranklin whispered. "Sometimes she gets loose, and we have to leave her locked in here scuttling around until morning."

For now, she was secured. Tied to the bed by sturdy lengths of cord, each of her limbs strained against the knots. Hale shook his head. He nodded to me and Lorne.

"Hold her," he said. I indicated that Lorne ought to grab the same limb I held. "Hold her tight there, blacksmith. What's in her makes her a hell of a lot stronger than any eight-year-old girl has any business bein'."

Lorne got his first real look at her face and began to pull back. I pressed my shoulder against him to keep him in place. I wrapped my hands around her upper arm.

"Try not to look at her face. She's not controlling her muscles right now. That face you see, that's a mask that it has put there to scare you."

"It?" Lorne whispered. Although I could feel him trembling, his grip remained true.

Hale loosened the knots. He discarded their rope and replaced it with a length of our own cord. Using the complicated techniques he'd taught me, he secured her arm. He caught the pastor's questioning look.

"Knots are tricky things. Or they can be. Yours ain't tricky at all and, no offense, I only trust my own rope. No wonder she's been gettin' loose on ya. You gotta use a few tricks and magic them a little bit to keep this thing from workin' them loose."

There was no magic involved. Just tight and exactingly convoluted knotwork that would leave the best of sailors scratching their heads. Hale moved from limb to limb as Lorne and I assisted. As we went, the girl struggled with all her might, but Lorne and I were strong enough to keep one limb held while the other three were tied.

So far, she hadn't said a word. Sometimes they can't speak, or won't speak. Most of the time, however, they've got something to say. Up until now, she'd kept her vocalizations to hisses and growls, but that was all about to change.

Finishing his last knot, Hale gestured for Lorne and me to step back. We watched as the little girl's body arched and struggled, testing the limits of her newly secured wrists and ankles. Wood creaked, and the ropes flexed under the strain, but Hale knew what he was doing. The girl stopped thrashing and regarded Hale for the first time.

"I was wonderin' when you'd notice me," Hale said. "You got an inkling of what I am?"

The stream of vile profanities that spilled from that little girl's chapped and bloodied lips would wilt my quill and curdle this ink, diluted though it is, should I mark them here in this account. Even Lorne the blacksmith cringed at the filth that assaulted our ears.

"Well, that's just fuckin' charming," Hale said as the girl stopped for a breath. He looked to the mayor and Pastor Ranklin. "Can either of you tell me if she's able to move stuff without—"

The bowl of broth flew from the table and struck the wall. It impacted with such force that shards no bigger than a fingernail and a wet splatter across the wall were all that remained. The wooden spoon stood up on the table and began to spin. Hale grabbed the spoon and handed it to me.

"Small wonder your knots ain't been holdin' her." He moved his hand to touch the girl's forehead. She strained against her bonds and snapped at his fingers with her teeth. She laughed and rolled her eyes until only the whites showed.

Hale placed his palm on her forehead. All hell broke loose.

The bed lifted from the floor, rattling from leg to leg. The table shot straight up and shattered against the ceiling, sending a shower of plaster and fine dust down upon all of us. The door snapped open, then slammed shut. The four lamps swung inward on their hooks, straining toward the girl.

Hale pulled back his hand. The bed fell with a crash. Everything was still. Sweat stood out on Hale's forehead. I figure I'm the only one who noticed. He ran his tongue around the inside of his mouth before he spoke to me.

"So, Tod," he said. "I promised you you'd get a turn and you will. This one...this one seems a tad ornery. It's been in there a long time. Likely pretty firmly planted. You'll get your turn, I promise. Soon. Just not tonight. That fine by you?"

I looked at the girl, the smashed bowl, and the shattered table. I looked at the plaster on the floor and shook the dust from my hair. Tilting my head, I caught Hale's eye.

"Figure I'll let you take this one," I said.

"Mighty generous of you." Hale crossed to the door. "She ought to be quiet for a bit. We'd best get her outside quick. One man to a corner. Tod, you be ready to step in should she wake up."

Neither the mayor nor the pastor seemed interesting in being near the girl's head. After the language that had spewed from that mouth, I suppose I could hardly blame them. They picked up the bed down by her feet while Hale and Lorne grabbed the headboard. As they made their way out of the house, the girl stirred, growled, and twitched, but that was all. On the front porch, they lowered the bed to take a rest.

"Where to now?" the mayor asked.

Hale wandered off the porch. He stood, stretching his back, looking up at the stars. The night was clear, and though the moon hadn't risen, there was plenty of starlight to see by. Hale didn't look like he'd heard the mayor at all.

"We need to get her in the center of those torches," I told them. "I'll take Hale's corner."

We moved her across the town square. As we drew closer to the circle of torchlight and our kilns, the bed seemed to grow heavier. When I glanced down, the little girl was awake, and her bloodshot eyes glared at me.

"Let me go," she rasped and arched her back. The ropes strained, but I wasn't worried. Hale knew his knots, and I myself had woven those cords. She spat at me. A hefty gob of bloody phlegm spattered against my cheek. Hale wouldn't have flinched. She looked at Lorne. "I know you." The voice was different now. It was as close to a little girl voice as that parched throat could manage. "I know all about what you like to do. I know the way you look at me. I'll wager you wish you were down the other end so you could be looking up my nightdress like dear daddy and the pastor are."

"Don't listen," I said. "It speaks only lies. That's all it knows."

A pair of glaring soul-emptied eyes fixed me in their stare.

"And just who the fuck are you?" The guttural voice was back, and I was glad. That little girl voice was apt to break the resolve of those who knew her. I noticed that the knots were writhing. If Hale hadn't fixed them, she'd have been loose by now. "You think your little fucking tricksie ropes will hold me for long?"

I forgot my own advice and answered.

"They'll hold long enough."

We were among the torches, and I told the others where to place the bed. The girl's head moved from side to side, looking for an object that might be turned into a weapon, hurled about like the bowl and the table in her room. There'd be no joy on that count. All of our equipment, right down to the five torches that surrounded us and every last brick in our kilns had be charmed against such use. In the end, all she could do was throw up the odd frustrated blast of dust from the ground.

I motioned for the others to retreat beyond the torches. Pastor Ranklin protested.

"I am a man of God," he said, his prayer book and crook produced from some pocket in his vestments. "My place is here with the afflicted."

"Your place," said Hale stepping from the shadows, "is in full view of your flock but well out of my way. Stand over there in the torchlight and say some prayers if you're so inclined, but that burlap bag's in easy reach if I need it."

The pastor moved beyond our ring of torches.

"Nice of you to join us," I said to Hale. "See anything interesting up there in the sky?"

Hale just shook his head. He looked down at the little girl, then back at me. "You two been talkin'?"

"A little. Just the usual."

The face scowled at Hale. A snarl split her lips. The bed trembled, but here, in our circle, a little lift and rattle was all it could manage.

"Does that holy man know what you are, sorcerer?" The girl's body twisted against the ropes, accompanied by grunts of exertion.

"He suspects," Hale said, "but dealin' with me is a hell of a lot more palatable than leavin' you where you're at. Tod, get busy."

Taking my cue, I gathered the blowpipe and opened to door on the furnace. A wave of intense heat blasted my face, stealing the moisture from my eyes. Blinking, I looked within. There in the center, in the depression of the crucible, bubbled the bright orange-red brilliance of molten glass. With a practiced twirl, I loaded the end of the blowpipe. As I prepared the glass, I watched Hale out of the corner of my eye.

"You've had a whole month to get yourself a pretty good hold on that girl," Hale said, pulling a small leather pouch on a string from within his shirt. "It ain't good enough."

The girl spat and smiled. "You think this pitiful circle can hold me? You're fucked if you think that, sorcerer."

Hale licked the tip of his finger, then loosened the drawstring.

"You're the one what's fucked. As long as you're in bonds, that little girl's body is your prison. Now the church..." Here Hale inclined his head toward

Pastor Ranklin as he slipped his moistened fingertip into the pouch. "The church tends to either burn or drown afflicted folks, which don't really solve the problem at all. You bastards just wait until the body dies then fuck off into someone else." Here the girl laughed, and the sound sent a chill through me despite the heat of the furnace. "Or, if they're feelin' especially clever, they'll lock the poor child away in some dark pit for years and years. But eventually all flesh dies…and eventually your kind always goes free."

The girl was grinning now. "Time is on our side," she said. "Like you say, sorcerer, all flesh dies. I have all the time in the world."

Then Hale smiled, and in its own way, that smile was a lot more frightening.

"You got that much right," he said as he withdrew his finger from the pouch. The end was blackened, stained by the powder that clung to its moistened tip. Without warning, his finger was in the girl's mouth and swept once in an arch between her lips and teeth. She snapped in a frenzy, but Hale was quick and had never yet lost a finger.

Her tongue writhed inside her mouth and she spat.

"What…what…"

"That there's a little somethin' an old witchy-woman taught me how to make. She used to mix it up for wives whose asshole husbands got busy with their fists when they'd been drinkin'. A little pinch in that last tankard and they'd be in no shape to raise a hand against anyone."

Hale looked over at me. I'd readied the glass and started the initial blow. The glass was quality, and I'd loaded a little more from the crucible to make it thick. Coloring stood at the ready on a metal plate on the ground. With a nod, I knew Hale was ready and began adding color to the glass.

"You see," Hale said, returning his attention to the girl tied to the bed, "the church has their ways of dealin' with the likes of you…and I have my own. The church operates on…ah, what do you call it?"

"An assumption?" I offered, quickly returning my lips to the pipe.

"That's the word. Thank you, Tod. The church has this assumption that your kind are purely spiritual. Now, you and me…we know better. Your kind are like a zephyr. Like a hot wind, full of spite and menace and a longin' to act in the world. But you're weak. All spaced out and loose-like until you happen upon someone like this little girl here. Tired…a little sickly…scared. You drift over and wait to be breathed in with the air. Once you're in, you bide your time. Parents'll notice a little willfulness that weren't there afore, but they'll put it down to her just growin' up. Then things'll start gettin' bad. That sweet little girl'll start gettin' mean. Start breakin' things. Start hurtin' and killin' little things. Like a chick maybe. Maybe a kitten. Maybe a baby brother or sister. And it only gets worse."

Hale paused and checked my efforts. I had a solid thick globe started that I kept returning to the glory hole to stay pliable. He nodded to me, then put his hand on the girl's cheek and gently pushed her head to one side. There was no resistance.

"Given enough time, this little girl would be yours for the rest of her life. Truth be told, there's only ever a small window of opportunity to get you out of there. Coming over the hill this morning was a real stroke a luck for me and the boy. And for the folks of this town. Not so lucky for you, though.

"Flesh and blood always fail and die, but quality glass…"

Exhaling, Hale seized the girl's head, pressing his lips against hers. The strain visible across his shoulders, Hale breathed deep. The girl's back arched. She rose from the bed, each limb drawing the rope holding it tight. Hale continued to breathe in, his head trembling from the effort. The girl's eyes were open and panicked, but Hale held the seal of their lips, drawing all of it in.

At last, he pulled away, teeth clenched behind clamped shut lips. Hale's eyes were glazed and bloodshot. He motioned for the blowpipe. I pulled the pipe and its small ball of near molten colored glass from the glory hole, swinging the business end of the pipe to Hale's outstretched hands.

Spinning the pipe to keep the sphere from drooping, Hale pressed his lips against the blowpipe. His body shuddered, and the edges of his eyes creased with the wracking pain the exhalation caused him. Forcibly pulled from one body, the entity fought for all it was worth to keep from being expelled from this new one. Had it been me, it might have grabbed hold and taken up residency in my mortal shell, but it wasn't me. It was Hale. The entity never stood a chance.

I stepped to Hale's side as he rattled to the end of his lung-emptying exhalation. He nodded, and I squeezed my metal pincers against the stem of glass where the globe met the blowpipe, crimping the glass and sealing the sphere. Only then did Hale move his mouth away.

After a huge breath of fresh air, he grinned. It was a thing of bloodied teeth and split gums. Hale looked at the cloudy mass swirling inside the globe, speaking directly to the entity within.

"As I was saying: Flesh and blood will always fail and die, but quality glass—if kept safe and sound—well, quality glass will last forever."

Hale moved the sphere over to the soaked, shaped block of wood for removal. There was a depression in the block the perfect depth for a globe this size. Hale moved into position.

"Have at 'er, Tod," he said, then whispered, "but make it quick. I can scarcely hold the pipe."

I rasped our fine-toothed saw along the top of the crimp in quick, sharp strokes, scoring the glass around the circumference. With my pincers, I tapped the blowpipe three times before the scored glass snapped and the pipe came free from the globe. I stepped away and opened our cooling kiln—the annealer. I held out the carrying tongs for Hale.

"You'd best do it," he said, lowering the glass-caked end of the blowpipe to the ground, leaning on it like a staff for support. "My arms are shaking like the devil. I don't dare trust in my strength right now. I'm like as not to drop the damn thing. Get it in quick. Don't want to shock the glass."

It had never taken this much out of Hale before, but I couldn't dwell on that. He was right. If I didn't get the globe into our cooling kiln quickly, all of our work would be for naught. Gingerly, I lowered the tongs over the globe and brought them together so the globe rested on them like an egg on an eggcup. I'd checked a dozen times during the afternoon that the path between the blowing station and the annealer was clear of any debris that was wont to trip me up. I still measured every single step with an extra dose of caution. It felt like I took far too long, but soon the globe was nestled safe in the cooling kiln. I closed the door and wired it shut.

I heard the girl gasp at the same instant I saw Hale tumble to the ground. Instinct sent me to Hale's side. Lorne, the mayor and Pastor Ranklin rushed to the girl. I threw a glance toward the bed. The mayor's daughter, now freed from the influence of the entity, struggled frantically with panic in her eyes.

"Untie her," I called as I cradled Hale's head in my lap. His eyes were bloodshot, his teeth stained by the blood from his gums. He reached up to pat the side of my face but only mustered enough strength to make a half-hearted effort before gravity dragged his arm down.

"Holy shit," he said, and his voice was a papery, raspy thing. "That one had a good little hold on 'er." He coughed some blood-speckled spittle to his chin. I rubbed it away with my sleeve. "Don't worry none. I got it all out and breathed it all into the globe. Sure as hell put up a scramble when it realized I aimed to blow it out, though. I'm getting too old for this, Tod. Figure I'll let you handle the next one."

"Tod," Lorne called, "we could use a little help over here. The girl's mighty distressed, but there's not a one of us can figure out these knots."

"You go help," Hale said, gathering enough strength to pull his hat down over his eyes. "I'll just rest up here a bit."

"Be sure resting is all you do," I said, lowering his head to the ground and finding my feet. "Don't you go dying on me or anything. Glassblowing's a two-man job. You taught me that."

The next day Hale was up at the break of noon, and though I'd already taken orders for bottles, jars, and such from half the townsfolk, he told me I was a slacker who would never amount to anything. To his credit, once he'd checked the fires and the amount of glass I had prepared in the crucible, he turned his attention to the girl.

"How's the globe?" he asked. "Coolin' without no flaws, I hope."

"I looked in on it an hour ago. Cooling nicely."

"And the girl? You been up to see her?"

I waved my hand around our set up and pointed to the annealer.

"I haven't been idle, Hale. There's more than just the globe in there, you know. I've been filling orders. It's hard making quality glass all by yourself."

"Hard work's good for the soul. Just ask Pastor Ranklin. I reckon I'll go and see him and the mayor. See what's what."

"Fine, but I'm starting on bottles soon. I'll need your help with the shaping. Don't be long."

Hale found me at the inn as I finished a bowl of beans. He settled on the bench across from me and ladled himself a helping from the pot. Reaching into his pocket, he found a small stoppered jar and placed it on the table.

"Pastor Ranklin sends his regards," he said around a mouthful of beans. "Says you two had some sort of deal."

"He offered a barrel. I only need a jar." I drained the last of my beer, wiping my mouth with my sleeve. "It wasn't easy making those bottles by myself, you know..."

"If this job were easy, folks wouldn't be lining up for our services."

Three days after the exorcism, it was time for us to leave. Everyone from miles around who needed glass had called on us, and the last of our wares had been picked up that morning. Only one item remained. I'd finished hammering the box together with some nails Lorne had been kind enough to supply. I'd offered to pay for the nails, but our money was no good.

Hale lined my new box with a handful of straw. From the back of our wagon, he found a canvas bag that once held a hundred-count of fine silk scarves bought at considerable cost in a distant port town out east. Hale removed one of the handful remaining and crammed it into his pocket.

"Look lively, Tod," he said, inclining his chin across the town square. "Here comes the mayor and his young 'un."

Father and daughter walked side by side, though as they drew near, the mayor lagged back. Hale had sent only for the girl.

She walked forward bravely. Only a little wisp of a thing, she couldn't have weighed more than a bag of feed grain. She was pale, but there was color in her cheeks. Only the dark rings under her eyes spoke to the ordeal she'd been through.

Hale gathered the globe, slowly cooled over three days, into his bare hands and dropped to one knee. The girl's steps became less sure as her gaze lighted on the sphere. Through the colored glass she could see the dark mass swirling within. She came forward, stopping an arm's length away.

"You and me," Hale said, "ain't been properly introduced. My name's Hale, and this here's Tod."

"I'm...Anya." She looked from Hale to me, her eyes settling once more upon the globe. "Is that...is that what was in me?"

Hale shifted the globe, holding it one handed, perched on his fingertips. He turned it slowly, letting the sunlight dance about the surface.

"It surely is," he said. "Don't look too hard. We build some pretty color into the glass, but nothin' can really mask the ugliness inside. It's an ugliness no one should ever have to look at."

Anya bit her lip, mustering the courage for her next question.

"Is it trapped in there?"

"So long as the glass don't break, it is well and truly trapped. That's the thing, Anya. This glass, though as thick as I can make it, is fragile. It's gotta be cared for."

"Will you do that?"

"Nope," Hale said, pulling the silk scarf from his pocket with a flourish and wrapping it around the globe. "It ain't for me to look after it. That's way too responsible a job for a couple of travelin' men like Tod and me." Hale gently placed the wrapped sphere into the box I'd made, fluffing the straw about the edges so it nestled within like some sort of giant egg. "You see, Anya." Hale paused and spoke to the townsfolk in the square who had been edging ever closer to listen in. "The rest of you might as well hear this too, so gather in. The thing in the globe has a taste for you now, Anya. It knows its way in, and if it gets free, it won't hesitate to take up residence in you again. That'll be a problem. If it gets in there again, it'll take a better man than me to draw it out."

Hale held out the box.

"This is yours to care for. Keep it safe and secure and you got nothin' to fear. Only problem is, the thing in that globe has a taste for you, and it's a taste that don't stop with you. Any children you have and any children they have and so forth—all of 'em are…damn it, Tod, what's that word I always forget?"

"Susceptible," I told him.

"That's the one. Thanks, Tod. All of 'em are susceptible to this thing should it get free. So, keep it safe and secure and pass along to your children and their children just how hellish a thing this globe—this family heirloom—is."

She took the box in both hands, retreating to her father's side without a word. The mayor opened his mouth to speak. Hale shook his head and rose to his feet. He brushed the dust from his knee and looked about.

"You got everything packed and ready to go, Tod?"

"I do."

"Good," he said, climbing onto the wagon's bench seat, pulling his hat down over his eyes.

I put my foot on the rail, about to pull myself up to join him when I felt a hand on my shoulder. I turned my head.

"I gotta know," Lorne said. "How is it that a man who has his words and letters and the manners and speech of a gentleman…how is it that you come to be rattling around the countryside as an apprentice to a…to a man like this?"

I dropped my voice so only Lorne could hear.

"I tell you this only because I like you, Lorne," I said. "Hale won't be around forever, and this is work that will always need to be done. I had good reason to sign on as Hale's apprentice and learn this trade. My little sister has just such a globe safe at home in her possession."

I mounted the wagon and gave the reins a shake. There was another village out there somewhere waiting for us.

There was always another village waiting for us.

BELLY SPEAKER

Nicole Givens Kurtz

THERE ARE MOMENTS WHEN THE GROWTH OF ONE'S PERSON SHIFTS FROM being centered around the outside forces to those internal. Honeysuckle Wynn knew this with all the thriving beat of her heart.

The sharp New Mexican wind lodged grit in the corners of her mouth. She wiped her lips with the back of her sleeve and spat onto the dirt. Morning broke the horizon. She squinted against the shimmering light. All around, the desert landscape changed like so many towns before with tall poles and colorful canopies, exotic wildlife, and strange odors. Tucked into the crook of Honey's arm, Momma Wynn watched with unblinking eyes as the rainbow of tents sprouted up against the flushed sky. Early morning laborers' grunts and shouts broke the new day's quiet. Fires snapped and crackled from makeshift pits. Smoke wafted across the field, snaking across the grounds, seeking freedom.

"Honey! Git over 'ere and lend a hand. Ya know Anna's wit child!" Carnival owner, Bob Mathers, gestured his meaty and chapped hands toward Anna, swollen and pink, who rubbed the small of her back.

"I'm practicing." Honeysuckle adjusted Momma Wynn against her knee, and then gestured with her head to the doll.

"Practicing what? How hard is it to make that stupid log of wood talk? Git over 'ere," Bob barked.

Don'tcha go over to 'em. Bloated pale pig. Momma Wynn's hoarse voice held hints of anger.

"You say somethin'?" Bob crossed his arms across his round belly and glared. "Eh?"

"Nothing!" Honeysuckle squinted at Momma Wynn and met her glass glare. In a whisper, she added, "Shush you. He the boss. We the workers."

You the slave and he the massa.

"We ain't slave no more. Thank ya, Mr. Lincoln, God rest his soul. We found freedom doin' this work. Now come on. No rockin' the boat." Honeysuckle sighed and sat Momma Wynn down beside her chair before heading over to the carnival owner.

People crawled around—some she knew, some she didn't. Honeysuckle found comfort in strangers. Her dark robe brushed the tops of her boots as she walked. They fell in a shush across the desert floor but shot little dusty clouds in her wake.

Even once she reached Big Bob, she could hear Momma Wynn whispering in her mind. *Don listen to 'em. Don't listen to 'em. Devils! Demons!*

"You walk so slow, lazy ass." Bob grunted and started toward the big tent. "Hercules could use some help with the cages."

Honeysuckle let it go, as her people had practiced doing for decades, letting the rancid bark of those supposedly superior flow from their scarred and marred backs. Holding her head high, she reached Hercules.

"Big man."

"Witch." He rumbled in greeting as he stood tall against the rising sun. Already drenched with sweat, he pushed a punishing hand through his shoulder-length hair. A mountain of a man, Hercules hadn't been his real name. After the war, everyone became someone else, even the nobodies. Carnival work gave them labels, allowed them to become strong men, funny men, belly speakers.

"I told you not to call me that." Honeysuckle reached down for the sledgehammer. "My momma was killed by witchcraft."

"Ah." Hercules had a sheen of anxious sweat dripping down his forehead. A hulking dark figure, he reached out for the sledgehammer. Callused rough hands waved her toward him. "Gimme, *witch*."

He smirked outright, fleshing out a dimple. If he hadn't been so cruel, he might've been handsome.

A cold chill filtered up from her belly, gushing like a geyser inside her. *Thack!*

She swung the heavy sledgehammer with ease, as if she had an extra set of hands. Honeysuckle watched the scarlet wound blossom across Hercules' upper chest, at the base of his throat, where the hammer's chipped edge snared his tanned flesh. The red stain inked its way through his thick fingers, clawing at his throat, dark eyes bulging as he fought to breathe.

Round, unblinking eyes took it all in.

"You don't hear too good. Do ya?" The sledgehammer smacked the dirt as it slid from Honeysuckle's grasp.

The icy burn began to recede, and as it did, she came back to herself. Her limbs tingled with pinpricks as if she'd been out in the cold too long. At once, Bob's shouting and Hercules' wheezing screams rent the dry air, and the thundering of running feet joined.

"What the hell you doin?" Bob shoved Honeysuckle aside. "Here! Here! Anna, get the doc!"

Honeysuckle's belly balled into a knot of gnawing fear. *What happened?*

She stumbled forward, tripping over the hammer's handle but catching herself before she hit the ground.

Bob snatched himself around to her, red-faced and spitting, fat bushy eyebrows crouched down in fury over angry, beady eyes. "You ain't right in the head. Git outta my sight! Where the hell is Doc? Herc's turnin' blue!"

Honeysuckle pushed through the thin crowd and marched back to her trailer, scooped up Momma Wynn, and retreated to its comforts. Inside, the oily smell of kerosene overpowered the scents of old tomes and the passage of time. The lantern's soft glow cast shadows into heavy curtains and worn, leather-bound books. She plopped down on the edge of her bed and grabbed a bottle of whiskey from the floor beside. As she fingered the capped mouth, the amber liquid sloshed about half empty.

Just like Honeysuckle.

"What happened?" Honeysuckle whirled around to Momma Wynn sitting on the loveseat.

The miniature doll with its hand-painted clothing, shoes, and facial features shook and then began to grow. The wood rings pulsated in hypnotic fashion. Her soulless eyes widened, as did she—long wooden legs stretched out until the four-toed feet touched the throw rug. Lanky, thin, branch-like arms creaked as she reached out with four-fingered hands. The oblong head swelled till it reached the ceiling. Leafy branches sprouted around her head to create a verdant afro.

Her lipless mouth opened, and Momma Wynn spoke. "Nothin'."

"Nothin'! He could die! If Hercules dies, Imma be headed for the noose, and you to the fire."

"Squashin' a bug. Riddin' the area of pests. Nothin' more." The gravelly voice clashed with Momma Wynn's faux cheery face. Somehow it made her words more sinister.

Honeysuckle swallowed to ease her dry throat before trying again.

"There's a big difference between bugs and people."

Momma Wynn's shimmering laughter shook her leaves, making them rustle in the small space, forcing the shadows to flicker. It raised gooseflesh along Honeysuckle's arms and tightened the knot in her belly.

Ever since she could remember, she'd had Momma Wynn. The wooden doll had spoken to her when she'd been old enough to fetch water from the well back in Tennessee, but never had she been in such a predicament as this. With mounting fear, Honeysuckle gaped at Momma Wynn, reclining on the loveseat unabashed. The grinning mouth, stretched to accommodate the now larger face, mocked Honeysuckle's fury. At the moment, all Honeysuckle could do was wait.

"Momma, we can't just attack a white man, even all the way out here! There's gonna be hell to pay, even if Hercules don't die."

"Ain't nobody gonna call me outta my name. Not no more."

"He didn't. He was talkin' to me..."

"Same as talkin' to me."

"But, Momma..."

"Hush now, chile."

A series of shouts and the sounds of laborers outside jolted Honeysuckle awake. Through bleary eyes and a pounding headache, she looked over to Momma Wynn. Though still seated on the loveseat, the doll's feet were now suspended high above the throw rug. Honeysuckle closed her eyes and breathed through the thundering at her temples. How'd she read the stars so wrong? Joining up with Bob's Traveling Circus had given her a place to stay, a way to see the country, and money, her own freedom. She peered over at Momma Wynn. Had she really achieved that freedom? Yeah, from bondage and servitude, sure. Although never alone, she *was* alone all the time. Momma Wynn didn't like people, especially those being friendly with Honeysuckle. The doll had helped her ice over the grief of her momma's death and helped her talents as a belly speaker grow. But, the doll had also crept up inside of her and tore a hole that she couldn't fix.

"My head just feels in pain. I hate this."

"No, you don't. You just ain't use to what you like." Momma Wynn snickered.

"I know this is wrong!" Honeysuckle climbed to her feet, using the bed as leverage. Held down by her side, her fist shook as she stepped closer to the smirking dummy. The big painted-on smile and those wide, unblinking eyes stared straight ahead. It infuriated Honeysuckle.

"It's better to feel pain than nothin' at all."

Honeysuckle pulled back her hand from where she'd reached for Momma Wynn. The doll laughed. Despite the mirth, it held warning.

"How would you know? You don't feel anything! Just a stupid dummy." Honeysuckle crossed her arms in a huff. Momma Wynn had a way of reducing her from her twenty-five years to twelve.

"Your bones gonna be dust, forgotten and absorbed into the black earth, soon enough, so take pleasure in sufferin'! That's all there is anyway."

"Just cause my skin is dark don' mean Imma just lay down and die. Yeah, we suffer, Momma, but we live too. We fight hard, but we rise up and live. Imma keep on livin'."

Honeysuckle sighed as the cool springs rose from her belly, filtering through her body, like rushing waters. She'd pushed too far.

"Momma..." She hated how it sounded so much like a whine. "Somehow, you make me feel like I can't live without you, and I'm big enough now to get on."

"Out here folks live by the loaded gun. Only one gonna defend ya and keep ya safe, baby girl. *Me*."

A shudder rocketed through Honeysuckle. Momma Wynn's words rattled around inside her, down into her empty belly where all manner of darkness swirled, or so she imagined. Thanks to Momma Wynn, she could never trust her own eyes, for the magic altered how she saw things. Honeysuckle did know there was something beyond *this*.

I can get away from her, but...

Banging interrupted her thoughts.

"Honey! Open this blasted door 'fore I tear it off!" Bob's knocking shook the trailer.

"Comin'! I'm comin'." She dropped the empty whiskey bottle, and it clattered to the floor.

With her head full of regret, Honeysuckle went to the door and peered through the thin curtain. Sure enough, Bob's balding and sunburned head turned to face her.

"Open the door!"

With a sigh, she unlocked the door and retreated farther inside. If the mob wanted her, they'd have to come in and get her. She wasn't gonna make it easy for them. The trailer sagged under Bob's weight. He squeezed into the tiny room, filling it with the odor of sweat and filth. He got almost to the loveseat before he quit trying to get closer.

Honeysuckle climbed to the rear of her bed where a small window rested at her back. Crouched on her heels, she held Momma Wynn in one hand. The roaring in her ears grew louder, and Momma Wynn's whispered chuckle served as an unsettling undercurrent. The air hung heavy with tension.

"What you want?" Honeysuckle clutched the doll tighter, and her skin grew colder.

"Now, Honey, ain't nothin' to be frightened 'bout." He shot her a greasy smile. "Old Herc's gonna live. May not talk again, but he'll live."

Honeysuckle held her breath and waited for the rest. Experience had taught her that white men always repaid back in kind what they perceived as defiance. The pull of the icy blackness welled up from her belly and pressed against her lips. She kept her mouth closed, but the pressure continued to build.

Bob's beady eyes shifted down to the doll and then back to Honeysuckle. "You, uh, use magic for that thing, huh? To make it talk?"

Honeysuckle shook from the freezing cold that exploded inside of her. The corners of her trailer went white. Frost crawled up the windows behind her, and her breath escaped in puffs. The kerosene lanterns flickered in warning. Then suddenly laughter spilled out of her. Chills skated along her flesh in concert with the stream of maniacal mirth. Across from her, Bob scowled in confusion, at first, and then took a pained step backward, clearly unnerved.

"Where you goin'?"

The voice's coarseness shocked Bob, and he glanced down to Momma Wynn.

"You heard me. Why the rush to run?"

His head snapped up to Honeysuckle. "Shut that dummy up 'fore it git you hurt."

Honeysuckle swallowed but held her lips shut. Truth was, she couldn't open them if she tried.

"Just, uh, keep yourself to yourself. Ya hear me?" With that, Bob squeezed out of the wagon so fast he snared his sleeve on the door's latch. He cursed and banged around the door's frame before disappearing into the blushing morn.

But the tone of his voice had held warning.

"That's it?" Honeysuckle blinked in disbelief.

He didn't answer.

She already had her answer. That wasn't the end. No way they would just leave her unscathed after she attacked Hercules. Her reckoning had only been postponed. The West stayed wild despite all the attempts to tame it, claim it, and abuse it. A fierce rejection of conformity. This wide expanse of nothing held a kinship with Momma Wynn—barren and unyielding. Perhaps that's why Momma Wynn was so strong out here.

"Imma go out. Get food. I'm starvin'." Honeysuckle picked up her rifle and took a breath.

She glanced over to the doll and awaited the rebuke.

Silence.

Honeysuckle headed out into the yucca-scented air of a new day.

In the arid, high desert, few animals stirred this early. Honeysuckle pointed her rifle at the dawn and marched across the open space in search of food. Soon she happened upon a group of rodent-like animals, peeking out of a mound. It seemed some stood as sentries watching out for bigger predators, like her. She crouched down slowly and remained still. Bob called them prairie dogs and told her to keep it to herself. Although the idea of eating dog turned her stomach, Bob had assured her that they tasted gamy and weren't real dog. Now, she just had to get one because her hunger was so real even the yucca looked tasty. It'd make a solid morning meal. From this distance, the camp's din punctured the quiet. The aroma of roast meat wafting from their campgrounds made her belly growl and her mouth water.

The wind whipped about something fierce, driving some of the prairie dogs back into their mound. They weren't the only ones on the prowl. Once the wind died, the heavy shuffle of feet snared her attention. Honeysuckle rose from the sparse brush, rifle in hand.

"Who's there?"

The wind roared again, stealing some of her words, but not her rising alarm. The hunter turned prey. A way of life for women in the West and in these lawless times.

A few feet away, Bob and a cluster of dusty men stopped. The two on horseback wore cowboy hats and apathetic glares. Bob and Hercules stood, horseless. The animals whinnied in greeting. They must've followed her, tracked her like an animal through the brush. Hercules carried a thick rope in one hand, and an angry scowl marred his face. The deep purple bruise across his neck spoke louder than any words he could say. That shut him up. The others wore gun belts slung low on their waists.

A lynch mob.

She warned Momma Wynn this would happen. Reckoning would come, and as always with men, so would violence.

"Go easy, Honey." Bob gestured with his fat left hand for her to lower her weapon.

"Mornin' again, Bob. Gentlemen." Honeysuckle sweetened her words but kept her rifle raised. The familiar feeling in her belly stirred.

"You know why I'm here." Bob nodded at Hercules. "We gotta make this right."

The others grunted in agreement.

"You sayin' my apology ain't enough?" Honeysuckle shuddered as the iciness flowed throughout her person. The wind picked up, again, but she held her weapon firm. Her fingers ached.

"Now, Honey, you attacked, hell, damn near killed 'em." Bob jerked a thumb at Hercules. "Aint' no savage gonna get at my crew. We can't have that kind of doin' 'round 'ere. We civilized folk."

"Ask the Indian 'bout that," Honeysuckle whispered.

"What? Speak up!" Bob moved closer, but still out of striking distance. "Quit ya mumbling."

Honeysuckle trained the gun on him. "No closer or she bangs."

The men on horseback drew their guns. At this, she finally took them in. Two shiny stars had been pinned to their shirts—a sheriff and a deputy.

Four men.

Three guns.

Two horses.

One Honeysuckle.

As the rising panic pressed against her throat, she squeezed her fingers tighter around the rifle, but she couldn't make them stop trembling.

Ain't no man gonna hurt my baby.

"Momma..."

The ache eased from her fingers, and a cool calm settled over her. She sighed as the internal whispers offered assurance and comfort. Nothing to fear.

Momma promised she'd protect her. A low drone, a hum of laughter, rippled up from her belly.

"Now, dontcha go beggin' for ya ma. You hurt Herc. The sheriff here says that's a hangin' offense." Bob adjusted his pants and gun belt.

Behind him, on the gray horse, the thin sheriff tipped his hat and spat at wad of tobacco. Thin rivulets of tobacco streamed down his chin into his beard. His pistol remained in his hand, ready to render judgment.

"You ain't got no arrest papers, no jury or trial. This is still America." Honeysuckle swallowed. "And I have rights now. Not as many as you, but I got 'em."

The men chuckled, then sobered.

"Out here, all this openness. Who gonna find ya?" Bob asked, wiping the sweat from his face.

"Who'd care?" the sheriff snorted.

"One less blackie to bother us," the other added with a shrug.

"Killing me kills your profit. I bring a fair bit of coin to you, paying customers who like my show." Honeysuckle knew her act provided good attendance. Curious people loved her "exotic" looks and the strangeness of her belly speaking abilities. They'd often try to touch her hair, her skin, and of course, Momma Wynn. Honeysuckle didn't like equating her life's worth with money—that happened all too often to her people—but that seemed all men like Bob understood.

Your grace is wasted on 'em.

Bob paused and studied her as he stroked his double chins.

The others' hard chuckles tapered off, and in the void, silence swelled.

Your good heart gonna get you chewed up.

"Ain't you got somethin' to say, Hercules?" The words thundered, spooking the men.

"Who said that?" Bob asked, looking around, pistol slicing through the air as he waved it.

"Don't all you men folk got all the answers?" the same voice jeered.

"She said it!" The sheriff nodded at Honeysuckle.

"Nuh uh. Her lips didn't move," the deputy countered.

They looked around, at each other, and then back to Honeysuckle. No one else had arrived. She hadn't moved. Instead, Honeysuckle held Hercules' dark, angry gaze. The voice clearly wasn't hers.

"Oh. You can't, can you?" She smirked, but not on her own accord.

Hercules lunged at her, and she fired… wide. It was enough to force the sheriff and his deputy to return fire.

Confusion erupted around them as Momma Wynn's anger rose. A crack of electricity made the deputy's horse whinny and then collapse to the ground, rolling onto the man's leg. Agonized howls joined the chorus of shouts and cursing.

Hercules dropped to the ground and tossed his arms over his head.

Bob shouted in fury and with fist raised, spun to face the sheriff. "Ya almost shot me!"

"Shut up! She's gettin' away!"

"Ma leg! Ma leg!" the deputy screamed.

Honeysuckle ran, scattering the prairie dogs and other creatures as she fled. She'd used her talent for mischief before, but this time it may have saved her life.

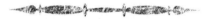

The tiny fire's flames licked at the skinned rabbit with eagerness. Still daylight, Honeysuckle hunched down in an abandoned hogan, a home the Dine had used as a dwelling. Perhaps they'd had nothing left to fight for so they'd pushed on. Or were too weary of war. Honeysuckle had collected tumbleweeds and wood pieces scattered around the truncated trees to make a feeble fire. After that, she'd managed to catch a rabbit, snapping its neck to avoid alerting Bob to her location. Her hunting knife did the rest. The fire's smoke only spoke to an occupant, not necessarily her. Still, an anxiousness settled around her. Each animal scuttling and twig snapping made her jump.

Full, with greasy fingers still tender from pinching the searing meat, Honeysuckle blew out a breath. She couldn't stay here forever. Momma Wynn waited, as did the rest of her own belongings, back in her trailer. With her fear in full bloom, she didn't dare chance a return without a plan. For now, the fizzing ceased inside, but everything felt just beyond her grasp.

She rubbed her arms, but that offered little ease from the raw anxiety crawling across her skin. Using the last stores of energy she had, she stood and peered out across the New Mexican landscape. The setting sun flushed the horizon with pinks and oranges. Such a glorious place for such ugly things to occur.

But she and chaos were old friends. Her life's map bore many memories of conflict and close calls. Each time, Momma Wynn had been there, an ever-present pillar of maternal strength. This time Honeysuckle would have to be bold, and her boldness would need to stand alone.

But did she have to do it alone?

Don't underestimate the things Imma do, Momma Wynn had told her this more than once. The dummy's protection had saved Honeysuckle, too. Momma Wynn's cold sensations left her feeling hollow like this hogan.

Why battle alone against the mob? Across the flat land, Honeysuckle glimpsed something in the falling light. Almost at once, she blended back into the hogan's shadows cloaking herself in its darkness. The rustling grew louder as the minutes ticked by. She crawled over to the fire where her pack rested and fished out her hunting knife. Her rifle would announce her location to others, but she picked it up anyway. The blade would do, but having both made her feel prepared. She scurried back to her previous position by the door.

The wind stilled and thickened with each breath. A thatch of cacti shuddered moments before the wooden doll emerged. Momma Wynn. Some rogue debris stuck to her hair and clothing, but she reached the outer edge of the yard.

"Momma!" Honeysuckle dropped the weapons and raced out to retrieve her.

Once she scooped the doll up, the cold crawling inside her returned. Despite this, she was comforted.

"Be calm," Momma Wynn whispered.

"How'd you get here? How'd you find me?" Honeysuckle searched the surroundings. No one. She pivoted back inside with her heart pounding.

Stunned, she sat down beside the fire. As she plucked the debris out of Momma Wynn's hair, she peered at the doll's short wooden legs.

"Momma?"

"Yeah?"

"How'd you find me?" Honeysuckle's mouth had gone dry.

"I'll find you no matta where ya go. We one." Momma Wynn laughed as if the question was ridiculous.

It raised chills across Honeysuckle's arms. "What that mean?"

Honeysuckle cradled Momma Wynn in her lap, both facing the fire. Momma Wynn's head suddenly turned 180 degrees to face Honeysuckle.

"I men' what I said. We gonna be together always."

Momma Wynn's painted-on mouth jeered at her.

"What if I find a man I like?"

"Then you find him dead."

Honeysuckle froze. An impulse to throw Momma Wynn into the flames shot through her. It might sever the tethered link between them. Would she wither if their link did? She squeezed the dummy. She just didn't know. One toss and drop, then it would be all over. A moment of hesitation made her hands shake.

With a sigh, she set Momma Wynn down beside her in the dirt. The twisted head didn't sit right with her.

Momma Wynn righted herself and then stretched out—her hair becoming leaves, limbs lengthening to adult size. Momma Wynn became more, a full tree of life. Now, as big as Honeysuckle, Momma Wynn scooted away from the fire, as if she knew Honeysuckle's previous dark thoughts. Honeysuckle couldn't ever be sure. Their bond left them tethered both physically, but how else did Momma Wynn find her? Sometimes, Honeysuckle suspected the doll could read her mind, too. Momma Wynn had taken control of her body before, so why not her mind?

At this, a chill skated over Honeysuckle.

"You think you gonna be done with me." It wasn't a question, but a heated declaration. "You want your freedom."

"I do."

Not until that moment did it solidify for Honeysuckle that she *did*. She'd never liked being shackled. Once she got her freedom, she loathed to lose it. Although Momma Wynn had brought her success and a job, she'd also cost her. Honeysuckle's life was too high a price to pay for Momma Wynn's temper. If Momma Wynn killed any or all of the men in the mob, then things would only be worse. Momma Wynn's unpredictable nature threatened any chance Honeysuckle would have for a safe and normal life.

"Not gonna happen." Momma Wynn's branches rustled in warning. "We gonna be together alway."

"You don't want me to be happy."

"Thought you'd be happy breathin'," Momma Wynn mocked.

Honeysuckle glowered and crossed her arms in a huff. Across the fire pit, Momma Wynn chuckled at her pout.

"Only me gonna save ya."

"I don't need savin'." Honeysuckle grunted at the hard resentment staining each of those words. The boast sparked an idea inside her, but instead of speaking it aloud, she tucked it away for later.

"Yeah, you do." Momma Wynn rose and moved around the circle, closer to Honeysuckle.

"Savin' is for sinners." Honeysuckle stood up.

"You ain't no saint."

"You ain't neither."

Momma Wynn's leaves rustled in the ensuing silence, but she didn't jeer. No snapping comeback. Maybe she heard the resolve in Honeysuckle's voice.

Good. Honeysuckle grinned. It felt good to stand on her own feet.

As the day bled to night, Honeysuckle wondered how long before Momma Wynn knocked her to her knees.

Or Bob hanged her by the neck.

The crisp New Mexican wind whipped, and Honeysuckle rubbed the sleep out of her eyes with one thought. *Water.* Clutching her knife, it took several fast blinks before she oriented herself. She took in the shadowy and strange surroundings with fear pumping through her. The blackened fire pit still sent a thin trail of smoke into the air. It stained the room with the scent of burnt hair and soot. Farther away, between the pit and the entrance, Momma Wynn lay face down in the dirt.

The wind wasn't the only thing that snatched her awake. Crunching of boots on dirt and snapping twigs alerted her through sleep's thin veil to something approaching. With her hunting knife, she stood up and crept to the sole window. On tiptoes, she peered out into the new day. Just before dawn, only a sliver of sunlight provided illumination. Figures stumbled around in the gloom. Their lanterns bobbed like fat junebugs lazily bouncing in the air. The curses sounded human enough.

Darn it! They found her!

She had minutes, maybe, to plan a way out. She rubbed the remainder of sleep from her eyes with the back of her blouse. As she stepped back, she tripped over Momma Wynn. She caught herself, and she stared down at the dummy. Honeysuckle braced for the familiar belly speaker to start.

No cold inkling erupted inside.

"Momma?" she whispered.

Nothing. Only the rawness of her own terror. A strangely new emotion that made her a bit ill.

"Honey!" Bob shouted and brought her back to the situation.

"Come on outta there."

Honeysuckle gripped the knife's hilt tight, thought about the number of pistols out there, and picked up her rifle. The round space made her a sitting duck. Trapped, it was too late to leave. Swearing, Honeysuckle pressed herself flat against the wall beside the entrance. With luck, she'd be able to use the element of surprise to take out a couple of them before she died. She'd go down fighting, not on her knees pleading for mercy.

The first man inside caught the rifle butt with his face. He howled and swung blindly. Thankful for her dark skin, she blended into the shadows. When her assailant stalked by her, unaware, she swung, and then ducked into the next patch of shadow. She repeated this several times, extending the element of surprise. The narrow entranceway forced them to enter one at a time.

"Git her!" the sheriff howled.

Honeysuckle rolled across the dirt and tripped the second guy. Easy enough, since he dragged one of his legs. He fell on top of the other man. The deputy's youthful voice coughed out a groan. The men's frustrated shouts as they struggled to untangle themselves amused her.

"That's enough, Honey." Bob's tone made Honeysuckle's pause.

She stood up and turned to face him. He held a pistol in one hand and a lantern in the other. An oily grin emerged from the dark stubble crawling across his double chins.

"Git on up now." Bob pushed his girth farther into the space and directed her with the gun.

Hercules silently followed behind and squeezed into the narrow available space.

"This is a real shit hole, innit?" Bob barked out a laugh.

Bob and Hercules threatened on her left, the sheriff and the deputy to her right. She couldn't see a way out, but then the cold burst blossomed up from her belly. Honeysuckle shuddered, not in fear nor from cold, but rather from Momma Wynn's unfurrowing full fury.

"Beware."

That simple word thundered.

"Who said that?" Bob searched around.

"My belly's speakin'," Honeysuckle explained. "You oughta listen."

Hercules' pinched and pained expression conveyed his anger. The dawn's light illuminated the inside of the hogan and the men therein. They put their lanterns down in the dust.

"She doin' it again," the deputy stammered as he got to his feet. He held a hand to the left side of his head, where blood trickled between his fingers. He'd been sent in first.

"A trick. Nothin' more," Bob countered.

At this, the wind roared through the hogan so powerful it blew off the cowboys' hats. Momma Wynn's power unraveled in the confined area, stirring up dust in hungry gusts.

Momma's coming.

As soon as she thought it, the air shifted.

Spooked, the sheriff shot toward the exit. "Git outta my way!"

Bob blocked the door, and the sheriff shoved at the mass. He failed to move the huge man. Bob didn't budge. "You ain't leavin'."

Roughly the same height as Bob, the sheriff leaned in close and poked him with his own gun. "You gonna stop me? Didn't think so."

Without waiting for a reply, he wedged himself through a sliver of space and out the hogan.

The deputy bolted, too. "Ain't worth this witchcraft shit."

"Buncha yella-bellied bastards!" Bob shouted after them before putting his attention back on Honeysuckle. "Welp, the law ain't here, so we ain't gonna follow any rules now, Herc."

The wind began again and coupled with the laughter, wild and evil. Honeysuckle's insides froze. Wincing, she struggled to stay conscious. Bob and Hercules staggered as the world shook. They toppled over onto each other. Once one men hit the ground, the weeds scrambled up from the earth. They pinned the men against the dirt and choked them. Gagging sounds rose up against the day. Honeysuckle fought the frost from consuming her by trying to stay awake. If she blacked out, she'd fail. Momma Wynn threatened to take over, and she'd kill them. The vegetation coiled around their necks. Their faces paled before turning to shades of blue. The men's gurgling faded as Momma Wynn sucked the life out of them.

Honeysuckle staggered over to the men. Momma Wynn's roaring laugh echoed in malicious glee.

"Not again!" Honeysuckle couldn't tolerate the callous disregard for life any longer.

"They mean to kill ya. Let them die!" The wind whirled in greater intensity, crushing the life out of them. Momma Wynn controlled everything, even *her*. Now. This was the time. If Bob and Hercules died, there would be more bounty on her head. Not only that, but their deaths would resolve nothing. She wanted to be in control of her life.

"Stop!" Honeysuckle's heart thundered in her chest, and it burned, hot in outrage. "Enough!"

She screamed so loud, it pulled from the depths of her being. It shot through her like a geyser, flooding her with fire. Honeysuckle raced to the men and began tearing at the weeds. As she tore through the restraints, not only those from the ground, but also inside herself, she beat back the icy feeling. It retreated with each snap. The yuccas cut and scratched her skin, tearing at her flesh with eager defiance. She grinned at the pain, and the cold recoiled further back into her belly.

What you doin? Momma Wynn shrieked. Panic stretched the words thin.

"I'm gettin' back my voice!" Honeysuckle grunted.

"Let me up!" Bob yelled. He thrashed about, his pudgy parts flailed against his bonds and strained against them. They didn't yield.

Honeysuckle crawled over to her hunting knife where it'd been discarded in the whirlwind. She hurried back to Bob and Hercules and sliced through the vegetation. Covered in dirt and slashes, Bob lumbered to his booted feet. Beside him, Hercules scurried back from her, got to his feet, and fled.

"Honey?" Bob croaked, rubbing his neck beneath his fleshy chins. He then patted his holster for his pistol, but it lay several feet away. His eyes darted to Honeysuckle as realization dawned across his face. He licked his lips.

"Shut. It." She stood up and poked him in the flabby folds of his chest. "Imma go and you ain't gonna follow me. Ever. Got it?"

Bob opened his mouth but closed it quick. Instead, he nodded before walking out the hogan, grumbling under his breath.

After he left, Honeysuckle picked up her rifle, sheathed her knife, and shouldered her satchel. A numbness took up residence inside her. Momma Wynn's familiar cold comfort had gone. With a glance down at the broken and battered doll, Honeysuckle took in a deep, steadying breath. Now, she'd do the next shows of her life alone. It felt both strange and exciting. An internal quiet made her uneasy, but in time, she'd adjust.

At last she'd found her voice.

Her belly would speak for her no longer.

WALK THE DINOSAUR

A BUBBA THE MONSTER HUNTER SHORT STORY

John G. Hartness

I STEPPED OFF THE AIRPLANE AND WOBBLED A LITTLE, BUT I DIDN'T FALL down. I also didn't drop to my knees and kiss the tarmac, although I can't say the thought didn't cross my mind. I stood there for a minute, blinking against the bright sun pounding through my sunglasses, and waited for my stomach to settle.

"Rough flight?" asked the man sitting on the tailgate of a rust-and-blue GMC pickup truck, maybe a '70 or so model.

"What makes you say that?" I asked. I was pretty proud of myself for not puking, but I did want to know if I was particularly green.

"I've seen a lot of people fly into here, and I never seen Randell puke before." He pointed off behind me, and I turned. The pilot was bent over by the front of the plane, revisiting the pizza he'd put down in Atlanta just before we took off.

"Yeah, there was a little thunder boomer a ways back," I said. "The landing wasn't the smoothest thing I've ever seen, either."

"Well, you know what they say about landings," the man said. I took a better look at him, now that the horizon had stopped swaying. He was a tall fella, big, rangy, John Wayne-looking dude with deep valleys around his eyes from squinting into the sun for years and years. His skin had that rough, reddish tone that comes from a lot of wind and sun, and his hands were big and looked solid. He wore a faded chambray work shirt, sleeves rolled up to show some cheap homemade, or maybe prison tattoos, and his jeans were also faded and worn thin at the knees. He wore a battered brown cowboy boot on his right foot and a blue walking cast on his left.

"I reckon you're Tyson," I said, walking over and shaking hands with the injured Hunter.

"What gave it away? My rugged good looks, devastating smile, or the footwear?"

"Might have something to do with you being the only person anywhere around this shitheap airport not wearing coveralls and driving a fuel truck." I swept the area with my gaze, but the little four-seater plane I'd arrived in was the only thing that looked like it had moved any time recently.

"You okay over there, Randell?" Tyson hollered.

"Kiss my ass, you old gimpy bastard!" the pilot yelled back.

"He's fine," Tyson said. "Get your crap and let's roll. I'll fill you in while we drive."

I walked over to the side of the plane and opened the back door. I grabbed a small backpack with my clothes in it and two duffels full of weapons. I tossed the duffels in the back of the pickup, pitched my backpack on top of them, and then reached into the cockpit to grab Bertha from where she hung on the back of my seat. I slipped the shoulder rig on and fastened it to my belt, checking to make sure the Desert Eagle was snapped in and secure. I did not want any fifty-caliber surprises coming at me if I had to move fast.

"Thanks for the ride, Randell," I said, waving to the pilot. "Sorry about your shoes." He looked down at the vomit on his right foot and set off into a fresh tirade. I laughed under my breath and walked over to the truck.

I pulled out my phone and turned it on, then pressed the button to wake up the Bluetooth transmitter in my earbud. "Skeeter, you there?"

"Yeah, I'm here, Bubba. How was your flight?"

"Shitty. Dumbass Randell drove us right through that thunderstorm you warned him about. Some crap about not wanting to add any more time onto the journey."

"That dipshit," Skeeter's shrill voiced laughed in my ear. "How many times did you throw up?"

"None, thank you very damn much," I replied. "I drank a bottle of Pepto in the airport before we left Atlanta. I won't poop for a week, but I didn't paint the inside of the plane, either."

"I reckon we can call that a win. You met up with Tyson yet?"

"Yeah, just got into his truck."

"Put me on speaker, then." I pulled out my phone, and Tyson pointed to a mount set into the dash. I slid my phone into it and pressed a button on the screen.

"Alright, Skeeter, you're on speaker."

"Hey, Tyson," my technical expert and best friend since middle school said. "Pleased to kinda meet you."

"Pleasure's all mine," Tyson said.

Skeeter continued. "I've got our giant friend here wired up to a satellite phone connection, and I pretty much don't ever break it, unless I need to sleep or he feels the need to go to a strip club, which happens way more often than I like. So if you need anything researched or the big guns called in, y'all just let me know."

Tyson chuckled and looked over at me. "You're saying you've got some bigger guns than this giant?"

Skeeter's shrill laugh about made my ears bleed. "No, but I've got a few that bring even bigger guns. Anyway, if you need anything, I'm never further away than Bubba's Bluetooth. You need me, just holler."

"Will do," Tyson said.

"I'm gonna go back to watching *Hap & Leonard* on Netflix. Bubba, try not to get dead." He beeped off, and I put the phone back in my pocket.

"Let's roll," Tyson said. He clicked his seatbelt into place and put the truck in gear. We didn't move; he just sat there staring at me. I took a minute to figure out what he wanted, then I put my own seatbelt on. Once I was properly restrained, he took his foot off the brake and started driving toward the exit of the Grant County Airport, south of Hurley, New Mexico. It was a little one-runway job that looked like it might see ten planes a week if it got real busy.

Once we got out of the airport gate, Tyson continued. "I appreciate y'all helping me out while my foot heals. Damn Gila bastard almost took it off, but I got him good."

"You said it was a were-lizard?" I asked. "I ain't never heard of such a thing."

"I don't know if it was technically a lycanthrope, or maybe some variant on a skinwalker, or just some type of shapeshifter. I can't rightly tell you since there wasn't but the one, and he wasn't too talkative when I was done with him. All I know is it was the biggest damn lizard I ever seen, and I've lived out here my whole life. No way in hell that thing was natural. I put him down, but he got one good bite in, right through my damn boot, and that venom has completely wrecked my foot. I've got a healer coming in from one of the reservations twice a week working with me on it, and he says it oughta be back right in another four or five treatments, but for now I can't run, jump, or climb anything."

"That sounds like a good way to get dead in our line of work," I said.

"Don't I know it," Tyson agreed. "That's why you're here. This thing out in the flats has got to be dealt with, and I can't do it. So I'm glad the Church had somebody they trusted enough to send."

I didn't want to tell him that trust probably had very little to do with it. I wasn't the closest Templar to Tyson's territory, but I was the one who was usually the biggest pain in the Church's ass. So if there was a chance somebody was gonna get killed hunting down whatever was out in the desert, it made sense to send the Knight they thought of as the most expendable. That was me in a nutshell.

We rode along for another forty-five minutes, shooting the shit, arguing about whether Chris Stapleton was better than Jason Isbell, about whether Colt or Sig made a better .45, and about whether barbecue was supposed to be made out of a pig or out of a cow. You know, the kind of crap guys talk about. Finally, we pulled up in front of Tyson's house, a wide old adobe-style ranch with not so much a driveway as an area of slightly flatter dirt than the dirt just off the road.

A good-looking woman in her mid-forties came out to meet us, her dark hair blowing in the wind. "Hey there, you must be Robert," she called as she came forward to give me a big hug.

"Call me Bubba," I said. "Nobody calls me Robert but the Bishop and the police when they pull me over for speeding."

"I'm Vanessa. I'm Ty's wife," she said. "Ty, you get your ass on in that house. Gerald will be here in an hour for your treatment. And no whiskey. You know how loopy you get after he works on your foot. We don't need you trying to dance in the swimming pool again."

"We ain't got a swimming pool, woman," Tyson said with a grin. I noticed he didn't slow down as he limped toward the house, though.

"That's my point, jackass. You were so stoned after Gerald's doctorin' and one beer you thought you were doing damn water aerobics in the middle of the desert."

"I woulda paid to see that," I said.

"Oh no, you wouldn't, either," Vanessa said, laughing. "He was doing it butt-naked!"

I shook my head, wishing I'd packed some brain bleach for the trip. "Yeah, I'd like to amend my earlier statement," I said. "Hey Tyson!" I hollered at his back. "You leave the keys in the truck?"

"Yep," he called back. "It's all you, buckaroo!"

"You're not coming in?" Vanessa asked.

"No ma'am," I said. "As much as I appreciate the offer, I figure I oughta let you and Tyson get his foot worked on in peace. I'm gonna go ahead and drive out to where the weird things are and see what I can find."

"Well, give me your suitcase. I'll put it in the guest room," she said, looking up at me. "Try not to get dead."

I laughed. "That's always the goal, ma'am. Always the goal." I handed her the backpack with my clothes in it, grabbed my duffels full of weapons and tossed them in the cab of the truck, then slid behind the wheel. I put the old GMC in gear and pulled back onto the highway.

I pressed a button on the Bluetooth ear thingy Skeeter made me wear all the time and said, "Where am I going, Skeet?"

Skeeter's voice came through the thousands of miles just like he was sitting beside me in the truck. I wasn't entirely convinced this was a good thing. "Head east for another thirty miles, then take the next road off to the north. All of Tyson's reports are coming from a couple of old homesteads in that area."

"Anything around there?"

"Dirt and wind, as far as I can see," Skeeter said.

"And were-lizards," I added.

"Poisonous were-lizards," Skeeter clarified.

I pulled up to an abandoned homestead about an hour later, having made one wrong turn and stopping at one gas station for a couple of hot dogs and a Pepsi. One thing is universal—it don't matter how far you travel, gas station hot dogs all taste like shit. The house had seen better days. I couldn't tell you when those better days were, but they weren't any time this century. The roof was all caved in, every window in the place was busted, and the porch only had one step left where three used to be. I barely trusted the porch, much less the steps, so I just stretched a little and hopped up there to take a peek inside.

The roof was indeed laying in the house, obscuring anything that might have been left behind when it was abandoned, but this didn't look like the kind of place anybody was cherishing any memories about. Frankly, I couldn't see why anybody would be out here to even report on anything weird.

"Skeeter, do Tyson's notes say what these people were doing out here in the first place?" I asked.

"One couple claimed they were stargazing and needed to get away from all the light pollution." I looked up through the open space where the ceiling should have been, and while it was still too light out for stars, there also weren't any street lights anywhere in view.

"That kinda makes sense," I said. "I can see it being darker than the inside of an elephant's butthole in a couple hours out here."

"That's poetic, Bubba," Skeeter remarked.

"I try. What about the other strangeness?"

"That was a couple of high school kids. Two boys and two girls. They didn't say what they were doing, but I reckon you can guess."

"Yeah, I can probably figure it out. I'm gonna poke around here for a little while, then gear up and wait for dark. Oughta only be about another two hours. Then if I'm lucky, I can see whatever they saw, shoot the shit out of it, and be on the first plane out of here tomorrow morning."

"Sounds like a plan. I'm gonna go watch *Z Nation* on Netflix and laugh my ass off. Call me if you need me."

"Will do, brother. Will do." I clicked off the comm and continued my poking around in the rubble. I couldn't see anything that would make me think the place was haunted, and nothing about it looked particularly demonic, either. There were a few piles of random animal poop laying around, but nothing seemed at all supernatural. Maybe I'd get lucky and the folks just got spooked by a coyote.

Yeah, I didn't think so, either.

It was full dark for a couple hours before anything weird happened, and I had to admit, the stars were real pretty. I was geared up as heavy as I could be and still move, with Bertha under one arm, a Mossberg pistol-grip 12-gauge on a sling over my right shoulder, a pair of silver-edged kukris strapped to my back, my Judge revolver in a paddle holster at the small of my back, and a silvered boot knife on my right leg. If it was magical, I was ready. I had silver, cold iron, and white phosphorous rounds for Bertha and the shotgun, and enough silver blades to gut anything short of a dragon.

I was dozing a little bit, playing Ray Wylie Hubbard low on my phone to set the mood. I was sitting in the driver's seat of the pickup with the windows down to make sure I could hear anything approaching, but I figured I was safer there than in the house, which looked like it was liable to collapse in on me at a stiff breeze.

A howl split the night open like a machete through a watermelon, and I fumbled around to make the music stop. I held still, but no more sound came. Opening the door, I slid out down to one knee and took cover beside the truck, drawing Bertha as I did. "Skeeter," I whispered. "You got me?"

"Yeah, what's up?"

His voice came through my earpiece at his normal volume, enough to make me cringe in the dark silence. I knew if there was anything close enough to hear Skeeter in my ear, then I was probably already dead, but that didn't make me any less jumpy.

"Something just howled," I said.

"Bubba, you're in the desert of New Mexico. I reckon there might be a coyote within a hundred miles. I'd be surprised if there *wasn't* something howling."

"It didn't sound like a coyote," I whispered back, then the howl came again. This time it did sound like a coyote, until it cut off in a sharp yelp, followed by a series of snarls and barks, then another bunch of yips, yelps, and whines. The noise trailed off, and everything around me was silent again. "That sounded like a coyote, but it sounded like a coyote having a real bad night," I said.

"Let me see if I can get any kind of satellite over you," Skeeter said. A few seconds passed, then he came back. "Nothing. Sorry, Bubba. I got nothing."

"That's fine, Skeet. I reckon this is as good a time as any to try your new toy." I reached back into the cab of the truck and slipped on the heat vision goggles Skeeter insisted I pack. I kinda hated the things because they screwed up what little crappy night vision I had, but if they let me find whatever just had itself a nice coyote dinner, I was happy to have them.

"Can you tell what direction the sound came from?" Skeeter asked.

"I think it came from the hills over to the west," I said, starting in that direction. The terrain was a weird range of greens and yellows, and when I looked down at my hands, they glowed bright red. I scanned the horizon as I walked, holstering Bertha and keeping the shotgun out in front of me. With my vision shot to shit, I figured I'd need the spread the Mossberg gave me.

I walked west for a good twenty minutes, occasionally hearing some scrabbling sounds off to the left or right of me, but whenever I looked, nothing showed up in the infrared. I came over a low hill, and down in a depression was a wide area giving off an orange glow, telling me it was warmer than the surrounding dirt. I didn't see anything red, or moving, so I flipped up the goggles and clicked on the flashlight I had slung under the barrel of the shotgun.

The scene that lit up in front of me was like something out of a horror movie. The sand was churned up and turned to red mud with all the blood spilled. It looked like whatever went down out here was fast, mean, and bloody as hell. I pulled a couple of chemical light sticks out of my back pocket, snapped them, and jabbed them into the dirt. The whole area lit up with a blue-white glow, making the blood look almost black in the artificial light. I stuck the butt of the shotgun into the sand, wedging the gun upright, and took the flashlight off the barrel. I walked into the depression, playing the light over everything trying to see if there were any clues I missed.

I pulled out my phone and snapped a bunch of pictures of tufts of hair, one loose coyote leg laying half-buried in bloody sand, and some piles of blood-muddied dirt. "Skeeter?" I said.

"Yeah, what you got?"

"I'm sending you some pictures to look at. Wait, never mind. I can't send data out here."

"Bubba, the only reason you have cell service is because I put that portable repeater in your bag. What do you see?"

"Looks like some kind of animal attack. Shitload of blood and hair. I'd guess coyote, but I've only got about one leg to go by."

"That's disgusting," Skeeter said.

"Yeah, I'm a little surprised there ain't more guts and stuff laying around, though. This is a real clean kill, like whatever did this hauled the coyote off somewhere to eat."

"Sounds smart," Skeeter said.

"I hate hunting smart monsters," I said.

"You hate hunting monsters that are smarter than you," Skeeter replied.

"Yeah, ain't that what I said? Anyway, there's a blood trail. I'm gonna see what I can find if I follow it."

"Don't get lost. It gets cold out there at night."

I didn't get lost. I also didn't find shit, even after traipsing around half the night in the cold-ass desert. The sun was coming up, setting the horizon ablaze by the time I trudged back to my truck. I made it back to Tyson's house right about the time Vanessa was setting the breakfast table.

"That does not look like a hunter coming home triumphant," she said. "Leave your boots on the porch if you've got anything nasty on them."

I didn't think I did, but I took them off anyway. She was walking around barefoot in the kitchen, so I wasn't sure if they were some of those folks that don't like shoes in the house, but either way it felt good to get my poor feet out of them boots for a while.

"What do we look like when we're triumphant?" Tyson said, limping around the corner and sitting down at the head of the table.

"Oh, sweetie, y'all are downright insufferable," Vanessa said, sliding a plate piled high with eggs and bacon in front of him. She turned to me. "You want to get cleaned up before breakfast?"

"Yeah, I oughta at least get a quick shower. Otherwise I'm liable to put you off your feed," I said, following her finger down the hall to the spare bedroom where she stashed my clothes. I grabbed a shower and sat down at the table ten minutes later, feeling almost human. I told them about my night while I shoveled food in my mouth, finishing up with the fact that the coyote's leg was in the back of Tyson's pickup.

"Seriously? You hauled a bloody coyote leg back here in my truck?" Tyson griped.

"Son, looking at that truck, I could have strapped it into the seat next to me and you wouldn't even have noticed another stain," I said, pushing back from the table.

Tyson gave me a sour look, but Vanessa just laughed. "He's got you there, Ty. What's next, Bubba?"

"Well, I'm gonna sleep most of today, I reckon. I'll take some pictures of the leg and send them to Skeeter before I crash, then tonight I reckon I'll go back out there with more lights and try to hunt this thing down."

"I can take the pictures for you," Tyson said. "You go sleep."

"You sure?"

"Let me feel like I ain't completely useless with this damn bum foot," he said, lurching to his feet and clumping across the kitchen. "I'll go get my camera."

"Just use my phone," I said, handing him my cell. "The camera's good enough, and Skeeter's got it all synced up with his computer so it transmits any picture I take straight back to him."

"That's useful," Vanessa said.

"Yeah, long as I remember to turn it off when I want to take pictures of my girlfriend," I said.

"You're terrible," she said with a grin.

"You ain't wrong," I grinned back. "But I'm also whooped. I'm gonna go sleep for a few hours, then when I get up, we can figure out the next step. Thanks for breakfast. It was awesome." I stood up and swayed a little on my feet. Between flying halfway across the country and being up all night, I was wore slap out. I lumbered back to the spare bedroom, unbuttoned my pants, and intended to lay back on the bed for just a minute before I got undressed and crawled under the covers.

The sun had moved all the way across the sky by the time I woke up, still flat on my back with my pants and shirt on. Somebody, Vanessa I reckoned, had come in and thrown a blanket over me at some point during the day. Tyson was a nice enough fellow, but he seemed about as nurturing as a drill sergeant, so I didn't expect it to be him. If I'd woke up with a dick drawn on my forehead, then I'd think my fellow Hunter might be responsible.

First thing I did after I went to pee was make sure there wasn't a dick drawn on my forehead. It was clear, so I washed my face, ran a comb through my hair, pulled it back into a ponytail, and freshened up my deodorant. I didn't see a whole lot of point in another shower, so I just brushed my teeth and wandered out into the house.

Tyson was sitting at a desk typing on a computer and waved me over as soon as he noticed me. "Come look at this," he said. He pointed at the screen, which showed an image of short, razor-sharp teeth.

"What's that?" I asked.

"That's a computer model of the teeth of the thing that killed your coyote," Skeeter's face popped up in a corner of the computer screen, like a less-helpful Microsoft Paperclip. He went on. "That tooth pattern doesn't match anything in any of our files or in DEMON's database."

"Skeeter, did you hack the government again?" I asked. The Department of ExtraDimensional Monsters and Occult Nuisances was the federal agency that didn't officially exist, but didn't exist specifically to handle the kind of threats that Skeeter and I dealt with every day.

"No, Amy ran a check against the computer model," he huffed. I would have apologized if he hadn't shown a tendency in the past to hack anything he felt like whenever he felt like it. Knowing he asked my girlfriend for help made me feel a lot better about the odds of us not getting sent to Gitmo this week.

"So we don't know what it is, but we know it's got a shitload of teeth. What else in this part of the world fits that description?" I felt a little shiver run up my spine. It was exciting, hunting something new for a change. After all these years, I'd put down enough werewolves and wrestled enough naked sasquatches to last a lifetime.

That number for naked sasquatch wrestling is one, by the way.

"Skeeter," I started, barely able to contain myself. "Do you think…could we be on the trail of the elusive…chimichanga?"

Tyson looked at me like a cat watching somebody pee in the toilet. It was like he was pretty sure he understood the words I was using, but he didn't quite comprehend how they were put together.

"Wait, I got it wrong again." I held up a hand. "Don't tell me…it's a chalupa!"

Still staring.

"Churro?"

Nothing.

"Chorizo?"

"Bubba what the hell are you trying to say? Are you hungry or something?" Tyson looked at me like I had a second head growing out my neck, and this one had a green face.

"He means a chupacabra," Skeeter said. "I don't know if it's a mental block at this point or if he just thinks he's funny, but he has never been able to get away from the menu at a Mexican restaurant when we're talking about a chupacabra. Which I don't think this is, by the way."

"Why not? Do we have a quesadilla's bite to compare it to?" I asked.

"No, we do not," Skeeter said. "But by all reports, the chupacabra drains the blood from its victims, which indicates fangs. There are no fangs in this bite pattern." He rotated the image on the screen, and no matter how many ways I looked at the imaginary digital teeth, there weren't any fangs there.

"Maybe they're retractable, like vampire fangs," I said.

"You said there was a lot of blood at the scene," Skeeter said.

"Yeah, there was so much it made a mud blood puddle. Heh, that sounds like something out of a Harry Potter book," I said with a chuckle.

"Not a very good bloodsucker if it leaves a bunch of blood behind," Tyson remarked.

"Et tu, Tyson?" I asked.

"Hey, man, don't get all Latin on me," he protested. "Just because it ain't a chupacabra don't mean we don't need to shoot it."

"*We* don't need to shoot nothing, Hopalong," I said, motioning to his leg. "I couldn't catch up to that thing with two good wheels, how you gonna do it with one?"

"I ain't," he agreed. "I'm gonna catch it with four."

An hour later we pulled out of Tyson's driveway with a trailer hitched behind his pickup. A pair of four-wheeled ATVs with high-powered spotlights mounted on the front were strapped down the trailer, and we were loaded for bear. Or enchilada. Or really any damn thing we might run into. I had Bertha, my Mossberg, and a pair of H&K MP-5 submachine guns mounted to the handlebars of one ATV. Ty had his Colt 1911 loaded with hollow point .45 rounds, a Benelli M4 shotgun, and a Remington 700 with a night scope across his ATV's gear rack. I didn't so much think we were in danger of anything that might be out there as I thought we might be in danger of being mistaken for an invading army if we got anywhere near the Mexican border. We also had a couple of battery-operated flood lights and a flare gun with white phosphorous flares to light up the whole area if we needed it.

We pulled up to the house where I stopped the night before and unloaded the ATVs. I turned to Tyson. "You sure you're up to this?"

"Son, that's at least the fourteenth time you've asked me that since we left my house. For the last damn time, yes, I'm fine. I ain't gonna go running after the damn thing. I'm gonna hang back and shoot the shit out of it." He threw his leg over the four-wheeler and cranked the machine to life. We pulled our night vision glasses on and rolled out toward where the chalupa killed the coyote the night before.

Once we got to the creature's known hunting ground, we started our search there. We made concentric circles on the ATVs, spiraling out from the kill zone at center in an ever-larger radius. After two hours of literally driving around in circles, I slowed down to let Tyson pull up alongside me and we turned off our rides.

"This ain't working," I said.

"It's early yet," Tyson replied.

"We ain't seen so much as a coyote in the last hour," I argued. "We're making too much damn noise. Ain't nothing going to come near us on these things."

"Shit." Ty nodded his agreement. "I was a little bit afraid that might be the case."

"But you couldn't stand the thought of being left out," I finished the thought for him.

I reckon he was glad it was dark so I couldn't see him blush. I didn't blame Ty, though. We weren't the kind of men who sat at home and made plans or watched the computer screen. We were meant to be out here, in the middle of the shit, and anybody who didn't believe that had no place being a Hunter. "Alright, so now what?" I asked.

"Well, my ideas ain't worked out so good so far, so I don't reckon I know."

"Well, I ain't an expert in desert hunting, so even though this was a shitshow, I reckon I'll still take any ideas you got," I said.

He didn't have time to tell me any ideas he might have because just then I heard another coyote scream. This one sounded closer than the one last night, and it only took me a second to get the general direction locked in. I thumped Tyson on the shoulder and said, "Let's go!"

He looked at me, rubbed his shoulder a little bit, and cranked his four-wheeler. We headed in the direction the howl had come from, and this time we had wheels. We crested a rocky dune and looked down into another small depression, where this chimichanga obviously liked to do its hunting. There was an orange spray of blood painting the ground in my night vision, but two bright red shapes still circled each other in the bottom of the ditch.

"Lights," I said, stripping off my goggles and flipping on the spotlights mounted to my handlebars. The xenon lamps cut through the dark like lasers, illuminating a battered coyote dancing and jumping around something that I couldn't quite identify. It was black and orange striped, about five feet tall at the shoulder, and about ten feet long, with a thick tail and a stubby head. It moved fast as lightning on its four stubby legs, and the coyote kept getting nipped when it went in to try and snap at the thing.

"Son of a bitch," I heard Ty murmur behind me. He had the high-powered LED floodlight out of the case and up on its stand, shining down into the depression like a miniature blue sun.

"What the hell is that, Ty?" I asked.

"That's another one of them damn were-lizards that bit me, only this one's about twice the size," he said.

"That ain't no were-lizard," Skeeter said into our earpieces. "That's a giant Gila Monster, and if it gets hold of you, it'll chew your damn leg clean off."

"A giant Gila Monster? Is that even a thing? Or are you just messing with me and really it's a churro?" I asked.

"That ain't no kind of chupacabra, Bubba. That thing looks like a Gila Monster, just five times the normal size. That means five times as venomous."

"Wait, you mean it ain't just a giant lizard with a shitload of teeth—it's a *poisonous* giant lizard with a shitload of teeth?"

"That's exactly what I mean," Skeeter said. "Try not to get dead."

"Always the goal," I said. I pulled Bertha from her shoulder holster and ran down the sand to about twenty yards from the lizard. I still wasn't convinced that it wasn't a chalupa, but either way, it looked a lot like something that was in serious need of killing. I drew a bead on the thing and squeezed the trigger. Bertha jumped a little in my hands, and a sound like a thunderclap came from her.

The fifty-caliber slug smacked into the lizard right in the side, a little high, but I was elevated and shooting down, so I gave myself a pass on a little bit of accuracy. Truth be told, I was a wee bit excited to be shooting something I'd never put a bullet in before, so that might have made me a little jumpy, too. The bullet hit home with a solid *thwack*, and the lizard turned and looked at me, its baleful yellow eyes boring holes into me as if to say, "Okay, asshole, you got next."

"Shit," I said. "That shoulda put a hole the size of a damn pie plate in that thing." Instead, there was a tiny trickle of blood where it looked like I broke the skin, but just barely. "Ty, did you say you killed one of these things with that Colt?"

"Yeah, but I reckon I got the runt of the litter," Tyson hollered back. "Get clear so I can put a few into its head!" I ran around to the right to get clear of Ty's line of fire, and he put five .308 rounds in the lizard's head and neck within half a dozen seconds. The lizard let out a screech and decided we were way more a threat than the coyote.

It spun around, looking for the critter that hurt it, and since Ty was way back at the ATVs shooting with a rifle like a sane person, I was the first thing the super-Gila found. It scurried up the hill way faster than anything with them stubby little legs ought to run, and I emptied Bertha's magazine at it as it came. One round caught it square in the snout, and that pissed it off enough to stop for a second and let out a bellow that sounded a lot like a dragon screwing a really upset billy goat, then it got right back after me.

I holstered Bertha and squared up like I was back at UGA getting after a quarterback. I didn't know which way I was gonna have to juke, I just hoped

I'd be fast enough and the stupid idea that popped into my head was gonna work. Ty reloaded and put another couple rifle slugs into the critter's side before it got to me, then it was go time. The lizard came at me like a dead run, and I was facing down more ugly death than I'd seen since the last time I had all-you-can-eat fajitas as La Casa del Fuego on dollar Budweiser night. It ran straight at me, and I jumped just far enough to the right to miss getting a gut full of pissed off lizard teeth.

I landed, spun around, and jumped again, landing on the Gila-Gigante's back just forward of its front legs. It bucked, and I wrapped my legs around its neck like a stripper on a wobbly pole, holding on for dear life. I managed to squeeze tight enough to lock my feet under the monster's throat, and it wasn't shaking me loose come hell nor high water. It thrashed, jumped, and wiggled, but I was stuck tighter than a tick in a poodle's butt hair, and frankly, I was too scared to let go. It even rolled over one time, squashing all the air outta my lungs and mashing one ball flatter than a penny on a railroad track, but I still hung on.

Ty couldn't shoot no more, on account of him kindly not wanting to kill me, and the lizard couldn't shake me, so I was the one in the catbird seat. Or maybe the lizardbird seat. Super-Gila kept running around and thrashing, but I just unslung that big Mossberg 12-gauge from my back, pressed the barrel to the back to the lizard's head, and cut loose with eight shotgun shells right into its brainpan. The first three didn't penetrate, but even the toughest hide can only take so much abuse, and a twelve-gauge shotgun at point-blank range is a hell of a lot of abuse. The lizard stopped moving after six shots, but I plugged a seventh one in there just for good measure. The eighth was just cause my nuts hurt and I was pissed off.

The creature flopped to the dirt on its belly, its skull a destroyed mess all over my shoes. I unhooked my feet, my ankles and knees screaming at the abuse I heaped on them, and I collapsed right beside the lizard. Tyson cranked his four-wheeler and drove down next to me, stopping a couple feet from my head.

"You alright?" he asked.

"I ain't dead, but my knees are shot and my balls hurt, and if this don't give me a ferocious case of hemorrhoids, I'll eat your hat," I said.

"So what you're saying is you're fine."

"Yeah, I'm alright."

"Good, cause we seem to have another problem." Tyson pointed past me to the other side of the little gulley the lizard was hunting in. Just on the edge of the floodlight's throw was a cave, just about the perfect size for this Uber-Gila to crawl into. Poking out of the mouth of the cave were a pair of little lizard heads. By little, I mean they looked to be the size of normal Gilas, about a foot high and probably two feet long.

"Son of a bitch," I said.

"Yup," Tyson agreed. "I reckon the one I killed last week was Papa."

"And I just killed the mama. Shit."

I pressed the button on my earpiece, but Skeeter was already listening. "I got you, Bubba. What are you gonna do with two baby Giant Gila Monsters?"

"Why do I even have an off switch on this thing if you can just turn it on whenever you want?"

"So you have the illusion of being in control of one thing in your life. Don't avoid the question. What are you going to do with them baby super-lizards?"

I let out a sigh and dug my phone out of my pocket. To my surprise, it was still intact after being rolled over by me and a giant lizard. Them Otterbox things are the bomb. I scrolled through some contacts until I got to the M's. I pressed a button, and a big goofy face filled my screen.

"Bubba? Is that you?" a voice came on the other end.

"Mason, I need a favor," I started. I explained what I needed, then hung up the phone. A minute later, I looked at Ty. "It's handled."

"What are you doing? You ain't killing them things are you?" he asked.

"Nah, looks like they only got to be real feisty when they had babies. This lizard's probably been hunting around here for decades without hurting anybody. It just had to widen its hunting ground because the babies needed fed. No need to exterminate what might be the last two just because their territory shrank the same time their family grew. I got a guy in Missouri. He's friends with a…dude that runs kind of a wildlife preserve for the wildest kind of life. He'll take these little guys out there where they can make friends with a couple gowrows and some other critters, and they won't need to bother nobody."

Ty thought about it for a minute, then nodded. "That sounds good. I reckon if they didn't have to hunt for food for their babies, I never would have run afoul of the papa."

"Yeah, but papa turned manhunter. It was only a matter of time before some hiker or camper ended up out here and became lizard food. This way they've got a safe place, and we don't need to kill 'em," I said.

"What are we gonna do with that?" Ty asked, pointing to the dead lizard.

I looked at it for a long minute, then grinned up at him from my spot on the ground. "Well, son, I've heard fried lizard tastes like chicken. Be a shame to let all that meat go to waste."

"I'll call Vanessa, tell her to break out the big skillet." He helped me to my feet, and we started back to the truck.

We got about twenty feet when something hit me. I looked over at Ty and said, "You know the rule she's gonna enforce, right?"

"What's that?"

"We killed it. We gotta clean it."

THE TIME TRAVELING SCHOOLMARMS OF MARLBOROUGH COUNTY

Barb Hendee

AS I LISTENED TO THE ROLLING WHEELS OF THE COACH AND WATCHED the barren landscape slip past outside the window, I couldn't help remembering an image of my grandmother, with her back straight and her head drawn high, looking down me.

"Decisions made in haste are always regretted."

This was a motto by which she lived—and one she had tried to impress upon me. Clearly, her advice had not taken. As those words turned over and over in my mind, the coach began to slow, approaching my final destination, and I wished that I'd listened to her.

But she was gone, in a grave, as was my father, and in truth, the overly hurried decision I'd made three weeks past had been the best of several options.

The coach stopped. A moment later, the door opened.

I was the only passenger remaining. The journey from Philadelphia that had seemed endless had finally ended. I'd used nearly the last of my money for the initial train fare to Denver and then the coach ride into Marlborough County, Colorado.

But I was here. I'd reached my new home, and my life was about to change dramatically.

"Winston," I said. "We're here."

Beside me, on the bench, my dog jumped to his feet. I fully believed he understood everything I said. Winston was a fox terrier. He'd been a gift from my father for my fifteenth birthday, but over the years, he'd become my closest friend.

Outside the coach door, the driver reached in for me. I picked up my parasol, took his hand, and allowed him to help me down. My back ached, but I tried my best not to show my discomfort.

As my small boots touched the ground, I took in my surroundings. Winston jumped down beside me. The town itself was called Spruce, apparently named for the variety of scattered blue spruce trees that dominated an otherwise sparse and rocky landscape.

Not having any idea what to expect—and fearing the worst—I must say I was pleasantly surprised. For all knew, the place could have constituted four dilapidated buildings and a watering trough. But Spruce appeared to be a thriving small town. From where I stood I could see down the main street and to the side streets. There was a red brick bank, two saloons—both brightly painted—and what appeared to be a courthouse. Squinting a little, I could see a dry goods store just up the street.

The driver climbed up on top of the coach to get my trunk. Everything I now owned was inside that trunk—including my books.

"Miss Miller?" someone said.

Half turning, I found myself looking up at a tall man with a silver star pinned to a leather vest. He looked to be perhaps thirty years old. His close-trimmed beard was a shade of light brown, and a wide-brimmed hat covered his hair.

"Sheriff Ward?" I responded.

When I'd first answered the advertisement for a teacher, a Sheriff Ward had written back to me with details and instructions—though I must admit the details were scant.

Staring at me, his mouth hung partway open, as if we'd both made a mistake. I'd expected to come as somewhat of a surprise. For one, I was a little younger than I'd represented myself to be, but at twenty-two, I was well educated enough to teach a schoolhouse full of children in a place like this.

I knew well that I was considered quite pretty by society men in Philadelphia. Though I was of small stature, with a trim figure, my chestnut hair was abundant and piled on top of my head with a few curled strands hanging down. Even when staying at hotels and traveling by coach, I was careful with my appearance. Grandmother always impressed upon me the value of a good first impression. With this advice, I had at least tried to listen.

Unfortunately, Sheriff Ward appeared more uncomfortable than impressed.

"Miss Miller?" he repeated, as if uncertain.

Behind him, a few people going about their daily business had stopped in their tracks, watching us.

"Yes, sir," I answered. "I am pleased to meet you. I do thank you for your kind letter."

His letter had been quite matter-of-fact, but I wasn't certain what else to say. Several more people stopped to stare at me.

It was then that I realized how out-of-place I must appear. The women wore drab dresses of tan or faded brown. Most of them wore their hair under some kind of equally drab scarf. While I wore a simple traveling dress, it was a lovely shade of royal blue—with white buttons—and a ruffled hem. My parasol matched the dress.

The glances directed my way were not admiring.

Indeed, I felt like a bluebird standing amidst a flock of rather judgmental sparrows.

Sheriff Ward suddenly seemed to remember his manners. "You must be tired. Let me load your trunk. I'll drive you out to your house."

Your house.

Again, I could only imagine what this meant.

"Thank you," I answered. "That would be so kind."

He hefted the trunk from the driver and began walking up the street. With little choice, I followed after, with Winston trotting at my heels. I didn't look back at the small, gathered crowd.

A wagon with two harnessed horses waited about thirty feet away.

Sheriff Ward loaded my trunk into the wagon. Turning back, he held out his hand to help me up, and as I reached for it, I saw that his discomfort had only grown.

"You're not what I expected," he said.

Though unaccustomed to such a blunt statement, I couldn't help asking, "And what did you expect?"

"Not you."

I had no response to that. Where I was raised, men did not speak their thoughts so openly to a lady.

Grasping his hand, I pulled myself up to the wagon's bench. Winston jumped after me.

Perhaps I was not what Sheriff Ward had expected, but that was irrelevant. He'd offered the post, and I had accepted. He was stuck with me now.

Or . . . at least I hoped he was.

I had nowhere else to go.

After that, we rode in silence for the most part. Occasionally, the sheriff offered bits of information.

"The teacher's house is about a mile east of town," he said, "but it's not far from the schoolhouse."

"Why is the school located so far from town?" I asked.

"Because most of the children don't live in town. They live east."

As the wagon rolled on, I had to admit the landscape possessed a unique beauty, varying between open spaces and blue spruce trees. The sky was clear, and the mountains loomed in the distance.

I'd never seen anything like it before.

"There," he said, pointing.

Up ahead, I saw a small, clapboard house. It had once been white, but was badly in need of paint. There was no yard, but I could see what might be the remnants of a kitchen garden. The outside of the house did not bode well. Still, beggars could not be choosers. Winston and I must do our best to keep up brave faces.

Sheriff Ward pulled up the horses and helped me down. Then he hefted my trunk.

"I doubt the door's locked," he said. "Nobody would ever bother Miss Peabody's things."

"Why is that?"

He shrugged. "She was Miss Peabody. She'd been our town's teacher for twenty years."

This was the first news I'd heard of my predecessor, and it daunted me somewhat considering the town could not have been founded much longer than twenty years ago. From what I'd read, people out here didn't care much for change. Was I replacing the only teacher these people had known?

Rather a tall order.

Hurrying over, I opened the door for Sheriff Ward, so he could bring my trunk inside. Winston ran through the open door to begin exploring our new home, but after setting down the trunk, the sheriff went back to the wagon and returned with a large burlap sack.

"I figured you might be too tired to shop for supplies," he said. "So I put some things together for you—some coffee, flour, beans, jerky, cheese, and a few apples."

"Oh, that was kind of you."

This time I meant it. I was grateful, and it gave me a graceful path toward a delicate question. "Um . . . when will I be receiving my first . . . my first . . ."

"Your first pay?" he finished.

I nodded curtly.

"Come see me at the end of the month. I handle paying anyone who works for the town, always at the end of the month."

I nearly sighed with relief. That was only two weeks away. I had enough money to support us for that long.

"Thank you."

He turned away. "Well, I'll let you get settled." He stopped, and when he glanced back, his expression had gone even more serious—if that was possible. "Are you *like* her?"

"Like who?"

"Miss Peabody."

How could I possibly know that? My confusion must have shown because he rushed on.

"I mean . . . you must have exchanged letters . . . known each other. Or else why would you have applied for the post?"

"No." I hesitated. "I found myself in need of a position, and I saw your advertisement at the post office."

His expression shifted to concern. "So, you've no connection to the Marlborough County schoolmarms?"

"Forgive me. I'm not sure what you mean."

"I mean the league of county schoolmarms. Miss Peabody had been preparing her replacement for a few years, a Miss Abigail Swenson over in Central City. Then Miss Peabody . . . she died suddenly from a stroke."

"Oh, I am sorry."

He nodded. "Thank you, but when I went to contact Miss Swenson, I learned she'd died of a fever in the same week. So I rode to Central City, and I paid the post office to place the advertisement. I had no idea it would be seen as far as Philadelphia, but when you answered, I just assumed . . . I assumed you were one of *them*."

As he spoke, I realized the situation was even worse than I'd first thought. Not only was Miss Peabody considered a beloved institution, she had been grooming a replacement who'd also died. I was now the unwelcome substitute.

"I am sorry," I answered, "but I belong to no teaching organizations. I saw the advertisement in the post office, and I answered it. Out of curiosity, why did you hire me?"

"You were the only one who applied."

I tried not to wince. "How flattering."

"Miss Peabody," he said. "She was special."

"I shall do my best to fill her shoes," I assured him.

My promise did not appear to make him feel better, and I had the strangest feeling that he and I were discussing two entirely separate things. But he gave up interrogating me.

"When you plan to start teaching?" he asked.

I saw no reason to put things off. "Tomorrow, if that's agreeable."

"Fine. I'll spread the word." With that, he left, closing the door behind him.

I was nonplussed. I would certainly need to learn a bit more about this Miss Peabody.

But at that point, I had my first opportunity to survey my new home. It was one room. There was a bed and a trunk on one side. There was a table with a single chair, a wood cook stove, and a cupboard for dishes and pots on the other side.

Was this to be my home? I thought on my father's beautiful three-story house in Philadelphia. I thought on my four-poster bed and silk comforter and the servants who had always changed my sheets.

Standing beside me, Winston looked up. His expression was dubious.

I stood straight. "There's nothing for it, Winston. We must make the best of things."

Then I noticed the shotgun leaning up against the cupboard. A note had been tied to the trigger guard. After walking over, I read the note:

Use this if necessary.

My confidence in my decision to come here did not rise.

Yet, I saw no other path but to continue investigating the contents of this new abode. Upon opening the cupboard, I found myself well set for cooking.

After a brief hesitation, I walked over and lifted the lid of the trunk at the foot of the bed, exposing three wool dresses, spare sheets, and several school books (including one math text and one for geography). At the bottom, I saw something that surprised me. At first I thought it might be jewelry. Then I realized it was too large.

Pulling back a sheet, I uncovered a large amethyst crystal in a setting of oval pewter. The crystal glittered by sunlight coming through the window. This object too had a note attached to it:

Abigail, as we discussed, you'll know what to do when the stone begins to glow. Be sure to keep it with you always. After all . . . you never know.

I gripped the crystal and re-read the note. It was written for the woman meant to replace Miss Peabody. But what did it mean?

The following morning, I arrived at the schoolhouse precisely at eight o'clock. I carried several books with me, and Winston trotted at my side. I had no intention of leaving him home alone all day.

The schoolhouse itself was of fair size, built from pine boards. A large bell hung over the door. I was concerned to see no children playing out front. I'd expected to find some of my students here by now, waiting for me to ring the bell and call them inside.

Upon opening the schoolhouse door, I braced myself for what I would find, and I was surprised to see about twenty children already seated at their desks.

Heads turned.

Children stared.

Right away, I felt at a disadvantage, as if I were late. But Winston trotted in ahead of me, and all attention turned to him.

"She has a dog," one child said.

"He's so small," said another.

Quickly, I entered and strode to the front of the room. Before saying anything, I wrote my name on the chalkboard. "I am Miss Miller," I announced, "and this is Winston. He will be accompanying me every day. I assure you he is well behaved."

Attention turned back to me. Today, I wore a simple wool gown—though it was bright purple. I didn't own any dresses in drab colors. My chestnut hair was piled on top of my head as usual, with a few strands around my face.

Sheriff Ward had promised there would be a piano here, and I was gratified to see a sturdy "upright" against one wall.

My eyes scanned the room. The youngest child appeared to be about seven years old, a boy. But there was another boy in the front row who appeared to be at least fifteen years old. He was tall, with clearly developing muscles, on the brink of manhood. Looking at me, he'd gone pale in what appeared to be shock.

The rest were a mix of boys and girls of ages in between. Most of the girls wore braids. For the first time, I imagined how this situation must feel to them. Many of them had spent their days with the same woman for years, and now here I was, walking in as her replacement.

"I've heard you were all fond of Miss Peabody," I began. "But I promise to teach you as best I can. I'd like to begin by learning your names." Turning to the tall boy, I asked, "You are?"

It took him a few seconds to find his voice. "Graham Ward, miss."

Ward? That was the sheriff's last name. I wondered if they were related. But for now, I was focused on meeting the rest of my students and looked to a girl sitting beside him. She appeared to be about twelve, with a shy demeanor.

"Matilda, miss," she said quietly. "Matilda Johnson."

I smiled at her, and she dropped her eyes to her desk. But I pressed on, trying to remember all their names as they introduced themselves. The youngest boy was called George.

It seemed best to launch right into a lesson. In my youth, I'd been tutored, but my various tutors all planned a lesson schedule. I'd given this a good deal of thought over the past three weeks. To me, it seemed best to begin with mathematics, while minds were fresh and breakfast was not far behind. Then, I would switch to letters or a writing lesson. By then the children might be growing tired or getting hungry for lunch, so a history or geography exercise would keep their minds active. After lunch, and a short rest, we could switch to literature and then finish the day with music. School ended at 2:00, so the children could get home to help with chores.

But . . . this being my first day, I decided not to begin with mathematics. Something of a more interactive nature was in order.

Turning to the blackboard, I wrote: *The Lewis & Clark Expedition.*

"How many of you are familiar with the adventures of Meriwether Lewis and William Clark?"

At first no one responded, and then Graham said, "They traveled west . . . after the Louisiana Purchase."

"Very good," I said. I wrote the dates 1804-1806 on the blackboard.

Looking back to the students, I said, "George, will you come and play Meriwether Lewis for us? Matilda, you can play William Clark. I'll be Thomas Jefferson and give you the commission."

George seemed pleased to be called up to take part, but Matilda's eyes widened. "But I'm a girl, miss. I can't play Clark."

"Nonsense," I said. "Of course you can."

She hesitated, but just as she was beginning to rise, the door to the schoolhouse slammed open, and a stocky man stood in the doorway, glaring inside.

"Tildy!" he shouted. "I told you to gather the eggs and clean up our breakfast afore you went to school! Now you git up or I'll whip you all the way home."

Matilda's face went white. "Ma said I could come. She told me to go to school."

"You git up!"

As he strode up the aisle between the desks, Matilda appeared to melt into her chair, gripping her desk.

He was not a tall man, but he was wide, and he was slurring his words. I suspected he was drunk before nine o'clock in the morning. He had the look of a ne'er-do-well to me, and a bully.

Whoever he was, Matilda was clearly afraid of him, and at present, she was in my charge.

I had never liked bullies.

A stout wooden pointer was leaned up against the chalkboard. Grabbing it, I quickly moved between them.

"You will stop, sir," I ordered, channeling my grandmother and using her haughtiest tone.

He stopped, taking me in with bleary-eyed surprise.

"Matilda is at her lessons," I said. "Her mother gave her permission to attend at the start of the day. Are you her father?"

Both my diction and tone had taken him aback, but he was recovering and sneered at me. "Nathan Johnson. Her uncle."

All the children sat frozen, watching us. I gripped the pointer tightly. I could certainly ram it into one of his eyes if necessary.

"Her uncle? I see," I said. "Well, her mother has sent her to school, and Matilda wishes to stay. Please leave immediately. You are disturbing these students' lessons."

He blinked in surprise at both my words and demeanor, and did not move to leave. By the smell of him—which had now reached me—he was most likely a drunkard who had crossed purposes with the law once or twice.

I couldn't be sure of this, but I took a chance. "Sheriff Ward had engaged me to teach these students. I'm sure he would not be pleased to hear of you bursting in here and frightening the entire class. Leave now, or I will make a full report of your actions."

The children waited breathlessly, as if wondering who would back down first.

Nathan Johnson's eyes widened briefly and then narrowed. Hatred passed through them, and I knew I'd made an enemy of him, but that hardly mattered now.

Standing my ground, I let the threat sink in. Thankfully, it worked. He began backing toward the door. Glowering at Matilda, he said, "I'll see you at home."

Then he was gone.

The children looked to me in stunned silence, but I could see relief on their faces. Something had just shifted. I simply wasn't sure what.

"Where were we?" I asked. "Ah, yes. Lewis and Clark."

At the end of the day, as the students filed out, I asked Matilda to stay a few moments and help me clean the blackboard.

Once we were alone, I asked her, "Will you be . . . all right when you get home?"

"You mean from Uncle Nate? Yes. Ma will stand by me."

Well, that was good news. I'd been worrying about the girl's safety.

As we finished the board, she seemed to want to ask me something else. I waited.

"Miss Miller," she began. "Did you know he was coming? You grabbed that pointer right quick."

Did I know? How could I?

Before I could say anything, she rushed onward. "I mean are you *like* Miss Peabody?"

She was the second person to ask this since my arrival.

"In what sense?" I asked.

"She knew things. She knew what was going to happen. She was a Marlborough County schoolmarm, and they protect their own."

A Marlborough County schoolmarm.

Again . . . Sheriff Ward had used that exact same phrase.

I sighed. "I'm just a woman who's come a long way to be your teacher. But I hope I can live up to Miss Peabody's example, and I do promise I will protect you."

She nodded. "Yes, miss."

That night, at home, I considered my limited choices for supper and decided I would need to walk into town and do some shopping soon. Winston and I could not live on coffee, beans, and cheese.

There was flour and a little lard. Perhaps I could make some biscuits.

I had brought a little tea in my traveling trunk, and I was longing for a cup. I preferred it with milk, but fresh milk would be a luxury here. Still, biscuits, a sliced apple, cheese, and tea would make an adequate meal.

However, as I walked toward my own trunk, I stopped at Miss Peabody's. Kneeling, I opened it and drew out the amethyst crystal in the oval of pewter.

The attached note caused me a moment of melancholy on two levels. First, this object had been meant for Abigail Swenson and not me. Second, Miss Peabody had lived here for twenty years, and at the end of her life, she'd had no one to whom she could leave her belongings besides the replacement teacher. She'd lived a life of duty and sacrifice, and it seemed she'd died alone.

Was this to be my future?

Against my will, the melancholy gave way to mild despair, and for the first time in three weeks, I let my thoughts slip back to the events that had brought me here. I'd lived a privileged life without even knowing it: a large house, servants, fine food, and clothes . . . afternoon teas and dinner parties. My father had owned a silver mine inherited from his own father. My grandfather died before I was born, and my mother died the night I was born, so my father and grandmother raised me. I loved them both and needed them both. Where she was stern and dependable, he liked to laugh. He took nothing too seriously, and he was wonderful company. I thought the world a perfect and safe place until my grandmother died shortly after my twentieth birthday.

I missed her terribly, but I thought Father and I would do well together. I was so blind to the truth. The first hints came when I heard him arguing at the back door with our butcher. The butcher was demanding payment, and my father promised to pay soon. I'd been confused and embarrassed and not asked him about this. Such scenes continued. Sometimes, my father would suddenly have money, and he'd pay off the people banging on our door.

A few months later, the banging would start again.

Our friends stopped inviting us to dinners.

Then they stopped inviting us to tea.

Shortly after my twenty-second birthday, my father locked himself in his room and shot himself in the head.

When our family lawyer read the will to me, I couldn't believe it. I was too shocked to weep. I had nothing. The house was mortgaged, and he owed money to nearly everyone we knew. Apparently, the silver mine had played out years ago, and he'd not lifted a finger to change our style of living. He'd simply borrowed. I was expected to leave our house by the end of the month. All of its furnishings would be sold to pay debts, but I was allowed to take my clothes and my books.

I was frightened. I had nowhere to go. I tried writing to a few of our friends, but no one answered—with one exception.

One family, the Van Horns, did write. They offered me a post as governess to their three daughters. They made it clear that I would eat apart from them and would no longer socialize with any of their guests, but that they "sympathized" with my situation. That was the word they used.

A governess.

For the Van Horns.

The very thought was unbearable. And what would become of Winston? Would they allow me to keep him?

But then an even worse option presented itself. My second cousin, Oliver, arrived at the house and proposed marriage. He'd always wanted to marry me, but had never dared ask openly before. He was slightly built with pockmarks and thick spectacles. Those things I could have easily overlooked, but he was also overly attached to his mother, prone to imagined illnesses, and he wrote down every penny he spent in a pocket notebook out of frugality. He was not for me.

I was on the verge of accepting the humiliating offer from the Van Horns (and begging them to allow me to keep Winston) when I visited the post office one afternoon and saw an advertisement for a teacher in Colorado . . .

Winston whined and brought me out of my unwanted memories. Then he licked my face. I was still kneeling by Miss Peabody's trunk. After taking a long breath, I ran my hand down Winston's back.

"Of course you're right," I said to him. "We could be much worse off than this."

I shivered at the thought of having to live with Oliver . . . and his mother.

Closing the lid to Miss Peabody's trunk, I set the crystal on top, in plain view. Something about it grounded me to my situation. Going to my own trunk, I dug out the packet of tea. Then I built a fire in the wood stove.

I was about to set the kettle onto the stove when Winston's whole body stiffened. He whirled for the door, and a low snarl escaped him.

"What is it?" I asked in alarm.

He rarely snarled.

I waited, but nothing happened, so I set the kettle on the stove. Perhaps there was a coyote or some raccoons outside.

"Whatever you smell out there," I said, "I assure you it cannot come inside."

His body remained tense, and he did not take his eyes off the door.

Just then . . . the amethyst crystal began to glow, softly at first, and then brighter than the candle lantern on the table. Without thinking, I hurried over and picked up the crystal.

Instantly, the entire world went dark, but only for a few seconds. Then, I found myself standing across the room from where I had been standing . . . and I was looking at myself. The self I saw seemed unaware there were two of us. She did not see me. Neither did Winston, though he still maintained his vigil near the door. The kettle that I'd just placed on the stove was now belching steam, and the other me reached for it.

With no warning, the front door burst open. Nathan Johnson stood in the doorway. His eyes were bloodshot.

The other me stepped back, looking wildly toward the shotgun leaning against the cupboard. It was too far away.

I tried to run for it myself, but I couldn't move.

Nathan rushed for her, grabbing her by the throat and holding her against the wall. Winston barked savagely and attacked his leg, but Nathan somehow half-turned and kicked the dog across the room.

I gasped, but no one heard me.

Nathan leaned close to the other me. "You come here and think you can start telling *men* what to do," he hissed into her face. "You got another thing comin'."

She shoved at him wildly, still looking toward the gun, but used his body to pin her—me—more tightly against the wall. He seemed to be enjoying himself now.

"Another thing comin'," he repeated.

Everything around me went black again, and suddenly I was standing by the stove with the crystal in my hand. Nathan was nowhere to be seen. There was only one of me now, and the teakettle was just beginning to boil. Winston still stared at the door.

Setting the crystal on the floor, I ran to the cupboard, grabbed up the shotgun, and dropped the barrel to see if it was loaded.

It was not.

But I'd seen a box of shells in the cupboard earlier, and I hastened to load the weapon. It was a single barrel that took only one shell, but that was good enough at close range.

Then I aimed it at the door.

Two breaths later, the door slammed open, and Nathan Johnson stood on the other side. I pointed the gun at his chest. Winston began to bark, but held his ground.

"If you take a step inside that door," I said, "you will not leave until someone drags out your body."

Nathan's eyes widened in shock.

"Are you one of them?" he asked. "You can't be . . . Tildy said you hailed from Philadelphia."

I had no idea what he meant, and I didn't care. Gripping the shotgun tighter, I said, "You have to the count of three."

With his eyes still wide, he turned and ran into the night.

Hurrying over, I closed the door. Then I locked it.

What had just happened? Had I just glimpsed in the future . . . and then changed it?

Walking slowly over to the crystal, I looked down, and Matilda's words about Miss Peabody echoed in my ears.

She knew things.

The next day, after only a brief hesitation, I dropped the crystal into my book satchel before leaving the house. Although I'd not completely accepted my own interpretation of the events of the night before, the note—still tied around the crystal—was beginning to make more sense.

Abigail, as we discussed, you'll know what to do when the stone begins to glow. Be sure to keep it with you always. After all . . . you never know.

Did the crystal begin to glow when something was about to happen? Had Miss Peabody used it to see into the future and then alter events?

As a logical-minded person, I could hardly believe it, and yet . . . the crystal had saved me last night.

That morning, in the schoolhouse, I did begin with a math lesson. Then we worked with letters and sentences, and I moved about, looking at the students' desk-sized chalkboards, to get a sense of their various levels. Then we continued our discussion of Lewis and Clark. After lunch, I began reading *Great Expectations* aloud, and we discussed the characters. The children seemed to enjoy this even more than acting out the Lewis and Clark expedition. I was pleased by their interest in learning.

However, I'd made a firm decision about the events of the previous night, and once school was finished for the day, Winston and I walked the mile into town.

Upon reaching Spruce, I found myself wishing it was feasible for me to live here—as I was accustomed to people and buildings and shops—but come winter, I would not enjoy walking a mile to the school and back.

Several people on the street glanced at me, and I realized I had no idea where to go.

A thin woman with a pinched face stopped in front of me. She carried a burlap sack, as if shopping. "You the new teacher?" Her voice was guarded but not unfriendly.

"I am," I answered. "Miss Miller. I am pleased to meet you."

She nodded. "My George is the youngest in the school. He thinks well of you. Last night, he came home talking about Meriwether Lewis."

As this was most gratifying, I smiled. "Thank you. He is a fine student." Thinking perhaps I could use our pleasant exchange to my benefit, I said, "I came to see Sheriff Ward. Do you where he might be found?"

"Sheriff Ward? He'd most likely be at the jail this time of day." She pointed down the street. "Backside of the courthouse."

I smiled again. "Thank you."

With Winston trotting beside me, I managed to round to the backside of the courthouse and enter a small brick building. Inside, Sheriff Ward sat behind a desk. He appeared to be working in an accounts book.

As he looked up and saw me, a moment of blank surprise crossed his features. In a way, he was a handsome man, and the close-trimmed beard suited him.

"Miss Miller?" he said, standing up. "It's a pleasure to see you. Graham came home last night already looking forward to going back to school today. He says you're a good teacher."

I then remembered they shared a last name. But the sheriff hardly looked old enough to be father to a fifteen-year-old.

He must have read my expression. "Oh, Graham's my brother."

That seemed an equal stretch. "Your brother?"

"Yes. My ma died when I was ten."

"Oh, I am sorry."

"Thank you. My pa remarried later, and Graham came along."

For some reason, I could not help asking, "But you . . . are you married?"

His steady gaze met mine. "No, miss. I never married."

Why had I asked that? This conversation had taken an awkward turn, but he rescued me from further embarrassing myself.

"This don't seem like a social call," he said. "Is anything wrong?"

"Yes." Now that I was here, I wanted to put this carefully. I had no intention of stirring up trouble, but I also wanted the sheriff informed of the situation— should it grow worse. "Yesterday, a Nathan Johnson burst into the schoolhouse. I believe he was intoxicated, and he verbally accosted his niece, Matilda, and tried to make her leave her lessons."

"I'm sorry that happened, but it doesn't surprise me. Nate likes his whiskey, and he likes to throw his weight around. I'll check on Matilda."

"I believe she is fine. I ordered him to leave."

Taken aback, he said, "You got Nate Johnson to leave without her?"

"Yes, of course. He's a bully. Bullies are always cowards. But that incident is not my main concern. Last night, he broke into my home and tried to attack me."

A moment of silence followed, and his body went rigid. "He what?"

"He broke into my home to attack me."

"Did he hurt you? Did he put his hands on you?" Now his voice was growing quietly angry, much angrier than I'd expected.

"No. I managed to get the shotgun loaded quickly, and I was able to run him off."

He sighed in relief. His eyes moved over my face, up to my hair, and down to my face again. "Don't worry. I'll make sure he never bothers you again."

For goodness sake. I'd not meant to instigate some manly feud. "Please don't do anything. I simply wanted you know what took place."

His eyes were dark. "I'll take care of it."

Perhaps I should not have made my report, but there was little else to say, and I had some supply shopping to do.

"Good day, Sheriff," I said in mild concern.

His eyes were still dark, but he nodded.

The following morning, I decided to stop fretting over the sheriff. What was done was done. Hopefully, once he'd thought it over, he'd allow his cooler head to prevail.

The morning at school passed swiftly, and the mathematical level of my students impressed me. Miss Peabody had been an excellent math teacher. But I—though I do flatter myself—appeared to be better with history and literature.

At the lunch break outside, Matilda approached me shyly. "Miss Miller?"

"Yes?"

"Did you . . . did you go to the sheriff telling tales on Uncle Nate?"

The wording of her question alarmed me, but I was more concerned about why she was asking. "Why?"

"The sheriff came to our house last night, and I never seen him so mad. He told my uncle he'd lock him up if he ever went near you or the schoolhouse again. When Uncle Nate yelled back, the sheriff shoved him down into a chair right in front of Ma and everybody."

"Oh, dear."

"Did you tell any tales?"

This was a difficult question. "I did make a report of some difficulties I've had with your uncle."

She didn't look accusing, only worried. "Maybe you ought not of done that."

Perhaps she was right.

Near dusk that night, I was home contemplating what to make for supper—now that I had a few more choices. I'd set the crystal on the center of the table. It seemed the right place.

I was just about to get the fire started when a knock sounded on the door. Winston glanced over but didn't bark. I opened to the door to find Graham Ward on the other side. At fifteen, he already towered over me. He was going to be a tall man—like his brother.

But then my eyes dropped to his hands. He carried a covered baking dish, and a delicious scent wafted up.

"Ma stewed some chickens today," he said. "She thought you might like one."

My mouth watered at the thought of a stewed chicken. And Winston would be so pleased. He and I could eat on that for days.

"Oh, please do thank her. That was very kind." As he handed me the dish, I asked, "Would you like to come in? I could make us some tea."

"No, miss. I'd better get back, but . . ."

"But what?"

"Might I borrow *Great Expectations* for tonight? I'll bring it with me to school in the morning for class, but I can't stop wondering what will happen next. I could read more tonight."

My face broke into a smile. "Of course you may. I'll just get it."

Quickly, I set the chicken on the table and fetched him the book.

"Thank you, miss."

He headed off, and I called after him, "Be sure to thank your mother for me."

After closing the door, I was just walking back toward the table when the crystal began to glow. Again, it was soft at first but growing brighter. Hurrying over, I picked it up.

The room went dark.

When I could see again, I found myself in an alley beside the courthouse in town. As opposed to dusk, it was fully dark outside, but I could see well enough via scant illumination from street lamps behind me. I heard the sound of a door close. Then I heard footsteps. Someone was coming toward me.

It was Sheriff Ward.

He'd come only halfway down the alley when someone else stepped from a darkened doorway and clubbed him over the head with what appeared to be a short branch. He fell face first to the ground, never having seen his attacker.

But I saw.

It was Nathan Johnson.

Dropping the branch, Nathan reached down and rolled the sheriff over onto his back. Something that glinted appeared in Nathan's hand. A hunting knife.

"No!" I shouted, but he did not hear me.

With great force, he drove the knife into Sheriff Ward's chest.

"No!" I cried again.

The world went black, and then I was standing beside the table of my own house, panting and shaken. I set down the crystal. Whirling, I rushed for the shotgun, which was still loaded, and I dropped three more shells into my pocket. Then I ran out the front door.

"Winston! Come!"

He ran beside me. Up ahead, Graham could still be seen on the path. He turned as we reached him, and his eyes searched my face. "You saw something? Fire? Fever coming? What is it?"

"Your brother," I answered, gripping the gun. "We have to hurry."

I kept up with Graham as best as I could as we ran the mile to town.

My first thought was to try to make it to the jail before the sheriff left, thereby stopping the tragedy before it happened and hoping he'd believe me.

But when Graham, Winston, and I reached the jail, the front door was locked.

I didn't hesitate and bolted for the alley.

I almost made it.

Up ahead, I saw Nathan step from the darkened doorway and club Sheriff Ward from behind. He dropped the branch and drew the knife.

Raising the shotgun, I shouted. "Stop!"

Nathan whirled. At the sight of me, his eyes first widened in surprise and then narrowed in rage. He glanced down at the sheriff. This time, I did not wait. Taking three steps forward, I aimed and fired.

The kick knocked me backward, but not as hard as I expected . . . for the shell had not been projected. The gun had misfired. Perhaps the shell was bad.

Nathan realized this in the same instant as myself, and he rushed me with the knife. I had no time to check the gun or reload, and he was almost upon me with the knife. Gripping the gun, I braced myself, my mind churning in spite of my panic over this turn of events.

But just as Nathan reached me, Graham came out of nowhere and grabbed the shotgun from my hands. Using it like a club, he swung. Nathan was coming too fast to slow down.

The stock cracked against the side of his head, and he dropped like a sack of grain. Graham, however, was not done and swung the gun downward, cracking the other side of Nathan's head as he lay on the ground.

Never underestimate either the strength or determination of a fifteen-year-old boy.

Then we both stood panting and staring at each other.

Down the alley, the sheriff groaned and half pushed himself up. Graham and I both hurried to help him up. I did not have to say much as Graham quickly accounted for the past few moments, but then he pointed to me.

"She knew," Graham said. "She's a Marlborough County schoolmarm."

Leaning on his younger brother, Sheriff Ward said to me, "I asked you. I asked *plainly*. Why didn't you just say?"

On instinct, I knew I couldn't tell them about the crystal. I knew that somehow I was privy to a secret that must be kept.

Pitching my tone to sound mildly flirtatious, I answered, "Well, a woman likes to keep some secrets."

"But you're one of them?"

Though I still wasn't entirely sure what this meant, I was sure of one thing, and I nodded to him. "Yes, I'm a Marlborough County schoolmarm."

And apparently . . . I was.

Rainmaker

Margaret S. McGraw

Overnight, the dust had seeped between my eyelids and stung my eyes. I scrubbed at the grit with my knuckles and rolled on my side, burying my face in her long, blond hair. It was foolish to wish for a little more sleep, a little more time.

She turned toward me, and the whiskey bottle fell off the bed with a loud clatter. Her fingers explored the lines etched into my neck and down my chest, but she didn't ask me about them. Her hand strayed under the tangled sheet. I pulled it up to kiss her fingertips.

"Glad you paid to stay the night, mister. Wanna stay a little longer?"

"I surely would, sweetheart, but I got to get going. Duty calls."

She watched me dress, sleepy smile and narrowed eyes tempting me as much as her bare body under the sheet. I pressed two more coins in her palm. She sucked her cheeks in and whistled her appreciation.

"Who are you, mister? What's your business in town, anyway?"

I stood and pulled my hat low over my brow, swinging my pack over my shoulder. "I'm the rainmaker, darlin'. Time to call the rain."

She burst out laughing. "Honey, there's been no rain in the sky for over two years now. You go give it a try if you gotta, then you come back to my bed. Ask Jason downstairs for Sally, okay?"

I nodded, though I knew I wouldn't see this room again. Once the rain came, I had to move on.

I closed the door quietly and headed out of the saloon to find the preacher. I'd need his help to round up the townsfolk for the hard work ahead. Sometimes keeping a frustrated, fearful crowd under control was as much of a challenge as bringing down the rain.

I found him in the cemetery behind the church, and I leaned against the shaded wall to wait for his notice. He walked down a row of headstones, placing his hand on each one as he paused before it. Will I have earned my spot when my time comes? Will I ever get that rest?

A crow cawed a doubtful reply as it flew over, and the preacher saw me. I walked down the dusty aisle to meet him. He shook my hand, meeting my eyes without fear or judgment. He stood a head shorter than me, and his loose gray hair and smile-lined face told the story of a compassionate man, not a fire-and-brimstone Bible-thumper. He eyed the marks on my neck and my wrist and said, "I prayed for help. Has God sent an answer? Can you do it, son?"

"Yes, sir. I can. I'll need help."

"I'll call the people in," he said and led me to the front of the church. While he untied the long bell rope and began to pull, he muttered, "I wish I'd known you were coming. I would have tried to get people ready. Not everyone will be eager to accept your help, I'm afraid."

"I never know where I'm headed next, Preacher. I have faith you'll convince them." He lifted an eyebrow as the bell began to swing.

When the chimes rang out, a young boy ran up the steps and took the rope from the preacher, jumping up and down as the bell swung from side to side. Soon people were trickling in, greeting the preacher and eying me curiously. He welcomed everyone by name and sent them to get settled in the pews.

I stood to the side and watched them all. Hard was the word that came to mind. Hard bodies, hard lives. Towns like this were filled with folks who had come out in homesteading caravans when the government was handing out property titles like religious tracts. They were worn down and dried like the hard clay that stretched to all horizons.

When the townsfolk were all gathered, talking among themselves, the preacher stood at the front and waited for their silence. "The drought has been long and hard on all of us," he said, and people muttered agreement. "But God has sent help, if we take it."

The people looked around in confusion. Questions and comments rang out.

"What do you mean, Preacher?"

"Why wouldn't we take it?"

"It's not raining," someone cracked, and a few people chuckled.

The preacher nodded to me, and I walked to join him. A voice from the back said, "He don't look like much help to me." A few snickers sounded, and more whispered questions as people eyed me warily.

The preacher held up my arm and pulled down my sleeve so they could see the marks. A couple of ladies gasped. A man in back said, "Hell no. Pardon me, Preacher, but I got no use for charlatans or fools." He stomped down the aisle and out the doors, his spurs jangling angrily with every step.

The preacher held up his other hand and waited for the crowd to quiet once more. "My first ministry was thirty years ago, down in Nacogdoches."

I understood his ready belief then.

He continued. "I was there two years when the drought came. Crops died, cattle died. People left or they'd die too. Until the rainmaker came. I was there. I saw what he did. I saw these same marks on him. He made it rain, and this young man can do it, too. Can't you, son?"

Without waiting for my answer, he continued, "You know who that was, don't you?"

"Yessir. That was my father."

The crowd erupted with noise. After a long moment, an old lady sitting in the front row pulled herself standing and turned around to face the rest. The preacher held up his hands and waited for silence, then asked, "Ms. Alma, what would you like to say?"

In a reedy voice, Ms. Alma said, "The Lord sent this man to us." Her voice strengthened as she continued. "If we don't show the Lord we accept His gift, He might think we don't want it. Don't deserve it." She turned around and nodded to me, then sat down. I bowed my head to her in silent thanks.

There were more angry murmurs, but no one else left the church. By lunchtime, we had an agreement and a plan.

The preacher invited me to join him for lunch in his study in back of the church. We sat at his table and ate thick slices of old smoked ham with a little dried cheese rind on crusty, stale bread. I was surprised when he pulled out a water skin full of cold well water to wash it down. He smiled ruefully. "There's no rain from above, but our wells run deep. They can't save the crops, but they've been enough to keep us alive, long as we're careful. Now you're here, the rain will come again."

He apologized for the poor fare, and I had to laugh. I couldn't remember the last time I'd enjoyed such a fine meal.

I pulled out a small pouch of dried cherries, and his eyes lit up. "Son, you could trade those for just about anything you want in Abe's store. Not that there's much left there, I'm afraid."

I shook my head and slid the pouch across the table. "I don't need much, Preacher, and you've been mighty kind to me so far. Please take these." He carefully counted out three for each of us and stowed away the rest.

We chewed on the cherries while we studied the map he unrolled on the table. I said, "I'm glad you saw my father's work, Preacher. It helps that you know what's going to happen. I understand folks being doubtful, even suspicious. I'm glad you're willing to help me convince your townsfolk to have faith." He simply nodded, so I continued. "It's best if I'm up on high ground and out of town. You already know from before that the townsfolk have to be there, too. Maybe Ms. Alma's right. Maybe the Lord does want to see they want it."

He glanced up from the map with raised eyebrows, but said nothing as he tapped against his chin. He put his finger down on the map. "We're here," he said, and slid his finger about a hand's span along the map. "Here. They call it Outlook Rise. It ain't much, but I reckon it's the best we can do. You think that's far enough from town for what you got to do?" It was my turn to nod agreement, and he said, "Let's ride out so you can see for yourself if it will do."

After lunch, we walked over to the saloon. The preacher recruited two men to ride with us. If Outlook Rise would meet our needs, they'd come back and let the townsfolk know to join us out there. They went to saddle the horses and collect gear, and we returned to the church.

While he packed a small bag, the boy who'd rung the bell ran in and skidded to a stop at the door. Without looking up, the preacher said calmly, "Yes, Peter?"

"Preacher, take me with you," the boy said breathlessly. His eyes darted to me, then back to the preacher. "I can help you with the horses, and camp, and whatever you need."

"Does your mother approve?"

The boy had the grace to blush. The preacher clearly knew his flock.

"You know she don't care. She ain't even woke up through all the excitement."

"Nonetheless, you will ask her," the preacher said with a stern voice. "*When* she says yes, you may meet us at the stables." The boy ducked his head and sprinted away.

I raised my eyebrows to the preacher.

"Peter's a good boy. His mother works in the saloon. She does love him, but she lets him run wild. He has a passion for books and learning, though, so he's as likely to be here or in school as getting into any trouble."

The boy looked nine or ten. Our stories had started similar, but by his age, I had already left home.

The preacher read my mind as he stopped in front of me at the door and put a hand on my shoulder. "It's a hard hand you've been dealt, son. No doubt about it. But I'm glad you're here now."

The five of us rode to Outlook Rise. It was hardly worthy of the name, little more than a bump in the dusty, red, barren landscape. No one spoke while I shaded my eyes and peered horizon to horizon. When I nodded, the preacher turned to the other men. "You two go back and tell everyone they got to come in the morning. We'll camp here tonight and get started at dawn."

They turned to leave, and he stopped them. "You remind anyone who's thinking of staying behind that it's on their head if the rain don't come."

The two men left, and the preacher, the boy, and I set up camp for the night. There was no shade and no water, of course, so we just put down where we had stopped. We hobbled the horses and fed them the hay we'd brought out from town. Peter's horse was loaded with full skins of well water, and he'd brought a shallow wooden kneading bowl to serve as a trough for the horses. I spilled a little water on the ground and watched it disappear into the desperate earth.

Dusk brought a winter chill, so we lit a fire and spread our camprolls around it. The preacher had brought more ham and bread, and Peter had wheedled a stewpot of rice and beans from the saloon cook. His eyes lit up when he got his first taste of dried cherry.

The preacher had a fiddle, and Peter pulled out a finger whistle. They played a dozen tunes or more, and then Peter settled down and fell asleep hard and fast, the way children do. I felt a rare sense of…family. I never stayed any place long enough for that.

Poking the fire and watching embers drift up into the night sky, the preacher asked me, "Is it the same for you as your father?"

I shrugged. "Can't say for sure. You saw him work more than me." I drank from a lukewarm canteen.

"He came through town about twice a year. He'd bring presents for Mama and me. We'd stay up all night in Mama's room over the saloon, listening to his stories about how he brought the rains." I emptied the canteen.

"He said he'd take me on the road with him when I turned ten. It didn't work out that way."

The preacher asked quietly, "He died?"

"Yessir. In Portland, Oregon. In '61."

He sucked in his breath. "Your father caused the Great Flood?"

I glanced at him, then up to the stars. "Yessir. He brought the rain with him. He'd been traveling along the Columbia. They say he was fighting pneumonia when he rode into Portland. They didn't know any better, and I guess he was too sick to keep moving on his own by then."

The preacher stared at me with a sadness in his eyes. "How old were you, son?"

"I was eight. I was playing outside when I called my first rain." I rubbed my shirt over the faded lines along my ribs.

"The sheriff came to the saloon that night and told Mama I had to leave the next day. The town gave me a horse and some supplies. Mama didn't want me to go, but she knew the rain wouldn't stop if I stayed. I've been on the move ever since."

"Do you ever go back to see your Mama?"

I didn't answer right away. Finally, I blew out a breath. "I was too late. I was angry for years, feeling like she cast me out. When I finally knew better, I went back. But she'd moved on. I've haven't found her or heard from her since."

We sat in silence for a while. I thought about the lives lost in the Great Flood, including my father's. I thought about my mama and the family she had sacrificed for the rain. What did the preacher say? A hard hand, indeed.

The preacher picked up his fiddle and played quietly. I watched the stars twinkle in the black sky, some dropping from time to time in long trails across the horizon.

In the gray early light before dawn, we shook off the gritty layer of red dust that clung to our skin and clothes. Peter had three hard-baked eggs and thick slices of bacon we warmed in the last embers of the campfire. The preacher handed us tin cups of lukewarm well water, and I wished for some strong coffee or hard whiskey to get me moving. He smiled and raised his cup toward me in a silent salute.

We watched the townspeople riding out on horses and carts, noisy and cheerful, loaded with food and camping supplies. I guess they'd decided this was some kind of revival. Well, in a way, it was. I directed them to set things up away from the base of the rise, and the preacher got everyone praying and singing.

He came over and handed me a small, heavy pouch. I didn't open it. I never told a town how much they should pay. I nodded my thanks and tucked it into my gear.

I walked up to the top of the rise alone and lifted my arms to the sky. "God, here I am again. These good people need the rain. I'm ready to make the sacrifice for them," I said loud enough for them to hear. It didn't really matter, but folks liked to see me do something, or they didn't feel like they were getting their money's worth. But God provided the real show.

I never knew how long it would take. Once, when I was about twelve, clouds rolled in ten minutes after I started, and the townspeople tried to hold back my pay, saying the rain had already been coming. I'd learned my lesson and collected up front since then. Folks didn't like it, but I always promised to return it if I didn't bring the rain. I'd never left a town empty-handed.

I walked in circles up on the rise through the morning, praying out loud for God to send the rain. He would in His own good time. I just hoped it would be before the townsfolk got too frustrated. A hawk flew up from the brush and circled high over me. Folks pointed to it, wondering aloud if it were a sign. There was only one sign I was waiting for. Only one that counted.

Peter brought up a tin cup of water every hour or so. I could see everyone in front of me, but he took his role to heart and reported on the crowd's mood and activities. This early in the day, they were all pretty hopeful. Some were praying and singing, while others set up tables for lunch.

At noon, the preacher brought two plates up to me, and we sat cross-legged in the dirt and ate.

After we finished, we sat in silence for a while under the cloudless sky. Scuffing my heel against the hard clay, I said, "They say God is good and merciful. They say things happen for a reason, even if we don't know it. My father called rainmaking a gift from God. He said it was an honor to be the sacrifice to bring the rain."

I turned to find him watching me. It had been a long time since I felt kinship with anyone. I didn't usually get enough time. Or maybe I just didn't meet the right people. I wasn't used to the feeling. The words piled behind my lips, but I swallowed them down. All I said was, "Preacher, it's likely I'll need your help to move on when this is over."

He stood and reached down a hand to help me up. "I know, son. I remember. Don't you worry, I'll make sure everything's taken care of."

I left the rainmaker on the hill and took our plates back down to where the women had set up a kitchen area. They rolled their eyes as I cleaned up, but I was used to taking care of myself. They had enough to do, preparing food for everyone and watching the little ones playing around our impromptu camp.

Through all the chatter and prayer and song, people kept a close eye on the rainmaker. I remembered what happened with his father in Nacogdoches, though, and I kept an eye on the sky. When the clouds rolled in, things would happen plenty fast. There was just no telling how long that would take.

I went from group to group, leading prayers and reassuring folks that their faith was well placed in the rainmaker. We carried on through the long, hot day without a single cloud to mar the sky. By dinnertime, I could feel the rising doubt and frustration running like a river current through the crowd. I called everyone together and got the choir leading them in songs.

I took a couple of cups of water up the hill. The rainmaker and I sipped slowly, gazing out across the town camp, the red dust that stretched to the hills on the horizon.

"They're losing faith, huh, Preacher?" he said with a knowing smile.

I shrugged. "Faith's a funny thing, isn't it?"

His eyes widened with surprise. "I wouldn't expect to hear that from you, Preacher."

"Who better to question faith than someone who's made it their life's work?"

He nodded slowly and sipped his water. "Well, Preacher, how's your faith?"

I smiled and took his empty cup. "Son, I don't know you from Adam, but I have complete faith in the Lord."

He gave a shout of laughter that turned heads below us. I tipped the empty cups to salute him and headed back down to lead my people in prayer. The rainmaker was sacrificing himself for us. We had to be ready to welcome God's gift with open arms when it came.

Twilight lasted a long time on the open plains. When darkness finally came, it fell fast and absolute, wrapping us up in the velvet, starry sky. People lit fires and settled down, playing music and cards and telling stories. It was a rare day out of time, everyone together and away from our usual routines of home and work.

The rainmaker had been on his feet the whole day, except when I brought him lunch and supper. Peter was the only other one willing to go up the hill to take him water, and I appreciated the boy's kind heart and clever mind. He reminded me of myself, and perhaps the son I never had. He sat with his mother and Sally. I didn't judge them, nor anyone. Every one of us had to walk our own road to reach Heaven's gate. Some were harder than others, that's for sure.

Peter came over and sat by me a while, and we joined some of the choir singing evening hymns. He leaned against me and asked quietly, "Preacher, why don't God just make it rain?"

I held back a bitter laugh. The boy asked aloud the question I had hidden in my heart. I hadn't known what to expect all those years ago in Nacogdoches.

Now I dreaded what was coming, as much as I knew we needed the rain.

"I don't know, Peter. I guess God's the only one who knows that."

He tilted his head back and gazed up at the stars. "Maybe because we don't live like He wants us to. He needs a sign from us to know we still believe in Him."

I wrapped my arm around his shoulders and gave him a hug. "You're wise beyond your years, Peter. Go on back over with your momma now, okay? I'm going to check on our friend."

Peter stood and turned his head toward the rainmaker. "He's our friend even though some of the people here don't trust him much. Why, Preacher?"

I followed his gaze. "Takes a whole lotta love in your heart to be a sacrifice for people who don't trust you, don't you think?"

Peter nodded thoughtfully. "Guess we'll have to be his friends then, Preacher, so he knows it's worth it."

I ruffled his hair. "That's right, son. Now, go on."

I slept fitfully for a couple of hours before dawn, dreaming of Nacogdoches. I flung myself upright and out of sleep, breathing hard. Twisting in my bedroll, I saw the rainmaker still standing at the top of the rise, his arms raised high. My gaze shifted to the cloudless sky, and my heart constricted as dread and hope churned inside me.

I smelled coffee brewing and headed for the kitchen campfire. Over the ladies' protests, I filled two pitchers and carried them around to everyone already stirring. As I poured coffee, I listened to their fears and reassured them that God would answer our prayers. Finally, I took two steaming mugs up to the rainmaker.

He sipped the coffee and said, "I smell it, Preacher. Storm's comin'."

Dawn was just spreading reds and golds up from the horizon, but the sky was still barren. He smiled as I scanned the sky. "Don't lose faith now, Preacher. After all these years, if there's anything I know, it's when the storm approaches. Can't you smell it? Feel it in the air?"

I shook my head helplessly. He finished his coffee and gestured down the hill. "When it starts, tell everyone they should move back a mite. The other side of the camp should be fine. I don't recommend the ladies or children watch, but seems they always do. Will you ask Peter to saddle my horse? That'll keep him occupied, at least."

I put my hand on his shoulder and marveled that he was comforting me, not the other way around. "Son, I remember everything from when your father called the rain. This town is going to survive because of you. You will always be welcome here." I tried to quiet the feelings in my heart. It wasn't up to me to question God's ways.

He took my hand and shook it with a firm grasp. "Preacher, you been the closest I had to a friend in a long time. I thank you for that, in case I don't have the chance to say goodbye later."

I gripped his hand in both of mine and went back down as the light roused the last of the late sleepers.

"Rainmaker says rain's comin' soon," I told everyone. "We got to be ready."

"How long we got to wait, Preacher? We got work to do. We can't stay out here forever," Tom Miller grumbled. He'd been the one to storm out of the church, and I wasn't surprised he was one of the first to complain now.

"This is a waste of time." Tom threw his pack on his shoulder and turned toward the horses. Others agreed, anger and frustration swirling through the crowd.

I stepped in front of Tom, searching for words to sway him. He pushed past me, knocking me off balance. As I fell to the ground, the crowd's angry mood spilled over. I don't know who shoved first, who swung a fist, but suddenly the men were fighting, and the women were pulling children out of the way. I scrambled to my feet, shouting. "Stop! All of you! This isn't the way—"

Thunder rumbled across the sky. Everyone froze in mid-motion. Then dark clouds roiled across the western sky. I called out, "People, look west! There's storm clouds gathering. God's answering our prayers at long last. We got to move ourselves back from the rise."

The crowd's anger evaporated in new excitement. I urged them to move to the far side of our camping area. Glancing back to the rainmaker as I moved through the makeshift camp, I saw he'd pulled off his shirt and was unbuttoning his pants. Some of the ladies tittered. Some of the men started toward him. I reached out a placating hand, urging them to continue away from the rise. "No point in him wasting those clothes. Ladies, don't look if you're easily offended. Folks, let him do his job, and let's get out of the way."

They grumbled but continued with me to the far side of the camp. I saw some of the women peeking back. More than one man grabbed his wife by the arm in consternation. Didn't matter. He wouldn't be sticking around to cause any trouble.

Peter ran to my side. "Preacher! What can I do to help?"

I put my hand on his shoulder. "You go saddle the rainmaker's horse. Give it some hay and water and tuck a water skin into the saddlebags, okay? He's going to have to get moving when the rains come, or they won't stop."

Peter's eyes grew wide at the thought. He took his charge seriously and ran off toward the horses. I was glad the rainmaker had thought of sending him away, sparing him the shock of what was coming. I wished I could spare him. I turned my face to the darkening sky. *Why, Lord? Why?*

The clouds raced across the dawn sky, hiding the rising sun. Chased by thunder, they hung dark and low, heavy with rain. We all watched in awe. It had been so long, and I had forgotten how beautiful, how powerful thunderstorms could be.

The clouds filled the sky, but the thunder rumbled to eerie silence. A wild energy filled the air, making it hard to breathe, and the hairs on my arms stood on end, a feeling I still remembered after all these years. I called out, "Here it comes! Shield your eyes or look away!" I knew they wouldn't—I couldn't.

The first lightning bolt struck the rainmaker full on the chest, surrounding him in a shower of white and gold sparks. He arched back, and the lightning speared through him into the ground.

Even from this distance, I could smell burning flesh and hair. Bile and anger filled my chest. Several ladies screamed, and children hid behind their parents. Some of the men shouted and even moved toward the rise. I held up my hands and called out over them all. "Keep back! We got to keep back!"

Another bolt followed the first. It struck the rainmaker on his shoulder, and he spun around and doubled over. The next speared his back, and he flipped up and arched like a bow till I thought he would fall to the ground. The sparks filled the air around him, bright as a fireworks display.

Two more bolts struck at once, and I swear flames flickered all along his body and dropped down to the ground. They disappeared in the blink of an eye. He stood with his arms outstretched, suspended in midair for a moment. Then he collapsed. No one moved.

Out of the silence, thunder rolled across the plains. The rain came down. Gentle drops at first, single splatters that exploded up from our dry skin, the dusty ground.

Dear old Ms. Alma raised her hands and voice in worship. "Praise God! Rain!"

The rain fell harder, a steady pour. Everyone moved at once. They were dancing, shouting, laughing, kissing. No one spared a glance up to the rise.

I pulled free of grabbing hands and headed to him. Sally came out of the crowd and met me on the way up the hill. She was white as a sheet, but I recognized that determined look on her face and didn't waste breath trying to turn her away. When we reached him, she gasped. "Is he dead, Preacher?"

I shook my head, unable to speak.

He lay unconscious, stretched out on his back in the rain. His hair was burnt, and it had burned completely off his arms and chest. Sparks still flared along the fresh lightning streaks that glowed a fierce red across his chest and arms. Old lines ran all over his stomach, his legs. They'd be on his back as well.

Sally dropped to her knees and reached out a hand, hesitant to touch him. Her eyes filled with tears. "What can we do for him, Preacher?"

Peter came running up the hill and stood stock-still when he saw the rainmaker's limp body. *Too late to spare him now.* He stared, wide-eyed, and held out a small tin. "Mama said to put this on him, Preacher. She got it from the cook." He shook his head doubtfully. "I don't think there's enough..."

I opened the tin. Precious aloe salve. It must have cost the cook a small fortune. I breathed a prayer of thanks for unexpected generosity and handed it to Sally. "Can you rub this on the new marks? Just a little, so you can cover all of them."

Peter was staring at the rainmaker's body. "Wow," he breathed. "They're kind of pretty, ain't they, the way they run all over in loops and squiggles like that. Jeez, he's even got them on his—"

"Peter," I interrupted. "Why don't you go get his horse and lead it up here. And see if you can find a bedroll sheet that will be softer than a blanket to wrap him in." He raced off down the hill.

Sally cried out, and I spun around. She pointed as the rain washed over his skin. Where the water touched, the sparks flickered out, and the angry red lines began to fade. Sally lifted the jar of salve in inquiry.

"Let the rain wash over his skin first, then rub a little of the aloe on," I advised. She nodded agreement, bending over the rainmaker's body in the rain as she gently traced the salve with one finger over the new lines. How long would it take him to heal, I wondered? Perhaps not as long as I'd thought. Another of God's gifts. He didn't abandon His sacrifice after all.

Feeling helpless, I walked over to where he had neatly folded his clothes. He wouldn't be putting them on any time soon. When I picked up the pile, a pocket watch dropped to the ground. I snapped it up, and the front popped open. There was a tintype of a beautiful woman who looked like him. I remembered his story and thought she must be his mother. Pressing it against my shirt to dry the raindrops, I gently closed it and tucked it more securely into his pants pocket.

Sally had carefully covered all the fresh lightning strikes on his chest and legs. I helped her roll him over to attend to his back. We both gasped at the sight. The fiery marks ran across his back and crisscrossed over his buttocks and down his legs. Even with the rain and the aloe, he'd be in agony riding like that.

By the time Peter walked the rainmaker's horse up the rise, Sally was crying in earnest as she traced the lines, covering them with the precious salve. "Preacher, we can't run him out of town like this! It ain't right!"

I grimaced in frustration. The rainmaker had made it plenty clear what had to happen.

Peter thrust a sheet and the horse's reins in my hand without a word and ran back down the hill. I didn't blame him for feeling overwhelmed. I was feeling some strong emotion myself, tightening my gut and constricting my chest. I thought I might be angry at God, and I didn't want to examine that too closely yet. I was supposed to be grateful for His blessings. His mercy. But where was mercy for the rainmaker?

As Sally and I debated the best way to wrap the rainmaker in the rain-soaked sheet and get him on his horse in any shape to ride, I heard a change from the crowd below us. Silence. The celebration stilled, and the people separated to make way for a horse and cart as it rolled up the rise.

I had misjudged the boy. Peter sat in front with Jason Bloom, the saloon owner. Jason hopped down and handed the reins to Peter. He stared at the rainmaker and whistled. "Holy smokes! Pardon me, Preacher. Peter was right, he's not riding anywhere like that. Let's take him back to the saloon, and—"

I shook my head, and he raised his eyebrows in inquiry. "He's got to leave town, or the rain won't stop. That's the flip side of the blessing God gave him."

Jason whistled again and turned back to the rainmaker. "You sure it's a blessing, Preacher? Sounds more like a curse."

I shrugged in resignation. My faith, so firm before the rain, failed me now.

Jason returned to the business at hand with his usual efficiency. "Okay, let's load him up. Sally, can you come with me to take him across to Murdoch? Preacher, you reckon that's far enough?"

I peered through the rains to the distant hills. Even if they were receiving God's gift, surely He would not begrudge the rainmaker rest there? I nodded and helped Jason pick him up and get him settled in the cart. Sally climbed in back and rested his head on her lap.

Peter wanted to go, but Jason told him to help his momma and the cook in the saloon, and he'd pay him a whole dollar when he got back. I put my arm around his shoulder, and we watched them leave for as long as we could see them in the rain.

Eight months later, the desert bloomed. I hadn't seen it so green in years. Tall grasses waved in a soft carpet, mixed with lavender thistle and brilliant yellow flowers. The long drought was over. The town was thriving once again. I had a full house for Sunday worship, and I was trying to believe my own sermon of praise and thanks when we all jumped at a clap of thunder.

Lightning speared through the air, and Sally gasped. Her eyes widened, and her hands jumped to cover her round belly in a protective embrace. Peter sat between her and his momma, and he reached around to give her a hug and lean his head against her stomach. She lifted a hand to stroke his hair.

She smiled up at me, but her eyes held a sadness I understood all too well. I continued the service by rote, thinking her child would grow up with lots of people to love and help him. Even if he never found his father, he wouldn't have to face this life alone. But he would have to leave, and keep moving, when it came his turn to bring the rain.

I raised my hands high to finish the service, and they all stood. My own voice sounded hollow to my ears, but everyone raised their hands and voices to fill the church in giving thanks. "Praise God from whom all blessings flow."

OUT OF LUCK

Jeffrey Hall

"**LUCKY LIZA REYNOLDS. THE RED REVOLVER OF RIO ANNE. HERO** of the Spindlelands," called Groden as he and his men walked down the main, long-abandoned street of Diago, their weapons drawn. Behind them, the mast of their sail-stage, the wind-powered vehicle that had brought the outlaws there, flapped angrily in the dry air. "They'll soon be calling you the Fool of Fiasco when they see me parading you through those dusty roads by your guts."

Liza peeked through the window cut into the squishy green walls of a deserted hut-cactus, the giant vegetation the denizens of Diago had made their homes in years past before the savages slaughtered them down to the last man. She could still see the bones of the place's former citizens hanging from the pole-sized barbs that covered the plants' exteriors. A scenery that only added to her current situation.

She breathed heavily. Blood ran down her arm from where a bullet had nicked her shoulder. Lying beside her, and in much worse condition than she, was her one-eyed, chestnut mare, Wink. Three bullets were lodged in the horse's hindquarters. A deep gash had opened up on her ankle, maybe from a bullet, maybe from the madness of their escape from Groden's hideout. Liza ran a hand through the horse's mane, trying to keep her quiet, whispering with her touch that she would be all right. *We'll find a way out of this like we always do, girl*, thought Liza.

Though she wasn't sure she believed it herself.

Bam! A bullet hole erupted a foot above her head, splattering the wet sinew of the cactus over her legs and Wink's head. The horse startled, but Liza kept her quiet by gripping her snout. It was a shot meant to scare them out of hiding. Nothing more. Or at least so she hoped.

"Just how lucky are you?" said Groden. His gruff voice echoed strangely into the domed roof of the hut-cactus. "Lucky enough to escape six of my best guns? Lucky enough to escape all them savages chasing our tails?"

Liza leaned her head against the wall and whispered to herself. "Not nearly as lucky as you think." She opened the cylinder to her pistol. The dust-dirtied light coming in from the window caused the red metal of the demon's gold gun to gleam like blood. She counted three bullets before dropping her hand to her ammo pouch and finding it empty.

Lucky indeed.

There's no such thing as luck, her mother had always told her as people began to forget her as simply Liza Reynolds of Old Canyon and started adding the pseudonym to the front of her name to account for good fortune that seemed to follow her entire life as a free-gun. I*t wasn't luck. Only the good things that happen to people with good hearts*, her mother had said.

But despite the accolades and medals received from sheriffs and governors, she didn't have a good heart. She had stolen. She had cheated. She had left lovers still naked in beds as she crept out into the night. She had killed people; hell, a dozen of Groden's men lay frozen in the dust back there because of her red revolver. She hadn't survived as long as she had because of a good heart. It was luck, plain and simple.

A luck that seemed to be running out.

She peered out the window once more to see Groden sending his men into cover, a subtle expression of fear on the man's bearded face. For a brief moment, she wondered why the sudden nerves, but then she heard it. A thunder of hoof beats and a squall of yips and growls approaching from the west.

Savages.

"You hear that? They caught up quick, didn't they? Don't matter. Savages ain't gonna send us running. We ain't leaving until I get back what's mine." Groden swept his silver rifle across the street. "Who you think they're going to dehoove first? A man who rolled into this place by wheel and wind, or a woman who's saddled up one of their gods?"

She crawled to the other side of the hut-cactus and looked out the window in the direction of the open plain. Emerging from a cloud of dust, like a collection of wraiths released from the fogs of hell, were a dozen centaurs of the Rainbow Back Tribe. The brown of their furs looked like something gleaned from the Spindlelands itself. The man portion of their bodies were draped in the blood-stained furs of plain beasts, those of jackalopes and were-bison and puma-men. The long black hair running down their backs had been crusted with the rainbow clays taken from faraway riverbeds that ran through the higher points of the Spindlelands. And the rest of them, the horse part, was painted for war. Snow-white etchings covered them. Depictions of arrows and axes, the cleaved feet of all the men they had killed, and the outlines of their gods. The free horses of the plain. The ones they had killed those men for. But the worst decorations of all, the ones that Liza in all of her wanderings and misdeeds had never stopped being unnerved by, were the dead men they had tied upon their backs. Headless, feetless, saddled bareback upon the centaurs' backs like incomplete riders to make some hellish statement were the rest of Groden's men. A dozen of them that had fallen either to Liza's gun or by the savages' arrows during her mad escape from the outlaw's hideout.

"You hear? Give me back my chain and we can all be on our merry way," cried Groden.

"It ain't yours," she dared to yell back, knowing he wouldn't find her before the centaurs arrived. "It belongs to Commander Bethel and you know it."

Another bullet blasted through the cactus wall, breaking the wall inches away from her left ear. Wink whinnied, but Liza was at her side again, comforting her before the wounded animal could try to rise in flight.

"That chain is mine," said Groden, as Liza watched him backpedal into a taller hut-cactus. "Everything in this cursed land is mine. Including your ass when I wrench that chain from your cold hands. I'll mount it next to the head of that blind bitch horse of yours, I promise you."

"Come and get it then," she shouted just before the cacophonic arrival of the centaurs drowned out her voice. She thumbed the chain tucked inside her shirt pocket. It was heavy. A thing made solely from the metal of Mount Murder. It was rumored to imbue its wearer with the gift of a long life. It might have been the most valuable thing she had ever carried besides her gun. But if she could somehow find her way out of this mess, she wouldn't sell it. No. It was Commander Bethel's, head of Fort Fiasco, and he wanted it returned to him in exchange for sparing Liza's mother's head. Liza owed too much to the old bag of bones to let her hang for missed taxes.

Now it seemed there was only one way she was getting it back to the commander's hand: kill Groden.

Put a bullet in his soul and the rest of his men would scatter like flies on scat. The savages she could hide from long enough so they'd eventually mosey along to other game, but the men wouldn't stop tailing her until there was no one left to tell them not to.

Liza thumbed the hammer of her revolver, the metal making its odd whisper she had become so accustomed to as it clicked into place. She patted Wink on her neck, trying not to look at the pool of blood welling beneath the horse. "Stay here, alright? I'll be back for you faster than you can lick up a gnat. You done good, girl. This ain't the end of our adventures."

Wink's ears flattened, as if to disagree. It took all of Liza's might to leave her there in such a state. Wink was her first and only horse. She was the one that had carried her through the countless miles of this land, the one she had talked to in her lonely life as a free-gun. But when Liza stepped cautiously out of the hut-cactus, she refused to look back. She was doing this for them both. Worry wouldn't stop Groden. Only a steady hand and a stout heart.

She peered to either side of the cactus as she stepped out into Diago. To the west lay a knot of tangle-tack, prickly vines growing like a wall to outline the deserted town's border. To the east, a row of small hut-cacti lay on the other side of the main street. West meant a few cuts in her caboose, east meant exposing herself to a hole in her head.

She chose west.

She crept toward the tangle-tak, ducking beneath the hut-cactus's barbs. The sound of the centaurs seemed to accompany her movements like a terrible song as they darted in and out the abandoned structures in search of the men foolish enough to encroach on their territory. The vine wall provided a narrow avenue between the houses, bringing her farther north to where she had seen Groden run off. She kept close to the vines, catching herself on more than one pricker as she snuck between the gaps of the huts. She could see the shadows of the centaurs reaching down the alleyways like hungry, black claws as she passed. Her heart thrummed inside her chest waiting for the descent of their arrows as she ran, but she passed each alleyway without incident.

She came to a spire-like hut-cactus about four dwellings down from where she had left Wink. It grew so close to the tangle-tak that she had to use its barbs to climb over the thorny knot or risk cutting an artery. It was during her climb that she peeked through the hut's window and saw one of Groden's men huddled beneath a cobweb-ridden table, facing the doorway, a pistol in each hand. Liza aimed her gun, sliding it through the broken glass of the window, but retracted it. Though her strange gun needed no special ammunition to do what it did, bullets were precious when they were scarce. Why give one to a man whose life was not worth its value, especially when he was doing nothing to ask for it?

She circumvented the knot of the tangle-tak, and just as she put her feet to the ground, gunfire erupted from the hut-cactus. Gunfire and the call of the savages. She dared to look once more into the window.

Groden's man had flipped down the table in front of him and fallen on his back. There, he leveled his weapons, firing them into the massive chest of a centaur as its hooves bore down upon him and the toppled furniture. Four wounds blossomed upon the savage's torso, yet they were not enough to stop it from swiping away the man's guns and picking him up by the scruff of his shirt. He dragged Groden's man out into the dirt, screaming and kicking like a captured rodent.

Liza looked away. She didn't need to see the horrors happen to be more afraid than she already was. The screams were enough. She moved on, a new chord of agony added to the song played by the centaurs, her hand still steady on her red revolver's trigger.

She hurried to the next alleyway, her attention still partially upon the disturbing noises now at her back. She crouched and peeked around the corner and saw a striped vest coming straight for her.

The two collided. The man's buckle connected with her nose in a crunch, sending her sprawling. The impact itself luckily caused the man to tumble forward into the tangle-tak. Groden's man pried himself away from the vine, biting his lip to keep himself from screaming, and Liza, dazed and bleeding, could see why. One of the vine's prickers had gone straight through the man's shooting hand, causing him to drop his weapon altogether. Making him defenseless, unable to retaliate against Liza in her compromising position.

He peeled himself away from the wall and dove for his weapon. Liza raised her gun and pulled the trigger.

The hammer fell, the muzzle flashed, and a cackle of laughter echoed out from the gun's mouth. A hole sizzled in the man's sleeve, the arm he had used to reach for his weapon, but no blood spurted from it. Only a waft of red smoke. Not a killing shot, unfortunately, nor could she afford to give him one. So she watched as the bullet from the demon's gold gun bled away his soul.

The man's hard, scarred face turned from an expression of shock into confusion. Then began the subtle shake of his eyebrows, the watering of his eyes, the twitch in his cheeks. Soon his pupils widened to the size of nickels and he was wobbling to his feet.

"No, no, no," said the man, the red smoke still rising from his arm. "I can see it!" he shouted.

See what? The coming darkness? The reel of his life cascading beneath their fading conscious like a waterfall? Hell? Liza never knew what those nonfatal victims of her weapon saw. The dust mystic she had won it from on a lucky hand in a game of flatdeck never told her anything. The only thing he ever said to her was that the gun had been forged from prospecting in the mythical Stream of Tears that ran through the deep desert of the Skull Orchard. After seeing so many faces like the man's before hers now, she was certain she did not want to know.

He put his hands to his face, clawing at his eyes, screaming louder, "I CAN SEE IT!" as he stumbled past her and into the alleyway where a centaur rounded the corner to meet him. The great savage raised its cleaver with two hands and brought it down into the nape of the man's neck. The man escaped the terrible vision Liza's gun had given him in tendrils of blood.

She rolled forward, behind the next cactus-hut, unsure if the centaur glimpsed her amidst his victory. Her head swam. She could feel blood trickling from her nose. She tried to quiet her own mind and listen.

Yip! Yip! Yon Yen! she heard the savage celebrate and then the *slink* of its weapon as it left flesh. *Keep going, you sunnova bitch*, she pleaded, and with any luck, it would. But then she heard the soft patter of its hooves as it crept down the alleyway toward the tangle-tak. She cursed to herself and hurried down between the back of the houses and the side of the thorny wall. She ducked into the next alleyway just as she looked back to a hoof rounding the corner from where she had just left. She was exposed to the main street there, but at the moment, nothing occupied it. She cocked the hammer of her gun once more, and it whispered, a sound only slightly louder than the heaving of her breath, a sound much quieter than the fall of the still-coming savage.

"Pssst," whispered a voice in her ear. She nearly pulled the trigger then and there as she swung her gun up. She half expected to see Groden peering out a window, his rifle pointed into her skull, that toothless grin of his plastered on his face as he spent the last of her luck with a bullet. Instead she saw a tumbleweed stuck on the edge of one of the hut-cacti's barbs. "Help me out here," said the wandering plant, its twiggy body quivering as if to emphasize its predicament.

"Damn it," she whispered back. "I nearly blew you to bramble."

"I wouldn't mind so long as it got me off this pricker. Free me."

"I'm busy here," she snapped. She dared to peek around the corner of the house. The centaur crept up the path, its weapon raised, looking into the tangle-tak as if ready to bisect anything that crawled out of it.

"What is it? One of them savages I hear yipping about?" said the tumbleweed. "Free me and I can help you with your problem."

"What are you gonna do, give it a rash?" said Liza. Tumbleweeds were strange creatures. Slaves to the wind and the land. Things that traveled in packs in search of enlightenment as they journeyed lazily across the world. They'd no business in a shootout, much less squaring up against a savage.

"Please," said the tumbleweed. "My posse has already moseyed along days ago now. I'll shrivel out here by my lonesome if you let me be."

Liza, fed up with its clamber, and perhaps feeling a little sorry for the thing even with the centaur stomping closer by the second, pulled it free. It rolled over the ground with joy. "Thank the stars," it said, and then it rolled to Liza's side. "You're lucky you found me."

"I'm lucky?" she snapped.

Without a response, the tumbleweed rolled out of the alleyway and toward the savage. The massive centaur froze, its hairy face widening with fear at the sight of the plant rolling toward it. It backed away, turning, despite the gouge of the tangle-tak against its horse parts, and galloped away.

The tumbleweed turned back to Liza. "See?" it said, and rolled on its way and out of sight.

She gathered her breath and looked out of the alleyway and across the main street of Diago where another row of hut-cacti, these ones blossoming sagging purple flowers upon their roofs, stood.

Come out, Groden, she thought to herself. *Come out and one of us can leave this hell.*

A bullet answered her thoughts. She heard the crumble of the cactus above her head before the report of the rifle echoed to her ear. She ducked to the ground, her pistol raised, but with so many windows pocketing the cacti, she could not see where it had come from.

Dust exploded an inch from her chin. The sound of the rifle chased after it. She scurried away, back toward the wall, trying to find cover before—

A bullet bit the back of her thigh.

She screamed, but quickly bit down on her lip to quiet herself, remembering the savages still roamed the streets. She clawed herself to safety.

"What did I say?" she heard Groden's voice follow her down the alleyway. "That ass is mine."

She wiped the wound, and her hand came back sticky with blood. She dried it on her chaps, brought her gun before her, and tried to think away the pain.

Focus, Liza. It's only a bullet. You've a dozen scars on your hide from such a bite. It ain't fatal. You'll live.

And somehow those thoughts allowed her to put the pain of the bullet aside and concentrate on giving one back to Groden.

But the return of the hoof-beats in the main street made that task much more difficult. She could hear them stirring up dust on the other side of the hut-cactus, interested by the sudden commotion on the northern part of town.

Liza inched her way around the hut-cactus and the tangle-tak until it stopped altogether. She had gone as far north as she could go by that route. There was nowhere else to hide. She peered around the other side of the cactus and saw the tumult of savages inspecting the area, turning over dry troughs, dragging furniture out into the streets, cutting down dead cacti, anything that could be used as a hiding spot. Yet even with such a presence in the main street, Groden's rifle still crackled. A bullet grazed Liza's cheek, where once more she howled from the touch of it.

"I'll nibble away at you until there ain't nothing left but that chain of mine lying in the dirt," cried Groden. Liza took cover once more. She hadn't even seen a muzzle flash. Where was he shooting from? It seemed not even the centaurs could find him. She could still hear their agitated yipping as they tore away the town of Diago in search of their prey. Their rancorous hunt was coming closer by the second. It wouldn't be long before it turned up Liza, which meant it wouldn't be long before she was a footless trophy upon their backs.

But just as the calamity grew to its pinnacle and it seemed the savages were cutting down the very hut-cactus she hid behind, it stopped.

Gon Gah Yin, she heard one of the centaurs say. There was a slow parade of hooves and then only one set clopping weakly against the packed dirt of the street.

"What luck," she heard Groden cry. "That blind bitch of a horse of yours decided to come out of hiding."

Liza scrambled back round the other side of the hut-cactus and peered out through the alleyway. The centaurs had lined either side of the main street with their heads bowed and their weapons lowered as one of their gods limped down its center.

It was Wink.

The horse's rear was crusted with red. A pink froth bubbled out from the corner of her snout. Her one good eye scanned the street wildly.

Liza knew the horse well enough to know that she wouldn't disobey her orders without a good reason, and the only reason that ever seemed to be was when Liza was in danger.

Damn my screams.

The centaurs whispered prayers to the mare as she passed them, quiet asks of one of the deities that they idolized, the creatures they had watched humans wrangle away from the plains and harness. But Liza hadn't broken Wink like a stubborn stallion wrestled from the wilderness. She had embraced her as a friend, as family, when her mother first took her to the stables and she picked out the half-blind foal with so much spirit. Since then, she had never even brought a spur into the horse's hindquarters, let alone cause any harm to her other than the fruits of the hazards of their trade. She wasn't about to let anything happen to her now.

"Think I can hit her other eye?" cried Groden. The rifle thundered, and a pop of dust exploded beside the horse's hoof. Wink flinched, but still she hobbled onward. "I ain't gonna miss again!"

Liza could tell in the man's voice he wasn't bluffing. In a moment, her best friend would be put down for good. She'd be damned if she let her die alone, surrounded by savages, bleeding out on the dust of a foreign, deserted place like Diago. Liza hurried forward, each step aggravating her wound, and pushed aside a pair of centaurs blocking the alleyway. They were in such a deep state of prayer that they startled as she scurried past, not even raising their weapons to cut her down. She lunged in front of Wink, gathering the mare's head in her arms just as Groden fired again.

She felt the bullet enter her shoulder and dropped. Wink fell to the ground with her in a heap of horse and rider. A fire like she had never felt before rose from where it had connected. Her eyes swam with tears, yet even still, she spread out her arms to cover as much of Wink as she could, waiting for another burst of the rifle. But it never came, and when her eyes cleared, she realized she was in the darkness of shadows.

The centaurs stood over them, looking down. The greatest of the creatures, and what must have been their chief as symbolized by the necklace of severed feet it wore around its neck, pointed at her and said, *Ga Goa La.* The pocked stones of the creatures' tremendous cleavers hung at their sides like gravestones under which she would soon be buried. Like the shot of the rifle, those weapons never came. Instead, the savages were content just to stare at her.

Wink whinnied beneath her and began to lick at Liza's wound. Liza blinked, and with the centaurs providing a broad-chested barrier against the overhead sun and the glisten of the hut-cacti's roofs, she could only see through the fence of their legs. It was with that narrowed view that she finally saw Groden.

The man had burrowed beneath the floor a hut-cactus and propped himself up between the shadowy tangle of the giant plant's exposed roots. In that darkness his protruding gun only looked like another barb. A perfect place to pick her apart unless she happened to be on the ground at a certain angle just like she was.

Lucky indeed.

Though she knew the centaurs could butcher her at any moment, she'd be damned if she let the sunnova bitch that served her up to them go on living without her. She lunged through the legs of the savages, brought up her revolver, and with a clear shot, pulled the trigger.

Her gun laughed so loudly that it even startled the centaurs. A red spark flew from where the bullet connected with Groden's rifle, shattering the weapon into a hundred tiny pieces, the shrapnel raking the man's face in the process. Groden scurried out of his hole yelling, holding the flaps of his face. He ran for it, exiting the town, and retreating for the open plain.

Though he no longer posed a threat and it was her last bullet, Liza thought that he had earned the gift of such a valuable thing.

The demon's gold laughed once more, and Groden dropped. A tendril of red smoke rose up from the back of his head, but his brains were still intact. They were just now in the hands of whatever purgatory the gun had taken him to.

Liza rolled onto her back, exhausted. All of her hurt. Above her the twilight-filled sky was as orange as embers, and the clouds that lay strewn upon it as gray as rotten bodies thrown into its fire to burn to ashes. It was a beautiful thing to die beneath.

The shaggy, dark faces of the savages appeared beneath it. She waited for the fall of their cleavers once more and wished they'd just hurry up and get on with it. Somewhere by her feet she felt Wink scuttle to be beside her. The horse laid her head down upon Liza's legs. It felt good to know that she wouldn't die alone.

In the distance, she heard the voices of men. The rest of Groden's crew was fleeing just as she expected. To her surprise, all the centaurs picked up their heads and suddenly left her vision. She heard their hooves trot away. She dared to sit up. Heading in the direction of south, the savages pursued three fleeing figures into the open plain, only the chief remained behind.

The great centaur reached into the quiver at its side and pulled out five blossoms of prairie pinch, the rare purple flower used to stop bleeding and numb pain. The chief knelt before Wink and placed three petals on the horse's wounds. The other two, he placed at Liza's feet.

Then, before Liza could even react, the great centaur rose and galloped away to join its tribe, the dismembered body upon its back bobbing like some strange gesture of farewell.

"You saved one of their gods," came a voice at her back. The tumbleweed rolled into view. "Lucky for you, they take kindly to creatures who treat their deities with respect."

"It ain't luck," said Liza as she picked up the flowers and put them over her wounds. Already she could feel their touch cooling the fire of the bullets. "I've done run outta that."

"Well then, maybe it's not that," said the tumbleweed. "Maybe it's another thing that I heard once upon a time during my wandering."

"What's that?" said Liza, too tired to tell the thing to brush off. She ran her hand through Wink's mane. The horse snorted and struggled to her feet, helping Liza up with her.

"That there is no such thing as luck, only good things that happen to people with good hearts."

Liza forced a laugh at that. "You sound like someone I know."

"Then maybe that person is smarter than you think."

"That person is set to dangle from the gallows. She's the reason I got into this mess in first place. I ain't got no good heart."

"You risked your own neck to save someone. Don't sound like you got a bad heart to me," said the weed.

Liza went to respond, but kept her mouth closed. Beside her, Wink trotted a bit as if to show her she could ride, the prairie pinch already taking effect. She climbed aboard and looked out into the open plain, feeling the weight of commander's chain in her pocket. There were miles to go before they reached Fort Fiasco. Though bullets were still buried beneath their skins and other wounds had marked their hides for good, their bleeding had stopped and their pain was numbed... for now. They would make it there as they always had, somehow eking a way forward through the treacheries the Spindlelands put down before them. Together. Not by luck.

Liza turned Wink westward, and the horse trotted forward. The tumbleweed called at their backs.

"This will be quite the story to tell my posse when I finally catch up."

"I hope they enjoy it," called back Liza.

"Tell me, what's your name?"

"Liza," she said. "Liza Reynolds."

"That it?" said the tumbleweed.

"That's it."

Together they left Diago.

ROLLIN' DEATH

Jake Bible

"WE SHOULD REALLY GO BACK, CLAY."

Clay MacAulay didn't reply. He sat there in his mech pilot's chair and chewed on his fourth hunk of jerky. It was making him unbearably thirsty, but he wasn't going to say so. Not to Gibbons. The AI could kiss his unwashed butt.

"Clay?" Gibbons said, the AI co-pilot's voice tinny over the ancient speaker system set into the mech cockpit's ceiling. "Clay, I know you can hear me. Stop ignoring me."

"Start saying something worthwhile, and maybe I'll start responding," Clay replied.

He kicked his legs up over the pilot's seat's armrest and stared out into the unforgiving landscape they were clomping across. Scrub brush. Deep, dry ravines. Mesas carved by winds that could strip a combat roller of its outer armor. Not a cloud in sight. Hadn't been for days.

"So, we just let them die?" Gibbons asked.

Clay adjusted his wide-brimmed hat, struggling against the sweat-soaked band that stuck to his forehead. He pushed the hat back and stared straight into one of the vid cams Gibbons used to see Clay. The stare became a glare; the glare became an eye roll.

"We aren't letting anyone die, Gibbons," Clay said. "Those folks made their choice. We told them that the Cabenero Pass was not safe. We told them that even with fifteen rollers training along, they didn't stand a chance against the scavengers that live in those mountains. We told them all of this. They didn't listen."

"They didn't listen because they assumed we'd help them get through the pass," Gibbons said.

"That was stupid of them," Clay replied. "One more stupid move on their part."

"Clay, what good is having a fifty-foot battle mech if we aren't going to help people?" Gibbons asked, his voice filled with frustration.

"To keep us alive until we get to where we're going," Clay said. "That's always been the point."

"Not anymore and you know it," Gibbons replied. "I'm sorry, but you are a great disappointment, Clay. If you want to waste this mech, then you start piloting it."

The mech slowed its walk across the landscape then stopped as it powered down.

Clay waited. And waited. But the mech didn't come back online.

"You suck, Gibbons," Clay snapped. "You really suck. What could we do? Honestly, explain it to me."

"We could have escorted them through the pass," Gibbons said. "It would have only added three days, maybe four, to our journey."

"Four days when we're low on gray?" Clay asked. "When was the last time we came across any gray? Geothermal only fills the power cells so much, Gibbons. Heading over that pass is the wrong move. There's gray this way. Map shows it. Old reactor about, what? A hundred kilometers north? That's why we aren't helping those folks and their foolhardy dreams of freedom out West."

"Dreams are not foolhardy," Gibbons replied, his voice low and mournful. "We have dreams."

"I have dreams," Clay said and laughed. "You're an AI. Artificial intelligence. You don't dream."

"You are being particularly nasty right now," Gibbons snapped. "So, you know what I'm going to do about it? Do you, Clay?"

Clay didn't respond.

"I'm going to go help some fine folks who have dreams," Gibbons continued. "If I can't have dreams of my own, then the least I can do is assist those who do."

Clay sat bolt upright. He planted his boots on the floor and grabbed the controls.

"Don't even think about it, Gibbons!" Clay snarled. "I'm the pilot!"

"You're the asshole is what you are," Gibbons said as the mech powered up and began to turn around. "I'm taking us back there, and we're going to help that roller train get through the pass. And there ain't a damn thing you can do about it."

"Oh, is that right?" Clay said. "Pilot override. Lock out AI. Full security protocols."

The mech continued to turn around until it was facing the opposite direction and a horizon lined with a far-off mountain range.

"I said pilot override!" Clay shouted. "Lock out AI! Full security protocols!" The mech began to walk. Gibbons began to hum.

Clay jumped to his feet and hurried to a small panel off to his right.

"I'll cut you," Clay warned.

"Yeah, Clay, you do that," Gibbons said, then went on humming.

Clay reached for the panel then paused. He pulled his hand back and turned to the vid cam.

"It's electrified, isn't it? You were gonna stun me and knock my ass out," he said. "I touch that and I sleep through most of the journey. Nice try."

"Huh? Don't know what you're jabbering about, Clay," Gibbons replied, the faux innocence mockingly thick. "You can touch that panel all you want. Go ahead. Touch it. Put both hands on it and yank it open. Then pull the six wires inside and take the mech back over. Go for it, Clay."

"I hate you," Clay said as he backed away from the panel and returned to his seat. "You know that?"

"All relationships go through rough patches," Gibbons said. "You'll get over it. You always do."

Gibbons was silent for a moment then added, "You grumpy asshole."

Clay grabbed another hunk of jerky and chewed it like he was gnawing on pure hate.

The mech stomped along, covering several kilometers before the sun began to set. Neither Clay nor Gibbons said another word that night.

Clay stretched and yawned before willing himself out of the uncomfortable seat so he could stumble to the latrine chute and relieve himself.

"Good morning, Clay," Gibbons said. "I would like to apologize for my part in our little fight yesterday."

Clay replied with a grunt.

"That's it? A grunt while you pee?" Gibbons asked. "I certainly hit the lottery with my choice of pilots."

"You didn't have to save me down in the Brazilian Empire, you know," Clay said as he zipped up and gave his hands a quick douse in sanitizer. "You could have left me down there. I was doing just fine."

"You were a dent destined to be... Never mind," Gibbons said. "We've been over this."

Clay opened a panel and pulled out a bottle of water and two bars of dehydrated fruit mush. The last two bars of dehydrated fruit mush.

"No wonder she wouldn't come with me," Clay muttered as he closed the panel and sat back down. "What do I have to offer? Over-salted jerky and a life where sand and dust fill your cracks and crevices. I wouldn't have gone with me neither."

"Is that what this is about?" Gibbons asked. "The woman? You're acting like a pissy little boy because that woman wouldn't come with us?"

Gibbons laughed long and hard. Clay glared out the cockpit's windshield at the slowly lightening landscape. They were approaching the mountains' foothills.

"You done?" Clay asked as Gibbons continued to laugh. "Really, you about got that out of your system?"

The laughter petered out, and Gibbons made noises like he was trying to catch his breath, which was impossible for an AI to do.

"Clay, she would have come with, but you didn't ask her," Gibbons said. "Humans are idiots."

"What the hell do you mean I didn't ask her?" Clay said around a mouthful of fruit mush. He swallowed hard, almost choking on the gooey chunk, then took a drink of water before continuing. "I asked her. She said no."

"Clay, you didn't ask her," Gibbons said. "I heard all of your conversations and not once did you explicitly come out and ask her to come with us."

"Don't listen to my conversations," Clay said.

"Then turn off your pocket watch," Gibbons replied. "What else do I have to do but live vicariously through you? Not like there are many mechs or AIs of my caliber left in the land. Your sad love life is the highlight my existence. Which is pretty damn sad in and of itself."

"It's creepy," Clay said and took another drink of water. "Okay, eavesdropper, I'm going to set the record straight. Two nights before we left, I rolled over and asked her point blank to come with me. I remember it distinctly because she was just lying there singing some old song, the blanket down at her waist, and damn if she wasn't the most beautiful woman I had ever seen."

"Yep, I know exactly what night you are referring to," Gibbons said. "Care for a replay?"

"You recorded it?" Clay asked.

"My system records everything," Gibbons said. "Here. Listen."

There was a crackle of static in the speakers, then the quiet sound of a woman singing a haunting tune. She continued singing for a couple of minutes then slowly let the song die away.

"What?" she asked.

"That was incredible," Clay's voice replied. "You're so beautiful."

Then the distinct sounds of kissing could be heard followed by more urgent sounds.

"I'll stop it there," Gibbons said. "You know what comes next."

"That's not it," Clay said, but didn't sound too convinced of himself. "You played the wrong night."

"I didn't play the wrong night and you know it," Gibbons replied.

"Son of a bitch," Clay muttered. "I didn't ask her?"

"You didn't ask her," Gibbons stated.

"I asked her in my head," Clay said.

"That doesn't count," Gibbons replied. "Might I point out that even if you did ask her, the very idea of letting a group of people die at the hands of those Cabenero Pass scavengers because she said no is still pretty shitty."

"Yeah, I know," Clay said. He shook his head and settled his hat back on his head. "Okay, okay, I'm a total shit. Admitted. How do we fix this?"

"Well, as you know, I am already fixing this by ignoring your pouty ass and heading us back to the pass," Gibbons said. "I pray we aren't too late."

"Give me an estimate," Clay said. "How fast the roller train can move through the mountains in relation to how far we traveled before turning back. Can we get to them in time?"

Gibbons didn't respond.

"Gibbons? Can we get to them in time?" Clay asked again, his hands gripping the seat's armrests.

"No, Clay, we cannot get to them before they enter the pass," Gibbons said. "Not using this route."

"What other route is there?" Clay asked.

"We climb the south face of the mountain," Gibbons said. "You'll have to do that. I'm good, but there's a reason a mech like mine needs a human pilot. Otherwise we AIs would have ditched you fleshy fools centuries ago."

"And that is why the AIs were outlawed after the Bloody Conflict," Clay said. "Because you guys said crap like that."

"We only spoke the truth," Gibbons said. "Not my fault that humanity is a fascist race at heart."

"Hard to argue against that," Clay said. He leaned forward and began to strap himself into the pilot's seat. "Okay, find us the best route to climb, pal. I haven't done an ascent in a long time, so try to pick one that won't get us killed."

"There is only one route," Gibbons said. "At least that can withstand the weight of the mech. It is…challenging."

"Great," Clay said. "Challenging. Fine. I'll take challenging. Just get us there fast and I'll do the rest."

"Getting us there fast right now," Gibbons said as the mech broke into a steady jog then sped up to a full-on sprint. "Hang on."

One massive hand over one massive hand. A giant foothold here, a giant foothold there. The fifty-foot battle mech slowly climbed the mountain face while winds of nearly sixty kilometers an hour whipped at it. The sun was only an hour away from setting, and the mech still had a long way to go.

"Eight meters to the right and six meters up," Gibbons said as a red target lit up a ledge on the display screen that was superimposed across the windshield. "You see it?"

"I see it," Clay said as he piloted the mech's right hand to grab the ledge. He tightened the grip and tested the ledge's stability before he moved the left foot from its perch below. "What now? The shadows are too deep. I can't tell where to grab next."

"Hold on," Gibbons said. "I'm trying to scan, but there's something interfering. There used to be a lot of old mines in these mountains. That's where the scavengers hide. Could be some vein of metal messing with the scanners."

"Compensate," Clay ordered.

"Oh, gee, Clay, what a thought," Gibbons replied.

Another red target lit up off to the left.

"Thanks," Clay said and grabbed for it with the mech's left hand.

The ledge held, but barely, as parts of it began to crumble and fall to the ground that lay two kilometers below.

"I have a route," Gibbons announced, sounding more than a little relieved. "It is tricky, but it's the best I can do with the info the scanners are giving me."

"Plot it," Clay said.

A red line with specific points lit up the windshield. Clay studied it for a moment then nodded.

"That'll work," Clay said. "Light it up."

"Are you sure?" Gibbons asked. "We'll be visible for kilometers when I turn on the floodlights."

"I don't trust the night vision," Clay said. "Not after what happened in La Stoli."

"Oh, yes, that," Gibbons said. "You are right. Floodlights are the safer option."

The mountain face was illuminated by several thousand watts of powerful floodlights. Clay began grabbing onto ledges and placing the giant feet into deep depressions at a rate that wasn't exactly safe. No choice once they were lit up for half the region to see. They were on the clock even more than before.

Three hours passed before Clay could swing a metal leg over the top edge of the cliff that made up part of the mountain's summit. He hoisted the mech up onto the top and then rolled it a few meters before coming up into a crouch.

"What we got, Gibbons?" Clay asked, the right arm out and up, a heavy-caliber belt gun aiming into the darkness. "You see the pass?"

"I do," Gibbons said. "It is half a kilometer to the northwest."

"Movement? Signs of life? Anything?" Clay asked.

"No," Gibbons stated.

They both left it at that as Clay stood the mech up and started walking carefully across the jagged terrain towards a pitch-black line that was darker than the rest of the night. Cabenero Pass.

Forty-two minutes later, they arrived. No movement, no signs of life.

But all the signs of death.

"God dammit," Clay muttered.

"I am sorry, Clay," Gibbons said. "I'll continue to scan the area, but I am not seeing any signs of life."

"I know," Clay said. "I'm going down there."

"Clay!"

"I have to, pal," Clay said. "I have to."

Clay holstered his pistol when he found her. He stood there for several minutes before he could summon the courage to kneel down and take her lifeless body into his arms.

"I'm sorry," he whispered. "I'm so sorry. I don't know why I didn't say it out loud."

Even in death she was beautiful, maybe more so. Dark skin, jet black hair, pronounced cheekbones and brow. A nose that lifted at the tip. Slate gray eyes that stared off into nothing.

"I could have saved all of you," Clay said. "All I had to do was think of someone other than myself for two seconds. I've been so obsessed with getting to where we're going that I forgot life happens along the way."

He rocked her back and forth and began to sing. It was her song. Nowhere near as beautiful, but Clay's rendition was filled with enough emotion to make up for the lack of musicality.

When the song was finished, Clay cleared his throat and set her corpse gently down to rest on the rocks. He stood up and wiped at his eyes. Clay stared down at the ground, and something tickled the back of his mind.

Where was the blood?

Then he drew his pistol and spun around, firing into the dark at a shape that darted from one huge boulder to another.

"Gibbons!" Clay shouted.

"I'm scanning! I'm scanning!" Gibbons replied into the comm in Clay's ear. "I don't see it on the scanners, Clay!"

"But you saw it with the vids, right?" Clay asked.

"I did, I did," Gibbons replied. "But it's not coming up on the scanners at all."

"Go to infrared," Clay ordered. "Keep an eye on me. I'm going to go find it."

"That is not a good idea, Clay," Gibbons said. "Climb back up into the cockpit and wait until morning. We'll track whoever it is then."

"It's one of the scavengers, I know it," Clay said. "I'm going to find the son of a bitch now and make them all pay for what they did."

"Yes, but how about we make them pay together? In the morning? When there's better visibility?" Gibbons pleaded.

Clay began walking towards the boulder, the hammer cocked on his pistol, his eyes hunting the darkness for any signs of movement.

"Clay, please stop," Gibbons said. "I can't have your back. The targeting system is useless without the scanners. Clay?"

"Quiet," Clay said as he approached the boulder.

He spun to the side and nearly opened fire, but there was no one there. Nothing was hiding behind the boulder.

"Son of a bitch," Clay muttered. "I know I saw something."

"Clay!" Gibbons cried.

Clay turned, his finger tightening on the trigger. The blast lit up the area, and the last thing Clay saw was a very large rock coming straight for his head.

Then the darkness of night became the pure blackness of unconsciousness.

Clay looked forward to the day when he awoke in a strange place without a massive headache. Whether the headache was from too much drink or from blunt force trauma, he didn't care. He just wanted to wake up not in agony for once in his life.

Slowly, because anything faster would have ripped his head open, Clay opened his eyes. Or tried to. It took a couple minutes of concentrated effort to get the gummy lids to peel apart.

When he did get them open, he wasn't exactly happy with what he saw.

Bodies. Several dozen bodies, all in different states of being. Some were alive, he could just make out sunken chests moving. Some were definitely not alive, evidenced by the desiccated state of the corpses. Many were a coin toss.

He cleared his throat and was instantly answered by urgent hushes.

"Where am I?" Clay asked.

More urgent hushes with a couple of frightened whimpers.

"Come on, folks, give me a clue here," Clay grunted. "This a cave? A mine? A big hole in the ground dug by giants?"

"Giants ain't real," a man replied from a few meters away. "Don't be an idiot."

"Can't make any promises there," Clay said. "Current circumstances point to that."

"You need to be quiet," the man warned. "They hear ya talkin' and they'll come for ya. Hook you up like the others. They wait to see who wakes up first. Tells them yer strong."

"Tells who?" Clay asked, but the man didn't reply. "Chicken shit."

Clay adjusted his position, but could only get so comfortable on account of his legs and wrists being shackled to heavy chains that were anchored to the rock wall he was sitting against. He studied the shackles and the chain, but there was no way he was getting loose with brute force. The whack on the head had sapped his energy, and it was a struggle to simply remain conscious. But despite that, the metal used was too thick to even think of breaking.

Too thick, but still kind of soft. Not pillow soft, but more like wood soft. Still plenty solid and strong, yet it sure as hell wasn't iron.

A thought nagged at him. When he'd found the bodies, they'd had their skulls bashed in or necks snapped, but no throats cut or guts stabbed. Blunt force trauma, just like the blow to the back of his head. Kept the bloodshed down.

Because blood shed was blood wasted…

"Drinkers," Clay said. "Hey Mister? I need to ask you something."

The man didn't respond.

"Come on, pal, you gotta help me out here," Clay said. "The bodies, the dried out ones, how'd they get that way? They were drained, right? The people that have us here are coming and draining them of all their blood. Come on! Just tell me if I'm right or wrong."

"You're about to find out for yerself," the man replied.

Two shapes appeared in the gloom by the entrance to whatever space Clay was being held in. He squinted and studied the area as fast as he could. A mine. He was in a side branch of a mine. Then the two shapes were on him, their stink as strong as the hands that grabbed at his wrists and ankles.

Clay tried to fight them off, but a third shape came in and pointed a pistol right at his face. Clay stopped struggling as the chains were pulled free from the wall, but kept snug through the shackles.

"That's mine," Clay said, staring straight into the barrel of the pistol. "Not a fan of having my own pistol pointed at me."

"Then quit yer fightin'," the shape replied.

A man, from the voice. Clay couldn't tell by looking at him since the man was bundled in rags that were wrapped over every inch of his skin. But it was a man. That he knew.

"Listen, pal, you are going to want to let me go," Clay said. "I have a partner that's looking for me."

"The mech," the man stated.

"Yeah, that's right, the mech," Clay said. "My partner is in the mech, and he will crush your ass when he finds me."

"You'll be dead," the man said. "Nothing to find very soon."

"Doesn't have to be that way," Clay said. He shook his shackles, and the two shapes that carried him—Clay assumed they were men, also from their size—growled. "Just making a point, okay? Calm down."

"Be back for you," the man said to an old man chained to the mine wall as they passed by.

"See!" the old man shouted. "I knew I shouldn't have talked to you!"

"Sorry," Clay said as he was carried past. "Don't worry. I'll come back for you all."

Clay was carried out of the side branch and into a much wider space.

Ancient, cracked bracing crisscrossed the ceiling, but it looked like it would hold. At least long enough for Clay to get out.

"Hey, listen, you're going about this all wrong," Clay said. He shook the shackles again, ignored the growls, and focused on the man leading them down the mine shaft. "This is lead, right? We're in a lead mine. All this metal is made out of lead. Come on! Answer me, pal! Am I right or not?"

"Don't know what metal it is," the man replied. "Just metal."

"No, no, it's not just metal," Clay said. "It's lead. Guess what? Lead is poison. Too much exposure will kill you. That's why you're draining folks. You're using their blood as transfusions to keep you all alive. I've seen it before."

The man stopped and turned around. All Clay could see was the man's eyes behind the bundled rags. They burned with hate and fire.

"You ain't seen us before," the man said.

"No, I don't mean you specifically. I mean drinkers," Clay said. "Sick folks that take healthy folks' blood. Radiation. Viral infections. Hemos. There are groups like you all over the damn place. I don't know why you think taking blood will help. All you have to do is move. Get your people out of here."

"This is our home," the man replied. His eyes lost some of the hate. Some.

"I get that, I do," Clay said. "Never really known a home myself, but I've come across folks who would rather die than leave. Home is where the heart is and all that cow crap. But the thing is, pal, your home is killing you. It's also driving you ten kinds of bonkers. You can't think straight with all this lead exposure."

"This is our home," the man repeated.

"Right…" Clay responded. "But. It. Is. Killing. You."

The man shrugged and turned back to lead the way.

"Oh, come on! You have more than enough rollers after killing those settlers," Clay said. "Just hop in the rollers and drive away. Find yourselves some pit or cave or ravine to live in. Just get out of this mine."

"No," the man said.

"Oh, for Christ's sake," Clay muttered.

The man led them into a second side branch. They'd only gone a couple of meters before Clay really realized how much trouble he was in. The distinct smell of copper was everywhere. Blood. So much blood.

"This isn't helping!" Clay said as he was set onto a soiled table. "All you are doing is putting off death! You're still going to stay sick no matter how much blood you take! Y'all are crazy!"

"You're the crazy one," the man said as he leaned over Clay while other shapes busied themselves around the table.

"Oh, those don't look sanitary," Clay said as a shape that could have been a woman held up a couple coils of rubber tubing. "You ever wash those tubes?"

"Washing takes away the properties," the man said, then left Clay's line of sight.

"Properties? Come on!" Clay shouted. "Listen to me! I can help you people if you just listen to me!"

"Taint gonna hurt but a bit, sugar," a woman said as she slid a large gauge needle over one end of the tubing. "Just relax and soon you'll be all sleepy like."

"Do not stick me with that!" Clay shouted as he struggled against his restraints. The metal gave slightly since it was lead, but not enough for him to work his hands free. "Back off!"

Clay's trousers were pulled down, and the woman eyed his inner thigh.

"It goes right there," the woman said. "You got pretty legs, you know that? I seen legs that ain't near as pretty as yours. What you do?"

"What the hell do you mean what do I do?" Clay shouted. "Stop making small talk and just let me go!"

"Ain't no need to be rude," the woman said. "Just trying to be friendly. You'll be here for a few days, so thought I'd get to know you."

"Days? What?" Clay asked. Then he cried out as the heavy gauge needle was shoved into his leg. "Sweet God!"

He tried to thrash, but heavy hands held him down as his life was slowly sucked from him. After a couple of minutes, his vision swam, and he lost consciousness.

Had to have been days. No way he would have survived as many drainings as he did. Clay knew that, even though thinking was about as useful as punching fog.

Clay lay there, the shackles beginning to chafe his skin, blisters forming, oozing pus a part of his waking life, and waited for the next bout with the heavy gauge needle and rubber tubing. He had a distinct feeling it would be his last. Pretty much everyone that had been in the side branch of the mine when he woke up had died. The old man was long gone.

His body shook, and Clay guessed shock had finally set in. He was surprised he even had the energy to shiver the way he was. Then a solid and loud boom grabbed his attention, pulling his mind from the constant fog punching that had become his mental pastime.

Clay wasn't shaking, the floor of the mine was. More accurately, the entire mine was. Ceiling, wall, floor, everything. Dirt clods and rocks began to fall everywhere, and Clay tried to cover his head, but the shackles didn't afford him enough slack.

"After all of this, I die in a damned earthquake," Clay mumbled.

The few people still alive began to weep and cry. Clay wanted to weep and cry with them, but he was just too dried out, and it took a lot of energy to cry.

Then the world around him became a nightmare of falling rock and choking dust. The little light that his captors had allowed him to experience from the three candles stuck into the walls of the side branch was snuffed out.

"Hello darkness, my old friend," Clay chuckled before the air was squeezed from his lungs.

Again, Clay looked forward to the day he came awake and wasn't hurting like all hell.

"Holy shit!" he yelled as he sat upright then proceeded to collapse back onto the metal floor. "Holy shit…"

"Clay?" Gibbons asked. "Clay? Can you hear me?"

"I hear you," Clay whispered. "I was trying to take a nap, pal. But, man, was I having one messed up dream. It was all so…"

Clay looked about the cockpit. Why was he on the floor?

"Gibbons?"

"Yeah, Clay?"

"What happened?"

"Do you remember the pass?"

"Yes."

"Do you remember what happened after?"

Clay sat up again, although without as much enthusiasm as before. The smell hit him hard. The cockpit stank. Clay looked down at his pale, emaciated body and realized he was what was stinking up the cockpit. He was coated in his own filth.

His fingers traced the huge bruise on the inside of his thigh.

"Gibbons?"

"Yeah, Clay?"

"How am I alive? How did I get here?"

"Both excellent questions," Gibbons replied. "The answer to the first is that I have been giving you small electric shocks to keep your heart going these past two days."

"Two days?" Clay exclaimed as he rolled onto his hands and knees. He grabbed the edge of the pilot's seat and struggled up into it. "Keep talking."

"Sure," Gibbons said. "Just waiting for you to get settled. That must have been hard."

"It was," Clay said.

"The answer to the second question is I dug," Gibbons said. "I dug through the mountain until I found you. Took three days. The digging was the easy part. Finding you wasn't."

"Because of the lead," Clay said.

"Yes!" Gibbons exclaimed. "It was the lead ore that was messing with the scanners."

"Messing with my body, too, pal," Clay said. "I'm a dead man. I was exposed to lethal levels."

"It is a good thing I have plasma stores for you," Gibbons said. "I can also perform a purge of your liver as well as kidneys and bladder. Did you eat anything they gave you?"

"They didn't give me anything except water," Clay said.

"Good then your intestines should be fine," Gibbons said. "Can I stop to help you perform these tasks?"

"Yeah, that would be great," Clay said.

The mech stopped moving, and the sudden stillness gave Clay the shivers. He hadn't realized just how comforting the movements of the mech were to him until they stopped.

"What now?" Clay asked.

"Now comes the hard part," Gibbons said. "I'll talk you through it all."

For the next twelve hours, Clay fought to stay coherent enough to perform the tasks needed to keep himself alive. Gibbons was expert in giving instructions, but the fog continued, and Clay struggled to get through each procedure.

"Okay, you aren't going to die right away," Gibbons said. "Get some sleep, Clay."

Clay started to give Gibbons a thumbs-up, but he barely lifted his hand off the seat's armrest before he was in a deep sleep.

No dreams, no subconscious torture or moral lessons filled his mind. All he experienced was the sublime nothingness of true unconsciousness. When he finally came back awake, he felt better than he had in a long time, although still weak.

"Thirty-eight hours straight," Gibbons announced as Clay stood on shaky legs and shuffled to the latrine chute. "I didn't have to shock your heart once."

"Yay," Clay said.

"However, we do have a slight situation on our hands," Gibbons said. "I'd take care of it, but once again I am faced with the reality that even AIs need physical pilots."

"Slight situation?" Clay chuckled. "The only time you use that phrase is when we're about to get into a fight. What fight could we possibly get into out here in the middle of nowhere? We're not encroaching on anyone's territory."

"Yes, that is true," Gibbons said. "But we are being pursued."

"Pursued?" Clay asked as he made it back to his seat and fell back into it, exhausted.

"Your captors," Gibbons said. "They are using the settlers' rollers to track us down. I have kept ahead of them, but it appears they will overtake us within the next few hours. I have not had a chance to recharge the power cells. We are totally out of gray and running off geothermal stores alone."

"Weapons?" Clay asked as a sinking feeling gripped his guts.

"Well, without full power cells, plasma cannons will be useless," Gibbons replied. "That leaves eight RPGs and the belt guns."

"And fists," Clay said. "There are always fists."

"Yes, well, you aren't in the shape needed for hand to hand," Gibbons stated.

"Not fighting another mech, pal," Clay said. "This will be hand to roller combat. Much easier."

"Is that so? Then perhaps give it a try," Gibbons suggested.

Clay strapped in and powered up. He integrated and engaged with the mech controls and gave a couple of tentative swings with the massive fists. Then he slumped in the seat and took several deep breaths.

"Ow," he muttered.

"Yes, well, perhaps a nap will do you some good," Gibbons said. "Sleep, Clay. I'll wake you when they are thirty minutes out. That will give you a couple hours of rest."

"A couple hours?" Clay laughed. "I'll be fine with a couple of hours."

"Yes, of course you will," Gibbons replied.

Clay came awake on his own. He opened his eyes and could see diagnostics being run on all systems. Gibbons was busy triple checking the mech for battle worthiness.

"How long was I out?" Clay asked.

"Two hours on the dot," Gibbons said. "I was about to wake you up. How do you feel?"

"Like hell," Clay replied. "But I can do this. No choice, right?"

"That is true," Gibbons said.

"What's the status?" Clay asked as he stood and stretched.

He bent each limb as far as it would go, then made sure he could twist and turn his back and at the hips. Fighting was fighting, whether one-on-one with bare fists or piloting a fifty-foot battle mech. You sure as hell didn't want to cramp up in the middle of the violence.

"Five rollers," Gibbons reported. "Your captors have adapted them. Three have large canons on top while the other two have belt guns. They all have very sickly looking people hanging on to the outsides, armed with rifles or pistols."

"I'm amazed they've hung on for so long," Clay said. "Those people should be dead."

"They would be if they hadn't been feeding their veins with stolen blood," Gibbons said. "If they are willing to do that, then what else have they been doing to themselves?"

"Excellent point, pal," Clay said.

"How should we handle this? Head on?" Gibbons asked.

"I think that works best," Clay said. "Ready, Gibbons?"

"As always, Clay," Gibbons replied.

The mech began to jog toward the rollers. Instantly the drinkers opened fire. Plasma blasts hit the ground in front of the mech, gouging out two-meter-wide holes and sending rock and dirt ten meters up into the air, almost as high as the mech's cockpit.

Clay ignored the attacks. If they got hit, they got hit. Nothing he could do about it since maneuverability was severely hampered by the low power cells. Every detour taken from the head-on path lessened the impact of the attack that Clay was counting on.

"The plasma cannon on the right is locked onto us," Gibbons said. "Sending RPG now."

"Good call," Clay replied, his focus on the rollers in the center of the horizontal line of vehicles racing at them.

The rocket propelled grenade flew from its launcher in the mech's shoulder and spat fire as it sped toward the farthest roller to the right. The drinkers saw it coming, and those hanging on to the outside leapt blindly, obviously deciding that the risk of breaking a limb, or their necks, was better than getting blown to smithereens.

The roller itself was not so lucky. Even a last minute evasive turn couldn't save it. The vehicle was destroyed instantly, sending shrapnel flying in all directions. The roller closest to it took the brunt of the onslaught of hot metal and melting plastic. Half of that vehicle's cockpit was shredded down to the struts, leaving a torso-less corpse in the driver's seat.

"Two down," Gibbons announced.

"Send all the RPGs," Clay ordered.

Gibbons followed the orders, and the remaining RPGs launched from the mech. But the rollers were prepared as they fired their plasma cannons, ripping the rockets apart while they were still in the air. Fire and smoke blocked the view between the two forces, and for a second, it was impossible to see the oncoming rollers.

Then the smoke cleared, and the three remaining rollers came speeding toward the mech, belt guns firing hot lead, and plasma cannons belching energy blasts. Clay sent the mech into a forward dive, tucking the massive machine's shoulder so it could tumble under his control and come up one knee, its own belt guns returning fire.

A third roller was ripped apart by the mech's heavy caliber bullets. The vehicle's engine compartment exploded and flames engulfed the entire roller. The screams of burning men and women could be heard all the way inside the mech's cockpit, but they quickly died out as the drinkers became crispy corpses.

Bullets tore into the midsection of the mech and warning klaxons began to blare.

"Gibbons!" Clay shouted as he executed a sideways roll to get out of the line of fire.

"We're going to lose the left side hydraulics soon!" Gibbons replied. "You need to end this, Clay!"

Clay knew that. He almost snapped back with some hurtful, sarcastic reply, but he held his tongue. Gibbons was doing his job and keeping the mech operational. That's all Clay really needed.

He emptied the belt guns into another roller, and the vehicle became more air than metal. Blood spurted from the windows and doors as those inside were aerated, completely torn apart in less than two seconds. The shredded roller lost its front wheels and came to a crashing halt as its nose was driven into the ground.

A plasma blast hit the mech in the left leg, and the machine collapsed onto the desert floor. Clay pushed up onto its hands, but a second plasma blast hit it in the left bicep, and the mech fell back down.

"Gibbons! I need to get up!" Clay yelled.

"Yes, I am aware of that, Clay!" Gibbons replied. "I'm trying to work around this, but the leg is crumpled. I may be able to reroute fluid and power to the left arm so we can sit up, but no promises!"

Two more plasma bolts hit the mech, and half the warning klaxons cut off.

"Well, that ain't good," Clay said. "Gibbons? I'm going out. Pop the hatch."

"Whoa, what?" Gibbons shouted. "Clay, no!"

"I got this, just pop the hatch," Clay said as he struggled up out of the pilot's seat and crawled across the sideways cockpit to the weapons cabinet.

He pulled out a carbine and grabbed a magazine, slapping it into the weapon. Clay pulled the action and moved toward the cockpit hatch.

"Gibbons?" Clay said.

"Fine," Gibbons replied as he popped the hatch open, forcing it down against the ground so it afforded just enough room for Clay to squeeze through.

Clay watched as two more plasma blasts hit the mech. He grunted and walked a few meters from the fallen machine before taking a knee and putting the carbine to his shoulder. The drinkers hanging on to the side of the roller started to open fire with their pistols and rifles, but they were horrible shots. Clay actually laughed for a second.

Then he opened fire with the carbine and dropped three drinkers before aiming directly at the driver's side of the roller's windshield. Two shots.

The roller slowly came to a stop as the windshield was painted with the driver's skull, brains, and hair. The mess dripped slowly as Clay stood up and limped his way closer.

The last two drinkers still hanging on to the side jumped down and ran in the opposite direction. Clay dropped them both, putting holes squarely in their backs. It wasn't very honorable, but the last thing he needed was for one of them to come sneaking back in the night to slash his throat.

By the time Clay reached the stopped roller, he was exhausted. He leaned against the hood and took several deep breaths.

"Clay? Can you hear me?" Gibbons asked over the comm.

"I hear ya, pal," Clay replied. "Just taking a breather. Give me a second."

It was closer to three minutes before Clay was able to push away from the roller and keep walking. He surveyed the destruction and made a note of what parts could be salvaged from the vehicles to help repair the fallen mech.

Then he plopped down on his ass and closed his eyes.

It was Gibbons's constantly calling that finally woke him back up.

"Here, here," Clay mumbled. "Sorry."

"Thank whatever Lord AIs get to pray to," Gibbons said. "Can you get up?"

"Yep," Clay said as he used the carbine as a cane and slowly got to his feet.

He hobbled his way back to the mech, climbed in through the open hatch, and collapsed again as soon as he was inside.

"Just gonna take a little nap," Clay said. "You gonna be good?"

"I'll keep watch," Gibbons said. "Any parts worth using?"

"A few, a few," Clay whispered. "I'll get to them once I feel a little better."

"Understood, Clay," Gibbons said. "Sleep well."

Clay mumbled something unintelligible then was out. Gibbons used what power the mech had left to dial up the scanners and keep watch over the sleeping pilot. He'd be fine. They'd both be fine. They'd faced much, much worse and made it.

No reason they couldn't make it through this.

It took a week for repairs and another week of walking slowly until they reached the old reactor. It would have taken only four days, but they had to stop periodically to drill down and recharge on geothermal.

Gibbons scanned the reactor once they'd reached it and gave a sad, slow sigh.

"Not nearly as much gray left in that cooling tower as we thought," Gibbons said.

"Is it enough to get us back to the pass?" Clay asked.

"Get us back to the what?" Gibbons replied. "Clay? I know you haven't been in the best of health, and living off lizards and birds hasn't helped much, but have you gone completely nuts?"

"Not completely, no," Clay replied.

"Then please tell me why we would go back to the pass," Gibbons said.

"Because I have to," Clay said. "If I don't, I'll never forgive myself. Gonna be hard enough as it is."

Gibbons grumbled for a minute, but didn't argue.

"I'll get the hose ready," Clay said as he stood up and then popped open the cockpit hatch. "You prep the holding tank."

"Will do, Clay," Gibbons said as Clay climbed over the edge of the cockpit and was lost from sight.

It was another week of walking before they reached Cabenero Pass. But, instead of scaling the cliff, they took the long way and hiked up the roller trail. It added a day, but Clay knew he had time.

When they finally reached the sight of the massacre, Clay sat on the edge of the cockpit for a good hour before he could bring himself to climb down and do what needed doing.

"I can use my hands and dig for you," Gibbons said.

"No, pal, I have to do this myself," Clay said as he unfolded the shovel and began testing the ground for soft areas to dig in. "This is my penance."

"Clay…"

"I can't explain it," Clay said. "It's just something I have to do."

Clay dug for a few hours then began dragging bodies over to the huge grave. He did that through the night, Gibbons illuminating the area with the mech's floodlights. By the time Clay had covered over the mass grave, dawn was breaking and the pass was bathed in a pinkish-orange glow.

"One more," Clay said.

He took great care to dig the last grave, a single plot, as deep as he could. It wasn't the standard six feet, but it was deep enough that animals shouldn't be able to defile it and dig up the body.

When he was finished, he sat next to the grave and stared into the hole for a long while, trying to muster the courage to do what needed doing. Finally, as the sun stood at high noon, Clay got up and walked to the last body.

He couldn't say the words he wanted to say. His throat was nothing but a grief-stricken, constricted mess. Tears streamed down his dirt-smeared cheeks, cutting clean furrows through his filthiness.

He knelt and took her in his arms one last time, then stood, his back popping and joints creaking. Clay walked her over to the grave and struggled to get her down inside without her tumbling in a heap.

Then he was done, and her body rested at the bottom of the dark hole. He smiled through his tears and nodded down at her, then began to fill in the grave.

An hour later, the plot was smoothed over, and he walked back to the mech.

"Here, Clay," Gibbons said, and a square of metal fell to the ground. "Wasn't easy to do, and it may not look like much, but I believe it is appropriate."

Clay picked up the square and read the words on it. The tears started up again, but he grimaced and forced them to stop before he wiped his eyes with the back of his hand and returned to the grave. He jammed the end of the metal into the ground and pushed down hard, making sure it wouldn't be blown away anytime soon.

Then he smiled at the words and returned to the mech.

Clay and Gibbons were long gone when more settlers finally traveled across the Cabenero Pass. It was a single roller with only a young man and a young woman in it, all of their worldly possessions packed in the hold behind their backs.

"What's that?" the young woman asked, and pointed at a thin piece of metal flapping in the wind.

"Grave marker," the young man said.

"Stop," the young woman said. "I want to read it."

"Come on, we need to get—"

"I said stop." The tone of her voice would not allow dissent.

The young man laughed and eased the roller to a stop. He got out and helped the young woman down, then they both approached the crude grave.

"*Here lies a woman who was loved. A woman who deserved more. A woman who will never be forgotten. I am sorry, my love. I am sorry, my sweet Netha Kane. You will always be in my heart. I will do right by you. I swear this to my end.*"

"Wow," the young woman said, taking the young man's hand. "You better write something like that for me."

"It'll be better," the young man said. "And it will be decades from now. And, if we're lucky, it will be our children writing the words so that we can go off in peace together."

The young woman smiled and gave him a kiss. Then they climbed back into their roller and drove across the pass, ready for a new life. A life they both hoped would be long and full of love, but neither of them expected to be easy.

Nothing ever was. Not anymore.

About the Authors & Editors

DAVE BEYNON: Originally from Britain, Dave Beynon came to Canada as an infant, growing up on a farm just outside of Dundalk, Ontario. He has been a cow milker, a residence manager at the Hamilton Downtown YMCA (there's a novel waiting to be written about those four years), a factory worker and a purveyor of fine corrugated packaging and displays.

Dave writes speculative fiction of varying genres and lengths. In 2011, his novel, *The Platinum Ticket* was shortlisted for the Terry Pratchett Prize. Dave co-hosts a local cable TV show called *Turning Pages*, an in-depth interview show that highlights authors, writing, and publishing.

He lives in Fergus, Ontario with his wife, two children, three chickens and a pond full of feral goldfish. Find out more about Dave at www.davebeynon.com or follow him on twitter @BeynonWrites.

JAKE BIBLE is a Bram Stoker Award nominated-novelist with over 40 published novels including the bestselling Z-Burbia series set in Asheville, NC, the bestselling Salvage Merc One, the Apex Trilogy (*Dead Mech, The Americans, Metal and Ash*) and the Mega series for Severed Press; the YA zombie novel, *Little Dead Man*, the Bram Stoker Award nominated teen horror novel, *Intentional Haunting*, the ScareScapes series, and the Reign of Four series for Permuted Press; and the dark fantasy novel, *Stone Cold Bastards*, and urban fantasy series, *Black Box, Inc*, for Bell Bridge Books.

AUBREY CAMPBELL writes short fiction across a wide variety of genres, from paranormal romance to sci-fi westerns, as long as it's weird, full of swashbuckling adventure and may or may not have a happy ending. When she's not writing, she spends her time drawing, hiking, and daydreaming too much about fictional characters. She lives in the Midwest where she hoards so many books she'll never be able to read them all, an unhealthy amount of journals, and cats.

ALEXANDRA CHRISTIAN is an author of mostly romance with a speculative slant. Her love of Stephen King and sweet tea has flavored her fiction with a Southern Gothic sensibility that reeks of Spanish moss and deep fried eccentricity. As one-half of the writing team at Little Red Hen Romance, she's committed to bringing exciting stories and sapiosexual love monkeys to intelligent readers everywhere. Lexx also likes to keep her fingers in lots of different pies having written everything from sci-fi and horror to Sherlock Holmes adventures. Her alter-ego, A.C. Thompson, is also the editor of the highly successful *Improbable Adventures of Sherlock Holmes* series of anthologies from Mocha Memoirs Press. A.C. will also pen several Shadow Council Archives novellas starring everyone's favorite sidekick, Dr. John Watson, coming soon from Falstaff Books.

A self-proclaimed "Southern Belle from Hell," Lexx is a native South Carolinian who lives with an epileptic wiener dog and her husband, author Tally Johnson. Her long-term aspirations are to one day be a best-selling authoress and part-time pinup girl. She's a member of Romance Writers of America and Broad Universe—an organization that supports female authors of speculative fiction. Questions, comments and complaints are most welcome at her website: http://lexxxchristian.wixsite.com/alexandrachristian

DAVID B. COE, who also writes as D.B. Jackson, is the award-winning author of nineteen novels and more than a dozen short stories. Writing under his own name (http://www.DavidBCoe.com) he is the author of the Crawford Award-winning *LonTobyn Chronicle*, the critically acclaimed *Winds of the Forelands* quintet and Blood of the Southlands trilogy, the novelization Ridley Scott's *Robin Hood*, and the *Case Files of Justis Fearsson*, a contemporary urban fantasy published by Baen Books.

Writing as D.B. Jackson (http://www.DBJackson-Author.com), he is the author of the Thieftaker Chronicles (Tor Books), a series set in pre-Revolutionary Boston that combines elements of urban fantasy, mystery, and historical fiction. David co-founded and regularly contributes to the Magical Words group blog (http://magicalwords.net), and is co-author of How To Write Magical Words: A Writer's Companion. His books have been translated into a dozen languages.

A. E. DECKER, a former ESL tutor, tai chi instructor, and doll-maker with a degree in Colonial American history, lives in Pennsylvania. She is the author of the Moonfall Mayhem YA series published by World Weaver press, and works as an editor for the Bethlehem Writers Group. Her work has been published by *Beneath Ceaseless Skies, Fireside Magazine,* and *The Sockdolager*. Like all writers, she is owned by three cats.

GUNNAR DE WINTER is a biologist/philospher hydrbid who explores ideas through fictional fieldwork. Beware, he occasionally attempts tweeting (@ evolveon) and writing.

B.S. DONOVAN made his first short story sale in the esteemed *Lawless Lands: Tales from the Weird Frontier anthology*. The rest, as they say, was future history. Originally from Boston, he's had a wide and varied career, which has brought him to China and Japan, where he currently lives and works. His greatest ambitions are to raise two confident and happy children, reach 1st *dan* at Japanese calligraphy, and to see his name in a list with these wonderful authors again. You can read more about him on bsdonovan.com

JO GERRARD is a poet and writer who has been published in *Star*Line, Dwarf Stars*, the upcoming *Invisible 3, Sporty Spec,* and *Magic and Mechanica*. She is a native of the western United States and as such will talk your ear off about jackalopes, Wyoming, or California's deserts. (She'll be glad to listen to your turn at storytelling, too.) She believes there is not nearly enough speculative fiction set in western (or Western) America. Jo can be found in inland Southern California, accompanied by one elderly guinea pig.

LAURA ANNE GILMAN is the Nebula- and Endeavor-award nominated author of two novels of the Devil's West, *Silver on the Road* and *The Cold Eye,* and the short story collection *Darkly Human* as well as the long-running Cosa Nostradamus urban fantasy multi-series (Retrievers, PSI, and Sylvan Investigations), and the "Vineart War" epic fantasy trilogy. Her recent short fiction has appeared in *Daily Science Fiction* and the anthologies *Genius Loci* and *Strange California*.

A former New Yorker, she currently lives outside of Seattle, WA with two cats and many deadlines. More information and updates can be found at www.lauraannegilman.net, or follow her on Twitter: @LAGilman

JEFFREY HALL lives in a small suburb of Massachusetts with his wife and son. When he isn't exploring different worlds through the written word or spending time with his family, you can find him doodling, playing basketball, reading, and thumbing away at a videogame or two. He is the author of several nontraditional fantasy short stories and the book series Chilongua Tales, a dark fantasy anthology set in the jungle. To find out more about his fiction and to see some of his doodles visit him at www.hallwaytoelsewhere.com.

JOHN G. HARTNESS is a teller of tales, a righter of wrong, defender of ladies' virtues, and some people call him Maurice, for he speaks of the pompatus of love. He is also the award-winning author of the urban fantasy series The Black Knight Chronicles (Bell Bridge Books), the Bubba the Monster Hunter comedic horror series, the Quincy Harker, Demon Hunter dark fantasy series, and many other projects.

In 2016, John teamed up with a pair of other publishing industry ne'er-do-wells and founded Falstaff Books, a small press dedicated to publishing the best of genre fictions "misfit toys."

In his copious free time John enjoys long walks on the beach, rescuing kittens from trees and playing *Magic: the Gathering*.

BARB HENDEE is the national bestselling author of The Mist-Torn Witches series. She is the co-author (with husband J.C.) of the Noble Dead Saga. In addition to writing novels, she also teaches writing for Umpqua Community College. She and J.C. (and their two beloved cats: Ashes and Cinders) live in a quirky two-level townhouse just south of Portland, Oregon. When they first bought the townhouse, the large fenced patio area consisted of nothing but rocks. They spent six months carting out rocks in a wheelbarrow, then ripped up the ground, and now have a lush vegetable garden where they grow everything from peas to tomatoes to carrots to potatoes—while they struggle to keep the zucchini plants from taking over the world.

MATTHEW J. HOCKEY has now returned to England with his fiancée after two years teaching in Seoul South Korea. By the time you read this he might actually have his own place. His crime fiction has most recently appeared in *Fast Women and Neon Lights*, an anthology of 1980s inspired neon-noir short stories from *Crime Syndicate* Magazine/Short Stack Books. His first foray into weird/horror was published in *Cthulhu Lies Dreaming: Twenty-three Tales of the Weird and Cosmic* from Ghostwoods Books. He can be found most days at https://www.facebook.com/MatthewJHockey/.

FAITH HUNTER: New York Times and USAToday bestselling fantasy author Faith Hunter was born in Louisiana and raised all over the south. She writes two contemporary Urban Fantasy series: the Jane Yellowrock series, featuring a Cherokee skinwalker who hunts rogue vampires, and the Soulwood series, featuring earth magic user Nell Ingram. Her Rogue Mage novels are a dark, post-apocalyptic, fantasy series featuring Thorn St. Croix, a stone mage. The role playing game based on the series is *Rogue Mage, RPG*. Find her online at www.faithhunter.net, yellowrocksecurities.com/, or http://gwenhunter.com

PAMELA JEFFS is a prize-winning speculative fiction author living in Queensland, Australia with her husband and two daughters. She has had her short fiction published in various magazines and anthologies both nationally and internationally.

When she isn't being a writer, Pamela has a background in interior and exhibition design where she has had the good fortune to work with a multitude of talented artists. This exposure has given her an appreciation for art in all its forms including, graphic, sculptural as well as the literary.

For further details about Pamela, visit her at www.pamelajeffs.wixsite.com/pamela-jeffs or drop her a line via Twitter @Pamela_Jeffs

NICOLE GIVENS KURTZ is the author of the Cybil Lewis science fiction mystery series. Her novels have been named as finalists in the Fresh Voices in Science Fiction, EPPIE in Science Fiction, and Dream Realm Awards in science fiction. Nicole's short stories have earned an Honorable Mention in L. Ron Hubbard's Writers of the Future contest, and have appeared in numerous anthologies and other publications.

EMILY LAVIN LEVERETT is a writer and editor of speculative fiction, and a professor of medieval English literature. Medieval English Romance is the focus of her scholarship and influences her fiction. *Changeling's Fall* (2016), co-written with Sarah Joy Adams, is the first book in their contemporary epic fantasy the Eisteddfod Chronicles from Falstaff books. *Winter's Heir* will follow in fall 2017. She has co-edited several volumes, including *The Big Bad I and II*, *Tales from the Weird Wild West*, and *Lawless Lands: Tales from the Weird Frontier*. She has published short stories in a variety of anthologies and magazines. Emily lives in North Carolina and, when not writing, editing, or professoring, she and her husband are fans of the Carolina Hurricanes and of their two cats.

MISTY MASSEY is the author of *Mad Kestrel, Kestrel's Voyages* and the upcoming *Kestrel's Dance*. She co-edited *The Weird Wild West* and *Lawless Lands: Tales From The Weird Frontier*. Misty is a founding member of Magical Words, and recently became the audiobook editor for BellaRosa Books. When she isn't writing, she studies Middle Eastern dance, and performs at local events. She's a sucker for good sushi, African coffee, and the darkest rum you can find. Find her at www.mistymassey.com, Facebook, Twitter and Dreamwidth.

MARGARET S. MCGRAW is co-editor, with Misty Massey and Emily Leverett, of two anthologies of short stories about the wildest West that never was: *Weird Wild West* (eSpec Books, 2015) and *Lawless Lands: Tales from the Weird Frontier* (Falstaff Books, 2017). Margaret writes fantasy and science fiction; blogs about prompt-writing, con reviews, and book reviews at WritersSpark.com; and edits fiction, academic, and technical writing. Her imagination draws on her lifelong love of science fiction, fantasy, and anthropology. Her education and experience range from anthropology and communication through web design and IT management. Margaret lives in North Carolina with her daughter, an array of dogs, cats, Macs and PCs, and too many unfinished craft projects. Friend Margaret on Facebook or Goodreads at "Margaret S. McGraw", follow her on Twitter @MargaretSMcGraw, or visit her blog at WritersSpark.com.

SEANAN MCGUIRE lives, writes, and occasionally sleeps in the Pacific Northwest, where she shares her home with three fluffy cats, a very angry lizard, and far too many books, some of which she wrote. When not writing, Seanan enjoys horror movies, Disney Parks, and haunted cornfields, not necessarily in that order.

EDMUND **R. SCHUBERT** is the author of the novel *Dreaming Creek*, and over 50 short stories. Some of his early stories are collected in *The Trouble with Eating Clouds*; newer ones can be found in *This Giant Leap*. Schubert also contributed to and edited the non-fiction book, *How to Write Magical Words*. In addition to writing, Schubert served for ten years as head editor of the online magazine *InterGalactic Medicine Show* (including publishing three *IGMS* anthologies and winning two WSFA Small Press Awards), resigning from the post in 2016 to make writing his primary focus.

Schubert insists, however, that his greatest accomplishment came during college, when his self-published underground newspaper made him the subject of a professor's lecture in abnormal psychology. Declining a Hugo nomination for Best Editor in 2015 (because of the associated political game of thrones) comes in a close second.